Court Netherleigh by Mrs Henry Wood

Ellen Price was born on 17th January 1814 in Worcester.

In 1836 she married Henry Wood, whose career in banking and shipping meant living in Dauphiné, in the South of France, for two decades. During their time there they had four children.

Henry's business collapsed and he and Ellen together with their four children returned to England and settled in Upper Norwood near London.

Ellen now turned to writing and with her second book 'East Lynne' enjoyed remarkable popularity. This enabled her to support her family and to maintain a literary career.

It was a career in which she would write over 30 novels including 'Danesbury House', 'Oswald Cray', 'Mrs. Halliburton's Troubles', 'The Channings' and 'The Shadow of Ashlydyat'.

Sadly, her husband, Henry died in 1866.

Ellen though continued to strive on. In 1867, she purchased the magazine 'Argosy', founded two years previously by Alexander Strahan. She was a prolific writer and wrote much of the magazine herself although she had some very respected contributors, amongst them Hesba Stretton and Christina Rossetti. Although she would gradually pare down writing for the magazine she continued to write novel after novel. Such was her talent that for a time she was, in Australia, more popular than Charles Dickens.

Apart from novels she was an excellent translator and a writer of short stories. 'Reality or Delusion?' is a staple of supernatural anthologies to this day.

Ellen Wood died of bronchitis on 10th February 1887. He estate was valued at a very considerable £36,000.

She is buried in Highgate Cemetery, London.

A monument to her in Worcester Cathedral was unveiled in 1916.

Index of Contents

CHAPTER I

MISS MARGERY

In the midst of the Berkshire scenery, so fair and wealthy, this pleasant little place, Netherleigh, nestled in a sylvan hollow. It was only a small, unpretending hamlet at its best, and its rustic inhabitants were hard-working and simple.

On a wide extent of country, surrounded on all sides as far as the eye could reach, with its forests, its hills and valleys, its sparkling streams, sat many a noble mansion of ancient or modern architecture, and of more or less note in the county. Farm homesteads might be seen, surrounded by their outbuildings, their barns and substantial hayricks. Labourers' cottages were dotted about; and the men themselves toiled at their several occupations.

Flanking the village, and looking down upon it from its eminence, rose the stately walls of Court Netherleigh: an imposing and beautiful edifice, with which none of the other mansions in the distance could compare. It was built of red brick, curious but bright-looking, and its gables and angles were quaint and picturesque in a high degree. Winding upwards from the village, you came upon the entrance-gates on the left of the road—great gates of wrought iron, with two smaller gates beside them. The lodges stood one on each side the gates, roses and honeysuckles adorning the porches and lower windows. In one of these lodges, that on the left as you entered, lived the gatekeeper and his family; in the other the head gardener. Let us, in imagination, enter the gates.

It is Monday morning, the first of October, and a lovely day—warm and sunny. The gatekeeper's wife, a child clinging to her apron, runs to the door at the sound of steps, lest, haply, the great gates should need to be thrown open. Seeing only a foot-passenger, she drops a curtsy. Winding onwards through the drive that surrounds the park, we see the house itself—Court Netherleigh; a wide, low, picturesque house: or perhaps it is only its size that makes it look low, for it is three stories high. At the back, hidden by clustering trees, are the stables and out-offices. Extensive gardens lie around, which show a profusion of luscious fruits and choice vegetables, of smooth, green lawns, miniature rocks, and lovely flowers. Fine old trees give shade to the park, and the deer may be seen under their spreading branches. Altogether, the place is noble, and evidently well-cared for. Whosoever reigns at Court Netherleigh does so with no sparing hand.

We shall soon see her, for it is a lady. Ascending the three broad stone steps to the entrance-hall, rooms lie on either hand. These rooms are not inhabited this morning. We must make our way to the back of the hall, go down a passage on our right, and open a door at the end.

A rather small room, its walls white and gold, its furniture a pale, subdued green, glass doors standing open to the outer air—this arrested the eye. It was called Miss Margery's room, and of all the rooms in Court Netherleigh it was the one that Miss Margery loved best.

Miss Margery was seated in it this morning, near the table, sewing away at a child's garment, intended probably for one of the inmates at the lodge, or for some little waif in the hamlet. Miss Margery was not clever at fine work, she was wont to say, but at plain work few could equal her, and she was never idle. She was a little woman, short and small, with a fair complexion and plain features, possessing more than her share of good sense, and was very active and energetic, as little people often are. She always wore silk. Her gown this morning was of her favourite colour, violet, with a large lace collar fastened by a gold brooch, and black lace mittens under her lace-edged sleeves. She wore also a white clear-muslin apron with a braided border. The fashion of these aprons had come in when Miss Margery was a much younger woman, and she would not give them up. She need not have worn a cap, for her hair was still abundant; but in those days middle-aged ladies wore caps, and Miss Margery was turned fifty. She wore her hair in ringlets, also the custom then, and her lace lappets fell behind them. This was Miss Upton, generally in the house called Miss Margery, the owner of Court Netherleigh and its broad lands.

The glass doors of the French windows opened to the lawn, on which were beds of mignonette and other sweet-scented flowers, a fountain playing in their midst. At the open window, one of them just outside, the other within, stood two young girls in the first blush of womanhood. The elder, Frances, had light hair and a piquant, saucy face; it had no particular beauty to recommend it, but her temper was very sweet, and her manner was charming. Hence Frances Chenevix was a general favourite. Her sister, one year younger than herself, and just nineteen, was beautiful. Her hair and eyes were of a bright brown, her features faultless, and the colour on her cheeks was delicate as a blush-rose. The sisters were of middle height, graceful and slender, and eminently distinguished in bearing. They wore morning dresses of pink cambric—a favourite material in those bygone days.

The elder, standing outside, had her hand to her eyes, shading them from the light while she looked out steadily. The window faced the open country on the side farthest from the village, which lay on the other side of the house. About half-a-mile away might be seen the irregular chimneys of an old-fashioned house, called Moat Grange, with whose inmates they were intimate; and in that direction she was gazing.

"Do you happen to have some opera-glasses, Aunt Margery? she suddenly asked, turning to the room as she spoke.

"There are some in the blue drawing-room. Adela can fetch them for you. They are in the table-drawer, my dear. But what do you want to look at, Frances?" added Miss Upton, as Adela went in search of the glasses.

"Only at a group in the road there. I cannot make out whether or not they are the people from the Grange. If so—they may be coming here. But they seem to be standing still.

"Some labourers mending the road," quietly spoke Miss Upton.

"No, Aunt Margery, I don't think so; I am almost sure I can distinguish bonnets. Something is glittering in the sun."

"Do bonnets glitter, Frances?"

Frances laughed. "Selina has some sparkling grass in hers. Did you not notice it yesterday in church?"

"Not I," said Miss Upton; "but I can take your word for it. Selina Dalrymple is more fond of dress than a Frenchwoman. Want of sense and love of finery often go together," added Miss Upton, looking off her work to re-thread her needle: and Frances Chenevix nodded assent.

She stood looking out at the landscape: at the signs of labour to be seen around. The harvest was gathered, but much outdoor work lay to hand. Waggoners paced slowly beside their teams, with a crack now and again of the whip, or a word of encouragement to the leading horse. At this moment the sound of a gun was heard in the direction of Moat Grange. Frances exclaimed—

"Aunt Margery, they are shooting!"

"Well, my dear, is that anything unusual on the first of October?" spoke Miss Upton, smiling. "Robert Dalrymple would think it strange if he did not go out today to bag his pheasants—poor things! I dare say it was his gun you heard."

"And there's another—and another!" cried the young lady. "They are shooting away! Adela must have run away with the glasses, Aunt Margery."

Adela Chenevix had gone, listlessly enough, into the blue room: one of the magnificent drawing-rooms in front, its colours pale blue and silver. She opened the first table-drawer she came to; but did not see any glasses. Then she glanced about in other directions.

"Janet," she called to a maid-servant passing the door, "do you know where the opera-glasses are?"

"The opera-glasses," returned the girl, entering. "No, I don't, my lady."

"Aunt Margery said they were in this room."

"I know Miss Margery had them a few days ago. She was looking through them at the rick that was on fire over yonder. I'll look in the other rooms, my lady."

Adela, sat down near the window, and fell into a train of thought. The maid came back, saying she could not find the glasses: and the young lady forgot all about them, and sat on.

"Well," said Miss Margery, interrupting her presently, "and where are the glasses you were sent for, Adela? And what's the matter?"

Adela started up; the blush-rose on her cheek deepening to a rich damask.

"I—I am afraid I forgot all about them, Aunt Margery. I can't find them."

Miss Upton walked to the further end of the large room, opened the drawer of a small table, and took out the glasses.

"Oh," said Adela, repentantly; "it was in this table that I looked, Aunt Margery."

"No doubt. But you should have looked in this one also, Adela. I hope the child has not got that Captain Stanley in her mind still, worrying herself over his delinquencies?" mentally concluded Miss Upton for her own private benefit.

They went back to the other room together. Frances Chenevix eagerly took the delayed glasses, used them, and put them down with a disappointed air.

"They are road labourers, Aunt Margery, and nothing else."

"To be sure, my dear," calmly returned Miss Upton, settling to her sewing again.

The owner of Court Netherleigh, preceding Miss Margery, was Sir Francis Netherleigh; his baronetcy being of old creation. Sir Francis had lived at the Court with his wife, very quietly: they had no children: and if both of them were of a saving, not to say parsimonious, turn of mind, the fact might be accounted for, and justified by their circumstances. Some of his ancestors had been wofully extravagant: and before he, Sir Francis, was born, his father and grandfather had contrived together to out off the entail. The title had of course to go to the next male heir; but the property—what was left of it—need not do so. However, it was eventually willed in the right direction, and Francis Netherleigh came into the estate and title when he was a young man. He married a prudent, good woman, of gentle but not high lineage;

they cheerfully set themselves to the work of repairing what their forefathers had destroyed, and by the time Sir Francis was five-and-fifty years of age, the estate was again bringing in its full revenues of fifteen thousand a-year. Lady Netherleigh died about that time, and Sir Francis, as a widower, continued to live the same quiet, economical, unceremonious life that he and his wife had lived together. He was a religious, good man.

Naturally, the question, to whom Sir Francis would bequeath the estate, became a matter of speculation with sundry gossips—who always, you are aware, take more interest in our own affairs than we take ourselves. The title would lapse; that was known; unless indeed Sir Francis should marry again and have a son. The only relatives he had in the world were three distant female cousins.

The eldest of these young ladies in point of years was Catherine Grant; the second was Margery Upton; and the third was Elizabeth Cleveland. Margery and Elizabeth were cousins in a third degree to one another; but they were not related to Catherine. The young ladies met occasionally at Court Netherleigh; for Sir Francis invariably invited all three of them together; never one alone. They corresponded at other times, and were good friends. The first to marry was Catherine Grant. She became the wife of one Christopher Grubb, a merchant of standing in the City of London. That, you must understand, was thirty years before this month of October we are writing about: and this again was many years prior to the present time.

In those days, to be in trade, no matter of how high a class it might be, was looked upon by the upper classes as next door to being in Purgatory. For all social purposes you might almost as well have been in the one as the other. Trading was nothing less than a social crime. Opinions have wonderfully altered now; but many will remember that what I state is true. Therefore, when Catherine Grant, who was of gentle blood, so far forgot what was due to herself and her friends as to espouse Mr. Grubb, she was held to have degraded herself for ever. What with the man's name, and what with his counting-house, poor Catherine had effectually placed herself beyond the pale of society. A few sharp, severe letters were written to her; one by Sir Francis Netherleigh, one each by the two remaining young ladies. They told her she had lost caste—and, in good truth, she had done so. From that hour Mrs. Grubb was consigned to oblivion, the fate she was deemed to have richly merited: and it may really be questioned whether in a few years she was not absolutely forgotten. As the daughter of a small country rector, Miss Grant had not had the opportunity of moving in the higher ranks of society (except at Sir Francis Netherleigh's), and the other two young ladies did move in it. She had, consequently, been already privately looked down upon by Elizabeth Cleveland—whose father, though a poor half-pay captain, was the Honourable Mr. Cleveland: and so, said Elizabeth, the girl had perhaps made a suitable match, after all, according to her station; all which made it only the more easy to ignore Catherine Grubb's existence, and to forget that such a person had ever inhabited the civilized world. The next to marry was Elizabeth Cleveland. Her choice fell upon a spendthrift young peer, George Frederick Chenevix, Earl of Acorn: or, it may be more correct to say, his choice fell upon her. Margaret Upton remained single.

Years went on. Lord and Lady Acorn took care to keep up an intimacy with Sir Francis Netherleigh, privately hoping he would make the earl his heir. The earl needed it: he was a careless spendthrift. But Sir Francis never gave them, or any one else, the slightest sign of such intention—and Lord Acorn's hopes were based solely on the fact that he had "no one else to leave it to;" he had no male heir, or other relative, himself excepted. He, the earl, chose to consider that he was a relative, in right of his wife.

Disappointment, however, as all have too often experienced, is the lot of man. Lord Acorn was fated to experience it in his turn. Sir Francis Netherleigh died: and, with the exception of legacies to servants and sundry charities, the whole of his property was left unconditionally to Margery Upton. Miss Upton, though probably as much surprised as any one else, accepted the large bequest calmly, just as though it had been a matter of right, and she the heiress-apparent; and she took up her abode at Court Netherleigh.

This was fourteen years ago; she was eight-and-thirty then; she was two-and-fifty now. Miss Upton had not wanted for suitors—as the world will readily believe: but she only shook her head and sent them all adrift. It was her money they wanted, not herself, she told them candidly; they had not thought of her when she was supposed to be portionless; they should not think of her now. Thus she had lived on at Court Netherleigh, and was looked upon as a somewhat eccentric lady; but a thoroughly good woman and a kind mistress. And the Acorns? They had swallowed their bitter disappointment with a good grace to the world; and set themselves out to pay the same assiduous court to Miss Upton that they had paid to Sir Francis. "I don't think hers will be a long life," Lady Acorn said in confidence to her lord, "and then all the property must come to us; to you and to me: she has no other relative on earth."

The world at large took up the same idea, and Lord Acorn was universally regarded as the undoubted heir to the broad lands of Netherleigh. As to the peer himself, nothing short of a revelation from heaven would have shaken his belief in the earnest of their future good fortune; and, between ourselves, he had already borrowed money on the strength of it. There never existed a more sanguine or less prudent man than he. The young ladies now staying with Miss Upton were his two youngest daughters. In the gushing affection professed for her by the family generally, the girls had been trained to call her "Aunt Margery:" though, as the reader perceives, she was not their aunt at all; in fact, only very distantly related to them.

"Tiresome things!" cried Lady Frances, toying with the glasses still, but looking towards the distant group of labourers. "I wish it had been the Dalrymples on their way here."

"You can put on your hats and go to Moat Grange, as you seem so anxious to see them," observed Miss Upton. "And you may ask the young people to come in this evening, if you like."

"Oh, that will be delightful," cried Frances, all alert in a moment. "And that young lady who was at church with them, Aunt Margery—are we to ask her also? They called her Miss Lynn."

"Of course you are. What strangely beautiful eyes she had."

"Thank you, Aunt Margery," whispered Adela, bending down with a kiss and a bright smile, as she passed Miss Upton. Not that Adela particularly cared for the Dalrymples; but the days at Court Netherleigh were, to her, very monotonous.

The girls set forth in their pretty gipsy straw hats, trimmed with a wreath of roses. It was not a lonely walk, cottages being scattered about on the way. When nearing the Grange they met a party coming from it; Selina and Alice Dalrymple, the latter slightly lame, and a young lady just come to visit them, Mary Isabel Lynn: a thoughtful girl, with a fair, sweet countenance, and wonderful grey-blue eyes. Gerard Hope was with them: a bright young fellow, who was a Government clerk in London, and liked to run down to Moat Grange for Sundays as often as he could find decent excuse for doing so.

"So you are here!" cried Frances to him, in her offhand manner—and perhaps the thought that he might be there had been the secret cause of her impatience to meet the Dalrymples. "What have you to say for yourself, Mr. Gerard—after protesting and vowing yesterday that the earliest morning train would not more certainly start than you."

"Don't know what I shall say up there," returned Mr. Hope, nodding his head in what might be the direction of London. "When I took French leave to remain over Monday last time they told me I should some day take it once too often."

"You can put it upon the shooting, you know, Gerard," interposed Selina. "No barbarous tyrant of a red-tape martinet could expect you to go up and leave the pheasants on the first of October. Put it to him whether he could."

"And he will ask you how many pair you bagged, and look round for those you have brought for himself—see if he does not," laughed Mary Lynn.

"But Gerard is not shooting," commented Frances.

"No," said Gerard, "these girls kept me. Now, Selina, don't deny it: you know you did."

"What a story!" retorted Selina. "If ever I met your equal, Gerard! You remained behind of your own accord. Put it upon me, if you like. I know. It was not for me you stayed."

Frances Chenevix glanced at the delicate and too conscious face of Alice Dalrymple. Mr. Gerard Hope was a general admirer; but these two girls, Frances and Alice, were both rather dear to him—one of them, however, more so than the other. Were they destined to be rivals? Frances delivered Miss Margery's invitation; and it was eagerly accepted: but not by Gerard. He really had to start for town by the midday train.

"Will Miss Margery extend her invitation to Oscar, do you think?" asked Alice, in her quiet voice. "He is staying with us."

"To be sure: the more, the merrier," assented Frances. "Not that Oscar is one of my especial favourites," added the outspoken girl. "He is too solemn for me. Why, he is graver than a judge."

They all rambled on together. Gerard Hope and Frances somehow found themselves behind the others.

"Why did you stay today?" the girl asked him, in low tones. "After saying yesterday that it was simply impossible!"

"Could not tear myself away," he whispered back again. "For one thing, I thought I might again see you."

"Are you playing two games, Gerard?" continued Frances, giving him a keen glance. In truth she would like to know.

"I am not playing at one yet," answered the young man. "It would not do, you know."

"What would not do? As if any one could make anything of your talk when you go in for obscurity!" she added, with a light laugh, as she gave a toss to her pretty hat.

"Were I to attempt to talk less obscurely, I should soon be set down; therefore I never—we must conclude—shall do it," spoke he, in pained and strangely earnest tones. And with that Mr. Hope walked forward to join the others, leaving a line of pain on the fair open brow of Lady Frances Chenevix.

CHAPTER II

THE SHOT

They had brought down the pheasants: never had a first of October afforded better spoil: and they had lingered long at the sport, for evening was drawing on. Robert Dalrymple, the head of the party and owner of Moat Grange—a desolate grange enough, to look at, with the remains of a moat around it, long since filled in—aimed at the last bird he meant to hit that day, and missed it. He handed his gun to his gamekeeper.

"Shall I load again, sir?"

"No; we have done enough for one day, Hardy: and it is getting late. Come, Robert. Oscar, are you satisfied?"

"He must be greedy if he is not," broke in the hearty voice of the Honourable and Reverend Thomas Cleveland, the Rector of Netherleigh, who had joined the shooting-party, and who was related to Lady Acorn, though very distantly: for, some twenty years ago, the Earldom of Cleveland had lapsed to a distant branch.

"You will come home and dine with us, Cleveland?" spoke Mr. Dalrymple, as they turned their faces towards the Grange.

"What, in this trim? Mrs. Dalrymple would say I made myself free and easy."

"Nonsense! You know we don't stand upon ceremony. James will give your boots a brush. And, if you insist on being smart, I will lend you a coat."

"You have lent me one before now. Thank you. Then I don't care if I do," concluded the Rector.

He had not time to go home and change his things. The Rectory and the Grange stood a good mile apart from each other, the village lying between them—and the dinner-hour was at hand. For the hours of that period were not the fashionable ones of these, when people dine at eight o'clock. Five o'clock was thought to be the proper hour then, or six at the latest, especially with unceremonious country people. As to parsons, they wore clothes cut as other people's were cut, only that the coats were generally black.

"Look out, Robert," cried Mr. Cleveland to young Dalrymple. "Stand away." And, turning round, the Rector fired his gun in the air.

"What is that for?" demanded Oscar Dalrymple, a relative of the family, who was staying for a day or two at the Grange.

"I never carry home my gun loaded," was Mr. Cleveland's answer. "I have too many young ones to risk it; they are in all parts of the house at once, putting their hands to everything. Neither do I think it fair to carry it into the house of a friend."

Oscar Dalrymple drew down the corners of his mouth; it gave an unpleasing expression to his face, which was naturally cold. At that moment a bird rose within range; Oscar raised his piece, fired and brought it down. "That," said he, "is how I like to waste good powder and shot."

"All right, Mr. Oscar," was the Rector's hearty answer. "To use it is better than to waste it, but to waste it is better than to run risks. Most of the accidents that happen with guns are caused by want of precaution."

"Shall I draw your charge, Mr. Robert?" asked Hardy; who, as a good church-going man, had a reverence for all the Rector said, in the church and out of it.

"Draw the charge from my gun!" retorted Hardy's young master; not, however, speaking within ear-shot of Mr. Cleveland. "No. I can take care of my playthings, if others can't, Hardy," he added, with all the self-sufficiency of a young and vain man.

Presently there came up a substantial farmer, winding across the stubble towards his own house, which they were passing. He rented under Mr. Dalrymple.

"Famous good sport today, hasn't it been, Squire?" cried he, saluting his landlord.

"Famous. Never better. Will you accept a pair, Lee?" continued Mr. Dalrymple. "We have bagged plenty."

The farmer gladly took the pheasants. "I shall tell my daughters you shot them on purpose, Squire," said he, jestingly.

"Do," interposed Robert, with a laugh. "Tell Miss Judith I shot them for her: in return for her sewing up that rent in my coat, the other day, and making me decent to go home. Is the fence, where I fell, mended yet?"

"Mended yet?" echoed Mr. Lee. "It was up again in an hour after you left, Mr. Robert."

"Ah! I know you are the essence of order and punctuality," returned Robert. "You must let me have the cost."

"Time enough for that," said the farmer. "'Twasn't much. Good-afternoon, gentlemen; your servant, Squire."

"Oh—I say—Lee," called out Robert, as the farmer was turning homewards, while the rest of the party pursued their way, "about the mud in that weir? Hardy says it will hurt the fish to do it now."

"That's just what I told you, Mr. Robert."

"Well, then— But I'll come down tomorrow, and talk it over with you: I can't stop now."

"As you please, sir. I shall be somewhere about."

Robert Dalrymple turned too hastily. His foot caught against something sticking out of the stubble, and in saving himself he nearly dropped his gun. He recovered the gun with a jerk, but the trigger was touched, he never knew how, or with what, and the piece went off. A cry in front, a confusion, one man down, and the others gathered round him, was all Robert Dalrymple saw, as through a mist. He dropped the gun, started forward, and gave vent to a cry of anguish. For it was his father who had fallen.

The most collected was Oscar Dalrymple. He always was collected; his nature was essentially cool and calm. Holding up Mr. Dalrymple's head and shoulders, he strove to ascertain where the injury lay. Though very pale, and lying with closed eyes, Mr. Dalrymple had not fainted.

"Oh, father," cried Robert, as he throw himself on his knees beside him in a passion of grief, "I did not do it purposely—I don't know how it happened."

"Purposely—no, my boy," answered his father, in a kind tone, as he opened his eyes. "Cheer up, Charley." For, in fond moments, and at other odd times, they would call the boy by his second name, Charles. Robert often clashed with his father's.

"I do not believe there's much harm done," said the sufferer. "I think the damage is in my left leg."

Mr. Dalrymple was right. The charge had entered the calf of the leg. Oscar cut the leg of the trouser round at the knee with a penknife, unbuttoned the short gaiter, and drew them off, and the boot. The blood was running freely. As a matter of course, not a soul knew what ought to be done, whether anything or nothing, all being profoundly ignorant of the simple principles of surgery, but they stumbled to the conclusion that tying it up might stop the blood.

"Not that handkerchief," interposed Mr. Cleveland, as Oscar was about to apply Mr. Dalrymple's own, a red silk one. "Take mine: it is white, and linen. The first thing will be to get him home."

"The first thing must be to get a doctor," said Oscar.

"Of course. But we can move him home while the doctor is coming."

"My house is close at hand," said Farmer Lee. "Better move him there for the present."

"No; get me home," spoke up Mr. Dalrymple.

"The Squire thinks that home's home," commented the gamekeeper. "And so it is; 'specially when one's sick."

True enough. The difficulty was, how to get Mr. Dalrymple there. But necessity, as we all know, is the true mother of invention: and by the help of a mattress, procured from the farmer's, with impromptu bearings attached to it made of "webbing," as Mr. Lee's buxom daughter called some particularly strong tape she happened to have by her, the means were organized. Some labourers, summoned by Mr. Lee, were pressed into the service; with Oscar Dalrymple, the farmer, and the gamekeeper. These started with their load. Robert, in a state of distraction, had flown off for medical assistance; Mr. Cleveland had volunteered to go forward and prepare Mrs. Dalrymple.

Mrs. Dalrymple, with her daughters and their guest, Mary Lynn, sat in one of the old-fashioned rooms of the Grange, they and dinner alike awaiting the return of the shooting-party. Old-fashioned as regarded its construction and its carved-oak panelling—dark as mahogany, but handsome withal—and opening into a larger and lighter drawing room. Mrs. Dalrymple, an agreeable woman of three or four and forty, had risen, and was bending over Miss Lynn's tambour-frame, telling her it was growing too dusk to see. Selina Dalrymple sat at the piano, trying a piece of new music, talking and laughing at the same time; and Alice, always more or less of an invalid, lay on her reclining sofa near the window.

"Here is Mr. Cleveland," cried Alice, seeing him pass. "I said he would be sure to come here to dinner, mamma."

Mrs. Dalrymple raised her head, and went, in her simple, hospitable fashion, to open the hall-door. He followed her back to the oak-parlour, and stood just within it.

"What a long day you have had!" she exclaimed. "I think you must all be tired. Where are the others?"

"They are behind," replied the clergyman. He had been determining to make light of the accident at first telling; quite a joke of it; to prevent alarm. "We have bagged such a quantity, Mrs. Dalrymple: and your husband has asked me to dinner: and is going to accommodate me with a coat as well. Oh, but, talking of bagging, and dinner, and coats, I hope you have plenty of hot water in the house; baths, and all the rest of it. One of us has hurt his leg, and we may want no end of hot water to bathe it."

"That is Charley, I know," said Selina. "He is always getting into some scrape. Look at what he did at Lee's last week."

"No; it is not Charley for once. Guess again."

"Is it Oscar?"

"Oscar!" interposed Alice, from her sofa. "Oscar is too cautious to get hurt."

"What should you say to its being me?" said Mr. Cleveland, sitting down, and stretching out one leg, as if it were stiff and he could not bend it.

"Oh, dear!" exclaimed Mrs. Dalrymple, running forward with a footstool. "How did it happen? You ought not to have walked home."

"No," said he, "my leg is all right. It is Dalrymple's leg: he has hurt his a little."

"How did he do it? Is it the knee? Did he fall?" was reiterated around.

"It is nothing," interrupted Mr. Cleveland. "But we would not let him walk home. And I came on to tell you, lest you should be alarmed at seeing him brought in."

"Brought in!" echoed Mrs. Dalrymple. "How do you mean? Who is bringing him?"

"Hardy and Farmer Lee. Left to himself, he might have been for running here, leaping the ditches over the shortest cut; so we just made him lie down on a mattress, and they are carrying it. Miss Judith supplied us."

"Has he sprained his leg?"

"No," carelessly returned Mr. Cleveland. "He has managed to get a little shot into it; but—"

"Shot!" interrupted Mrs. Dalrymple, in frightened tones. "Shot?"

"It is nothing, I assure you. A very slight wound. He will be out with us again in a week."

"Oh, Mr. Cleveland!" she faintly cried. "Is it serious?"

"Serious!" laughed the well-intentioned clergyman. "My dear lady, don't you see how merry I am? The most serious part is the leg of the trousers. Oscar, taking alarm, like you, decapitated it at the knee. The trousers will never be fit to wear again," added Mr. Cleveland, with a grave face.

"We will turn them over to Robert's stock," said Selina. "I am sure, what with one random action or another, half his clothes are in ribands."

"How was it done?" inquired Alice.

"An accident," slightingly replied Mr. Cleveland. "One never does know too well how such mishaps occur."

"We must send for a doctor," observed Mrs. Dalrymple, ringing the bell. "However slight it may be, I shall not know how to treat it."

"We thought of that, and Robert is gone for Forth," said the Rector, as he turned away.

In the passage he met Reuben, a staid, respectable manservant who had been in the family many years; his healthy face was ruddy as a summer apple, and his head, bald on the top, was sprinkled with powder. Mr. Cleveland told him what had happened; he then went to the back-door, and stood there, looking out—his hands in the pockets of his velveteen coat. Selina came quietly up; she was trembling.

"Mr. Cleveland," she whispered, "is it not worse than you have said? I think you have been purposely making light of it. Pray tell me the truth. You know I am not excitable: I leave that to Alice."

"My dear, in one sense I made light of it, because I wished to prevent unnecessary alarm. But I assure you I do not fear it is any serious hurt."

"Was it papa's own gun that went off?"

"No."

"Whose, then?"

"Robert's."

"Oh!—but I might have known it," she added, her shocked tone giving place to one of anger. "Robert is guilty of carelessness every day of his life—of wanton recklessness."

"Robert is careless," acknowledged Mr. Cleveland. "You know, my dear, it is said to be a failing of the Dalrymples. But he has a good heart; and he is always so sorry for his faults."

"Yes; his life is made up of sinning and repenting."

"Sinning!"

"I call such carelessness sin," maintained Selina. "To think he should have shot papa!"

"My dear, you are looking at it in the worst aspect. I believe it will prove only a trifling injury. But, to see him borne here on a mattress, minus the leg of his pantaloons, and his own leg bandaged, might have frightened some of you into fits. Go back to the oak-parlour, Selina; and don't let Alice run out of it at the first slight sound she may chance to hear."

Selina did as she was told: Mr. Cleveland stayed where he was. Very soon he distinguished the steady tread of feet approaching; and at the same time he saw, to his surprise, the gig of the surgeon turning off from the road. How quick Robert had been!

Quick indeed! Robert, as it proved, had met the surgeon's gig, and in it himself and Dr. Tyler, a physician from the nearest town. They had been together to a consultation. Robert, light and slim, had got into the gig between them. He was now the first to get out; and he began rushing about like a madman. The clergyman went forth and laid hands upon him.

"You will do more harm than you have already done, young sir, unless you can control yourself. Here have I been at the pains of impressing upon your mother and sisters that it is nothing more than a flea-bite, and you are going to upset it all! Be calm before them, at any rate."

"Oh, Mr. Cleveland! You talk of calmness! Perhaps I have killed my father."

"I hope not. But I dare say a great deal depends upon his being kept quiet and tranquil. Remember that. If you cannot," added Mr. Cleveland, walking him forward a few paces, "I will just march you over to the Rectory, and keep you there until all fear of danger is over."

Robert rallied his senses with an effort. "I will be calm; I promise you. Repentance," he continued, bitterly, "will do him no good, so I had better keep it to myself. I wish I had shot off my own head first!"

"There, you begin again! Will you be quiet?"

"Yes, I will. I'll go and stamp about where no one can see me, and get rid of myself in that way."

He escaped from Mr. Cleveland, made his way to the kitchen-garden, and began striding about amidst the autumn cabbages. Poor Robert! he really felt as though it would be a mercy if his head were off. He was good-hearted, generous, and affectionate, but thoughtless and impulsive.

As the gamekeeper was departing, after helping to carry the mattress upstairs, he caught sight of his young master's restless movements, and went to him.

"Ah, Mr. Robert, it's bad enough, but racing about won't do no good. If you had but let me draw that there charge! Mr. Cleveland's ideas is sure to be right: the earl's always was, afore him."

Robert went on "racing" about worse than before, clearing a dozen cabbages at a stride. "How did my father bear the transport home, Hardy?"

"Pretty well. A bit faintish he got."

"Hardy, I will never touch a gun again."

"I don't suppose you will, Mr. Robert—not till the next time. You may touch 'em, sir, but you must be more careful of 'em."

Robert groaned.

"This is the second accident of just the same sort that I have been in," continued Hardy. "The other was at the earl's, when I was a youngster. Not Mr. Cleveland's father, you know, sir; t'other earl afore him, over at t'other place. Two red-coat blades had come down there for a week's sport, and one of 'em (he seemed to us keepers as if he had never handled a gun in all his born days) got the shot into the other's calf—just as it has been got this evening into the Squire's. That was a worse accident, though, than this will be, I hope. He was laid up at the inn, close by where it happened, for six weeks, for they thought it best not to carry him to the Hall, and then—"

"And then—did it terminate fatally?" interrupted Robert, scarcely above his breath.

"Law, no, sir! At the end of the six weeks he was on his legs, as strong as ever, and went back to London—or wherever it was he came from."

Robert Dalrymple drew a relieved breath. "I shall go in and hear what the surgeons say," said he, restlessly. "And you go round to the kitchen, Hardy, and tell them to give you some tea; or anything else you'd like."

Miss Lynn was in the oak-parlour alone, standing before the fire, when Robert entered.

"Oh, Robert," she said, "I wanted to see you. Do you fear this will be very bad?—very serious?"

"I don't know," was the desponding answer.

"Whose gun was it that did the mischief?"

"Whose gun! Have you not heard?" he broke forth, in tones of fierce self-reproach. "MINE, of course. And if he dies, I shall have murdered him."

Mary Lynn was used to Robert's heroics; but she looked terribly grieved now.

"I see what you think, Mary," he said, being in the mood to view all things in a gloomy light: "that you will be better without me than with me. Cancel our engagement, if you will. I cannot say that I do not deserve it."

"No, Robert, I was not thinking of that," she answered. Tears rose to her eyes, and glistened in the firelight. "I was wondering whether I could say or do anything to induce you to be less thoughtless; less—"

"Less like a fool. Say it out, Mary."

"You are anything but that, and you know it. Only you will act so much upon impulse. You think, speak, move and act without the slightest deliberation or forethought. It is all random impulse."

"Impulse could hardly have been at fault here, Mary. It was a horrible accident, and I shall deplore it to the last hour of my life."

"How did it happen?"

"I cannot tell. I had been speaking with Lee, gun in hand, and was turning short round to catch up the others, when the gun went off. Possibly the trigger caught my coat-sleeve—I cannot tell. Yes, that was pure accident, Mary: but there's something worse connected with it."

"What do you mean?"

"Mr. Cleveland had just before fired off his gun, because he would not bring it indoors loaded. Hardy asked if he should draw the charge from mine, and I answered him, mockingly, that I could take good care of it. Why did I not let him do it?" added the young man, beginning to stride the room in his remorse as he had previously been striding the bed of cabbages. "What an idiot I was!—a wicked, self-sufficient imbecile! You had better give me up at once, Mary."

She turned and glanced at him with a smile. It brought him back to her side, and he laid his hands on her shoulders and looked into her eyes by the light of the fire.

"It may be to your interest," he whispered, in agitation. "Some day I may be shooting you, in one of my careless moods. What do you say, Mary?"

She said nothing. She only leaned slightly forward and smiled. Robert threw his arms around her, and strained her to him in all the fervency of a first affection. "My darling, my darling! Mary, you are too good for me."

They were nice-looking young people, both of them, and in love with one another. Robert was three-and-twenty; she only nineteen; and the world looked fair before them. But, that she was too good for him, was a greater truth than Mr. Robert thought.

Stir was heard in the house now; the medical men were coming downstairs. Their report was favourable. The bleeding had been stopped, the shots extracted, and there was no appearance of danger. A little confinement, perfect quiet, and proper treatment, would, they hoped, soon set all to rights again.

Dinner had not been thought of. When the cook had nearly succumbed to despair, and Mr. Dalrymple had dropped into a calm sleep, and the anxious ones were gathered together in the oak-parlour, Reuben came in, and said the soup was on the table.

"Then I will wish you all a good appetite, and be gone," said the Rector to Mrs. Dalrymple.

"Indeed you will not go without some dinner."

"I am in a pretty state for dinner," said he, "and I can't worry Dalrymple about coats now. Look at me."

"Oh, Mr. Cleveland do you think we shall regard your coat! Is this a time to be fastidious? We are not very much dressed ourselves."

"No?" said the Rector, regarding them. "I am sure you all look well. You are not in shooting-jackets and gaiters and inch-thick boots."

"I am going to sit down as I am," interrupted Robert, who had not changed a thing since he came in. "A fellow with a dreadful care at his heart has not the pluck to put on a dandy-cut coat."

Mrs. Dalrymple ended the matter by taking the Rector's arm and bearing him off to the dining-room. The rest followed. Oscar met them in the hall—dressed. He was a small, spare man, cool and self-contained in all emergencies, and fastidious in his habits, even to the putting on of proper coats. His colourless face was rather unpleasing at times, though its features were good, the eyes cold and light, the in-drawn lips thin. Catching Selina's hand, he took her in.

It was a lively dinner-table, after all. Hope had arisen in every heart, and Mr. Cleveland was at his merriest. He had great faith in cheerful looks round a sick-bed, and he did not want desponding ones to be displayed to his friend, Dalrymple.

Before the meal was over, a carriage was heard to approach the house. It contained Miss Upton. The news of the accident had spread; it had reached Court Netherleigh; and Miss Upton got up from her own dinner-table and ordered her carriage. She came in, all concern, penetrating to the midst of them in her unceremonious way. "And the fault was Robert's!" she exclaimed, after listening to the recital, as she turned her condemning eyes upon the culprit. "I am sorry to hear that."

"You cannot blame me as I blame myself, Miss Upton," he said ingenuously, a moisture dimming his sight. "I am always doing wrong; I know that. But this time it was really an accident that might have happened to any one. Even to Oscar, with all his prudence."

"I beg your pardon, young man; you are wrong there," returned Miss Upton. "Oscar Dalrymple would have taken care to hold his gun so that it could not go off unawares. Never you fear that he will shoot any one. I hope and trust your father will get well, Robert Dalrymple; and I hope you will let this be a lesson to you."

"I mean it to be one," humbly answered Robert.

Miss Upton carried the three young ladies back to Court Netherleigh, leaving Oscar and Robert to follow on foot: no reason why they should not go, she told them, and it would help to keep the house quiet for its master.

"Will it prove of serious consequence, this hurt?" she took an opportunity of asking aside of Mr. Cleveland, as she was going out to the carriage.

"No, I hope not. I think not. It is only a few stray shots in the leg."

"I don't like those stray shots in the leg, mind you," returned Miss Upton.

"Neither do I, in a general way," confessed the Rector.

Thinking of this, and of that, Miss Upton was silent during the drive home. But it never did, or could, enter into her imagination to suppose that the fair girl, with the sweet and thoughtful grey-blue eyes, sitting opposite her—eyes that somehow did not seem altogether unfamiliar to her memory—was the daughter of that friend of her girlhood, Catherine Grant.

CHAPTER III

LEFT TO ROBERT

The eighth day after the accident to Mr. Dalrymple was a day of rejoicing, for he was so far recovered as to be up for some hours. A sofa was drawn before the fire, and he lay on it. The symptoms had all along been favourable, and he now merrily told them that if any one had written to order him a cork leg, he thought it might be countermanded. Mr. Cleveland, a frequent visitor, privately decided that the thanksgiving for his recovery might be offered up in church on the following Sunday—such being the custom in the good and simple place. They all rejoiced with him, paying visits to his chamber by turns. Alice and Miss Lynn had been in together during the afternoon: when they were leaving, he beckoned the latter back, but Alice did not notice, and went limping away. Any great trouble affected Alice Dalrymple's spirits sadly, and her lameness would then be more conspicuous.

"Do you want me to do anything for you?" asked Mary, returning, and bending over the sofa.

"Yes," said Mr. Dalrymple, taking possession of both her hands, and looking up with an arch smile: "I want you to tell me what the secret is between you and that graceless Robert."

Mary Lynn's eyes dropped, and her face grew scarlet. She was unable to speak.

"Won't you tell me?" repeated Mr. Dalrymple.

"Has he been—saying anything to you, sir?" she faltered.

"Not he. Not a word. Some one else told me they saw that he and Miss Lynn had a secret between them, which might possibly bear results some day."

She burst into tears, got one of her hands free, and held it before her face.

"Nay, my dear," he kindly said, "I did not wish to make you uncomfortable; quite the contrary. I want just to say one thing, child: that if you and he are wishing to talk secrets to one another, I and my wife will not say nay to it: and from a word your mother dropped to me the last time I was in town, I don't think she would either. Dry up your tears, Mary; it is a laughing matter, not a crying one. Robert is frightfully random at times, but he is good as gold at heart. I invite you and him to drink tea with me this evening. There."

Mary escaped, half smiles, half tears. And she and Robert had tea with Mr. Dalrymple that evening. He took it early since his illness; six o'clock. Mary made the tea, and Robert waited on his father, who was then in bed. When tea was cleared away, Mary went with it; Robert remained.

"This might have been an unlucky shot, Charley," Mr. Dalrymple suddenly observed.

"Oh, father! do not talk about it. I am so thankful!"

"But I am going to talk about it. To tell you why it would have been unlucky, had it turned out differently. This accident has made me remember the uncertainty of life, if I never remembered it before. Put the candles off the table; I don't like them right in my eyes; and bring a chair here to the bedside. Get the lotion before you sit down."

Robert did what was required, and took his seat.

"When I married, Robert, I was only the second brother, and no settlement was made on your mother: I had nothing to settle. The post I had in London in what you young people are now pleased to call the red-tape office, brought me in six hundred a-year, and we married on that, to rub on as we best could. And I dare say we should have rubbed on very well," added Mr. Dalrymple, in a sort of parenthesis, "for our desires were simple, and we were not likely to go beyond our income. However, when you were about two years old, Moat Grange fell to me, through the death of my elder brother."

"What was the cause of his death?" interrupted Robert. "He must have been a young man."

"Eight-and-twenty only. It was young. I gave up my post in town, and we came to Moat Grange—"

"But what did Uncle Claude die of?" asked Robert again. "I don't remember to have heard."

"Never mind what. It was an unhappy death, and we have not cared to speak of it. Moat Grange is worth about two thousand a-year: and we have been doing wrong, in one respect, ever since we came to it, for we have put nothing by."

"Why should you have put by, father?"

"There! That is an exemplification of your random way of speaking and thinking. Moat Grange is entailed upon you, every shilling of it."

"Well, it will be enough for me, with what I have," said Robert.

"I hope it will. But it would have been anything but well had I died; for in that case your mother and sisters would have been beggars."

"Oh, father!"

"Yes; all would have lapsed to you. Let me go on. Claude Dalrymple left many debts behind him, some of them cruel ones—personal ones—we will not enter into that. I—moved by a chivalrous feeling perhaps, but which I and your mother have never repented of—took those personal debts upon me, and paid them off by degrees."

"I should have done the same," cried impulsive Robert.

"And the estate had of course to be kept up, for I would not have had it said that Moat Grange suffered by its change of owners, and your mother thought with me; so that altogether we had a struggle for it, and were positively less at our ease for ready-money here than we had been in our little household in London. When the debts were cleared off, and we had breathing time, I began to think of saving: but I am sorry to say it was only thought of; not done. The cost of educating you children increased as you grew older; Alice's illness came on and was a great and continued expense; and, what with one thing and another, we never did, or have, put by. Your expenses at college were enormous."

"Were they?" returned Robert, indifferently.

"Were they!" echoed Mr. Dalrymple, almost in sharp tones. "Do you forget that you also ran into debt there, like your uncle Claude?"

"Not much, was it, sir?" cried Robert, deprecatingly, who remembered very little about the matter, beyond the fact that the bills had gone in to Moat Grange.

"Pretty well," returned Mr. Dalrymple, with a cough. "The sum total averaged between six and seven hundred a-year, for every year that you were there."

"Surely not!" uttered Robert, startled to contrition.

"It seems to have made but little impression on you; you knew it at the time. But I am not recalling this to cast reproach on you now, Robert: I only wanted to explain how it is that we have been unable to put by. Not a day after I am well, will I delay beginning it. We will curtail our expenses, even in things hitherto considered necessary, no matter what the neighbourhood may think; and I shall probably insure my life. Your mother and I were talking of this all day yesterday."

"I can do with less than I spend, father; I will make the half of it do," said Robert, in one of his fits of impulse.

"We shall see that," said Mr. Dalrymple, with another cough. "But you do not know the trouble this has been to me since the accident, Robert. I have lain here, and dwelt incessantly upon the helpless condition of your mother and sisters—left helpless on your hands—should I be called away."

"My dear father, it need not trouble you. Do you suppose I should ever wish to disturb my mother and sisters in the possession of their home? What do you take me for?"

"Ah, Robert, these generous resolves are easily made; but circumstances more often than not mar them. You will be wanting a home of your own—and a wife."

Robert's face took a very conscious look. "Time enough for that, sir."

"If you and Mary Lynn can both think so."

"You—don't—object to her, do you, sir?" came the deprecating question.

"No, indeed I don't object to her: except on one score," replied Mr. Dalrymple. "That she is too good for you."

Robert laughed. "I told her that myself, and asked her to give me up. It was the night of the accident, when I was so truly miserable."

"Well, Robert, you could not have chosen a better girl than Mary Lynn. She will have money—"

"I'm sure I've not thought whether she will or not," interrupted Robert, quite indignantly.

"Of course not; I should be surprised if you had," said Mr. Dalrymple, in the satirical tone his son disliked. "Commonplace ways and means, pounds, shillings and pence, are beneath the exalted consideration of young Mr. Dalrymple. I should not wonder but you would set up to live upon air tomorrow, if you had nothing else to live upon."

"Well, father, you know what I meant—that I am not mercenary."

"I should be sorry if you were. But when we contemplate the prospect of a separate household, it is sometimes necessary to consider how its bread-and-cheese will be provided."

"I have the two hundred a-year that my own property brings in—that Aunt Coolly left me. There's that to begin with."

"And I will allow you three or four hundred more; Mary will bring something and be well-off later. Yes, Robert, I think you may set up your tent, if you will. I like young men to marry young. I did myself—at three-and-twenty: your present age. Your uncle Claude did not, and ran into folly. And, Robert, I should advise you to begin and read for the Bar. Better have a profession."

"I did begin, you know, father."

"And came down here when you were ill with that fever, and never went up again. Moat Grange will be yours eventually—"

"Not for these twenty years, I hope, father," impulsively interrupted Robert. "You are spared to us, and I can never be sufficiently thankful for it. Why, in twenty years you would not be an old man; not seventy."

"I am thankful, too, Robert; thankful that my life is not cut off in its midst—as it might have been. The future of your mother and sisters has been a thorn in my side since I was brought face to face with death. In health we are apt to be fearfully careless."

"Hear me, father," cried Robert, rising, and speaking with emotion. "Had the worst happened, they should have been my first care; I declare it to you. First and foremost, even before Mary Lynn."

"My boy, I know your heart. Are you going down? That's right. I think I have talked enough. Bring a light here first. My leg is very uneasy."

"Does it pain you?" inquired Robert, who had noticed that his father was getting restless. "How tight the bandage is! The leg appears to be swollen."

"The effect of the bandage being tight," remarked Mr. Dalrymple. "Loosen it, and put plenty of lotion on."

"It feels very hot," were Robert's last words.

The evening went on. Just before bed-time, the young people were all sitting round the fire in the oak-parlour, Mrs. Dalrymple being with her husband. So assured did they now feel of no ill results ensuing, that they had grown to speak lightly of it. Not of the accident: none would have been capable of that: but of the circumstances attending it. Selina had just been recommending Robert never in future to touch any weapon stronger than a popgun.

"I don't mean to," said Robert.

"What a long conference you had with papa tonight after Mary came down," went on Selina. "What was it about, Robert? Were you getting a lesson how to carry loaded guns?"

"Not that," put in Oscar Dalrymple: "Robert has learnt that lesson by heart. He was getting some hints how to manage Moat Grange."

Robert looked up quickly, almost believing Oscar must have been behind the chamber wall.

"Your father has come so very near to losing it," added Oscar. "A chance like that brings reflection with it."

"Only to think of it!" breathed Alice—"that we have been so near losing the Grange! If dear papa had died, it would have come to Robert."

"Ay, all Robert's; neither yours nor your mother's," mused Oscar. "I dare say the thought has worried Mr. Dalrymple."

"I know it has," said Robert, in his hasty way. "But there was no occasion for it."

"No, thank Heaven!" breathed Selina.

"However things had turned out, my father might have been easy on that score. And we were talking of you," added Robert, in a whisper to Mary Lynn, while making believe to regard attentively the sofa cushion at her ear. "And of setting up our tent, Mary; and of ways and means—and I am to go on reading for the Bar. It all looks couleur-de-rose."

"Robert," returned Alice, "should you have sent us adrift, had you come into the old homestead?"

"To be sure I should, in double-quick time," answered he, tilting Alice's chair back to kiss her, and keeping it in that position. "'Sharp the word and quick the action' it would have been with me then. I should have paid a premium with you both, and shipped you off by an emigrant ship to some old Turkish Sultan who buys wives, so that you might never trouble me or the Grange again."

"And mamma, Robert?"

"Oh, mamma—I might perhaps, have allowed her to stop here," conceded Robert, with a mock serious face. "On condition that she acted as my housekeeper."

They all laughed; they were secure in the love of Robert. In the midst of which, the young man felt some one touch his shoulder. It was Mrs. Dalrymple.

"Dearest mamma," said he, letting Alice and her chair go forward to their natural position, and stepping backwards, laughing still. "Did you hear what we were saying?"

"Yes, Robert, I heard it," she sighed. "Have you a mind for a drive tonight?"

"A drive!" exclaimed Robert. "To find the emigrant ship?"

"I have told James to get the gig ready. He can go, if you do not, but I thought you might be the quicker driver. It is to bring Mr. Forth. Some change for the worse has taken place in your father."

All their mirth was forgotten instantly. They sat speechless.

"He complained, just now, of the bandage being too tight, and said Robert had pretended to loosen it, but must have only fancied that he did so," continued Mrs. Dalrymple, speaking to them generally. "It is much inflamed and swollen, and he cannot bear the pain. I fear," she added, sitting down and bursting into tears, "that we have reckoned on his recovery too soon—that it is far off yet."

Robert flew on the wings of the wind, and soon brought back Mr. Forth. Mrs. Dalrymple and Oscar went with the surgeon to the sick-chamber. Uncovering the leg, he held the wax-light close to examine it. One look, and he glanced up with a too-expressive face.

Oscar, always observant, noticed it; no one else. Mrs. Dalrymple asked the cause of the change, the sudden heat and pain.

"It is a change—that—does—sometimes come on," drawled Mr. Forth; who of course, as a medical man, would have protested against danger had he known his patient was going to drop out of his hands the next moment but one.

"That redness about it," said Mr. Dalrymple, "that's new."

"A touch of erysipelas," remarked the surgeon.

His manner soothed them, and the vague feeling of alarm subsided. None of them looked to the worst side—and a day or two passed on. Dr. Tyler came again now as well as Mr. Forth.

One morning when the doctors were driving out of the stable-yard—that way was more convenient to the high-road than the front-entrance—they met Mr. Cleveland. Mr. Forth pulled up, and the Rector leaned on the gig while he talked to them, one hand on the wing, the other on the dashboard.

"How is he this morning?"

"We were speaking of you, sir," replied Mr. Forth: "saying that you, as Mr. Dalrymple's chief friend, would be the best to break the news to the Grange. There is no hope."

"No hope of his life?"

"None. A day or two must terminate it."

Mr. Cleveland was inexpressibly shocked. He could not at first speak. "This is very sudden, gentlemen."

"Not particularly so. At least, not to us. We have done all in our power, but it has mastered us. Will you break it to him?"

"Yes," he answered, quitting them. "It is a hard task; but some one must do it." And he went straight to Mr. Dalrymple.

In the evening, Robert, who had been away all day on some matter of business, returned. As he went to his father's room to report what he had done, his mother came out of it. She had her handkerchief to her face: Robert supposed she was afraid of draughts. He approached the bed.

Mr. Dalrymple, looking flushed and restless, took Robert's hand and held it in his. "Have they told you the news, my boy?"

"No," answered Robert, never suspecting the true meaning of the words. "Is there any?"

Robert Dalrymple the elder gazed at him; a yearning gaze. And an uneasy sensation stole over his son.

"I am going to leave you, Robert."

He understood, and sank down by the side of the bed. It was as if a thunderbolt had struck him: and one that would leave its trace throughout life.

"Father! It cannot be!"

"In a day or two, Robert. That is all of time they can promise me now."

He cried out with a low, wailing cry, and let his head drop on the counterpane beside his father.

"You must not take it too much to heart, my son. Remember: that is one of my dying injunctions."

"I wish I could die for you, father!" he passionately uttered. "I shall never forgive myself."

"I forgive you heartily and freely, Robert. My boy, see you not that this must be God's good will? I could die in peace, but for the thought of your mother and sisters. I can but leave them to you: will you take care of and cherish them?"

He lifted his head, speaking eagerly. "I will, I will. They shall be my only care. Father, this shall ever be their home. I swear—"

"Be silent, Robert!" interrupted Mr. Dalrymple, his voice raised in emotion. "How dare you? Never take a rash oath."

"I mean to fulfil it, father; just as though I had taken it. This shall ever be my mother's home. But, oh, to lose you thus! My father, say once more that you do forgive me. Oh, father, forgive and bless me before you die!"

Death came, all too surely; and the neighbourhood, struck with consternation, grieved sincerely for Mr. Dalrymple.

"If Mr. Robert had but let me draw that charge from his gun, the Squire would have been here now," bewailed Hardy, the gamekeeper.

CHAPTER IV

AT CHENEVIX HOUSE

It was a magnificent room, everything magnificent about it, as it was fitting the library of Chenevix House should be: a fine mansion overlooking Hyde Park. What good is there to be imagined—worldly good—that fortune, so capricious in her favours, had not showered down upon the owner of this house, the Earl of Acorn? None. With his majority he had come into a princely income, for his father, the late earl, died years before, and the estates had been well nursed. Better had it been, though, for the young Earl of Acorn that he had been born a younger son, or in an inferior rank of life. With that spur to exertion, necessity, he would have pushed on and exercised the talents which had been liberally bestowed on him; but gliding as he did into a fortune that seemed unlimited, he plunged into every extravagant folly of the day, and did his best to dissipate it. He was twenty-one then; he is walking about his library now—you may see him if you choose to enter it—with some five-and-thirty good years added to his life: pacing up and down in perplexity, and possessing scarcely a shilling that he can call his own. His six-and-fifty years have rendered his slender figure somewhat portly, and an expression of annoyance is casting its shade on his clear brow and handsome features; but no deeper lines of sorrow are marked there. Not upon these careless natures does the hand of care leave its sign.

But the earl is—to make the best of it—in a brown study, and he scowls his eyebrows, and purses his lips, and motions with his hands as he paces there, communing with himself. Not that he is so much perplexed as to how he shall escape his already great embarrassments, as he is to contriving the means to raise more money to rush into greater. The gratification of the present moment—little else ever troubled Lord Acorn.

A noise of a cab in the street, as it whirls along, and pulls up before the steps and stately pillars of Chenevix House; a knock and a ring that send their echoes through the mansion; and the earl strides forward and looks cautiously from the window, so as to catch a glimpse of the horse and vehicle. It was only a glimpse, for the window was high from the ground, its embrasures deep, and the cab close to the pavement; and, for a moment, he could not decide whether it belonged to friend or foe; but soon he drew away with an ugly word, crossed the room to unlatch the door, and stood with his ear at the opening. What! a peer condescend to play eavesdropper, in an attitude that befits a meaner man? Yes: and a prince has done the same, when in bodily fear of duns.

A few minutes elapsed. The indistinct sound of contention approaches his lordship's ear, in conjunction with a very uncomfortable stream of wind, and then the house-door closes loudly, the cab whirls off again, and the earl rings the library-bell.

"Jenkins, who was it?"

"That impudent Salmon again, my lord. I said you were out, and he vowed you were in. I believe he would have pushed his way up here, but John and the porter stood by, and I dare say he thought we three should be a match for him."

"Insolent!" muttered his lordship. "Has Mr. Grubb been here?"

"No, my lord."

"What can detain him?" spoke the earl to himself, irascibly. "I begged him to come today. Mind you are in the hall yourself, Jenkins; you know whom to admit and whom to deny."

"All right, my lord." And the butler, who had lived with the earl many years, and was a confidential servant devoted to his master's interests, closed the library-door and descended.

It was not until evening that Mr. Grubb came, and was shown into the library. Do not be prejudiced against him on account of his name, reader, but pay attention to him, for he is worthy of it, and plays a prominent part in this little history. He is thirty years of age, a tall, slender, noble-looking man, with intellect stamped on his ample forehead, and good feeling pervading his countenance. It is a very refined face, and its grey-blue eyes are simply beautiful. He is the son of that city merchant, Christopher Grubb, who married Catherine Grant. Christopher Grubb has been dead many years, and the son, Francis Charles Christopher, is the head of the house now, and the only one of the name living.

His acquaintanceship with Lord Acorn had commenced in this way. When that nobleman's only son, Viscount Denne, was at Christchurch, Francis Grubb was also there; and they became as intimate as two undergraduates of totally opposite pursuits and tastes can become. Lord Denne was wild, careless, and extravagant; more of a spendthrift (and that's saying a great deal) than his father had been before him. He fell into debt and difficulty; and Mr. Grubb, with his ample means, over and over again got him out of it. During their last term, when young Denne was in a maze of perplexity, and more deeply indebted to his friend than he cared to count, the accident occurred that deprived him of life. A mad race with another Oxonian, each of them in his own stylish curricle, the fashionable bachelor carriage of the day, resulted in the overturning of both vehicles, and in the fatal injury of Lord Denne. During the three days that he lingered Mr. Grubb never left him. Lord Acorn was summoned from London, but Lady Acorn and her daughters were abroad. The young man told his father how much money he owed to Francis Grubb, begging that it might be repaid, and the earl promised it should be. The death of this, his only son, was a terrible blow to him: he would have been nine-and-twenty this year.

For this happened some nine or ten years ago; and during all that time Mr. Grubb had not been repaid.

Repaid! The debt had been only added to. For the earl had borrowed money on his own score, and increased it with a vengeance. He had borrowed it on the strength of some property that he was expecting yearly to fall to him through the death of an uncle: and Mr. Grubb, strictly honourable himself, had trusted to the earl's promises. The property, however, had at length fallen in; had fallen in a year ago; and Mr. Grubb had not been repaid one shilling. While Lord Acorn was yet still saying to him, I shall have the money tomorrow, or, I shall have it the next day, Mr. Grubb had now found out that he had had it months before, and had used it in repaying more pressing creditors. Francis Grubb did not like it.

"Ah, Grubb, how are you?" cried Lord Acorn, grasping his hand cordially. "I thought you were never coming."

"It is foreign post night; I could not get away earlier," was Mr. Grubb's answer, his voice a singularly pleasant one.

"Look here, Grubb: I am hard up, cleared down to the last gasp, and money I must have," began his lordship, as he paced the carpet restlessly. "I want you to advance me a little more."

"Not another farthing," spoke Mr. Grubb, in decisive tones. "It has just come to my knowledge, Lord Acorn, that you received the proceeds of your uncle's property long ago—and that you have spent them."

Remembering the deceit he had been practising, his lordship had the grace to feel ashamed of himself. His brow flushed.

"I could not help it, Grubb; I could not indeed. I did not like to tell you, and I have had the deuce's own trouble to keep my head above water."

"I am very sorry; very," said the merchant. "Had you dealt fairly and honourably with me, Lord Acorn, I would always have returned it in kind; always. Had you said to me, I have that money at last, but I cannot let you have it, for it must go elsewhere, I should never have pressed you for it. I must press now."

"Rubbish!" cried the earl, secure in the other's long-extended good feeling. "You will do nothing of the kind, I know, Grubb. You have a good hold yet on the Netherleigh estate. That must come to me."

"Not so sure. Lord Acorn, I must have my money repaid to me."

"Then you can't have it. And I want you to let me have two thousand pounds more. As true as that we are living, Grubb, if I don't get that in the course of a few hours, I shall be in Queer Street."

"Lord Acorn, I will not do it; and I will do the other. You should have dealt openly with me."

"Did you ever get blood from a stone?" asked the earl: and the careless apathy of his manner contrasted strongly with the earnestness of Mr. Grubb's. "There's no chance of your getting the money back until I am under here," stamping his foot on the ground, "and you know it: unless the Netherleigh estate falls in. I speak freely to you, Grubb, presuming on our long friendship. Come, don't turn crusty at last. You don't want the money: you are rich as Croesus, and you must wait. I wish my son had lived; we would have cut off the entail."

"The debt must be liquidated," returned Mr. Grubb, after a pause of regret, given to poor Lord Denne. And he spoke so coldly and determinedly that Lord Acorn wheeled sharply round in his walk, and looked at him.

"I don't know how the dickens it will be done, then. I suppose you won't proceed to harsh measures, and bring a hornets' nest about my head."

They faced one another, and a silence ensued. For once in his careless life, the good-looking face of Lord Acorn was troubled.

"There is one way in which your lordship can repay the debt," resumed Mr. Grubb. "And it will not cost you money."

"Ah!" laughed the earl, "how's that? If you mean by post-obit bonds, I'll sign a cart-load, if you like."

Mr. Grubb approached the earl in a sort of nervous agitation. "Give me your youngest daughter, Lord Acorn," he breathed. "Let me woo and win her! I will take her in lieu of all."

His lordship was considerably startled; the proud Chenevix blood rose, and dyed his forehead crimson. He had not been listening particularly, and he doubted whether he heard aright. In one respect he had not, for he thought the words had been your eldest daughter. Against Francis Grubb personally, nothing could be said; but against his standing a great deal. Many years had gone by since Catherine Grant lost caste by marrying a "City man," but opinions had not changed, for it was yet long antecedent to these tolerant days. Men in trade, no matter how high the class of trade, were still kept at a distance by the upper orders—not looked upon as being of the same race.

Therefore the demand was as a blow to Lord Acorn; and he dared not resent it as he would have liked to. His daughter descend from her own rank, and become one with this trader! Was the world coming to an end?

But as the two men stood gazing at one another, neither of them speaking, the earl began to revolve in his mind the pros of the matter, as well as the cons. Lady Grace was no longer young; she was growing thin and rather cross, for she had been before the world ten years, with no result. Would it be so bad a match for her?

"I will settle an ample income upon her," spoke Mr. Grubb. "And your unpaid bonds—there are many of them, my lord—I will return into your hands: all of them. Thus your debt to me will be cancelled, and, so far as I am concerned, you are a free man again."

"I cannot be that. I am at my wits' end now for two thousand pounds."

"You shall have that."

"Egad, Grubb's a generous fellow!" cogitated the earl, "and it will be a famous thing for Grace: if she can only think so. Have you ever spoken to Grace of this," he asked, aloud.

"To Lady Grace? No."

"Do you think Grace likes you," continued Lord Acorn, remembering how attractive a man the merchant was. "Do you think she will accept you?"

"I am not speaking of Lady Grace."

"No!" repeated the earl, opening his eyes wider than usual. "Which of them is it, then?"

"Lady Adela."

If Lord Acorn had been startled when he thought the object of this proposal was Grace, he was considerably more startled now. Adela! young, beautiful, and haughty!—she would never have him. His first impulse was indignantly to reject the proposition; his second thought was, that he was trammelled and dared not do so.

"I cannot force Adela's inclinations," he said, after an awkward pause.

"Neither would I take a wife whose inclinations require to be forced," returned Mr. Grubb. "Pray understand that."

"My lord," cried a servant, entering the library, "her ladyship wishes to know how much longer she is to wait dinner?"

"Dinner!" exclaimed the earl. "By Jove! I did not know it was so late. Grubb, will you join us sans cérémonie?"

It was not the first time, by many, Mr. Grubb had dined there. He followed the earl into the drawing-room. Lady Acorn was in it, a little woman, all fire and impatience; especially just now, for if one thing put her out more than another, it was that of being kept waiting for her meals. The five daughters were there: they need not be described. Grace, little and plain, but nevertheless with a nice face, and eight-and-twenty, was the oldest; Adela, whom you have already seen, twenty now, and a very flower of beauty, was the youngest. Four daughters were between them. Sarah, next to Grace, and one year younger, had married Major Hope, and was in India; Mary, Harriet, and Frances; Adela coming last. Not a whit less beautiful was she than when we saw her a year ago at Court Netherleigh.

"Here's the grub again," whispered Harriet, for the girls were given to be flippant amongst themselves. Not that they disliked Mr. Grubb personally, or wished to cast derision on him, but they made a standing joke of his name. He was in trade—and all such people they had been taught to hold in contempt. The house, "Christopher Grubb and Son," was situated somewhere in the City, they believed: it did business with India, and the colonies, and ever so many more places; though what the precise business was the young ladies did not pretend to understand; but they did know that it was second to few houses in wealth, and that their father was a considerable debtor to it. While liking Mr. Grubb personally very well indeed, they yet held him to be of a totally different order from themselves.

"Dinner at once," cried the countess, impatiently, to the butler. "Of course it's all cold," she sharply added, for the especial benefit of her husband.

Mr. Grubb went to the upper end of the room after greeting the countess, and was speaking with the young ladies there; Lord Acorn bent over the back of his wife's chair, and began to whisper to her.

"Betsy, here's the strangest thing! Grubb wants to marry one of the girls."

"Absurd!" responded the wrathful little woman.

"So it appears, at the first blush. But when we come to look at the advantages—now do listen reasonably for a moment," he broke off, "you are as much interested in this as I am. He will settle hundreds of thousands upon her, and cancel all my debts to him besides."

"Did he say so?" quickly cried the countess, putting off her anger to a less interested moment.

"He did," replied the earl, forgetting that he had improvised the hundreds of thousands. "And in addition to putting me straight, he will give me a handsome sum down. You shall have five hundred pounds of it for your milliner, Madame Damereau, which will enable you all to get a new rig-out," concluded the wily man, conscious that if his self-willed better-half set her temper against the match, the Archbishop of Canterbury himself could never tie it into one.

"Which of them does he want?" inquired the countess, snappishly, as if wishing to intimate that, though she might have to say Yes, it should be done with an ill grace. "He's talking now with—which is it?— Mary."

"I thought it was Grace," began the earl, in a deprecatory tone; "I took that for granted—"

"Dinner, my lady," came the interruption, as the door was flung open: and the earl started up, and said not another word. He thought it well that his lady wife should digest the news so far, before proceeding further with it. The countess on her part, understood that all was told, and that the desired bride was Grace.

Mr. Grubb gave his arm to Lady Acorn, and sat down at her right hand. Lady Grace was next him on the other side. He was an agreeable man, of easy manners. Could they ignore the City house, and had he boasted of ancestry and a high-sounding name, they could not have wished for a companion who was more thoroughly the gentleman. Unusually agreeable he was this evening, for he now believed that no bar would be thrown in the way of his winning the Lady Adela. He had long admired her above all women; he had long loved her, and he saw no reason why any bar should be thrown: what incompatibility ought to exist between the portionless daughter of a ruined peer and a British merchant of high character and standing and next to unlimited wealth? The ruined peer, however, had he heard this argument, might have said the merchant reasoned only in accordance with his merchant-origin; that he could not be expected to understand distinctions which were above him.

Lady Acorn rose from table early. She had been making up her mind to the match, during dinner: like her husband, she discovered, on reflection, its numerous advantages, and she was impatient to disclose the matter to Grace. Mr. Grubb held the door open as they filed out, for which the countess thanked him by a bow more cordial than she had ever bestowed on him in her life. Whether it had ever occurred to Lady Acorn that this City man was probably the son of Catherine Grant, cannot be told. She had never alluded to it. Catherine had offended them all too greatly to be recalled even by name: and, so far as Lord Acorn went, he did not know such a person as Catherine had ever existed.

The girls gathered their chairs round the fire in the autumn evening, and began grumbling. "Engagements"—he did not say of what nature—had been Lord Acorn's plea for remaining in town when every one else had left it. Adela was especially bitter.

"Papa never does things like other people. When we ought to be away, we are boxed up in town; and when every one else is in town, we are kept in the country. I'm sick of it."

"It's a pity, girls, you haven't husbands to cater for you, as you are sick of your father's rule," tartly spoke their mother. "You don't go off; any of you."

"It is Grace's turn to go first," cried Lady Harriet.

"Yes, it is—and one wedding in a family often leads to another," observed the wily countess. "I should like to see Grace well settled. With a fine place of her own, where we could go and visit her, and a nice town mansion; and a splendid income to support it all."

"And a box at the opera," suggested Frances.

"And a herd of deer, and a pack of hounds, and the crown diamonds," interrupted Adela, with irony in her tone, and a spice of scorn in her eye, as she glanced up from her book. "Don't you wish we had Aladdin's lamp? It might come to pass then."

"But if I tell you that it will come to pass without it," said Lady Acorn, "that it has come to pass, what should you say? Look up, Grace, my dear; there's luck in store for you yet."

Their mother's manner was so pointedly significant, that all were silent from amazement. The colour mounted to the cheeks of Grace, and her lips parted: could it be that she was no longer to remain Lady Grace Chenevix?

"Grace, child," continued the countess, "the time has gone by for you to pick and choose. You are now getting on for thirty, and have never had the ghost of a chance—"

"That is more than you ought to say, mamma," interrupted Grace, her face flushing, perhaps at her mother's assertion telling home. "I may have had—I did have a chance, as you call it, but—"

"Well, not that we ever knew of; let us amend the sentence in that way. What I was going to observe is, that you must not be over-particular now."

"Has Grace got an offer?" inquired Harriet, breathlessly.

"Yes, she has, and you need not all look so incredulous. It is a good offer too, plenty of substance about it. She will abound in such wealth that she'll be the envy of all the girls in London, and of you four in particular. She will have her town and country mansions, crowds of servants, dresses at will—everything, in short, that money can purchase." For, in her maternal anxiety for the acceptance of the offer, her ladyship thought she could not make too much of its advantages.

"Why, for all that, Grace would marry a chimney-sweep," laughed the plain-speaking Lady Frances.

"Grace has had it in her head to turn serious," added Harriet; "she may put that off now. I think Aladdin's lamp has been at work."

"Of course there are some disadvantages attending the proposed match," said Lady Acorn, with deprecation; "no marriage is without them, I can tell you that. Grace will have every real and substantial good; but the gentleman, in birth and position, is—rather obscure. But he is not a chimney-sweep: it's not so bad as that."

"Good Heavens, mamma!" interrupted Lady Grace. "'So bad as that'?"

"Pray do not make any further mystery, mamma," said Mary. "Who is it that has fallen in love with Grace?"

"Mr. Grubb."

"Mr.—Grubb!" was echoed by the young ladies in every variety of astonishment, and Grace thought that of all the men in the world she should have guessed him last; but she did not say so. She was of a cautious nature, and rarely spoke on impulse.

The silence of surprise was broken by a ringing laugh from Adela, one laugh following upon another. It seemed as though she could not cease. When had they seen Adela so merry?

"I cannot help it," she said apologetically, "but it did strike me as sounding so absurd. 'Lady Grace Grubb!' Forgive me, Gracie."

"It will not bear so aristocratic a sound as Lady Grace Chenevix," retorted the mother, tartly, "but remember the old saying, 'What's in a name?' It is you who are absurd, Adela."

CHAPTER V

"I have opened the matter to Grace, and there'll be no trouble with her," began Lady Acorn to her husband the next morning, halting to say it as she was going into her dressing-room. "No girl knows better than she on which side her bread is buttered!"

"To Grace!" cried the earl, who was only half awake, and spoke from the bedclothes. "Do you mean about Grubb?"

"Now what else should I mean?"

"But it is not Grace he wants. It's Adela."

"Adela!" echoed Lady Acorn, aghast.

"I don't think he'd have Grace at a gift—or any of them but Adela. And so you told her, making her dream of wedding-rings and orange-blossoms! Poor Gracie, what a sell!"

"Adela will never have him," broke forth the countess, in high vexation, at herself, her husband, Mr. Grubb, and the world in general. "Never!"

"Oh, nonsense, she must be talked into it. With five girls, it's something to get off one of them."

"Adela is not a girl to be 'talked into' anything. She would like a duke. She is the vainest of them all."

"Look at the amount of devilry this will patch up," urged the earl, impressively, as he lifted his head from the pillow. "If he does not get Adela, he is going to sue for his overdue bonds."

"You have no business with bonds, overdue or under-due," snapped his wife. "I declare I have nothing but worry in this life."

"I shall get the two thousand pounds from him, if this comes off; you shall have five hundred of it, as I told you; and my debt to him he will cancel. The man's mad after Adela."

"But she's not mad after him," retorted Lady Acorn.

"Make her so," advised the earl. And her ladyship went forth to her dressing-room, and allowed some of her superfluous temper to explode on her unoffending maid, who stood there waiting for her.

"There, that will do," she impatiently said, when only half dressed, "I'll finish for myself. Go and send Lady Grace to me." And the maid went, gladly enough.

"Gracie, my dear," she began, when her daughter entered, "I am so sorry; so vexed; but it was your papa's fault. He should have been more explicit."

"Vexed at what?" asked Grace.

"That which I told you last night—I am so grieved, poor child! It turns out to have been some horrible mistake."

Grace compressed her lips. "Yes, mamma?"

"A mistake in the name. It is Adela Mr. Grubb proposed for—not you. I am deeply grieved, Grace."

Lady Grace laid one hand across her chest: it may be that her heart was beating unpleasantly with the disappointment. Better, certainly, that her hopes had never been raised, than that they should be dashed thus unceremoniously down again. She had learnt to appreciate Mr. Grubb as he deserved; she liked and esteemed him, and would gladly have married him.

"Will Adela accept him?" were the first words she said. For she did not forget that Adela, by way of amusing herself, had not been sparing of her ridicule, the previous night, of Mr. Grubb and his pretensions.

"I don't know," growled Lady Acorn. "Adela, when she chooses, can be the very essence of obstinacy. I have said nothing to her. It is only now that I found out there was a misapprehension."

"Mother!" suddenly exclaimed Grace, "it has placed me in a painfully ridiculous position, there's no denying that: we have been talking of it among ourselves. If you will help me, it may be made less so."

"How?"

"Say that I was in your confidence; that we both know it was Adela; and that what was said about me was arranged between us to break the matter to her, and get her reconciled to the idea of him. And let it be myself, not you, to explain now to Adela."

"Yes, yes; do as you will," eagerly assented the mother: for she did feel sorry for Grace.

Grace went to Adela's room, and found her there, with Harriet. She had been recalling the past: and she saw now how attentive Francis Grubb had been to Adela; how fond of talking with her. "Had our eyes been open, we might have seen it all!" sighed Grace.

"How nicely you were all taken in last night!" she said, assuming a light playfulness, as she sat down at the open window. "Don't you think mamma and I got up that fable well about Mr. Grubb?"

"Got it up!" cried Harriet. "You hypocritical sinners! Did he not make the offer?"

"Ay; but not to me. It was better to put it so, don't you see, by way of breaking it to you."

"Then you are not going to be Lady Grace Grubb, after all!" said Adela. "Well, it would have been an incongruous assimilation of names."

"I am not. Guess who it is he wants, Adela?"

"Frances?" cried Harriet.

"No, but you are very near—you burn, as we children used to say at our play."

"Not Adela!"

"It is," answered Grace. "And I congratulate her heartily. Lady Adela Grubb will sound better than Lady Grace would."

"Thank you," satirically answered Adela; "you may retain the name yourself, Grace. None of your Grubbs for me."

"Ah, don't be silly, child. A grub, indeed! He is one of the best and most admirable of men; a true nobleman."

The words were interrupted by a laugh from Harriet; a ringing laugh. "Oh, Gracie, how unfortunate! What shall we do! Frances wrote last night to tell Miss Upton of your engagement, and the letter's posted."

Grace Chenevix suppressed her mortification, and quitted her sisters with a smiling face. But when she was safe in her own room, she burst into a flood of distressing tears.

Lord and Lady Acorn chose to breakfast that morning alone in the library. Afterwards Adela was sent for. Straightening down the slim waist of her pretty morning dress with an action that spoke of conscious vanity, she obeyed the summons. Lord Acorn threw aside the morning paper when she entered.

"Adela, sit down," he said, pushing the chair at his elbow slightly forward. "We have received an offer of marriage for you; and though it is not in every respect all that we could wish—"

"From the grub," interrupted Adela, merging ceremony in indignation, as she stood confronting both her parents, regardless of the seat proffered. "Grace has been telling me."

"Hush, Adela! don't give way to flippant folly," interposed her mother. "Have you considered the advantages of such an alliance as this?"

"Advantages, mamma! I don't understand. Have you"—turning to her father—"considered the disadvantages, sir?"

"There is only one disadvantage connected with it, Adela—that he is not of noble birth."

"But that is insuperable, papa!"

"Indeed, no," said Lord Acorn. "You will possess every good that wealth can command; all things that can conduce to happiness. Your position will be an enviable one. How many of the daughters of our order—in more favourable circumstances than yours—have married these merchant-princes!"

Adela pouted. "That is no reason why I should do so, papa. I don't want to marry."

"You might all remain unmarried for ever, and make five old maids of yourselves, and buy cats and monkeys to pet, if it were not for the horrible dilemma we are in," screamed the countess, in her well-known fiery tones, and with a wrathful glance at the earl; for her tones always were fiery and her glances wrathful when his unpardonable recklessness was recalled to her mind. "Mr. Grubb has been, so to say, the salvation of us for years—for years, Adela,—every year has brought its embarrassments, and he has helped us out of them. As well tell her the truth at once, Lord Acorn," she concluded sharply.

"Ugh!" grunted he, in what might be taken for a note of unwilling assent.

"And if we put this affront upon him—refuse him your hand, which he solicits with so much honour and liberality—it will be all over with us. We can't live any longer in England, for there's nothing left to live upon; we must go abroad to some wretched hole of a continental place, and lodge on one dirty floor of six rooms, and live as common people. What chance would there be of your picking up even a merchant then?"

Adela rose, smiling incredulously. "Things cannot be as bad as that, mamma."

"Sit down, Adela," cried her father, peremptorily, raising his hand to check the flow of eloquence his wife was again about to enter upon. "It is as bad. Grubb has behaved like a prince to me, and nothing less. And, if he should recall the money he has lent, I know not, in truth, where any of us would be. I should have to run; and be posted up as a defaulter, into the bargain, all over the kingdom." And, in a few brief words, he explained facts to her; making, of course, the worst of them. The obstinacy on Adela's countenance faded away as she listened: she was deeply attached to her father.

"You will be a very princess, if you take him, Adela," said Lady Acorn. "Ah! I can tell you, child, before you have come to my age you will have found out that there's little worth living for but wealth, which brings ease and comfort. I ought to know; for our want of it, through one absurd extravagance or another"—with a dreadful glance at her lord—"has been the worry and bane of my married life."

"You have been extravagant on your own score," growled he.

"But, papa, I don't care for Mr. Grubb. Apart from the disreputable fact that he is a tradesman—"

"Those merchant-princes cannot be called tradesmen, Adela," quickly interposed Lord Acorn, who could put the case strongly, in spite of his prejudices, when it suited his interest to do so.

"Well, apart from that, I say I do not like him."

"You cannot dislike him. No one can dislike Francis Grubb."

"I shall if I am made to marry him."

Her obstinate mood was returning; they saw that, and they let her escape for a time. Adela, the youngest and most beautiful of all their children, had been reprehensibly indulged: allowed to grow up in the belief that the world was made for her.

"Well, Adela, and how have you sped?" asked Grace.

"Oh, I don't know," was Adela's answer, as she flung herself into a low chair by her dressing-table. "Mamma is so fond of telling us that the world's full of trouble; and I think it is."

"Have you consented?"

"No. And I don't intend to consent."

"But why not? He is very nice; very; and the advantages are very great. Tell me why you will not, Adela—dear Adela?"

Adela turned her head away. "I do not care to marry yet; him, or any other man."

A light—or rather a doubt—seemed to break upon Lady Grace. "Adela," she whispered, "it is not possible you are still thinking of Captain Stanley?"

"Where would be the use of that?" was the answer. "He is fighting in India, and I am here: little chance of our paths in life ever again crossing each other."

"If I really thought your head was still running upon Stanley, I would tell you—"

"What?" for Grace had stopped.

"The truth," was the reply, in a low voice. "News of him reached England by the last mail."

"What news?"

"Well, I—I hardly know whether you will care much to hear it."

"Probably not. I should like to, for all that."

"He is married."

Adela looked up with a start, and her colour faded. "Married?"

"He is. He has married his cousin, a Miss Stanley, and it is said they have long been attached to each other. He was a frightful flirt, but he had no heart; I always said it; and I think he was not a good man in other respects."

The news brought a pang of mortification to Adela; perhaps a deeper pang than that. Some eighteen months back, she saw a good deal of this Captain Stanley; it was thought by shrewd observers that she had lost her heart to him. If so, it was now thrown back upon her.

And, whether it might have been this, or whether it was the persistent persuasion of her father and mother, ay, and of her sisters, Adela Chenevix consented to accept Mr. Grubb. But she bitterly resented the necessity, and from that hour she deliberately steeled her heart against him.

Daintily she swept into the room for her first interview with him. He stood in agitation at its upper end—a fine, intellectual man; one, young though he was, to be venerated and loved. She wore a pink-and-white silk dress, and her hair had pink and white roses in it; for Mr. Grubb had come to dinner, and she was already dressed for it. A rich colour shone in her cheeks, her beautiful eyes and features were lighted up with it, and her delicate figure was thrown back—in disdain. Oh, that he could have read it then!

He never afterwards quite remembered what he said when he approached her. He knew he took her hand. And he believed he whispered words of thanks.

"They are not due to me," was her answer, delivered with cold equanimity. "My father tells me I must marry you, and I accede to it."

"May God enable me to reward you for the confidence you repose in me!" he whispered. "If it be given to man to love a wife as one never yet was loved, may it be given to me!"

She twisted her hand from him with an ungracious movement, for he would have retained it, and walked deliberately across the room, leaving him where he stood, and rang the bell.

"Tell mamma Mr. Grubb is here," she said to the servant.

He felt pained: he understood this had been an accorded interview. Like all other lovers, he began to speak of the future—of his hope that she would learn to love him.

"There should be no misunderstanding between us on this point," she hastily answered; and could it be that there was contempt in her tone? "I have agreed to be your wife; but, until a day or two ago, the possibility of my becoming so had never been suggested to me. Therefore, the love that I suppose ought to accompany this sort of contract is not mine to offer."

How wondrously calm she spoke—in so matter-of-fact, business-like a way! It struck even him, infatuated though he was.

"It may come in time," he whispered. "My love shall call forth yours; my—"

"I hear mamma," interrupted Adela, drawing away from him like a second cruel Barbara Allen.

"Adela, where's your town house to be?" began one of the girls to her when they got into the drawing-room after dinner, the earl and Mr. Grubb being still at table. "Not in the smoky City, surely!"

"His house is not in the City; it's in Russell Square," corrected another. "Of course he won't take her there!"

"Ada, mind which opera-box you secure. Let it hold us all."

"Of course you'll be smothered in diamonds," suggested Lady Mary.

"One good thing will come of this wedding, if nothing else does: mamma must get us new things, and plenty of them."

"I wonder whether he will give us any ornaments? He is generous to a fault. Is he not, Adela?"

"How you tease!" was Adela's languid rejoinder. "Go and ask him."

"I protest, Adela, if you show yourself so supremely indifferent he will declare off before the wedding-day."

"And take one of you instead. I wish he would."

"No fear. Ada's chains are bound fast about him. One may see how he loves her."

"Love!" cried Adela. "It is perfectly absurd—from him to me. But it is the way with those plebeians."

The preparations for the wedding were begun. On so magnificent a scale that the fashionable world of London was ringing with them. The bridegroom's liberality, in all that concerned his future wife, could not be surpassed. Settlements, houses, carriages, horses, furniture, ornaments, jewellery, all were perfect of their kind, leaving nothing to be wished for. The Lady Adela had once spoken of Aladdin's lamp, in reference to her sister Grace's ideal union; looking on these real preparations, one might imagine that some magic, equally powerful, was at work now.

Lord Acorn had a place in Oxfordshire, and the family went to it in October. Mr. Grubb paid it one or two short visits, and went down for Christmas, staying there ten days. They were all cordial with him, except Adela; she continued to be supremely indifferent. He won upon their regard strangely; the girls could do nothing but sing his praises. Poor unselfish Grace once caught herself wishing that that early misapprehension had not been one, and then took herself to task severely. She loved Adela, and was glad for her sake.

But Adela was not quite always cold and haughty. As if to show her affianced husband that such was not her true nature, she would now and again be sweetly winning and gentle. On one of these occasions he caught her hand. They were alone, sitting on a sofa; Frances had run into the next room for a book they were discussing.

"Adela," he whispered passionately, taking both her hands in his, "but for these rare moments, I should be in despair."

She did not, for a wonder, resent the words. She glanced up at him, a shy look in her sweet brown eyes, a smile on her parted lips, a deeper rose-blush on her delicate face. He stooped and kissed her; kissed her fervently.

She resented that. For when Frances, coming back on the instant, entered, she met Adela sweeping from the room in a storm of anger.

Not to let him kiss her! And in six weeks' time she was to be his wife!

Mr. Grubb had an adventure on the journey home. They had passed Reading some minutes, when the train was stopped. A down-train had come to grief through the breaking of an axle, throwing a carriage, fortunately empty, right across the line; which in consequence was temporarily blocked up. The passengers of the down-train, very few of them, were standing about; the passengers of the up-train got out also.

"Can I be of any use?—can I do anything for you?" asked Mr. Grubb, addressing a little lady in a black-silk cloak and close bonnet, who was sitting on a box and looking rather helpless. And, though he had heard of Miss Margery Upton, he was not aware that it was she to whom he was speaking.

"It is good of you to inquire, sir; you are the first who has done it," she answered; "but I don't see that there's anything to be done. We might all have been killed. They should keep their material in safer order."

She looked up as she spoke. Some drops of rain were beginning to fall. Mr. Grubb put up his umbrella, and held it over her. To do this, he laid down a small hand-bag of Russian leather, on the silver clasp of which was engraved "C. Grubb." Miss Upton read the name, rose from her box, and looked him steadily in the face. "It is a good face and a handsome one," she thought to herself.

"Sir, is your name Grubb?" she asked.

"Yes, madam, it is."

"I read it here," she explained, pointing to the old-fashioned article.

"Ah, yes," he smiled. "It was my late father's bag, and that was his name."

"Was he Christopher Grubb?

"He was."

She put her hand on his coat-sleeve, apparently for the purpose of steadying herself while regarding his face more attentively.

"You have your mother's eyes," she said; "I should know them anywhere. Beautiful eyes they were. And so are yours."

"And may I inquire who it is that is doing honour to my vanity in saying this?" he rejoined, in the winning voice and manner characteristic of him.

"Ay, if you like. I dare say you have heard of me. I am Margery Upton."

"Indeed I have; and I have wondered sometimes whether I should ever see you. Then—did you know my mother, Miss Upton?"

"I did; in the old days when we were girls together. Has she never told you so?"

"Not to my recollection."

"I see. Resented our resentment, and dropped us out of her life as we dropped her," commented Miss Upton partly to herself, as she sat down again. "What a tinkering they keep up there! Is your mother living?"

"Yes; but she is an invalid."

"Is it you who are about to marry Lord Acorn's daughter?" continued Miss Upton.

"Yes. I have just come from them."

"I knew the name was Grubb, and that he was a City man and wealthy," she candidly continued; "and the thought occurred to me that it might possibly be the son of the Christopher Grubb I heard something of in early life. I did not put the question to the Acorns."

"It is by them I have heard you spoken of," he remarked. "Also by my sister."

"By your sister!" exclaimed Miss Upton, in surprise. "What sister? What does she know of me?"

"She was staying some fourteen or fifteen months ago with the Dalrymples of Moat Grange—it was at the time of Mr. Dalrymple's sad death—and she made your acquaintance there. She is Mary Lynn, my half-sister. My father died when I was a little lad, and my mother made a second marriage."

Miss Upton was silent, apparently revolving matters in her mind. "Did your sister know that I was her mother's early friend?" she asked.

"Oh no; I think not. She only spoke of you as a stranger—or, rather, as a friend of the Dalrymples. I never heard my mother speak of you at all—I do not suppose Mary has."

"That young girl had her mother's eyes," suddenly cried Miss Upton, "just as you have. They seemed familiar to me; I remember that; but I wanted the clue, which this name"—bending to look at the bag—"has supplied. C. Grubb—Christopher was your father's name."

"It is mine also."

"And Francis too!" she quickly cried.

"And Francis too—Francis Charles Christopher." It crossed his mind to wonder how she knew it was Francis, then remembered it must have been from the Acorns. Miss Upton had lifted her face, and was looking at him.

"Why did your mother name you Francis?" she asked, rather sharply.

"I was named Francis after my father's only brother. He was my godfather, and gave me his name—Francis Charles." And left me his money also, Mr. Grubb might have added, but did not.

"I see," nodded Miss Upton, apparently satisfied. "You have been letting Lord Acorn borrow no end of money of you on the strength of his coming into the Netherleigh estate," she resumed, in her open, matter-of-fact way, that spoke so much of candour.

Mr. Grubb hesitated, and his face slightly flushed. It did not seem right to enter upon Lord Acorn's affairs with a stranger. But she seemed to know all about it, and was waiting for his answer.

"Not on the Netherleigh estate," he answered. "I have always told Lord Acorn that he ought not to make sure of that."

"You would be quite safe in lending it," she nodded, a peculiar look of acuteness, which Mr. Grubb did not altogether fathom, on her face. "Quite."

Some stir interrupted further conversation. The tinkering, as Miss Upton called it, had ceased, and the down-line was at length ready for traffic. "Where are my people, I wonder?" cried Miss Upton, rising and looking around.

They came forward almost as she spoke—a man and a maid servant. The former took up the box she had been sitting on, and Mr. Grubb gave her his arm to the train, and put her into the carriage.

"This is the first time I have seen you, but I hope it will not be the last," she said, retaining his hand, in hers when he had shaken it. "I am now on my way to Cheltenham, to spend a month, perhaps two months. I like the place, and go to it nearly every year. When I return, you must come to Court Netherleigh."

"I shall be very much pleased to do so."

Mr. Grubb had left her, and was waiting to see the train go on, when she made a hasty movement to him with her hand.

"Perhaps I was incautious in saying that you were safe in lending money on the Netherleigh property," she whispered in his ear. "Take care you don't breathe a word of that admission to Acorn. He would want to borrow you out of house and home."

Mr. Grubb smiled. "I will take care; you may rely on me, Miss Upton." And he stood back and lifted his hat as the delayed train puffed on.

And it may be well to give a word of explanation whilst Mr. Grubb is waiting for his delayed train, which is not ready to puff on yet.

The house, "Christopher Grubb and Son," situated in Leadenhall Street, was second in importance to few in the City; I had almost said second to none. It had been founded by the old man, Christopher Grubb, father of the Christopher who had married Catherine Grant, and grandfather of the Francis who is waiting for his train. The two Christophers, father and son, died about the same time, and the business was carried on by old Christopher's other son, Francis. Catherine Grubb, née Grant, was left largely endowed, provided she did not marry again. If she did, a comparatively small portion only would remain hers, and at her disposal—about a thousand a-year; the rest would go at once to her little son, of whom she would also forfeit the personal guardianship. Mrs. Grubb did marry again; and the little lad, aged eight, was transferred to the care of his uncle Francis, in accordance with the terms of the will, and to his uncle's house in Russell Square. But Mr. Francis Grubb was no churlish guardian, and the child was allowed to be very often at Blackheath with his mother. Mrs. Grubb's second husband, Richard Lynn, who was a barrister, not often troubled with briefs, did not live long; and she was again left a widow, with her little girl, Mary Isabel. She continued in the house at Blackheath, which was her own, and she was in it still.

Upon quitting Oxford, where he took a degree, Francis entered the house in Leadenhall Street, becoming at once its head and chief. He showed good aptitude for business, was attentive, steady, punctual; above all, he did not despise it. When he had been in it three or four years, his uncle—with whom he continued to reside in Russell Square—found his health failing. Seeing what must shortly occur, he recommended his nephew to take a partner—one James Howard, a methodical, middle-aged, honourable man, who had been in the house since old Christopher's time. This was carried out; and the firm became Grubb and Howard. The next event was the death of the uncle, Francis Grubb. He bequeathed five thousand pounds to Mary Lynn, and the whole of his large accumulated fortune, that excepted, to his nephew, Francis the younger, including the house in Russell Square. Francis had continued to reside in the house since then, until the present time.

He was quitting it now—transferring it to Mr. Howard; who had taken a fancy to leave his place at Richmond and live in London. Of course, a house in Russell Square would not suit the aspiring tastes of Lady Adela Chenevix, and Francis Grubb had been fortunate enough to secure and purchase the lease of one within the aristocratic regions of Grosvenor Square.

The wedding took place in February. Miss Upton did not attend it, though pressed very much by the Acorn family to do so. She was still at Cheltenham, not feeling very well, she told them, not sufficiently so to come up; but she sent Adela a cheque for two hundred pounds—which no doubt atoned for her absence.

The bride and bridegroom took their departure for Dover en route for Rome: Lady Adela having condescended to express a wish to visit the Eternal City.

CHAPTER VI

ALL DOWN-HILL

The hot rays of the June sun lay on the west-end streets one Thursday at midday, and on three men of fashion who were strolling through them arm-in-arm. He who walked in the middle was a young man turned six-and-twenty, but not looking it; a good-natured, easy-going, attractive young fellow, who won his way with every one. It was Robert Dalrymple. From two to three years had elapsed since his father's death; and, alas, they had not been made years of wisdom to him. Impulsive, generous, hasty, improvident, and very fond of London life, Robert Dalrymple had been an easy prey to Satan's myrmidons in the shape of designing men.

These two gentlemen, with him today, were not precisely genii of good. One of them, Colonel Haughton, was a stout, elderly man, with a burly manner, and a mass of iron-grey hair adorning his large head; his black eyes stood out, bold and hard, through his gold-rimmed glasses. Mr. Piggott, much younger, was little and thin, with a stoop in the shoulders, and one of the craftiest countenances ever seen, to those who could read it. Suddenly Robert stood still, withdrew his arm from Mr. Piggott's, and gazed across the street.

"What now, Dalrymple?"

"There's my cousin Oscar! If ever I saw him in my life, that is he. What brings him to town? I will wish you good-day and be after him."

"To meet tonight," quickly cried Colonel Haughton.

"To meet tonight, of course. No fear of my not coming for my revenge. Adieu to both of you until then."

It is a sad story that you have to hear of Robert Dalrymple. How shall I tell it? And yet, while running into this pitfall, and tumbling into that, the young man's intentions were so good and himself so sanguine that one's heart ached for him.

In his chivalrous care for his mother, the first thing Robert did, on coming home from his father's funeral, was to break off the engagement with Mary Lynn. Or, rather, to postpone it—if you can understand such a thing. "We shall not be able to marry for many a year, Mary," he said, the tears that had fallen during the burial-service still glistening in his eyes, "and so you had better take back your troth. Moat Grange is no longer mine, for I cannot and will not turn my mother and sisters out of it; I promised him I would not: and so—and so—there's nothing to be done but part."

In the grey gloaming that same evening they went out under the canopy of heaven and talked the matter over calmly. Neither of them wanted to part with the other: but they saw no way at present of escaping from it. Robert had property of his own that brought him two hundred a-year; Mary had the five thousand pounds left her by Mr. Francis Grubb. Mary would have risked marrying, though she did not say so; Robert never glanced at the possibility. Super-exalted ideas blind us to the ordinary view of everyday life, and Robert could only look at housekeeping in the style of that at Moat Grange. It occurred to Mary that perhaps his mother and her mother might spare them something yearly, but again she did not like it to be herself to suggest it. So the open agreement come to between them was, to cancel the engagement; the tacit one was to wait—and that they were just as much plighted to each other as ever.

But the reader must fully understand Robert Dalrymple's position. He had come into Moat Grange as surely and practically as though he had had no mother in existence. Its revenues were his; his to do what he pleased with. It is true that the keeping up of Moat Grange, as his father had kept it up, would take nearly all those revenues: and Robert had to learn that yet, in something beyond theory. Mrs. Dalrymple instituted various curtailments, but her son in his generosity thought they were unnecessary.

Close upon his father's death, Robert came to London, attended by Reuben, and entered upon some rather luxurious chambers in South Audley Street. The rooms and the expenses of fashionable living made havoc of his purse, and speedily plunged him into embarrassment. It might not have been serious embarrassment, this alone, for he of course took to himself a certain portion of his rents; but unfortunately some of the acquaintances he made introduced him to that most dangerous vice, gambling; and they did not rest until they had imbued him with a love of it. It is of no use to pursue the course of his downfall. He had been gradually getting lower and lower since then in regard to finances, and deeper into embarrassments: and in this, the third season, Robert Dalrymple had hardly a guinea he could call his own; and Moat Grange was mortgaged. He was open-hearted, generous as of old. Ah, if he could only have been as free from care!

Dodging in and out among the vehicles that crowded Regent Street, Robert got over at last, and tore after his cousin. "Oscar, Oscar! is it you?" he called out. "When did you get here?"

"Ah, Robert, how are you? I was on my way to South Audley Street to find you."

"Come for a long stay?" demanded Robert, as he linked his arm within Oscar's.

"I came today and I return tomorrow," replied Oscar.

"You don't mean that, man. Visit London in the height of the season, and stay only a day! Such a calamity was never heard of."

"I cannot afford London in the season; my purse is not long enough."

"You shall stay with me. But what did you come for?"

"A small matter of business brought me," replied Oscar, "and I have to go down tomorrow—thank you all the same."

He did not say what the business was; he did not choose to say. Mrs. Dalrymple, still living at the Grange, had been tormented by doubts, touching her son, for some time past. Recently she had heard rumours that rendered her doubly uneasy, and she had begged of Oscar to come up and find out whether there was any, or how much, ground for them. If things were as bad as Mrs. Dalrymple feared, Oscar concluded that from Robert he should hear nothing. He meant to put a question or two to him, to make his observations silently, and, if necessary, to question Reuben. They were of totally opposite natures, these two young men; Oscar was all cool calculation, and the senior by half-a-dozen years; Robert all thoughtless impulse.

Oscar put the question to Robert in the course of the afternoon; but Robert simply waived the subject, laughing in Oscar's face the while. And from the observations Oscar made in South Audley Street, nothing could be gathered; the rooms were quiet.

They dined there in the evening, Reuben waiting on them. Robert urged various outdoor attractions on Oscar afterwards, but he urged them in vain: Oscar preferred to remain at home. So they sipped their wine, and talked. At eleven o'clock Oscar rose to leave.

"It is time for sober people to be in bed, Robert. I hope I have not kept you up."

Robert Dalrymple fairly exploded with laughter. Kept him up at only eleven o'clock! "My evening is not begun yet," said he.

"No!" returned Oscar, looking surprised, whether he felt so or not. "What do you mean?"

"I am engaged for the evening to Colonel Haughton."

"It sounds a curious time to us quiet country people to begin an evening. What are you going to do at Colonel Haughton's?"

"Can't tell till I get there."

"Can I accompany you?"

Robert's face turned grave. "No," said he, "it is a liberty I may not take. Colonel Haughton is a peculiar-tempered man."

"Good-night."

"Good-night, Oscar. Come to breakfast with me at ten."

Oscar Dalrymple departed. But he did not proceed to the hotel where he had engaged a bed. On the contrary, he took up his station in a shady nook, whence he could see the door he had just come out of; and there he waited patiently. Presently he saw Robert Dalrymple emerge from it, and betake himself away.

A little while yet waited Oscar, and then he retraced his steps to the house, and rang the bell. Reuben answered it. A faithful servant, getting in years now. Robert was the third of the family he had served.

"Reuben, I may have left my note-case in the dining-room," said Oscar. "Can I look for it?"

The note-case was looked for without success: and Oscar discovered that it was safe in his pocket. Perhaps he knew that all the while.

"I am sorry to have troubled you for nothing, Reuben. Did I call you out of your bed?"

"No, no," answered the man, shaking his head. "There's rarely much bed for me before daylight, Mr. Oscar."

"How's that?"

"I suppose young men must be young men, sir. I should not mind that; but Mr. Robert is getting into just the habits of his uncle."

Oscar looked up quickly, "His uncle—Claude Dalrymple?" he asked in a low tone.

"Ay, he is, sir: and my heart is almost mad at times with fear. If my dear late master was alive, I should just go down to the Grange and tell him everything."

An idea floated into the mind of Oscar as he listened. Mrs. Dalrymple had not mentioned whence she had heard the rumours of Robert's doings: he now thought it might have been from no other than Reuben. This enabled him to speak out.

"Reuben," he said, "I came up today at Mrs. Dalrymple's request. She is terribly uneasy about her son. Tell me all, for I have to report it at the Grange. If what we fear be true, something must be done to save him."

"It is all true, sir, and I wrote to warn my mistress," cried Reuben. "Should things ever come to a crisis with him, as they did with his uncle, I knew Mrs. Dalrymple would blame me bitterly for not having spoken. And I should blame myself."

Oscar Dalrymple gazed at Reuben, for the man's words had struck ominously on his ear. "Do you fancy—do you fear—things may come to a crisis with him, as they did with his uncle?" he breathed in a low tone.

"Not in the same way, sir; not as to himself," returned the man, in agitation. "Mr. Oscar, how could you think it?"

"Nay, Reuben, I think it! Your words alone led to the thought."

"I meant as to his money, sir. He has fallen into a bad, gambling set, just as Mr. Claude fell. One of them is the very same man: Colonel Haughton. He ruined Mr. Claude, and he is ruining Mr. Robert. He was Captain Haughton then; he is colonel now; but he has sold out of the army long ago. He lives by gambling. I have told Mr. Robert so; but he does not believe me."

"That's where he is gone tonight."

"Where he goes every night, Mr. Oscar. Haughton and those men have lured him into their toils, and he can't escape them. He has not the moral courage; and he has the mania for play upon him. He comes home towards morning, flushed and haggard; sometimes in drink—yes, sir, drinking and gaming mostly go together. He appeared laughing and careless before you, but it was all put on."

"Have you warned him—or tried to stop him?"

"Yes, sir, once or twice; but it does no good. I don't like to say too much: he might not take it from me. Those harpies won't let him rest; they come hunting after him, just as they hunted his uncle a score, or more, years ago. Nobody ever had a better heart than Mr. Robert; but he is pliable, and gets led away."

Oscar frowned. He thought Robert had no business to be "led away," and he felt little tolerance for him. Reuben had told all he knew, and Oscar wished him good-night and departed, full of painful thought touching Robert.

The night passed. In the morning Oscar went to South Audley Street to breakfast. Robert was looking ill and anxious.

"Been making a night of it?" said Oscar, lightly. "You look as though you had."

"Yes, I was late. Pour out the coffee, will you, Oscar?"

His own hands were shaking. Oscar saw it as Robert opened his letters. One of them bore the Netherleigh postmark, and was from Farmer Lee. Oscar hardly knew how to open the ball, or what to say for the best.

"I'm sure something is disturbing you, Robert. You have had no sleep; that's easy to be seen. What pursuit can you have that it should keep you up all night!"

"One is never at a loss to kill time in London."

"I suppose not, if it has to be killed. But I did not know it was necessary to kill that which ought to be spent in sleep. One would think you passed your nights at the gaming-table, Robert."

The words startled him, and a flush rose to his pallid features. Oscar was gazing at him steadily.

"Robert, you look conscious. Have you learnt to gamble?"

"Oh, it's nothing," said Robert, confusedly. "I may play a little now and then."

"Do not shirk the question. Have you taken to play?"

"A little, I tell you. Never mind. It's my own affair."

"You were playing last night?"

"Well—yes, I was. Very little."

"Lose or win?" asked Oscar, carelessly.

"Oh, I lost," answered Robert. "The luck was against me."

"Now, my good fellow, do you know what you had best do? Go home to Moat Grange, and get out of this set; I know what gamesters are; they never let a pigeon off till he is stripped of his last feather. Leave with me for the Grange today, and cheat them; and stop there until the mania for play shall have left you, though it should be years to come."

Ah, how heartily Robert Dalrymple wished in his heart that he could do it!—that he could break through the net in which he was involved, in more ways than one! "I cannot go to Moat Grange," he answered.

"Your reasons."

"Because I must stay where I am. I wish I had never come—never set up these chambers; I do wish that. But, as I did so, here I am fixed."

"I cannot think why you did come—flying from your home as soon as your father was under ground. Had you succeeded to twenty thousand a-year, you could but have made hot haste to launch out in the metropolis."

"I did not come to launch out," returned Robert, angrily. "I came to get rid of myself. It was so wretched down there."

Oscar stared. "What made it so?"

"The remembrance of my father. Every face I met, every stick and stone about the place seemed to reproach me with his death. And justly. But for my carelessness he would not have died."

"Well, that is all past and gone, Robert. You shall come back to the Grange with me. You will be safe there."

"No. It is too late."

"It is not too late. What do you mean? If—"

"I tell you it is too late," burst out Robert, in a sharp tone: and Oscar thought it was full of anguish.

He tried persuasion, he tried anger; and no impression whatever could he make on Robert Dalrymple. He thought Robert was wilfully, wickedly obstinate; the secret truth being that Robert was ruined. Oscar told him he "washed his hands" of him, and departed.

It chanced that same afternoon that Robert was passing through Grosvenor Square and met Mr. Grubb close to his house. Looking at him casually, reader, he has not changed; he has the same noble presence, the same gracious manner; nevertheless, the fifteen or sixteen months that have elapsed since his marriage, have brought a look of care to his refined and thoughtful face, a line of pain to his brow. They shook hands.

"Will you come in, Robert?"

"I don't mind if I do," was the answer—for in good truth Robert Dalrymple was too wretched not to seize on anything that might serve to divert him from his own thoughts. But Mr. Grubb paused in sudden remembrance.

"Mary is here today. Have you any objection to meet her?"

"Objection! I shall like it," answered Robert, with a flush of emotion, for Mary Lynn was still inexpressibly dear to him. "I wish with my whole heart that she was my wife—that we had never parted! It was all my foolish doing."

"I thought at the time you were rather chivalrous: I must say that," observed Mr. Grubb, regarding him attentively. "I suppose, in point of fact, you are both waiting for one another now."

"Why do you say that?" asked the young man, in evident agitation.

"Step in here, Robert," said Mr. Grubb, drawing him through the hall to his own room, the library. "Mary persistently refuses to accept good offers: she has had two during the past year; therefore, I conclude that she and you have some private understanding upon the point. I told her so one day, and all the answer I received consisted of a laugh and a blush."

It could have been nothing to the blush that rose to Robert's face now; brow, ears, neck, all were dyed blood-red. The terrible consciousness of how untrue this was, how untrue it was obliged to be, was smiting him with reproachful sting. Mr. Grubb mistook the signs.

"I think," he said, "that former parting was a mistake. It was perfectly right and just that Mrs. Dalrymple should have been well provided for, but—"

"You think I should have taken Moat Grange myself, and procured another home for my mother," interrupted Robert. "Most people do think so. But, if you knew how I hated the sight of the Grange!—never a single room of it but my poor dead father's face seemed to rise up to confront me."

"It might have been best that you should remain in your own home; we will not discuss it now. What I want to say is this—that if you and Mary have been really living upon hope, I don't see why you need live upon it any longer. A portion of your own revenues you may surely claim, a few hundreds yearly; and Mary shall bring as much grist to the mill on her side."

"You are very kind, very thoughtful," murmured Robert.

"But there must be a proviso to that," continued Mr. Grubb. "Reports have reached me that Robert Dalrymple is going headlong to the bad—pardon me if I speak out the whispers freely—that he is becoming reckless, a gamester, I know not what all. I do not believe this, Robert; I do not wish to believe it. I have seen nothing to confirm it, myself; you are in one set of London men, I am in another. In a young man situated as you are, alone, without home-ties, some latitude of conduct may be pardoned if he be a good man and true, he will soon pull himself straight again. If you can assure me on your honour it is nothing more than this, well and good. If it be more—if the worst of the whispers but indicate the truth, you cannot of course think of Mary. Robert, I say I leave this to your honour."

"I should like to pull myself up beyond any earthly thing," spoke the young man, in a flash of what looked far more like despair than hope. "If I could do it—and if Mary were my wife—I—I should have no fear. Let us talk of this another day. Let me see her!"

Mary was just then alone in what they called the grey drawing-room. A lovely room; as indeed all the rooms were in Mr. Grubb's house, made so by him in his love for his wife. He went in search of his wife, giving Robert the opportunity of seeing Mary alone.

Let no woman go to the altar cherishing dislike or contempt of him who is to be her husband. Marriages of indifference are made in plenty, and in time they may become unions of affection. But the other!—it is the most fatal mistake that can be made. Lady Adela treated her husband with scorn, did so systematically; she did not attempt to conceal her dislike; she threw his love back upon him. On the very day of their marriage, when she, in what appeared to be a fit of petulance, drew down all the blinds of the chariot as they drove away from Lord Acorn's door, and he, taking advantage of the privacy, laid his hand on hers, and bent to whisper a word of love, perhaps to take a kiss from her cheek, she effectually repressed him. "Pray do not attempt these—endearments," she said in a scornful tone, "they are not agreeable." Francis Grubb drew back to his corner of the carriage, and a bitter blight fell upon his spirit.

For some months past now, Lady Adela had been pale and thin, sick and ill. She resented the indisposition strongly, for it prevented her joining in the gaiety she loved, and went about wishing fretfully that her baby was born.

"Oh, Robert! Robert!"

Mary Lynn had started up with a cry, so surprised was she to see him enter. She stood blushing even to tears. And Robert? Conscious how unworthy he was of her, how impossible it was that he should dare to claim her, while the love within him was beating on his heart with lively pain, he sat down with a groan and covered his face with his hands. She thought he was ill. She went to him and knelt down, and looked up at him in appealing fear.

"Robert, what is it—what is amiss?"

And for answer, Robert Dalrymple, utterly overcome by the vivid sense of the remorseful past, of despair for the future, let his face fall upon her shoulder, and burst into a fit of heart-rending sobs so terrible for a man to yield himself to.

CHAPTER VII

DESPERATION

Alone in the oak-parlour at Moat Grange, playing soft bits of melody in the summer twilight, sat Selina Dalrymple, her very pretty face slightly flushed, her bright hair pushed from her face. Ordinarily of a calm and equable temperament, Selina was yet rather given to work herself up to restlessness on occasion. She was expecting Oscar Dalrymple; and though the excitement did not arise for himself, it did for the news he might bring.

"There he is!" she cried, as a step was heard on the gravel. "He has walked up from the station."

Oscar Dalrymple came in, very quiet as usual, not a speck of dust or other sign of travel upon him, looking spick and span, as though he had but come out of the next room. Oscar Dalrymple's place, a small patrimony called Knutford, lay some three or four miles off; he would probably walk on there by-and-by, if he did not sleep at the Grange.

"I thought you would come!" exclaimed Selina, gladly springing towards him.

"I told Mrs. Dalrymple I should return before Saturday," was his answer, as he took her hand, and kept it in his. "Where is she?"

"Gone with Alice to dine at Court Netherleigh," replied Selina. "I sent an excuse: I was impatient to see you."

"Thank you, Selina!" he whispered in low, warm tones. "That is a great admission from you."

"Not to see you; but for what you might have to tell," she hastened to say. "Oscar, how vain you are!"

She sat down in the bow-window, in what remaining light there was, and he took a chair opposite to her. Then she asked him his news.

"Do you know exactly why I went up?" he inquired with some hesitation, in doubt how far he ought to speak.

"I know all," she answered pointedly. "I saw Reuben's letter to mamma; and her fears are my fears. We keep it from poor Alice."

In a hushed voice, befitting the subject and the twilight hour, Oscar related to her what he had gathered in London. The very worst impression lay on his own mind: namely, that Robert was going rapidly to the dogs, money and honour and peace, and all; nay; had already gone; but he did not make the worst of it to Selina. He said that Robert seemed to be on a downward course, and would not listen to any sort of reason.

Selina sat in dismay; her soft dark eyes fixed on the evening sky, her hands clasped on the dress of blue silk she wore. The evening star shone in the heavens.

"What will be the end of it, Oscar?"

Oscar did not immediately answer. The end of it, as he fully believed, would be ruin. Utter ruin for Robert; and that would involve ruin for his mother and sisters.

"Does Robert really play?" pursued Selina.

"I fear he does. Yes."

"Could—could he play away our home—Moat Grange?"

"For his own life. That is, mortgage its revenues."

"But you don't, surely, fear it will come to this?" she cried in agitation.

"Selina, I hardly know what I fear. Robert is not my brother, and I could not—I had no right—to question too closely. Neither, if I had questioned, and—and heard the worst—do I see what I could have done. Matters have gone too far for any aid, any suggestion, that I could have given."

"What would become of us? Poor mamma! Poor Alice! Oh, what a trouble!"

"You, at least, can escape the trouble, Selina; you can let me take you out of it. My home is not the luxurious home you have been accustomed to here; but it will afford you every comfort—if you will only come to it. Oh, my love, why do you let me plead to you so long in vain!"

Selina Dalrymple pouted her pretty red lips. Oscar loved her to folly. She did not discourage him; did not absolutely encourage him. She liked him very well, and she liked his homage, for she was one of the vainest girls living; but, as to marrying him?—that was another thing. Had he possessed the rent-roll of a duke, she would have had him tomorrow; his income was a small one, and she loved pomp and show.

"Now, Oscar!" she remonstrated, putting him off as usual. "Is it a time to bring in that nonsense, when we are talking and thinking of poor Robert? And here come mamma and Alice, for that's Miss Upton's carriage bringing them. They said they should be home early."

And now we have to go back some few hours. It is very inconvenient, as the world knows, to tell two portions of a story at one and the same time.

Turning out of one of the handsomest houses in Grosvenor Square, in the bright sunshine of this same Friday afternoon in June, went Robert Dalrymple, his step spiritless, a look of perplexity and pain on his young and attractive face. He had been saying farewell to Mary Lynn, and he felt, in his despairing heart, that it must be for life. Just a hint he whispered to her of the worst—that he had been heedless and reckless, and was ruined; but, woman-like, fond and confiding, she had told him she never would believe it, and if it was so, there existed all the more reason for her clinging to him.

Ah, if it only might be! If the prospect just suggested to him by that good man, Francis Grubb, might only be realized! If he could pull up at any cost, and enter upon a peaceful life! If! None knew better than himself that there was no chance of it. All he had was gone—and, had not Mr. Grubb left it to his honour?

Robert Dalrymple was ruined. Bitterly was the fact impressing itself upon him, as he walked there under the summer sunlight. Not only were all his available funds spent, but he had entered into liabilities thick and threefold, far beyond what the rent-roll at the Grange would be sufficient to meet. He had told Oscar Dalrymple this very morning that he did not play much the previous night. Oscar did not believe it, but it was true. Why did he not play much? Because he had nothing left to play with, and had sat, gloomy and morose, looking on at the other players. Introduced to the evil fascinations of play by Colonel Haughton, he was drawn on until the unhappy mania took hold upon himself. To remain away from the gambling table for one night would have been intolerable, for the feverish disease was raging within him. Poor infatuated man!—poor infatuated men, all of them, who thus lose themselves!—he was positively still indulging a vision of success and hope. Every time that he approached the pernicious table, it was rife within him, buoying him up, and urging him on—that luck might turn in his favour, and he might win the Grange back—or, rather, the money he had lost upon it. Thus it is with all gamblers who are comparatively fresh to the vice; only the vile old sinners such as Colonel Haughton and his confederate, Piggott, know what such is worth. The ignis-fatuus, delusive hope, beckoning ever onwards, lures them to their destruction. Pandora's box, you know, contained every imaginable evil, but Hope lay at the bottom. Even now, as Robert is walking to South Audley Street, a feverish gleam of hope is positively rising up within him. If he had only money to go to the tables that night, who knew but luck might turn, and he could extricate himself from his most pressing debts, and so be able to tell the whole truth to Mr. Grubb?—and how carefully he would avoid all evil in future, when Mary should be his wife! But—where was the use of conjuring up these fantastic visions, he asked himself, as he flung himself into a chair in his sitting-room, when he had no money to stake?

Everything was gone, every available thing; he had nothing left but the watch he had about him, and the ring he wore—and a few loose shillings in his pocket. Nothing whatever, in the house, or out of it.

Yes, he had, but it was not his. Farmer Lee, wishing to invest a few hundred pounds in the funds, had prayed his young landlord to transact the business for him, and save him a journey to London. Robert good-naturedly acquiesced. Had any man told him he could touch that money for his own purposes, he would have knocked the offender down in his indignation. The cheque, for the money to be transferred, had come from Mr. Lee that morning. There it lay now, on the table at his elbow, and there sat Robert, striving to turn his covetous eyes from it, yet unable, for it was beginning to bear for him the fascination of the basilisk. He wished it was in the midst of some blazing fire, rather than lying there to tempt him. For the notion had seized upon his mind that it was with this money, if he might dare to stake it, he might win back a portion of what he had lost. With a shudder he shook off the idea, and looked at his watch. Was it too late to take the cheque to its destination? Yes, it was; the afternoon was waning, and business places would be closed. Robert felt half inclined to hand it to Reuben, and tell him to keep it in safety.

While in this frame of mind, that choice friend of his, Mr. Piggott, honoured him with a call. Whether that worthy gentleman scented the presence of the cheque, or heard of it casually from Robert, who was candid to a fault, certain it was that he did not leave Robert afterwards, but sat with him until the dinner-hour, and then took him out to dine. Robert locked up the cheque in his desk before he went.

About eleven o'clock he came home again, heated with wine. Opening his desk, he snatched out the cheque and hid it away in his breast-pocket, as if it were something he had a horror of looking at. Piggott and Colonel Haughton had plied him with something besides wine; alluring hopes. Turning to leave the room, buttoning his coat over what it contained, he saw Reuben standing there.

"Mr. Robert!—do not go out again tonight."

Robert stared at the man.

"Sir, I carried you in my arms when you were a child; your father, the very day he died, told me to give you a word of warning, if I saw you going wrong; let that be my excuse for speaking to you as you may think I have no right to do," pleaded Reuben, the tears standing in his faithful old eyes. "Do not go out again, sir; for this night, at any rate, stay away from the set; they are nothing but blacklegs. There's that Piggott waiting for you outside the door."

"Reuben, don't be a fool. How dare you say my friends are blacklegs?"

"They are so, sir. And you are losing your substance to them; and it won't be their fault if they don't get it all."

Robert, eager to go out to his ruin, hot with wine, would not waste more words. He moved to the door, but Reuben moved more quickly than he, and stood with his back against it.

"What farce is this?" cried Robert, in his temper. "Stand away from the door, or I shall be tempted to fling you from it."

"Oh, sir, hear reason!" And the man's manner was so painfully urgent, that a half-doubt crossed his master's mind whether he could know what it was he was about to stake. "Three or four and twenty years ago, Mr. Robert—I'm not sure as to a year—I stood, in like manner, praying your uncle Claude not to go out to his ruin. He had come to London, sir, as fine and generous a young man as you, and the gamblers got hold of him, and drew him into their ways, and stuck to him like a leech, till all he had was gone. Moat Grange was played away, mortgaged, or bartered, or whatever it might be, for the term of his life; there's a clause in its deeds, as I take it you know, sir, that prevents its owner from encumbering it for longer—and, perhaps, that's usual with other estates—"

"You are an idiot, Reuben," interrupted Robert, his tone less fierce.

"A night came when Mr. Claude was half mad," continued Reuben, unheeding the interruption. "I saw he was; and I stood before him, and prayed him not to go out with them, as I am now praying you. It was of no use, and he went. If I tell you what that night brought forth, sir, will you regard it as a warning?"

"What did it bring forth?" demanded Robert, arrested to interest.

"I will tell you, sir, if you will take warning by it, and break with those gamblers this night, and never go amongst them more. Will you promise, Mr. Robert?"

"Out of the way, Reuben!" was the impatient rejoinder. "You are getting into your dotage. If you have nothing to tell me, let me go."

"Listen, then," cried Reuben, bending his head forward, in his excitement. "At three o'clock that same morning, Mr. Dalrymple returned. He had been half-mad, I say, when he went, he was wholly mad when he came back; mad with despair and despondency. He came in, his head down, his steps lagging, and went into his bedroom. I went to mine, and was undressing, when he called me back. He had got his portmanteau from against the wall, opened it, and was standing over it, looking in, his coat and cravat off, and the collar of his shirt unbuttoned. 'Reuben,' said he, 'I have made up my mind to leave London, and take a journey.'

"'Down to the Grange, sir?' I asked, my heart leaping within me at the good news.

"'No, not to the Grange this time; it's farther than that. But as I have not informed any one of my intention I must leave a word with you, in case I am inquired after.'

"'Am I not to attend you, sir?' I interrupted.

"'No, I shan't want you particularly,' he answered; 'you'll do more good here. Tell all who may inquire for me, and especially my brother' (your father, sir, you know), 'that although they may think I did wrong to start alone on a road where I have never been, I am obliged to do so. I cannot help myself. Tell them I deliberated upon it before making up my mind, and that I undertake it in the possession of all my faculties and senses.' Those were the words."

"Well," cried Robert, impatient for the end of the tale.

"I found these words somewhat strange," continued Reuben, "but his true meaning never struck me—Oh," wailed the old man, clasping his hands, "it never struck me. My thoughts only turned to Scotland; for my master had been talking of going there to see a Scotch laird, a friend of his, and I believed he had now taken a sudden resolution to pay the visit; I thought he had pulled out his trunk to put in some things before I packed it. I asked him when he intended to start, and he replied that I should know all in the morning; and I went back to my bed."

Robert sat down on the nearest chair: his eyes were strained on Reuben. Had he a foreshadowing of what was to come?

"In the morning one of the women-servants came and woke me. Her face startled me the moment I opened my eyes; it was white and terror-stricken, and she asked me what that stream of red meant that had trickled from under the door of the master's chamber. I went there when I had put a thing or two on. Master Robert," he added, dropping his voice to a dread whisper, his thoughts wholly back in the past, "he had indeed gone on his long journey."

"Was he dead?"

"He had been dead for hours. The razor was lying beside him near the door. I have never quite got over that dreadful sight: and the thought has always haunted me that, had I understood his meaning properly, it might have been prevented."

"His trunk—what did he get that out for?" asked Robert, after a pause.

"To blind me, sir—as I have believed since—while he gave the message."

"Why did he commit the deed?" gloomily continued Robert, whom the account seemed to have partially sobered.

"He had fallen into the clutches of the same sort of people that you have, sir, and they had fleeced him down to beggary and shame, and he had not the resolution to leave them, and face the poverty; that was why he did it. His worst enemy was Captain Haughton. He is Colonel Haughton now."

"What do you mean?" cried Robert Dalrymple, after a pause of astonishment.

"Yes, sir, the same man. He is your evil genius, and he was your uncle's before you. The last time I saw him, in the old days, was when we both stood together over my master's dead body; he came in, along with others. 'He must have been stark mad,' was his exclamation. 'Perhaps so, Captain Haughton,' I answered, 'but the guilt lies on those who drove him so.' He took my meaning, and he slunk away out of the room. Mr. Robert," added the old man, the tears streaming down his cheeks, "do you know what I like to fancy—and to hope?"

Robert lifted his eyes.

"Why, that the punishment will lie with these wretched tempters, as well as the guilt. The good God is just and merciful."

Robert did not speak. Reuben resumed.

"The first time that Haughton called here upon you, sir, I knew him, and he knew me; and I don't think he liked it. He has never come here himself since; I don't know whether you've noticed it, sir, he has sent that Piggott—the man that's waiting for you outside now. Mr. Robert, you had better have fallen into the meshes of the Fiend himself than into that man Haughton's."

"My uncle must have been insane when he did that," broke from Robert Dalrymple.

"The jury said otherwise," sadly answered Reuben. "They brought it in felo-de-se; and he was buried by torchlight, without the burial-service."

The news had told upon Robert. His mind just then was a chaos. Nothing tangible showing out of it, save that his plight was as bad as his uncle Claude's had been, and that he was looking, in his infatuation, for that night to redeem it. Could he go on with his work—with that example before him? For a while he sat thinking, his head bent, his eyes closed; then he rose up, and signed to Reuben to let him pass. The latter's spirit sank within him.

"Is what I have told you of no avail, Mr. Robert? Are you still bent on going forth to those wicked men? It will be your ruin."

"It is that already, Reuben. As it was with my uncle, so it is with me: I am ruined, and worse than ruined, and after tonight I will know Colonel Haughton no more. But I have resolved to make one desperate effort this night to redeem myself; something whispers to me that I shall have luck; and—and you don't know how much lies upon it."

He was thinking of his union with Mary Lynn, poor infatuated man. Could he redeem himself in a degree this night, he would disclose his position to Mr. Grubb, entreat his condonation of the past, and forswear play for ever. A tempting prospect. Nevertheless the tale had staggered him.

"Don't go, don't go, Mr. Robert. I ask you on my bended knees."

"Get up, Reuben! don't be foolish. Perhaps I will not go. But I must tell Piggott: I cannot keep him waiting there all night."

Reuben could do no more. He stood aside, and his young master went forth, hesitating.

What strange infatuation could it have been, that it should so cling to him? Any one who has never been drawn into the fiery vortex of gambling would have a difficulty in understanding it. Robert Dalrymple was a desperate man, and yet a hopeful one, for this night might lift him out of despair. Moreover, the feverish yearning for play, in itself, was strong upon him: as it always was now at that night hour. As yet, the penalty he had incurred was but embarrassment and poverty: he was now about to stake what was not his, and risk guilt. And yet, he went forth: for the dreadful vice had got fast hold of him; and he knew that the hesitation in his mind was but worthless hesitation; a species of sophistry.

Mr. Piggott had been cooling his heels and his patience outside, not blessing his young friend for the unnecessary and unexpected delay, and not doing the opposite. He was of too equable a nature to curse and swear: he left that to his peppery partner, Haughton.

"I thought you were gone to bed," he said, when Robert appeared: "in another minute I should have come in to see after you."

And it was a wonder he did not go in. But Colonel Haughton had whispered a word of caution as to Reuben, and neither of them cared to pursue the master too persistently in the man's sight. Robert Dalrymple spoke of his hesitation, saying he was not sure he should play that night. He did want to keep the farce of prudence up, even to himself.

"You have that cheque in your pocket, I suppose?" sharply questioned Piggott.

"Yes. But—"

"Come on, then; we'll talk of it as we go along." And Robert linked his arm within Mr. Piggott's and walked on in the direction of Jermyn Street.

They entered the "hell." It is not a pleasant word for polite pens and ears, but it is an exceedingly appropriate one. It was blazing with light, and as hot as its name; and fiery countenances of impassioned triumph, and agonized countenances of vacillating suspense, and sullen countenances of despair were crowding there. Colonel Haughton was in a private room: it was mostly kept for himself and his friends, a choice knot of whom stood around. Poor Robert's infatuation, under Mr. Piggott's able tuition, had returned upon him. Down he sat at the green cloth, wild and eager.

"It is of no use to make fools of us," whispered Colonel Haughton. "You know you do not possess another stiver; why take up a place?"

"Now, Haughton, you are too stringent," benevolently interposed Mr. Piggott, laying hold of the colonel's arm, and giving it a peculiar pinch. "Here is Dalrymple, with an impression that luck will be upon him tonight, a conviction of it, indeed, and you are afraid of giving him his revenge. It is his turn to win now. As to stakes, he says he has something with him that will do."

Robert drew the cheque from his pocket, and dashed it before Colonel Haughton. "I am prepared to stake this," he said. "Nothing risk, nothing win. Luck must favour me tonight; even Piggott says so, and he knows how bad it has been."

Colonel Haughton ran his spectacles over the cheque. "I see," he said: "it will do. The risking it is your business, not ours."

"Of course it is mine," answered Robert.

"Then put your signature to it. Here by the side of the other."

It was done, and they sat down to play. "Nothing risk, nothing win," Robert had said; he had better have said, "Nothing risk, nothing lose;" and have acted upon it. A little past midnight, he went staggering out of that house, a doomed man. All was over, all lost. Farmer Lee's money, or the cheque representing it, had passed out of his possession, and he was a criminal. A criminal in the sight of himself, soon to be a criminal in the sight of the world; liable to be arrested and tried at the bar of Justice, a common felon.

He had tasted nothing since he entered, yet he reeled about the pavement as one who is the worse for drink. What was to become of him? Involuntarily the fate his unfortunate uncle Claude had resorted to came across his mind: nay, it had not been away from it. Even in the mad turmoil of that last hour, when the suspense was awful to bear, and hope and dread had fought with each other as a meeting whirlwind, the facts of that dark history had been thrusting themselves forward.

His face was burning without, and his brain was burning within. It was a remarkably windy night, and he took off his hat and suffered the breeze to blow on his miserable brow. And so he paced the streets, going from home, not to it. Where could he go? he with the brand of crime and shame upon him? He got to Charing Cross, and there he halted, and listened to the different clocks striking one. Should he turn back to South Audley Street? And encounter Reuben, who had tried to save him, and had failed? And go to bed, and wait, with what calmness he might, till the law claimed him? Hardly. Anywhere but home. The breeze was stronger now: it blew from the direction of the water. Robert Dalrymple replaced his hat, pulled it firmly on his head to hide his eyes from the night, and dragged his steps towards Westminster Bridge.

Of all places in the world!—the bridge and the tempting stream!—what evil power impelled him thither?

CHAPTER VIII

PERVERSITY

In the bed of a large and luxurious chamber, her delicate face pressing the pillow, her eyes closed to the shaded light, lay Lady Adela Grubb. The baby she so wished for had come at last. Not that it was the baby itself she wanted, but that she might be at liberty through renewed health to mingle with the great world again. To be deprived of its gaiety and obliged to keep herself very much at home had been to her a species of intolerable thraldom.

The baby was born on Friday night: a few hours subsequent to Robert Dalrymple's interview with Mr. Grubb and Mary Lynn. Mary, only in Grosvenor Square for the afternoon, returned to Blackheath unconscious of the close approach of the event. The illness had been a favourable one; and Adela, on this Sunday morning, was going on well towards recovery. She had taken her breakfast, and was ready to see her husband. The doctor had only now gone out.

A wee cry from the cradle caused her to open her eyes. An elderly woman, with soft step, bent over the cradle, and would have hushed the baby to sleep again.

"Put him here, nurse. I want to look at him."

The nurse took up the white bundle, and laid it in the great bed, beside Lady Adela. The little pale face was turned to her; for it was a pale face, not a red one; and she lay looking at it. The child opened its eyes: and, young though it was, one could see it had the beautiful grey-blue eyes of its father. Her own brilliant yet soft brown eyes grew fond as she gazed on the still face.

"Is he quite healthy, nurse?" she suddenly asked.

For the space of half a moment the nurse hesitated. "He was born quite healthy, my lady; but I think he might get on better if you nursed him. Some infants require their mother more than others do. I suspect this one does."

She made no reply; except by an all but imperceptible toss of the head: one can't toss effectively lying down. There had been some trouble with Lady Adela on the score of nursing the child. Nothing would induce her to do it. It would be well for her and well for the little one, Dr. Dove had said. Adela would not listen. Her mother, Lady Acorn, had treated her to a sharp scolding the day before, Saturday, and told her she was "unnatural." All the same: Adela indignantly demanded whether they thought she should give up the season for any infant in the world. She was also obstinate on another score—she would not allow, would not hear of, a nurse being sought to supply her place. And there she lay this morning: her own head on one pillow, the child's on another. One of the windows was open behind the drawn blind, admitting a breath of the warm June air. On a stand at Lady Adela's elbow lay a bouquet of sweet-scented, lovely hot-house flowers.

"Little wee thing!" she fondly cried, stretching out her fingers to stroke the baby's soft face, and its fragile hand that lay so still.

A tap at the door. The nurse answered it and admitted Mr. Grubb; she herself then retiring to the next room, which opened from this one. He came to the bed, bent over his wife and gently kissed her.

"Oh, don't!" she cried, turning her cheek ungraciously from him, just as she had for the most part done ever since their wedding-day. It had grown into a habit now.

"Adela," he whispered, biting his trembling lips to keep down the pain, "should not this little treasure, our child, teach you to be more of a loving wife to me?"

"I am very sorry it has come," she answered in fretful tones. "I'm sure I shall be if they are going to worry me over it. You should hear mamma go on:—and Grace, too!—with their old-fashioned notions."

"No one shall worry you," he fondly said. "Tell me, Adela, what you would like his name to be?"

"His name!" she repeated, looking up in quick surprise. "Time enough for that."

"Dr. Dove thinks it may be as well to have him baptized. He came into the library just now, as he went out; and, in talking of one thing and another, he chanced to mention this." Chanced to mention this! Mr. Grubb was cautious not to alarm his wife.

"The baby is not ill! Is it?"

"No, no, I trust not, Adela. It is a delicate little thing; all babies are, perhaps: and—and it is as well, you know, to be on the safe side."

"But I should like a christening. A grand, proper christening; to be held when I get well."

"Of course. His being baptized now will make no difference to that. I think it must be done, my dear."

"In this room, then; by my bedside. I should like to see it."

"You shall. And now, what name?"

Adela lay back on the pillow, her cheeks slightly flushed with their delicate pink, fresh and pure as the hue of a seashell, her eyes cast upwards in thought.

"I should like it to have papa's name—George."

"George Frederick?"

"Not Frederick: I don't care about the name. George—would you like also your own name—Francis?" she broke off to ask. "George Francis?"

"Would you care to have it Francis?" he returned, his tone one of emotion, bending over her until his face nearly touched hers.

She heard the tone, she saw the wet eyelashes shading the wonderful grey eyes, with their yearning, earnest expression. It flashed into her mind to remember how few men were his equals, in looks, in worth, in loving indulgence to a rebellious wife. Adela was not quite proof against her better nature. She was not always hard.

"Yes, I should; and he has your eyes," she whispered softly, in answer to the question, her own sweet eyes lifted to her husband's.

"Adela," he breathed, his voice low with its agitation, "you do love me a little! You surely do!"

"Just a very little—sometimes," she whispered in a half-saucy, half-loving tone. And, when he let his face fall on hers, she for once held it there, and welcomed the kisses from his lips.

It was all the work of the baby, his child and hers, thought he in his glad heart. But no. Now and again, at rare intervals, Adela did feel a spark of tenderness for him: though instead of letting it come to fruit, of allowing him to see it, she forced it back to the coldness she had taken up, and resolutely steeled her heart against him. Illness had just now somewhat softened her spirit.

He went round the bed to the side where the baby lay, and looked at it long and earnestly. The doctor had just told him that he did not feel altogether easy on the score of the child; could not be sure that it was likely to live.

"It is a pale little blossom, Adela. I thought babies were generally red."

"Frightfully red. I have seen them."

"Well, we will get it baptized; and then—"

"What?" she cried—for he had stopped.

"And then, I was going to say, whether it lives or dies, it will be safe in its Saviour's arms."

"But you do not think it will die?" she cried, taking up some alarm. "Oh, Francis, I should not like him to die, now he has come!"

He went round to soothe her, the word "Francis" causing his heart to leap. For in a general way she persistently called him "Mr. Grubb," and not graciously either.

"My darling, I assure you there is no cause for alarm. So far as I know, the child is not ill; it will, I hope, do well. Dr. Dove does not think him particularly strong—but what can be expected of a two-day-old baby?"

"True," answered Adela, feeling reassured again. "Francis, I do believe there's mamma coming up! Yes, it is her voice. Mind you don't tell her—"

Lady Acorn came swiftly in; and, what he was not to tell her, Mr. Grubb never knew. She had dressed early for church, and came round to see Adela on her way to it. Grace was with her. One of the daughters had married during the past year, but it was not Grace. It was Harriet; she had espoused a little Scotch laird, Sir Sandy MacIvor. Peppery and red, in came the countess, for she had just heard something that vexed her; Lady Grace, so calm and still, presented a contrast to her vivacious mother.

"Well, and now what's this I hear about things not going on well?" began Lady Acorn, subduing her voice with difficulty to the requisition of a sick-room.

"I am going on very well, mamma—how do you mean?" returned Adela, assuming the doubt must apply to herself. "I have made a famous breakfast. They let me have an egg and some buttered toast."

"You are all right, Dove says—we have just met him," returned Lady Acorn. "But he does not think the baby is. And you have yourself to thank for it, Adela."

The pink tinge on Lady Adela's cheeks increased to rose colour, as she armed herself to do battle with her mother.

"Dove says the baby wants its proper food; not that gruel stuff, or milk-and-water, or whatever rubbish it is, that it is being dosed with. And it is not too late for you to reform, Adela, and do what you ought."

"It is too late," retorted Adela, with flaming cheeks. "And if you begin about it again, mamma, you will make me ill. Francis"—stretching out her arm for her husband—"don't let me be worried. You promised me, you know."

With a loving word to his wife, a reassuring pressure of her hand, which he kept in his, he turned to Lady Acorn, and spoke to her in a low tone.

"Talk to her when she's better and more able to bear it!" repeated the countess, taking up his words aloud. "Why, my good man, it would be too late. And—you do not want to lose your child, I suppose!"

"Indeed, I do not. But, better lose my child than my wife."

"She is well enough, and safe enough," spoke the mother, secure in her superior knowledge. "Adela has been an indulged girl all her life, and you, her husband, continue the indulgence. It is not good for her; mark you that. With regard to this caprice of hers, the not undertaking the poor sickly baby, you ought to hold her to her duty, Mr. Grubb, and insist upon her fulfilling it."

He turned to his wife, his eyes unconsciously wearing a pleading look. "If you would only suffer yourself to be persuaded, Adela! For the child's sake."

Adela looked at them separately; at her husband, at her mother, at Grace, standing with a cold and impassive countenance that did not betoken approbation; and she took up an idea that they were in league with one another to "hold her to her duty," and enforce obedience. Had not the doctor talked to her that very morning: had not the nurse subsequently presumed to hint at an opinion? Yes, they were all in league together. Lady Adela turned rebellious, and flung her husband's hand away with passionate anger.

"Why do you come into my room at all?" she exclaimed to him. "You know I do not want you."

At that moment the nurse looked in from the adjoining apartment and made a sign to Mr. Grubb. He obeyed it at once, taking no notice of his wife or her cruel words.

"There! you have driven him away now!" cried Lady Acorn, on the eve of an explosion: for she had not seen the summons of the nurse. "You will never go to heaven, Adela, for your wickedness to your husband."

Adela did not make any answer: perhaps she was feeling a little sorry in her heart: and there ensued a silence. The sweet-toned bells, calling people to service, rang out on the air.

Mr. Grubb came in again. Feeling more alarmed in his heart at the doctor's words than he allowed to appear, and anxious for the child, he had written a note as the medical man left him, and sent it to a young assistant clergyman whose lodgings were close by. He had now called, on his way to church, ready to perform the ceremony at once if it were wished for, and a servant had come up to inform the nurse.

"Mr. Wilkinson has called, and is asking after you," began Mr. Grubb to his wife, voice and demeanour a model of quietness, not to say indifference. "It struck me, Adela, that he might as well baptize the child—as he is here. He has time to do it before service."

"What a hurry you are in!" she returned, ungraciously.

"As well take the opportunity of his being here, Adela. And then it will be over."

"Oh, well, yes—if it has to be done," conceded she. "I'm sure there's no necessity for it. Let Wilkinson come up."

Lady Acorn's sharp red nose turned purple. She had listened in surprise. Saying nothing to Adela, she trotted into the dressing-room, and shut the door.

"What's this, nurse—about the child being baptized?"

"I believe it is going to be done, my lady. Mr. Grubb has just said a word to me."

"Is it so ill as that?"

"Well, no, I did not think it was," acknowledged the woman. "Dr. Dove did not much like its look this morning; I saw that. I suppose he spoke to Mr. Grubb more fully than to me."

"Do you think it is in any danger?"

The nurse paused before replying. "One can never be quite sure of these very young infants. When it was born, I thought it a nice healthy little thing; yesterday it seemed quiet and peeky, and wailed a bit; this morning it seems anything but well, and does not take its food. Still, my lady, I can't say that it is in danger."

Lady Acorn nodded her head and her bonnet two or three times, as if not satisfied with affairs in general, and went back to her daughter's room.

The young clergyman came up; things were made ready; and they gathered round in a group at the bedside, kneeling down for the short preparatory prayers used in private baptism. When they arose, the clergyman took the child in his arms from Grace, who had held it.

"Name this child."

"George," promptly spoke the mother from the bed, her tone giving emphasis to the word. And Francis Grubb's face flushed as he heard it. Ah, what pain was often his!

The short service was soon over. Mr. Wilkinson departed for his church; Lady Acorn and Grace followed him. The nurse had gone back to the dressing-room. Mr. Grubb stood by the bed in which the quiet child had again been laid.

"I thought you were going to church?" said Lady Adela.

"Yes; directly." He wanted especially to go to church that day; to return thanks to God for the mercy vouchsafed him in the preservation of his wife. Though, indeed, he had not waited to be in church to do that.

"How quiet the baby was all through it!" cried Adela.

"Very quiet. Too quiet, your mother says."

"Mamma says all sorts of things when she is in a temper, as you have learnt by this time, and she is in one this morning," was Adela's light, and not over-dutiful remark. Not but that it was true.

Mr. Grubb had taken the child in his arms, and stood looking down upon it. Save that its eyes were open and that it breathed, it seemed still enough for death. He did not understand babies, but he did think this one was unnaturally quiet.

"Why are you looking at him so attentively?" asked Adela, by-and-by.

"I don't think he can be well."

"But—you don't think he is ill, do you?" returned she after a pause, and speaking quickly.

"Adela, I do not know. He seems to me to have changed a little in the last half-hour, since I first came in. Of course I may be mistaken."

"Suppose you send for Dr. Dove?"

"I can send if you like: he has only just gone, you know. The nurse does not seem to be"—alarmed, he was about to say, but changed the word—"anxious; so all may be well."

He put the baby in its place, and Lady Adela raised her head to look at it. "He gets paler, I think," she observed; "and, as you say, he is very, very quiet. Poor little thing! he has no strength yet."

"He cannot have much of that," remarked Mr. Grubb. "The nurse says she cannot get him to take his food. If he does not, he must sink, Adela."

Their eyes met. There was certainly no reproach in his, only a settled look of pain. Adela did not want her baby to die, and the fear of it was beginning to trouble her; she was aware that, looking at matters from their point of view, her enemies', she might not be altogether unconscious of meriting some reproach. Back she lay on the pillow again, and burst into tears.

Mr. Grubb went round, bent down, and sheltered her head on his breast. "I don't want him to die," she sobbed.

"Won't you try to save him?" he whispered in his tenderly persuasive tones, as he held her face close to his own.

"But the trouble!—and the sacrifice. Oh, how cross and contrary the world sometimes is!"

"Your own child and mine, Adela! It would be only a little sacrifice, a little trouble. When he gets older, he will repay you love for love."

A pause. "I suppose you will be very cross with me if I don't, Francis."

"Am I ever cross with you! I should grieve for the child, if he died; I should grieve for your grief, for I know you would feel it. Oh, my darling, won't you try to save him? To do so must be right in God's sight."

She cried silently for a minute longer, her wet cheek lying contentedly against his. "Perhaps I will," she whispered in his ear. "For his sake, you know."

"For all our sakes, Adela."

"Put him nearer to me, please. I will look at him again—whether he does seem ill. And how late you will be at church!"

"Not very: the bell is going yet," said Mr. Grubb. He placed the infant where she could look at it closely; gave her a farewell kiss, and departed. Adela rang for the nurse.

"You may throw away all the stupid gruel, nurse. I shall not let the baby have any more of it."

CHAPTER IX

JOSEPH HORN'S TESTIMONY

"Some one is waiting to see you, sir," said one of Mr. Grubb's servants to him, as he entered the house on his return from church.

"Who is it?"

"Mr. Dalrymple's man, sir. He has been waiting nearly an hour."

Reuben came forward from the back of the hall. The moment Mr. Grubb caught sight of his face, usually so full of healthy bloom, now pale and woe-begone, he was seized with a presentiment of evil.

"Come into the library, Reuben," he said. "Have you brought ill news of any kind?" he added, shutting the door. "What is it?"

And to make matters more intelligible to you, reader, we will go back to the past Friday night, when Robert Dalrymple left his lodgings in the company of Mr. Piggott, leaving poor Reuben in distress and despair.

Reuben sat up the livelong night. The light dawned after the brief interval of darkness, very brief in June, the sun came out, the cries and bustle in the streets gradually set in, and London had begun another day. At six o'clock Reuben lay down on his bed for an hour, and then got himself a bit of breakfast— which he could not eat. His master did not come.

Fearing he knew not what, and attaching more importance, in his vague uneasiness, to Robert's having stayed out than he might have done at another time, at nine o'clock Reuben betook himself to Mr. Piggott's. That gentleman did not live in very fashionable lodgings, and his address was usually given at his club, not there. Reuben, however, knew it. Some time before, Reuben had gone on a fishing tour, to catch what information he could as to the private concerns of Mr. Piggott and Colonel Haughton, and had found out where each lived.

The slipshod servant who came to the door could say nothing as to whether Mr. Dalrymple was staying the night there; all she knew was, that Mr. Piggott "warn't up yet." Reuben inquired as to the locality of Mr. Piggott's chamber, went up to it without opposition, and knocked at the door; a sharp, loud knock.

"Who's there?"

Another knock, sharper still.

"Come in."

Reuben walked in at once. "Sir," was his unceremonious address, "do you know anything of my master?"

"I!" cried Mr. Piggott, when he had recovered his surprise, and speaking from the midst of his bedclothes. "I do not. Why?"

"I thought you might know, sir, as you took him out last night. He said he was going to play with you and Colonel Haughton. He has not returned home, which I think very strange; and, as there is some important business waiting for him, I want to find him."

Reuben spoke out freely. But the "important business" was only an invention. He did not care to betray how uneasy he was, yet wanted an excuse for inquiring. Poor man! the fate of his early master lay ominously on his mind.

"He left us last night between twelve and one o'clock; to go home, as I suppose," said Mr. Piggott, somewhat taken aback.

"Between twelve and one, sir?"

"Close upon one it may have been; it had not struck. I know nothing more."

"Did he go home with Colonel Haughton?"

"That I am sure he did not. Colonel Haughton and I walked away together. I left the colonel at his own door."

"Away from Jermyn Street, I suppose you mean, sir!"

"You have no right to suppose anything of the kind," roared Mr. Piggott, aroused to anger. "What is it to you? Go out, and shut the door."

Reuben did as he was bid; there seemed to be no use in staying. He sought out Colonel Haughton, who (remembering past events) was civil, and who possibly felt some undefined uneasiness at the disappearance of Robert. His story was the same as Piggott's—that the young man had left them a little before one o'clock.

Trusting these gentlemen just as far as he could see them, and no farther, or their word either, Reuben went to the gambling-house in Jermyn Street. After some difficulty—for every impediment seemed put in the way of any inquiry; and, to judge by appearances, the place might have been the most innocent in the world—Reuben found a man attached to the house who knew Mr. Dalrymple. This man happened to be at the front-door when Mr. Dalrymple went out the previous night; it wanted about five or ten minutes to one. He watched him walk away.

"Which way did he go?" asked Reuben. "Towards home—South Audley Street?"

"No; the other way. He staggered a bit, as if not quite sober."

"Through the machinations of the wicked people that have been hunting him; he never drank but when incited to it by them," spoke Reuben, in his pain.

Back he went to South Audley Street, in the hope that his master might have now reached it. Not so. The day wore on, and he did not come. Reuben was half distracted. In the evening, he went to various police-stations, and told his tale—his master, Mr. Robert Dalrymple, had disappeared. It may, perhaps, seem to you, reader, that all this was premature; hardly called for; but the faithful old servant's state of mind must plead his excuse.

Another night passed. Sunday morning arose, and then tidings came of Robert and his probable fate. The police had been making inquiries, and one of them came to Reuben.

A hat had been found in the Thames, the previous day, floating away with the tide. Inside it was written "R. Dalrymple." The policeman had it in his hand; bringing it to Reuben to be owned or disowned. Reuben recognized it in a moment. It was the one his unfortunate master had worn on Friday night. How could it have got in the water?—and where, then, was Robert Dalrymple?

Little need to speculate. Some bargemen who were in their vessel, lying close to the side of Westminster Bridge, had disclosed to the police that about two o'clock on Saturday morning they had heard a weight drop into the water, seemingly from the bridge—"as if," said one of them, "a body had throwed hisself right on to the Thames o' purpose to make a hole in it."

It was this disastrous news that Reuben had now brought to Mr. Grubb. That gentleman sat aghast as he listened. The old man, seated opposite to him, broke down with a burst of anguish as he concluded, the salt tears raining on his cheeks.

"Can he have wilfully destroyed himself?" breathed Mr. Grubb.

"Only too sure, sir," wailed Reuben; "only too sure."

"And the motive? Embarrassment?"

"Not a doubt of it, sir: he was quite ruined."

"If he had only applied to me!—if he had only applied to me!" bewailed Mr. Grubb, rising from his chair to pace the room in excitement. "I would have saved and helped him."

"A dreadful set had got hold of him, poor young man," sobbed Reuben. "The same gamblers—one of them's the same, at any rate—that got hold of and ruined his uncle. Doubtless you know that story, sir. On this last Friday evening that ever was, I told it to Mr. Robert, hoping it would turn him back. But those wretched men had laid too fast a hold upon him. One was waiting for him outside in the street then. My belief is, sir, he couldn't break with them."

"Had the tale no effect upon him?"

"Some little it had; not enough. He must go forth to play that night, he said to me; he had given his word to Piggott to go, and, besides, he thought the luck would turn and favour him; but once the night was over, he would know that Haughton and the rest of the set no more. And I think he would have kept his word, sir."

"I suppose luck did not favour him? That shall, if possible, be ascertained."

Reuben shook his head. "No need to doubt, sir. The worst is—the worst is—I hardly like to say it."

"Can anything be worse, Reuben, than what you have told me?" was Mr. Grubb's sad rejoinder, as he took his seat again.

"Ay, but I meant as to his means, sir; his losses. He was quite cleared out; he told me that; everything, including Moat Grange, so far as his life interest in it went, was staked and gone. But that last night"—

Reuben's voice dropped to a dread whisper—"he took out with him what was not his to stake. And, no doubt, lost it."

"What was it?" questioned Mr. Grubb, in the same hushed tone, feeling rather at sea, yet afraid of he knew not what.

"It was a cheque that had come up that morning from Netherleigh. Farmer Lee wanted some money invested in some particular security, and he got my master to undertake to do it for him, to save himself the journey up. Mr. Robert had told me all about it—he mostly did tell me things. Ah, sir, his disposition was open and generous as the day."

"And the money came?"

"The cheque came, sir. It was for five hundred pounds. Piggott called that Friday afternoon and scented the cheque; saw it, most likely. He took Mr. Robert out to dinner, and plied him with wine, and between ten and eleven he brought him back again, staying outside while my master came in—come in for the cheque. It was then I tried to pull him up by telling him about his uncle Claude—how the man Haughton had lured Mr. Claude to his destruction, just as he was now luring Mr. Robert. He said he would have no more to do with Haughton after that night; but he went out to Piggott with the cheque in his pocket, and they walked away together arm-in-arm."

Mr. Grubb took out his pocketbook, and made a note in pencil. He would get that cheque back from the gamblers, if possible. At any rate, he would have a good try for it.

Reuben had not much more to tell. Mr. Grubb put on his hat and went with him to see the police inspector who had the case in hand. It was a terrible blow: terrible in all ways: Francis Grubb was feeling it to be so—and what then would it be to his sister Mary?

The inspector pointed out to Mr. Grubb that, in spite of the finding of the hat in the Thames, which hat was, beyond all doubt, Mr. Dalrymple's, it did not follow that Mr. Dalrymple was himself in the Thames; and the splash heard by the men in the barge might have been made by any one else. There was no proof, he urged, that Mr. Dalrymple had been on Westminster Bridge, or near it. And all this seemed so reasonable that Mr. Grubb felt his heart's weight somewhat lightened.

But, ere the Sunday afternoon closed in, testimony on this point was forthcoming, and rather singularly. It chanced that a young man, named Horn, who was an assistant to Robert Dalrymple's tailor, and had often measured Robert for clothes, was spending the Friday with some friends at South Lambeth. Horn, a very respectable and steady man, had stayed late, for it was a wedding feast, beyond the time of omnibuses, and had to walk home to his lodgings near Leicester Square. In passing over Westminster Bridge, it was then close upon two o'clock, he saw some one mounted on the top, leaning right over the parapet, hanging over it, as if he had a mind to fling himself into the water. Horn, startled at the sight, ran up, and pulled the man back; and then, to his unbounded astonishment, he found it was Mr. Dalrymple.

"I beg your pardon, sir," he said in apology. "I had no idea it was you."

"Good-night, Horn," replied Robert.

"Good-night, sir," returned Horn; and walked on.

But Horn felt uneasy; especially so at the remembrance of Mr. Dalrymple's face, for it looked full of trouble; and he turned back again. Robert was then standing with his arms folded, apparently looking down quietly on the water.

"Can I do anything for you, sir?" he asked. "Nothing has happened, I hope?"

"Oh, nothing at all," replied Robert. "I don't want anything done; thank you all the same, Horn. The night is warm, and I am enjoying the air: one gets it here, if anywhere. Good-night."

Joseph Horn wished him good-night again and walked finally away. On this day, Sunday, chancing to hear that Mr. Dalrymple was missing—for inquiries were now being made extensively—he came forward and related this.

It was just the one link that had been wanting. Poor Robert Dalrymple, utterly ruined, soon now to be pointed at as a felon, had found his trouble greater than he could bear, and had put an end to it. Of that there could exist no reasonable doubt. The melancholy tale speedily fled over London—how quickly such news does fly! Robert Dalrymple had drowned himself—another victim to Play.

"It runs in the family," quoth some careless people who remembered the former catastrophe. "Like uncle, like nephew! The name of Dalrymple must be a fated one."

"I would at least have used a pistol, and gone out of the world like a gentleman," was the bad remark of that bad man, Colonel Haughton, as he stood on the Sunday night—yes, the Sunday night—and listened to the news in that place with the hot name.

But the colonel changed his tone the following day, when Francis Grubb, the great East India merchant, whom all men, high and low, looked up to and respected, stood before him, and quietly informed him he must give up a certain cheque belonging to Mr. Lee of Netherleigh, or its value if it had been cashed; give it up, or submit to appear before a magistrate, and run the gauntlet of public exposure. After putting himself to a great deal of trouble, in the way of remonstrance, excuse, and grumbling, to which Mr. Grubb made no sort of reply, as he calmly waited the result, the colonel returned the cheque—which had not been cashed. Possibly the disappearance of Robert Dalrymple had put him and Mr. Piggott on their guard.

Meanwhile the Grange remained in ignorance of what was passing; but the terrible tidings would soon have to be carried thither.

When Mrs. Dalrymple returned home on Friday evening from dining at Court Netherleigh, she did not say much to Oscar about her son; but on the following morning, after breakfast, Oscar having slept at the Grange, she questioned him. Without making exactly the worst of it, Oscar disclosed the truth—that is, that Robert was undoubtedly falling into trouble through his gambling habits. He deemed it lay in his duty to tell this; and Mrs. Dalrymple, as the reader must remember, had been already warned by Reuben's letter. That letter had been a great shock to her; she knew how fatal the vice had already proved in the family.

It was a lovely midsummer morning, and she and Selina were sitting on the bench under the great elm-tree. The bees were humming, the butterflies sporting, the birds singing around them. The grass was green at foot; overhead, the blue sky could be seen through the branches of the flickering trees. Oscar leaned against the trunk of an opposite tree as he talked to them.

"What can be done?—what can be done?" exclaimed Mrs. Dalrymple, clasping her hands in distress. "Oscar, you ought to have brought him down with you."

"He positively refused to come. I might as well have tried to bring a mountain. Something ought to be done, and must be done," added Oscar; "you are quite right in saying that. The question is—what is it that can be?"

"The root of the evil lies in his having gone to London," said Mrs. Dalrymple. "He ought to have taken up his own proper station here, and ourselves have found a house elsewhere. But, in his chivalrous affection for me, Robert would listen to no remonstrance; some implied promise to his father, when he was on his death-bed, I believe, swayed him. Robert was always so good-hearted—and so impulsive. He—here is Alice," she broke off, in lowered tones.

Alice, with her sweet face, her slight figure, and her quite perceptible limp, came across the grass. "May I not be admitted to the conference?" she asked pleadingly. "I know you are talking of Robert."

"Oh, my dear, it is nothing that you need trouble yourself about," said her mother, soothingly. "Go back to your tatting."

"I have my tatting with me. Mamma—Oscar—do you not see that it will be well for me to hear what there is to hear. I know something is wrong about Robert; I could not sleep all last night, no, nor the night before, for dwelling on it. Whatever there is to hear, it cannot make me more anxious than I am—and it would end this suspense."

"Well, well, sit down," said Mrs. Dalrymple, giving way. "I hardly know myself how much or how little of evil there is to hear, Alice." And she went on to speak without reservation: "Robert had fallen into gambling habits; and there was no telling how deeply. All his own means were undoubtedly gone. Of course things must get worse night by night," she concluded. "Any night he may stake the Grange."

"Stake the Grange!" echoed Alice. "Mamma, what do you mean?"

"Stake it and lose it," confirmed Oscar. "When the mania for play sets in on a man, he is not content to confine his ventures to trifles."

"But I do not understand," returned Alice. "How could he stake the Grange? It is in the Dalrymple family, and cannot go out of it?"

"He might stake its value. Mortgage it, that is, for his own life."

"And could we not remain in it?" she quickly asked.

"Scarcely. It might take every shilling of its incomings to pay off the interest. You could not remain here upon nothing."

"Would it be sacrificed; useless to us for so long as Robert lived?" questioned Selina, not quite comprehending.

Oscar nodded. "I am only saying that he might do it: I do not say he will. He might so hamper himself, so involve the estate, that he could never derive further benefit from it. Or his family either, so long as he lived."

"Does it return to us at Robert's death? I wish to goodness he would be more careful of himself," added Selina, in her quick way. "Sitting up till daylight, night after night, cannot be good for him."

"It—would return into the family," spoke Oscar, hesitatingly.

Alice Dalrymple looked up from a reverie. A contingency had occurred to her which she had never thought of before: so entirely had the Grange been theirs in their father's recent lifetime, and in the certainty of its descending to Robert afterwards. "Suppose anything were to happen to Robert," she said, "whose would the Grange be? Mamma's?"

No one answered her.

"Oscar, I ask you, would it go to mamma?"

"No."

"To whom, then?"

"My dear," interposed Mrs. Dalrymple, "it would be Oscar's. It goes in the male line."

The answer took both the young ladies by surprise. They were really very ignorant of these matters. Each of them stole a glance at Oscar: a red, conscious light had flown into his usually pale cheek.

"I never knew it," breathed Selina.

"And it is of little import your knowing it now," gently spoke Oscar. "I am as likely to come into the Grange as I am of being made prime minister. Robert is a younger man than I am."

"Poor Robert!" lamented Alice. "He has been left to himself up in that great wicked town, he has had no one to turn to for advice or counsel, and I dare say he has only done what he has done from thoughtlessness. A word from mamma may set him right. Mamma, do you not think you ought to go to him?"

"Yes, Alice. It is what I have been resolving to do, now, as you were talking. And you must stay here over tomorrow, and go with me, Oscar. We will start by the nine-o'clock train on Monday morning."

"So be it," acquiesced Oscar. "It is the only thing. He may listen to you."

So Oscar Dalrymple stayed with them at the Grange until the Monday, revelling in the society of the one only being he loved on earth—Selina.

Mrs. Dalrymple had made ready for the journey—and how fervent, how imploringly earnest her prayers were that it might bear happy fruit, she and Heaven alone know. They all sat down to an early breakfast: even Alice, whose lameness was an apology for not rising betimes in general. In the midst of breakfast, James came in, and looked at Oscar Dalrymple.

"Will you please to step here, sir, for a minute?"

"What for?"

"Just for a minute, sir," repeated the man; and his eyes seemed to telegraph a momentary entreaty with the words.

Oscar went out hurriedly, for there was no time to spare, and the carriage to take them to the station had already come round. James shut the door.

"Here's Reuben come down, sir, by the early train," he whispered. "He told me to fetch you out to him, quietly, but not to say who it was."

Oscar walked quickly across the hall. Reuben awaited him in an empty room.

"What is it, Reuben? What has brought you from town?"

The old servant trembled with agitation, and grasped hold of the back of a chair. "Oh, Mr. Oscar, it is all over. My poor young master is gone."

Oscar sat down, seemingly unconscious what he did, and the red light came again into his cheeks.

"The very night after you left London, sir, those men drew him out again. Before he went, I spoke to him, trying to stop him, and he told me he was ruined and worse than ruined. He never came back. He has just followed in the steps of Mr. Claude Dalrymple, and has met with the same fate."

"Surely he has not destroyed himself?" breathed Oscar.

"He has; he has."

"But how? In what manner?"

"By drowning, sir. He jumped over Westminster Bridge right into the water during that same night. About two o'clock, they say. Oh, what distraction his poor mind must have been in, to urge him to such a death as that!"

Oscar rose and looked from the window. Cold as was his nature, the news could not fail to shock him— although he was the inheritor of the Grange.

"Has he been found?" he presently asked.

"No. Perhaps never will be. The officers say that not half the bodies that get into the Thames ever see the light again. But his fate is as sure and certain, sir, as though he had been found, and the drags are yet at work. Mr. Oscar, I'd rather it was my own death that had to be told of than his," added Reuben, breaking into sobs.

"It is sad indeed," cried Oscar, feeling, truth to say, terribly cut up. "I and Mrs. Dalrymple were on the point of starting for London. It is no use to go now. At least she must not."

"His hat was found in the Thames," said poor Reuben, regaining some composure; "and, curious to say, one Joseph Horn, a young man, who—"

"Oscar," called out the voice of Mrs. Dalrymple, "where are you? We have not any more time to spare."

"How shall I break it to them?" wailed Oscar to himself, knowing that it must be done, and without delay. "It is a terrible mission. Reuben, don't show yourself for a minute."

He walked across the hall, now his own, and re-entered the breakfast-room. He proceeded with his task as well as he could, and got through it, not telling them the worst, only that some accident had happened to Robert. By intuition however, they seemed to seize on the truth—that he was dead. Oscar felt almost thankful that Alice fainted and fell to the floor, because it caused some diversion to Mrs. Dalrymple's death-like shock.

And, ere the midday sun was at its height, the estate was ringing with the news that its generous young landlord had passed away, with his faults and follies, and that Oscar Dalrymple would reign at the Grange.

CHAPTER X

A COSTLY MANIA

The residence of Mrs. Lynn at Blackheath was a substantial, old-fashioned, roomy house on the heath, standing alone within a high wall surrounded by trees. And to this house, on the Monday morning, went her son, Francis Grubb, carrying with him his burden of ill news. The same fatal news which the old-serving man, Reuben, had already taken to Moat Grange.

In the morning-room sat Mary Lynn, glancing over a short letter she had just written. She started up in what looked like alarm when her brother entered.

"Oh, Francis!" she exclaimed, a hectic colour flushing her face, "what have you come today for—now? Is it to bring me ill news?"

"Why do you imagine that?" he asked, rather struck with her words—and her looks. "Can't a business man come out to pay a morning visit, Mary, without bringing ill news with him? My wife and the baby are going on well, if you are thinking of them."

He spoke in a half-jesting tone, making light of it at first. It was not usual with him to leave the City at this early hour. Mary glanced at the open letter on the table. She wore a cool muslin dress of a pinkish colour, and was looking altogether fresh and fair and pure—but sad.

"How is mamma?" he asked.

"Not at all well; she is keeping her room today," said Mary. Mr. Grubb, standing so near, could not fail to see that the letter was written to Robert Dalrymple. The reader may like to see its contents.

"My DEAR ROBERT,

"Considering that you and I ceased to correspond some years ago, you will be surprised at my writing to you. I have no doubt all proper-minded old ladies, including my mother, would shake their heads at me. Will you just drop me one line in answer, to say how you are, and how the world is using you, and please let it be by return of post. I have a reason for asking this. Pardon the trouble; and believe me ever affectionately yours,

"MARY ISABEL LYNN."

"Have you brought me ill news, Francis?" she repeated. "About Robert Dalrymple?"

Her brother looked at her. "Again I ask you, Mary, why you should put the question?"

"I will tell you," she said: "at the risk of your laughing at me, Francis; and that I know you will do. I have had a dream about Robert, and it has made me uneasy."

"A dream!" he repeated in surprise. But he did not laugh.

"It was last Friday night," she went on. "I came home from your house rather tired, and—and troubled; troubled about Robert. I had seen that he was in great trouble himself; in fact, he told me so; but he would not tell me its nature. The world was using him hardly—that was the most explicit admission he made. I could not get to sleep at first for thinking of him; not before one o'clock, I dare say; and then I had a terrible dream."

"You should not think of dreams, child," put in her brother. "But go on."

"I thought we were in some gloomy room, Robert and I. At the end of it was a small door, closed, with an opening at the top protected by iron spikes. Beyond that narrow opening nothing could be seen, for it was dark. Robert stood near this door, facing it in silence, as if waiting for it to open, and I stood some yards behind him, waiting also. Some trouble seemed to lie upon both of us, some apprehension, but I know not what; something that could not be spoken of: it filled my heart to sickness. Suddenly the door began slowly to open; and, as the intense darkness beyond began to disclose itself more and more—a black, inky darkness that seemed to reign in illimitable space—a most frightful terror took possession of me, a terror more awful than can ever be experienced in life. Robert turned and looked at me in token of farewell, still in silence—and oh, Francis, I shall never forget the despairing misery depicted on his face. He turned it away again, and took a step towards the door, now quite open. I rushed forward with a scream and caught his arm on its threshold. 'No, no, you shall not go out there!' I cried: 'stay, and pray for deliverance.' This awoke me; awoke me to the same vivid terror I had felt in the dream," concluded Miss Lynn; "and just afterwards the clock struck two."

"Two?"

"Two. I lay in the most extreme agitation for the rest of the night; instinct whispering me that some evil had befallen Robert. With the morning the feeling in some degree passed away, and the occupations of the day served still more to deaden it: several visitors called on Saturday. Nevertheless, the dream has haunted me over since like a nightmare. Not a word of the sermon yesterday morning could I take in. When mamma asked me what the text was when I got home from church, I was obliged to say I could not remember it. So, this morning, I thought I would write a line to Robert, asking if things are well with him—for anxiety and suspense yet cling to me."

Her voice ceased. Mr. Grubb made no comment.

"Has any ill happened to Robert?" she continued her face raised wistfully. "Have you come to tell it me?"

Oh, it was a hard task, this, that was imposed upon him. Far harder than the one that had fallen to Oscar Dalrymple at Moat Grange in Berkshire. For the natures of the two men were essentially different: the one stoically calm; the other warm, generous, loving. Francis Grubb took his sister gently by the hand.

"Let us go into the open air, Mary; to the quiet shrubbery. What I have to tell you, I will tell you there."

It was a most terrible thing to have come to pass. Better that the ill-fated Robert Dalrymple, when in the very act of self-destruction, had arrested himself, and prayed to God for deliverance as Mary Lynn seemed to have implored him to do in her dream.

And if any latent doubt lingered in the minds of fond relatives, this was to be extinguished. Some three weeks after the fatal night he was found in the water near Mill-wall: quite unrecognizable in himself, but identified by his clothes. The jury brought in a more merciful verdict than was passed on his uncle before him—"Temporary insanity;" and he was buried in the nearest churchyard.

As to his creditors, they were not paid. There was nothing to pay them with. With the exception, however, of his gambling debts, it turned out that Robert did not owe much. Mr. Grubb had got back Farmer Lee's five-hundred-pound cheque—and Mr. Grubb, Reuben, and Oscar, to whom it was alone known, kept that matter secret from the farmer and from the world.

Oscar Dalrymple had come into the Grange, and would take possession of it as soon as Mrs. Dalrymple could, at her convenience, move out. Oscar, cold and calculating though he was, could but come forward to Mrs. Dalrymple's rescue. It fell to him to keep her and her daughters now. He spoke to her in a kindly, generous tone, letting nothing appear of the inward wincing he possibly may have felt. She had absolutely no resource in the world, save Oscar. They had a distant relative indeed, one Benjamin Dalrymple, living in the West of England; a crusty old man, who was reported to be very rich, and had made his money at cotton-spinning; but this old man had created quite a deadly feud between himself and all the Dalrymple family; and Mrs. Dalrymple would starve rather than apply to him. Better be under an obligation to Oscar than to him: though she did not over-well like that. Oscar proposed (perhaps he felt he could do no less) that she and her daughters should still make the Grange their home; but Mrs. Dalrymple declined. A pretty little house on the estate, called Lawn Cottage, was assigned to her use, rent free; and two hundred pounds per annum. Oscar remonstrated against the smallness of the pittance, but she absolutely refused to accept more. With her poultry and fruit and vegetables, and the milk from her one cow, Mrs. Dalrymple assured him she did not see how she could spend even that. So she and her daughters removed to Lawn Cottage, and Oscar entered upon his reign at the Grange.

A year had gone by. London was in a commotion: nothing was talked of in its gay circles but the young and lovely bride, Mrs. Dalrymple. Peers were going mad for her smiles; peeresses condescended to court them. Panics do sometimes come over the fashionable world of this great metropolis: now it is a rage for speculation, like that railway mania which once turned people's sober senses upside down; now it is the new and very ugly signora who is ruling the boards and the boxes at Her Majesty's Theatre; now it is an insane sympathy—insane in the working—with all the black Uncle and Aunt Toms in the western hemisphere; but at the time of which we are writing, it was the admiration of one of themselves, a woman, the beautiful Mrs. Dalrymple.

She was charming; not because fashion said it, but that she really was so. Naturally fascinating, the homage she received in the gay world—a new world to her—rendered her manners irresistibly so. Some good wives, staid and plain, who had never been guilty of courting a look in their lives, and prided themselves on it, avowed privately to their lords that she laid herself out for admiration, and was a compound of vanity and danger; and the lords nodded a grave approval, and the moment they could get out of sight, went running in the wake of Mrs. Dalrymple.

A stylish vehicle, much favoured in those days by young fellows with little brains and less prudence, something between a brake and a dandy-horse, with two stylish men in it, especially in the extent of their moustaches, was driving down Regent Street. He who held the reins, Captain Stanley, was attending to some object at a distance rather than to his horse: his head was raised, his eyes were intently fixed far before him. A cab whirled suddenly round the corner of Argyle Place: Captain Stanley was too much absorbed to avoid it, and the two vehicles came into contact with each other.

No damage was done. All that came of it was a wordy war: for the cabman's abuse was unlimited, and Captain Stanley retorted in angry explosion.

"Is that the way you generally drive in London?" quietly asked his companion, as they went on again.

"An insolent reptile! he shall smart for it. I'll have him before the magistrate at Marlborough Street."

"Don't call me as a witness, then. It was your fault. You got into the fellow's way."

"I didn't get into his way."

"At any rate, you didn't get out of it, which amounts to the same thing. I ask if that is your usual mode of driving?"

"What if it is?"

"It is a careless one. The next time you offer me a seat, Stanley, I shall propose to take the reins."

"I thought I saw her carriage before us," explained Captain Stanley, in a more conciliatory tone, as he began to recover his good-humour. "It made me blind to everything else, Winchester."

"Who is 'her'?" demanded Lord Winchester, who had just returned from a prolonged sojourn on the Continent.

"The loveliest woman, Winchester. I can tell you you have a treat in store: you will say it when you get introduced to her. I couldn't exist," added the captain, twirling his moustache, "without a daily sight of that angel."

The viscount smiled. He knew, of old, Captain Stanley's propensity for going into heroics over "angels:" he did so himself upon occasion. "Mrs. Stanley to be?" asked he, indifferently, by way of saying something.

"No such luck. She's married. And so am I."

"Pardon, Stanley; I forgot it. When a fellow marries over in India, the fact is apt to slip out of one's memory."

"By Jove here she comes! She has turned back again. The green carriage and dark livery. I knew I saw it. Isn't she—"

"Take care of your horse," interrupted Lord Winchester; "here's another cab."

"Hang the cabs! Look at her."

An open barouche was approaching. One lady sat within it. Lord Winchester caught sight of an exquisite toilette, and then, the point-lace parasol being slightly moved, of an exquisite face. A young face, looking younger, perhaps, than it really was; clearly cut, delicate features; cheeks of a rich damask, brown glossy hair, and soft dark eyes of wonderful brightness.

"There's a picture for you!" murmured the enamoured Captain Stanley, letting his horse go as it would. "And the face is nothing to her fascination, when you come to talk to her. She has sent half London wild."

Off went his hat, for the bright eyes were smiling, and the fair head bowing to him. But off went Lord Winchester's also: for a brighter smile and a more familiar recognition, though one of surprise, greeted him.

"Halloa, Winchester! I say, that's too bad!" cried Captain Stanley, when they had passed. "You know her?"

"Knew her before I knew you. She's Selina Dalrymple."

"Selina? yes, that is her Christian name; I saw it one day on her handkerchief. Where was the use of your making a mystery over it? Why couldn't you say that you knew her?"

"I made no mystery, my good fellow. I did not know it was Selina Dalrymple you were speaking of. I used to meet her years ago at Court Netherleigh. Whom has she married? What's her name?"

"What is the matter with you?" cried Captain Stanley, looking at the viscount. "You call her Selina Dalrymple, and then ask what her name is. Do you suppose she bears one name, and her husband another?"

"She has never married Oscar Dalrymple!" exclaimed Lord Winchester, in lively tones. "Has she?"

"Her husband is the only Dalrymple I know of in the land of the living. A cold, dry, wizen-faced man."

"So he, Master Oscar! it is better to be born lucky than rich. Moat Grange and its fairest flower! You did not bargain for that, once upon a time. Poor Robert Dalrymple! he was nobody's enemy but his own."

"You mean her brother. He went out of the world ungenteelly, I believe, as Miss Bailey's ghost says. I did not know him."

"The Oscar Dalrymples are up in town for the season, I suppose?"

"Ay. They have taken part of a small house in Berkeley Street—not being rich."

"Anything but that, I should fancy."

"It is said that he did not want to come to town; hates it. Only, her heart was set upon it, and he can't deny her anything."

"Oh, that's it, is it," returned Lord Winchester.

That was it. Selina Dalrymple, the bride of a month or two, had made Oscar promise that they should spend part of the season in town. Vain, giddy, and thoughtless, Selina's heart was revelling in the pleasures of this London life, her head turned with the admiration she received. Alas! she had all too speedily forgotten the tragical end of her once-loved brother, though it came but a year ago. Amidst all this whirl of gaiety there was no time to remember that.

Mrs. Dalrymple's carriage had continued its course. It was now on its way to her dressmaker's, Madame Damereau. Dead now, and the once large business dispersed, Madame Damereau, a Frenchwoman, was famous in that gone-by day. An enormous custom—clientèle she used to call it—had she. Her house was handsome, and, so far as its appearance went, strictly private. It was in a private street, amidst other handsome houses, and there was nothing to betray its business except the brass-plate on the wide mahogany door—"Madame Damereau." It was as handsome inside as out; its rooms were a mixture of Parisian taste and English comfort, with their velvet carpets, rich crimson furniture, brilliant mirrors, and ornamental objects of porcelain, all delicate landscape painting and burnished gold. Surely, rooms so elaborately fitted up were not needed to carry on the business of a milliner and dressmaker, great though that business was! Needed or not, there they were. Madame Damereau had taste, and liked them. There was a hall and a reception-room; and a painted glass-door at the end of a passage, as the clientèle turned to ascend a handsome staircase that led to the show-rooms; through which glass-door might be caught glimpses of a paved court with green shrubs and plants. Above the stairs came an anteroom, and a trying-on room—and I know not how much more. Madame Damereau was as fascinating, in her line, as Mrs. Dalrymple in hers. Ask the ladies who were for ever paying her visits, and they would tell you that, once within reach of the fascinations of herself and her show-rooms, there they were contentedly fixed; there was no getting away, and there was no trying to get away. Madame's expenses were very great, and she had feathered her nest pretty well: somebody paid for it. When madame's nest should be sufficiently well feathered—or what she would consider so—it was her intention to return to La Belle France—pays chéri!—and quit England and its natives—les barbares!—for ever. Every thought of madame had reference to this enchanting finale: not a dress did she make, a bonnet sell, a mantle improvise, but the charges for them (very high generally) were elaborated with this one desirable end in view. Apart from this propensity to gain, madame was not bad at heart. Very good, in fact; and many a little kindness did she enact in private, especially to her poor countrymen and women domiciled here. What though she did stick on ruinous prices for those who could pay?—a person must live. Que voulez-vous?

There had been a Monsieur Damereau once upon a time. He had something to do with the theatres, though not in the way of acting. But he grew too fond of English porter and of fingering madame's profits. Madame inveigled him into a journey to Paris with her; let him have his fling a little while, and one fatal morning the poor deluded man woke to find that he and his wife were two; she had obtained a separation from him "de corps et de biens." Madame returned to England the same day, and what became of him she neither knew nor cared; except that he regularly drew the annuity she allowed to him, and which was to cease if he ever reset his foot in the British Isles.

At the period of which we are writing, a great mania had seized upon the gay London world. That other mania, admiration for Oscar Dalrymple's wife, which chiefly concerned the men, was but a small and private one; this was public and universal, and pertained to the women. It was a love for dress. A wild, rampant love for extravagant dress, not to be controlled within any limit. No fever yet known was like unto it; and Madame Damereau blessed it heartily, and petted it, and nursed it, and prayed—good Catholic that she was!—that it might never abate. We who have come to a certain age (than which nothing was ever more uncertain) can remember this, and the commotion it wrought. It was not the ordinary passion for finery that obtains in the beau monde, more or less, at all times, that is prevailing now, but something worse—different. In truth it was a very madness; and it ruined thousands. Few had fallen into this insidious snare as completely as Mrs. Oscar Dalrymple. Bred up in the country, in simplicity and comparative seclusion, London and its attractions had burst upon her with irresistible power, dazzling her judgment, and taking captive her senses. The passion for dress had been born with Selina. No wonder, therefore—example is so contagious, rivalry so rife in the human heart—that it had, with its means of gratification, seized frantic hold of her; just as another passion had formerly seized upon and destroyed her unfortunate brother. Not caring particularly for her husband, the world's homage had become as second life to her vain (and somewhat empty) mind; and of course she must dress accordingly and go out at all times and seasons armed for conquest. At breakfast gatherings; in afternoon visits; at teas, I was going to say, but kettledrums had not then come into vogue; in the parks, at dinners, at the play, and in the ball-room, she would be conspicuous for the freshness and beauty of her toilette.

Does the reader remember a remark made by Miss Upton, of Court Netherleigh? "Selina Dalrymple is more fond of dress than a Frenchwoman. Want of sense and love of finery often go together."

Poor Oscar Dalrymple, knowing nothing of the mysteries of a lady's toilette, or its cost, was content to admire his wife's as did other men. And, it may be, that no thought ever intruded itself into Selina's mind of the day of reckoning that must inevitably come.

CHAPTER XI

WITH MADAME DAMEREAU

Mrs. Oscar Dalrymple's carriage stopped at the door of Madame Damereau. Other carriages, waiting for their ladies, drew aside for it, and Mrs. Dalrymple descended. Rather tall, very elegant, her dress, a delicate lilac silk, flounced to the waist, became her well, and her rich white lace mantle became that. The Damereau footman threw open the door for her, and she went up to the show-room. A lady in plain black silk, but than which nothing could be more rich of its kind, with a small cap on her head of costly lace, and lappets of the same, disengaged herself from a group, to whom she was talking, and came forward, bowing; such bows as only a Frenchwoman can achieve. It was Madame Damereau. A clever-looking woman, with a fair skin, and broad smooth forehead.

What could she have the honour of doing today for Madame Dalreemp?

Mrs. Dalrymple scarcely knew. If put upon her conscience, she perhaps could not have said she wanted much. She would walk round first, and see. Was there anything fresh?

The Frenchwoman put the tip of one of her white fingers (very white they were, and displayed some valuable rings) upon the glove of her visitor, and then passed carelessly through the door to the next room. Madame Damereau certainly favoured Selina, who bought so largely of her, and never grumbled at the price. Selina understood the movement, and, stopping to look at a displayed article or two in her way, as carelessly followed her. That was madame's pet way when she was bent upon doing a good stroke of business.

"Tenez—pardon, madame," quoth she, as soon as Selina joined her, and speaking in scraps of French and English, as was her custom: though she spoke both languages almost equally well, barring her accent of ours—which was more than could be said for the clientèle, taking them collectively, and hence, perhaps, the origin of her having acquired the habit—"I have got the rarest caisse of articles arrived from Paris this morning. Ah! qu'ils sont ravissants!"

"What are they?" cried Selina, with breathless interest.

"I have not shown them to anybody: I have kept them en cachette. I said to my assistants, 'You put that up, and don't let it be seen till Madame Dalreemp comes.' Il-y-a une robe—une robe—une robe!" impressively repeated madame, turning up the whites of her eyes—"ma chère dame, it could only have been made for you!"

Selina's eyes sparkled. She thought herself the especial protégée of the Damereau establishment—as many another vain woman had thought before, and would think again.

"Is it silk?" she inquired.

"No. Dentelle. Mais, quelle dentelle! Elle—"

"Madame," said one of the assistants, putting in her head and speaking in a low tone, "the countess wishes to see you before she leaves."

"I am with her ladyship in the moment. Madame Dalreemp, if you are not too hurried, if you can wait till some of these ladies are gone, the caisse shall be brought out. I will not show it while they are here; I want you to have first view."

"I am in no hurry," replied Mrs. Dalrymple. "I have not been here for two days, so shall give myself time to look round."

As Selina did, and to gossip also. Several of her acquaintances were present. Lady Adela Grubb for one. Adela was looking a little worn and weary. A discontented expression sat on her face, not satisfactory to see, and she evidently did not take the enraptured interest in those fine articles, displayed around, that Selina took. Of course they were all "superbes" and "ravissant," as madame was given to observe: still a show-room, even such a one as this, tempting though it undoubtedly is, does not bear for every one quite the fascination of the basilisk.

Amidst other ladies who came in was Selina's old neighbour in the country, Mrs. Cleveland, the Rector's wife. Selina was surprised.

"I am only up for a day or two, my dear," she said. "I shall call in Berkeley Street before I go back."

"And how is mamma?"

"She is pretty well, my dear, and Alice too. Mary Lynn is staying with them."

"Oh is she? You never told me that," added Selina, turning to Lady Adela.

Lady Adela's mouth took rather a scornful curve. "Do you suppose Miss Lynn's movements concern me, that I should hear of them? When did you see Aunt Margery last, Mrs. Cleveland?"

"At church on Sunday."

"How beautiful!" exclaimed Selina, as they were slowly walking round the room, to look at the displayed wares: some on stands ranged against the walls, some on a large centre table. The ladies moved from one sight to another with enraptured gaze.

"What is beautiful?" asked Mrs. Cleveland. "That mantle?"

"Which mantle? That old dowdy black silk thing! I meant these sleeves. See; there's a collar to match."

"Yes, ma'am," interrupted one of the assistants, "we never had anything more beautiful in the house."

"What are they?" inquired Selina.

The young woman, attired in black silk only a degree less rich than madame's and a gold chain, her hair arranged in the newest fashion, carried the sleeves to her mistress.

"What am I to ask?" she said in a low tone.

"Twelve guineas."

"It is for Mrs. Dalrymple."

"Oh! I thought it was Madame Cliv-land. Fifteen guineas."

"They are fifteen guineas, madam," said the young person, returning. "And dirt cheap."

"I inquired what description of lace it was," said Mrs. Dalrymple. "Not the price."

"It is Venice point, madam. Real Venice point."

"I think I must have them," cried Mrs. Dalrymple. "Are they not tempting?

"Not to me," laughed Mrs. Cleveland. "I have too many little pairs of live arms to provide for, to give that price for a pair of sleeves."

"Only fifteen guineas!" remonstrated Selina. "And that includes the collar. I will take these sleeves," she added to the young woman.

"Thank you, madam."

"Those are pretty, that muslin pair."

"Very pretty, madam, for morning. Will you allow me to put these up with the others?"

"I don't mind—yes, if you like," replied Selina, never asking the price. "I saw Lord Winchester just now," she resumed to Mrs. Cleveland. "I did not know he had returned."

"Only a day or two since, I believe. My husband does not care to renew our acquaintance with him, so—"

"Oh, what a love of a bonnet!" unceremoniously interrupted Mrs. Dalrymple, as her eye fell on a gossamer article, all white lace and beauty, with something green sparkling and shining in it.

"Ah," said madame, coming forward, "ce chapeau me rend triste chaque fois que je le vois."

"Pourquoi?" demanded Selina, who was not quite sure of her French, but liked to plunge into a word of it now and then. In those days, French was not so universal a language, even in polite circles, as it is in these.

"Parce que je ne suis pas dame, jeune et belle. Ainsi je ne peux que le regarder de loin. Mais madame est l'une et l'autre."

Selina blushed and smiled, and fixed her eyes on the bonnet.

"It is a charming bonnet," observed Mrs. Cleveland. "What is the price?"

"Thirteen guineas, madam."

Thirteen guineas! Mrs. Cleveland shook her head. Such bonnets were not for her.

"It is a high price," observed Selina.

"High! Mesdames have surely not regarded it closely. These are emeralds. Look well, ma chère Madame Dalreemp. Emeralds. It is the very cheapest bonnet—for its real value—that I have shown this season."

"I think I will try it on," cried Selina.

Madame was not backward to follow the thought. In a twinkling the bonnet was on Selina's head, and herself at the glass. Twitching the border and the flowers, twitching her own hair, she at length turned round with a radiant face, blushing in its conscious beauty, as she spoke to Mrs. Cleveland.

"Is it not a sweet bonnet?"

"If you do not take it, it will be a sin against yourself," interposed the bonnet's present owner. "You never looked so well in all your life, Madame Dalreemp. Your face does set off that chapeau charmingly."

"I will take it," decided Selina. "What did you say it was? Fifteen guineas?"

"Thirteen, madam; only thirteen. Ah! but it is cheap!"

Mrs. Cleveland bought the mantle Selina had designated as dowdy, and a bonnet equally so. Selina told her they were frightful; fit for an almshouse.

"My dear, they are quiet, and will wear well. I cannot afford more than one new bonnet in a season. As to a mantle, it generally lasts me three or four years."

"Look at this handkerchief," interposed Selina, thinking what a dreadful fate Mrs. Cleveland's must be. "I really think it matches the sleeves and collar I have bought. Yes, it does. I must have that."

"That's a dear handkerchief, I know," cried Mrs. Cleveland. "What is it, Madame Damereau?"

"That—oh, but that's recherché, that," said madame, in a rapture. "Nine guineas. Ah!"

"Send it home with the other things," said Selina.

"I am going," said Mrs. Cleveland. "I have bought all I came to buy, and it is of no use staying here to be tempted, unless one has a long purse."

"The truth is, one forgets whether the purse is long or short in the midst of these enchanting things," observed Selina.

"I fear it is sometimes the case," was Mrs. Cleveland's reply. "Are you coming, my dear?"

"Not yet," answered Selina.

Lady, Adela went out with Mrs. Cleveland. She had not given a single order; had not gone with any particular intention of giving one, unless she saw anything especially to take her fancy. But Madame Damereau's was regarded as a favourite lounging place, and the gay world of the gentler sex liked to congregate there.

"Can I drive you anywhere?" asked Adela of Mrs. Cleveland, as they stood on the steps of Madame Damereau's handsome entrance-door. "Will you come home with me?"

"Thank you, I wish I could," was the answer. "But when I do come to London I have so many little commissions to execute that my time has to be almost entirely given to them. I shall hope to call and see you the next time."

"I wish you would come and stay with me for a week," cried Adela, quickly. "It would be a charity—an oasis of pleasure in my lonely life."

"Lonely from the want of children," thought Mrs. Cleveland, with a sad, faint smile.

"Are you quite well?" asked Adela, quickly, some delicacy in Mrs. Cleveland's face striking her.

"I—hope I am," was the hesitating answer. "At least, I hope that nothing serious is amiss. It is true I have not felt quite right lately, have suffered much pain; and one of my errands here is to see a physician. He has made an appointment for tomorrow morning."

Adela renewed her invitation, wished her good-day, and watched the rather fragile form away with a wistful look. They never saw each other again in life. Before two months had run their course, poor Mrs. Cleveland had gone where pain and suffering are not.

Meanwhile, when the show-rooms had thinned a little, Madame Damereau had the "caisse" brought out: that is to say, the contents of it. The caisse was taken for granted; the articles only appeared. The chief one, the lace dress, new from Paris, and secluded till that moment from covetous eyes, was of a species of lace that madame called Point d'Angleterre.

Madame shook out its folds with tender solicitude, and displayed its temptations before Mrs. Dalrymple's enthralled eyes. Madame did not speak; she let the dress do its own work: her face spoke eloquently enough. Selina was sitting on one of the low crimson velvet ottomans, her parasol tracing unconscious figures on the carpet, and her own elegant silk gown spread out around her.

"Oh dear!" she ejaculated, withdrawing her enraptured gaze. "But I fear it is very dear."

"Never let madame talk about that," said the Frenchwoman. "It is high; but—look at it. One could not pick up such a dress as that every day."

"How I should like to have it!"

"The moment we took this dress out of the caisse, I said to Miss Atkinson, who was helping me, 'That must be for Madame Dalreemp: there is no other lady who could do it justice.' Madame," she quickly added, as if an idea had just occurred to her, "fancy this robe, fine et belle, over a delicate pink glacé or a maize!"

"Or over white," suggested Selina.

"Or over white—Madame Dalreemp's taste is always correct. It would be a dress fit for a duchess, too elegant for many of them."

Some silks of different colours were called for, and the lace robe was displayed upon them successively. Selina went into ecstasies when the peach-blossom colour was underneath.

"I must have it. What is the price?"

"Just one hundred guineas, neither more nor less: and to anybody but Madame Dalreemp I should say a hundred and twenty. But I know that when once she appears in this before the world, I shall have order upon order. It will be, 'Where did you get that dress, ma chère Madame Dalreemp?' and madame will answer, 'I got it of Damereau;' and then they will come flocking to me. Ainsi, ma bonne dame, I can afford to let you have your things cheap."

"I don't know what to say," hesitated Selina, taking in, nevertheless, all the flattery. "A hundred guineas; it is a great deal: and what a bill I shall have! that lace dress I bought three weeks ago was only sixty."

"What was that lace robe compared with this?" was madame's indignant rejoinder. "That was nothing but common guipure. Look at what the effect of this will be! Ah, madame, if you do not take it I shall not sleep: I shall be vexed to my heart. Just as madame pleases, though, of course. Milady Grey did come to me yesterday for a lace dress: I told milady I should have one in a week's time: I did not care for her to see it first, for she is short, and she does not set off the things well. I know she would give me one hundred and twenty for this, and be glad to get it."

This was nearly the climax. Lady Grey, a young and pretty woman, dressed as extravagantly as did Mrs. Dalrymple, and there was a hidden rivalry between them, quite well known.

"There is another lady who would like it, I know, and she has but just gone out—and a most charming angel she is. I do speak of the Lady Adela—"

This was quite the climax, and Selina hastily interrupted. Lady Adela was even more lovely than was she herself: very much, too, in the same style of delicate beauty. What would Adela be in that lace dress!

"I will take it," cried Selina. "I must have a slip of that peach glacé to wear underneath it."

"It will be altogether fit for a queen," quoth madame.

"But could I have them home by tomorrow night for Lady Burnham's party?"

"Certainly madame can."

"Very well then," concluded Selina. "Or—stay: would white look better under it, after all? I have ever so many white glacé slips."

Madame's opinion was that no colour, ever seen in the earth or in the air, could or would look as well as the peach. Milady Grey could not wear peach; she was too dark.

"Yes, I'll decide upon the peach blossom," concluded Selina. "But that's not a good silk, is it?"

"Si. Mais si. C'est de la soie cuite."

"And that is all, I think, for today."

"What will Madame Dalreemp wear in her hair with this, tomorrow night?"

"Ah! that's well thought of. It must be either white or peach."

"Or mixed. Cherchez la boîte, numero deux," quietly added madame to an attendant.

Box, number two, was brought. And madame disentangled from its contents of flowers a beautiful wreath of peach-blossom and white, with crystallized leaves. "They came in only today," she said. Which was true.

"The very thing," cried Selina, in admiration. "Send that with the bonnet and sleeves today."

"Madame ought to wear amethysts with this toilette," suggested Madame Damereau.

"Amethysts! I have none."

"It is a great pity, that. They would look superbe."

"I was admiring a set of amethysts the other day," thought Selina, as she went down to her carriage. "I wish I could have them. I wonder whether they were very out-of-the-way in point of cost? I'll drive there and ascertain. I have had a good many little things there that Oscar does not know of."

She entered her carriage, ordering it to the jeweller's; and with her pretty face reposing amidst its lace and its flowers, and her point-lace parasol shading it, Mrs. Dalrymple, satisfied and happy, bowed right and left to the numerous admiring faces that met and bowed to her.

That same evening, Madame Damereau, having dined well and taken her coffee, proceeded to her usual business with her cashier, Mrs. Cooper. A reduced gentlewoman, who had tried the position of governess till she was heart-sick, and thankfully left it for her present situation, where she had less to do and a liberal salary. Miss Atkinson and Miss Wells, the two show-room assistants, came in. It was necessary to give Mrs. Cooper a summary of the day's sale, that she might enter the articles. They arrived, in due course, at the account of Mrs. Dalrymple.

"Dress of Point d'Angleterre," cried Madame Damereau. "One hundred guineas."

"Which dress is it she has bought?" inquired Mrs. Cooper, looking up from her writing. She had learnt to take an interest in the sales and customers.

"The one that the baroness ordered for her daughter, and would not have when it came," explained madame. "I then sent it to the Countess of Ac-corn, who was inquiring about a lace robe yesterday morning: but it seems she did not keep it. She never knows her own mind two hours together, that Milady Ac-corn."

"It is a very nice dress," remarked Mrs. Cooper.

"It is a beauty," added Miss Atkinson. "And Lady Acorn need not have cried it down."

"Did she cry it down?" quickly asked madame.

"She said it was as dear as fire's hot."

"Par exemple!" uttered madame, with a flashing face. "Did she say that?"

"Yes, madame. So Robert told me when he brought it back."

"She's the most insolent customer we have, that Femme Ac-corn," exploded madame. "And pays the worst. The robe would have been cheap at the price I asked her—eighty guineas."

"Mrs. Dalrymple, lace robe, one hundred guineas," read Mrs. Cooper. "What else?—making?"

"Making, two guineas. Peach glacé slip comes next."

"Peach glacé slip," wrote Mrs. Cooper. "The price, if you please?"

"Put it down in round figures. Ten guineas. She did not ask."

"I sold her those morning sleeves with the little dots," interposed Miss Wells. "There was no price mentioned, madame."

"What were they marked?" asked madame.

"Fourteen and sixpence."

"Put them down at a guinea, Mrs. Cooper. Making peach glacé slip—let me see, no lining or trimming—say fourteen shillings. White point-lace bonnet, thirteen guineas. Sleeves and collar—what did I say for that, Miss Wells?"

"Fifteen guineas, madame: and the handkerchief nine."

"Sleeves, collar, and handkerchief of Venice point, twenty-four guineas," read Mrs. Cooper. "She must be rich, this Mrs. Dalrymple."

"Comme ça, for that," quoth madame.

"She has had for more than a thousand pounds in the last six weeks. I suppose you are sure of her, madame? She is a new customer this season."

"I wish I was as sure of getting to Paris next year," responded madame. "Her husband has not long ago come into the Dalreemp estate. And the English estates are fine, you know. These young brides will dress and have their fling, and they must pay for it. They come to me: I do not go to them. The Dalreemps are friends of the Cliv-lands, and of those rich people in Grosvenor Square, the Grubbs, which is quite sufficient passe-port. You can go on now to Madame Cliv-land, Mrs. Cooper: one black mantle, silk and lace, three pounds ten shillings, and one fancy straw bonnet, blue trimmings, three guineas."

"Is that all there is for Mrs. Cleveland?"

Madame shrugged her shoulders. "That's all. I would not give thank you for the custom of Madame Cliv-land in itself; but they are well connected, and she is a gentle, good woman. I thought she looked ill today."

"There was Mrs. Dalrymple's wreath," interrupted Miss Atkinson, referring to a pencil list in her hand.

"Tiens, I forgot," answered madame. "What were those wreaths invoiced to us at, Miss Wells? This is the first of them sold."

"Twenty-nine and sixpence each, madame."

"Peach-and-white crystallized wreath, Mrs. Cooper, if you please. Forty-nine shillings."

"Forty-nine shillings," concluded Mrs. Cooper, making the entry. "That is all, then, for Mrs. Dalrymple."

And a pretty good "all," for one day, it was, considering Mr. Dalrymple's income.

CHAPTER XII

A LECTURE

A small, friendly dinner-table, Mr. Grubb and Lady Adela presiding. A thin, sharp-featured, insignificant little man, whose evening clothes looked the worse for wear, and who wore a black watered ribbon across his waistcoat in lieu of a gold chain, sat at Lady Adela's right hand. It was Colonel Hope. To look at him and his attire, you would have said he did not know where to turn for a shilling: yet he was the possessor of great wealth, and had seen hard service in India. Beside Mr. Grubb sat the colonel's wife, Lady Sarah; a tall, portly woman, whose face bore much resemblance to her mother's, Lady Acorn. Grace and Frances Chenevix and Mr. Howard, Mr. Grubb's partner, completed the party: the latter was a staid, stiff gentleman of sixty, with iron-grey hair and whiskers, and a stern face. He and the colonel had known each other in early life, when both had the world to fight for fame or fortune. Each had fought it well, and won; certainly so far as fortune was concerned. The colonel was just home from India, and Mr. Grubb had given the two early friends a speedy opportunity of meeting. One place at table was empty, and the young lady who sat next it, Frances Chenevix, did not look quite pleased at its being so. It was intended for Gerard Hope, who had somehow failed to make his appearance.

Colonel Hope had retired from the army and was come home for good. About a year ago he and Lady Sarah had lost their two sons, lads of seven and eight, from fever. They had no other children, and it was generally supposed the colonel would make his nephew, Gerard, his heir. The colonel and his wife were both tired this evening, having been looking at houses all day. Frances had been with them, but she seemed fresh and bright as a lark. The colonel had bought a pretty little property in Gloucestershire, but Lady Sarah wished for a town house also.

"I think I shall take it, though it is rather small," observed the colonel, talking of one of the houses they had seen. "There'd be room for a friend or two as well as for ourselves: and for Gerard also, if I decide to adopt him. By the way—what is your opinion of that young man, Grubb?"

"As to looks, do you mean, colonel?" smiled Mr. Grubb. "They are good. I don't know much else of him."

"Thought you did," growled the colonel, who was a hot-tempered man, and liked plain answers to his questions.

"I know nothing against him," said Mr. Grubb, emphatically. "I have seen but little of him, but that little I like."

"He is very nice and very good, and quite worthy to be adopted by you and Sarah, colonel," spoke up Lady Frances in her free way. "I'm sure the manner he slaves away in that red-tape office he is chained to, ought to be a gold feather in his cap."

"A gold feather?" repeated the literal colonel, looking at the speaker questioningly. While Mr. Howard, who knew what "slaving away" amounted to in a red-tape office, indulged in a silent laugh.

"Well, ought to tell in his favour, I mean," said Frances, mending her speech.

"I suppose he only does what he is put to do—his daily work," continued the colonel. "That, he cannot shirk: he has nothing to look to but his salary to pay his way. There's no merit in doing one's simple duty."

"I think there is a great deal, when it is such hard work as Gerard's," contended Frances. And this time Mr. Howard laughed outright at the "hard work."

"Perhaps the hard work is keeping him tonight," suggested Mr. Grubb, with just the ghost of a smile.

"No," said Frances, "I think the office closes at four."

"Oh," cried the colonel. "Where is he then? What does he mean by staying away?"

"He is run over, of course," said Frances, "and taken to the nearest hospital. Nothing short of that would have kept him away."

Lady Sarah Hope looked down the table at her sister. "Is Gerard in love with you, Frances?"

"In love with me!" exclaimed the young lady, her face flushing vividly. "What ridiculous fable will you imagine next, Sarah?"

"Is it a fable?" added Lady Sarah, struck with the flush.

"What else should it be?" laughed Frances. "Gerard could not think of falling in love upon nothing a-year. Nothing a-year, and find himself! That has been his case, poor fellow—or something akin to it."

"That may be remedied," remarked Lady Sarah. She had caught up an opinion upon the subject, and she held to it in the future.

As the small line of ladies filed out of the dining-room, Lady Sarah, walking first, turned just outside the door to wait for her sister Adela. Mr. Grubb, who was holding the door open, said something to his wife in an undertone as she passed him. Adela made no answer whatever; except that her lifted face put on a look of scorn, and her lips took a downward curve.

"What did your husband say to you?" asked Lady Sarah, having fancied that she heard her own name—Hope.

"I don't know—or care. As if I should listen to anything he might say!" contemptuously added Lady Adela.

Lady Sarah stared. "Why, child, what do you mean? He is your husband."

"To my cost."

"What do you mean? What does she mean?" continued Lady Sarah, appealing to the other two sisters, for Adela had not deemed it necessary to lower her voice. They did not answer. Grace took up an album, her face wearing a sad look of pain; Frances walked into the other drawing-room.

"I insist upon knowing what you mean, in saying that Mr. Grubb is your husband to your cost," cried Lady Sarah, returning to the charge. She was so much older than Adela—looking, in fact, old enough to be her mother, for India's sun and the loss of her children had greatly aged her—that she took her to task at will. Lady Sarah, like her mother, had always displayed somewhat of a propensity for setting the world to rights.

"It is to my cost," spoke Adela, defiantly. "That I should be his wife, obliged to stand as such before the world, a man of his name, a tradesman!" And the emphatic scorn, the stress of aversion laid on the "his," no pen could adequately express. "I never hear myself announced, 'Lady Adela Grubb,' but I shiver; I never see it in the Morning Post, amongst the lists at an entertainment, or perhaps at Court, but I fling the paper from me. As I should like to fling him."

"Bless my heart and mind, what's in a name?" demanded Lady Sarah, having listened as one astounded.

"Grubb! Grubb!" hissed Adela, from between her dainty lips. "There is a great deal in that name, at any rate, Sarah. I hate it. It is to me as a nightmare. And I hate him for forcing me to bear it."

"Forcing you to bear it! Why, you are his wife."

"I am—to my shame. But he had no right to make me his wife: to ask me to be his wife. Why could he not have fixed upon any one else? Grace, there, for instance. She would not have minded the name or the trade. She'd have got used to it—and to him."

Lady Sarah Hope nodded her head four or five times in succession. "A pretty frame of mind you are cherishing, Adela! Leave off such evil speaking—and thinking. Your husband is a true gentleman, a man that the world may be proud of; he can hold his own as such anywhere. As to the house in Leadenhall Street, it is of world-wide fame—the idea of your calling him a 'tradesman!'—Let me speak! Where can you find a man with so noble a presence, so refined and sweet a countenance? And I feel sure that he is as good and true and generous in himself as he is distinguished in reputation and person."

"All the same, I scorn him. I hate him for having chosen me. And it is the pleasure of my life to let him see that I do," concluded Adela, in sheer defiance, as she tossed her pretty head.

"Cease, Adela, cease!" interposed Grace, coming forward, her hands lifted imploringly. "You little know the wickedness of what you are saying; or the evil you may be laying up for yourself in the days to come. This is not your true nature; you are only forcing it upon yourself to gratify a resentment you have persistently taken up. How often have I prayed to you to be your own true self!

"Pray for it yourself, child," enjoined Lady Sarah, laying her hand with a firm grasp upon Adela's shoulder. "Pray upon your bended knees to Heaven, to snatch and shield you from Satan. Most assuredly he has got into you."

"What has got into me?" asked Adela, with languid indifference, not having caught the words.

"The devil," angrily amended Lady Sarah.

That infant of Lady Adela's, little George, did not live. Just for a month or two, just long enough for her to get passionately attached to him, to use every means to make him strong, he lingered. Then there came three days of illness, and the little soul fled from the feeble frame. No other child had been born, and Lady Adela seemed to be left with no end or aim in life, except that of cherishing resentment against Mr. Grubb. She took it up more fiercely than ever, and she let him feel it to his heart's core. The still, small voice of conscience, warning her that this was a forced and unnatural state of mind, could not always be deadened. The very fact of its pricking her caused her to resent the pricks, and to nourish her ill-omened temper the more persistently. Francis Grubb's life was not one of fair skies and rose-leaves.

"I should like to shake it out of her—and I wonder he does not do it," ran the thoughts of Frances Chenevix, as she opened the piano in the next room and began to play a dashing march.

Very especially just now was the Lady Adela Grubb resenting things in general. Captain Stanley—who had set up a flirtation with her when she was but a slip of a girl, and with whom it had pleased her to fancy herself in love after he sailed for India, though that was pure fancy and not fact—had taken no notice of her now that he was home again, beyond that demanded by the ordinary usages of society; and at this Lady Adela felt mortified—slighted. He had not as much as said to her, "So we are both married, you and I; we cannot sit in corners any more to talk in whispers:" on the contrary, he spent his time talking with newer beauties, Selina Dalrymple for one. It was quite the behaviour of a bear, decided Adela; and she was resenting it by showing temper to the world.

Frances Chenevix dashed through the march. Its last bars were dying into silence, when she thought she heard footsteps on the stairs. Going to the door, she saw Gerard Hope.

"Well, and what account have you to give of yourself?" began Frances, as he took her hand.

"I was at a water-party at Richmond," breathlessly answered Gerard, who had been having a race with time.

"Well, I'm sure! And here have I been vowing to them that nothing could have kept you but being run over in the streets; and Colonel Hope thinks you are detained over the red-tape duties. You might have come for once, Gerard."

"I couldn't possibly, Frances; I couldn't land; and then I had to dress. The tide kept us out. It has vexed me above a bit, I can tell you."

"You look vexed," she retorted, regarding his laughing countenance.

"I am vexed; but it is of no use to weep over it. You know I want to stand well with my uncle. I suppose you have finished dinner?"

"Ages ago."

"Where are the rest of you ladies?"

"In the next room, quarrelling. Lady Sarah is treating Adela to a bit of her mind—and she deserves it. Now, Gerard, behave yourself. What do you want to come so close to me for?"

For Mr. Gerard Hope was squeezing himself beside her on a small ottoman, meant for only one portly personage. He did more than that: he stole his arm round her waist.

"I believe Uncle Hope wants to adopt me," cried Gerard. "Won't it be jolly. No more scratch, scratch, scratch away with a pen all the blessed day."

"I called it 'slavery' to them just now," interrupted Frances.

"Good girl! No more getting up by candle-light in winter, and trudging off through the frost and through the thaw without breakfast, which you have not had time to take! It will be a change—if he does it. I'm not sure of it yet."

"You don't deserve it, Gerard."

"No! Why don't I? I'd try and be a good nephew to him—as dutiful as the good boy in the spelling-book. I say, Frances, has he been asking about me?—getting references as to character?"

"Yes, he has," was the perhaps unexpected answer. "Just as if you were a footman. Mr. Grubb said he did not know much of you; but what he did know he liked. Hark! They are coming out of the dining-room. And if you want any dinner, you had better go there and ring for it."

"Perhaps there's none left for me."

Frances laughed. "I heard Mr. Grubb whisper to his wife that if Gerard Hope came he was to go into the dining-room."

Gerard rose, went out, and met the gentlemen. Frances stayed where she was, and fell into a reverie. Did Gerard really love her? At times she thought so, at others she thought not.

The days wore onwards in their rapid flight. Time does not stand still even for those favoured ones who are plunged, for the first time, into the allurements of a London season: as was Selina Dalrymple.

One bright morning, when the sun was shining brilliantly and the skies were blue and the streets warm and dusty, she sat in the breakfast-room with her husband. The late meal was over, and Selina, a hot colour in her cheeks, was drumming her pretty foot on the floor, and not looking the essence of good-humour. She wore a richly embroidered white dress with pink ribbons. Mr. Dalrymple's eyes had rarely rested on a fairer woman, and his heart knew it too well.

"Selina, I asked you last night whether you intended to go to Lady Burnham's breakfast, at that rural villa of theirs. Of course, if you go, I will accompany you, otherwise I have some business I should like to attend to on Thursday."

"I can't go," answered Selina. "I have nothing to wear."

"Nothing to wear!"

"Nothing on earth."

"How can you say so?"

"I did think of ordering a suitable toilette for it, and was at Damereau's about it yesterday. But, after what you said last night—"

"My dear, what do you mean? what did I say? Only that you seemed, to me, never to appear in the same gown whether at home or out; and I begged you to remember that our income was limited."

"You said I changed my dresses four times a-day, Oscar."

"Well. Don't you?"

"But every one else does; Some change them five times. You would not like me to come down in the morning and go up to bed at night in the same dress, would you?"

"I suppose not. It's of no use asking me about dress, Selina. I scarcely know one gown from another. But it does strike me that you have a most extraordinary number of new things. Go out or come in when I will, there's sure to be the milliner's porter and basket at the door."

"Would you have me look an object?"

"You never do look an object."

"Of course I don't. I guard against it. I'd give the world to go to this fête at the Burnhams'. Every soul will be there, but me."

"And why not you, if your heart is so set upon It? I think all such affairs a stupid bore: but that's nothing."

"Would you wish me to go there in a petticoat?"

"No; I suppose not. I tell you I am no judge of a lady's things. I don't think I should know a petticoat from a gown. Those are gowns, are they not, hanging in rows round the walls in the room above, and covered up with sheets and table-cloths."

"Sheets and table-cloths! Oscar!"

"My dear, they look like it."

"Well—if they are gowns—there's not one I can wear."

"They are all recently new," said Mr. Dalrymple. "What's the matter with them?"

"There's not one I can wear," persisted his wife.

"But why?"

"Why!" repeated Mrs. Dalrymple, in quite a contemptuous tone, for she had no patience with ignorance. "You ought to know why!"

"My dear, I really don't. If you wish me to know, you must tell me."

"I have worn them all once," was the angry answer. "And some twice, and some three times. And one—Oscar," she broke off, "you remember that lovely one; a sky blue, shot with white; a robe à disposition?"

"What is à disposition?"

"Oh—a silk, flounced, and the flounces have some designs upon them, embossed, or raised, sometimes of a different colour. That dress I have worn five times. I really have, Oscar; five times!

"I wear my coats fifty times five."

"The idea of my being seen at Lady Burnham's in a dress I have worn before! No; I'd rather go in a petticoat, of the two evils, and hide my head for ever after."

Mr. Dalrymple was puzzled. "Why could you not be seen, there or anywhere else, in a dress you have worn before?"

"Because no one else is."

"Then what becomes of all the new gowns?" inquired the wondering man.

"For goodness' sake, do not keep on calling them 'gowns.'"

"Dresses, then. What becomes of them?"

"Oh—they do for the country. Some few, by dint of retrimming, can be made to look new for town. You don't understand ladies' dresses, Oscar."

"I have said I do not."

"Neither ought you," added Selina, crossly. "We do not worry ourselves to interfere between you and your tailors, or pry into the shape and make of your waistcoats and buttons and things, and we do not expect to have it done by us."

"Selina, let your grievance come to an end. I do not like to hear this tone of reproach."

"Then you must retract what you said last night. It was as if you wanted me never to have a new dress again."

"Nay, Selina, I only reminded you how small our income is. You must not overlook that."

"Don't be foolish, Oscar. Do you fear I am going to ruin you? What's the cost of a few dresses? I must have one for Lady Burnham's fête."

"My dear, have what you like, in reason," he said, in the innocence of his unconscious heart: "you are the best judge. Of course I can trust you."

The words were as the sweetest music in her ear. She sprang up, dancing to a scrap of a song.

"You dear, good Oscar I knew you were never going to be an old griffin. I think I must have that lovely green-and-white gauze. It was the most magnificent dress. I was divided between that and a cream-coloured damask. I'll have the gauze. And gauze dresses cost nothing."

"Nothing?"

"Next to nothing."

Selina flew upstairs. She pulled aside the "sheets and table-cloths," and glanced underneath. It was a goodly stock of robes; but yet not all the stock: for the lace, and muslin, and flimsy gauze, and delicate white, and delicate pearl, and delicate pink, and delicate other shades, were reposing in drawers, out of sight, between folds of tissue paper. Barège and balzarine: satin, plain and figured; velvet; silk, plain, damask, flowered, shot, corded, and of all the colours of the rainbow. Beautiful dresses; and yet—new, and rich, and elegant as they were, Selina Dalrymple could not go to the fête without a new one!

Away she went to Madame Damereau's. Astonishing that renowned artiste by the early hour of her visit.

"I want a thousand things," began Selina, in the blitheness of her heart. "Have you sold the green-and-white gauze dress?"

No, was madame's answer, she had kept it on purpose for Madame Dalreemp. Milady Ac-corn had come in yesterday afternoon late, and wanted it, but she had told milady that it was sold.

Selina took it all in. The fact was, madame had tried to persuade Milady Ac-corn into buying it, but milady was proof against the price. She had wanted it for Frances. It was only seventeen guineas, and that included the fringe and trimmings. Selina had told her husband that gauze dresses cost nothing!

"I want it for the breakfast on Thursday," cried Selina. "What mantle can I wear?"

A momentous question. They ran over in memory the mantles, scarfs, fichus, possessed by Mrs. Dalrymple, and came to the conclusion that not one of them would "go with" the gauze dress.

"I have a lace mantle," said madame—"ah! but it is recherché!—a real Brussels. If there is one robe in my house that it ought to go with, it is that green-and-white."

She brought it forward and exhibited it upon the dress. Very beautiful; of that there was no doubt. It was probably a beautiful price also.

"Twenty-five guineas."

"Oh my goodness—twenty-five guineas!" cried Selina. "But I'll take it. A breakfast fête does not come every day."

For a wonder—for a wonder—Selina, having exhibited her white lace bonnet with the emeralds only twice, came to the conclusion that that "would do." Not that she hesitated at buying another, but that it was so suitable to the green-and-white dress.

"And now for—Oh, stop; I think I must have a new parasol. My point-lace one is soiled, and I caught it in my bracelet the other day and tore it a little. You had a beautiful point-lace parasol here yesterday. Let me see it."

"The one you wore looking at yesterday will not do," cried madame. "It is lined with blue: Madame Dalreemp knows that blue can never go with the green dress. I have one parasol—ah, but it is a beauty!—a point-lace, lined with white. I will get it. It does surpass the other."

It did surpass the other, and in price also. Selina chose it. It was twenty guineas.

"My husband thought I could have worn one of my old dresses," observed Selina, as she turned over some gloves; "he says I have a great many. But one can only appear in a perfectly fresh toilette at a magnificent gathering such as this is to be." And madame fully assented.

Mrs. Dalrymple went to the breakfast, and she and her attire were lovely amidst the lovely, exciting no end of admiration. Very gratifying to her heart, then topsy-turvy with vanity. And so it went on to the end of the season, and her pleasurable course was never checked.

When they were preparing to return to the Grange, and her maid was driven wild with perplexity as to the stowing away of so extensive a wardrobe, and conjecturing that the carriage down of it would alone come to "something," it occurred to Selina, as she sat watching, that the original cost would also come to "something." Some hundreds, she feared, now she came to see the whole collection in a mass.

"Of course I shall not let Oscar see the bill," she soliloquized. "I'll get it from madame before I leave: and then there'll be no fear of its coming to him at the Grange."

Mrs. Dalrymple asked for the bill; and madame, under protest that there was no hurry in the world, promised to send it in.

Selina was alone, sitting in the drawing-room by twilight, when the account was delivered to her; it was enclosed in a large thick envelope, with an imposing red seal. She opened it somewhat eagerly. "What makes it such a bulk?" she thought. "Oh, I see; she has detailed the things."

Holding it close to the window, she looked at the bottom of the page, and saw ninety-four pounds.

"Ninety-four pounds!" ejaculated Selina. "What does madame mean? It must be much more than that."

She lighted the little taper on her writing-table; and then found she had been looking at one item only—the Venice point-lace for the decoration of a dress. So she turned the page and looked at the foot of the next.

"Antique robe, lace trimmings, and sapphire buttons, one hundred and twenty-five pounds. Tush!" impatiently exclaimed Selina.

With a rapid movement she turned the account over to the end, and gazed at the sum total; gazed at it, stared at it, and recoiled from it. Three thousand and odd pounds, odd shillings, and no pence! What the odd pounds were, whether one, or whether nine hundred ninety-nine, she did not catch in that moment of terror; the first grand sum of three thousand absorbed her eyes and her faculties. And there floated over her a confused consciousness of other bills to come in: one from the jeweller's, one for shawls, one for expensively trimmed linen. There was one shawl, real India—but she dared not think of that. "Oscar will say I have been mad," she groaned.

No doubt he would.

At that moment she heard his step, coming in from the dining-room, and turned sick. She crushed the bill in her right hand and thrust it down the neck of her dress. Then she blew out the taper, and turned, with a burning brow and shrinking frame, to the window again, and stood there, apparently looking out. Selina had never attempted to sum up what she had bought. At odd moments she had feared it might come to something like a thousand pounds.

Oscar came up and put his arm around her, asking whether it was not time to have the lights.

"Yes. Presently."

"What in the world have you got here?" cried he. "A ball?"

She pushed the "ball" higher up, and murmured something about "some paper."

"My dear, what is the matter with you here? You are trembling."

"The night-air, I suppose. It is rather chilly."

Yet the night was hot. Mr. Dalrymple immediately began to close the window. He was a minute or two over it, for one of the cords was stiff and did not go well. When he turned round again, his wife had left the room.

"Selina does not seem very well," thought Oscar.

CHAPTER XIII

FOLLY

There is no misfortune on earth so great as that of a troubled conscience: there is nothing that will wear the spirits and the frame like a burdensome secret which may not be told. It will blanch the cheek and sicken the heart; it will render the day a terror and the bed weary; so that the unhappy victim will be tempted to say with Job: When shall I arise and the night be gone? He is full of tossings to and fro unto the dawning of the day: his sleep is scared with dreams and terrified with visions.

Had Mrs. Oscar Dalrymple been of a different temperament, this unhappy state of mind would have been hers. But she had no very deep feeling. Troubled in a degree she undoubtedly was. That terrible secret, the debts she had incurred, lay on her mind always in a greater or a less degree; for she knew that when her husband paid them he would be half ruined; certainly crippled for years to come.

Another season had come round and was at its height; and Mr. and Mrs. Dalrymple had again come up to it. The past autumn and winter had been spent at Moat Grange, which Selina found insufferably dull, and where her chief solace and recreation consisted in looking over her beautiful and extensive wardrobe, and trying on portions of it in private. A very negative sort of enjoyment. Where was the use of possessing these divine dresses and adjuncts, when no field was afforded for their display? Selina had ventured to wear one costly robe on a certain evening that she dined at Court Netherleigh, and was severely taken to task by her mother, who was the only other guest, and by Miss Upton, for appearing in such "finery." They asked her what she meant by such extravagance. And that before Oscar, too! Selina blushed a little and laughed it off; but she mentally wondered what would have been said had she put on her very finest, or if they saw the stock at home.

During the winter Selina had a fever, brought on, it was thought, from exposing herself unduly to damp. She grew better, but was somewhat delicate and very capricious. Oscar, loving her intensely, grew to humour her fancies and to pet her as if she were a spoiled child. Her conscience reproached her now and then for the tacit deceit she was enacting, in thus suffering him to live in blissful ignorance of their true position; but on the whole it did not trouble her greatly. Alice, her sensitive sister, would have died under it; Selina contrived to exist very comfortably.

"If you found out that I had done anything dreadfully wrong, would you quite kill me?" she playfully said to him one day.

"Dare say I should," answered Oscar, putting on a face of mock severity. "Might depend, perhaps, upon what the thing was."

"Ah, no; you'd just scold me for five minutes, and then kiss and be friends. I always said you'd never turn out to be an old griffin."

That was the nearest approach Selina ever made towards confessing to her husband. And Oscar had only looked upon it as a bit of passing pleasantry.

Alice Dalrymple had left her mother's house to become companion to Lady Sarah Hope. During a week's visit that Colonel Hope and his wife made to Miss Upton in the autumn—it was soon after they had got into their new house in London—Alice had also been staying at Court Netherleigh. One day Lady Sarah chanced to say she wished she could find some nice young gentlewoman, who would come to her in the capacity of companion: upon which Alice said, "Would you take me?" "Ay, and be glad to get you," returned Lady Sarah, supposing that Alice had spoken in jest. Alice, however, was in earnest. She could not bear to be living on the charity of Oscar Dalrymple, for she shrewdly guessed that Selina threw as much expense on him as he could well afford; and Alice quite believed that her mother, devoted to the care of her poultry, her birds, and her flowers, would not miss her. So the bargain was struck. "And please remember, Lady Sarah, that I come to you entirely as companion, prepared to fulfil all a companion's duties, and not merely as a visitor," Alice gravely said; and she meant it.

Selina was vexed when she heard of the arrangement. She went straight down to her mother's cottage, and upbraided Alice sharply. "It is lowering us all," she said to her. "A companion is next door to a servant; every one knows that. It will be just a disgrace to the name of Dalrymple."

"Very well, Selina; then, as you think that, I will drop the name," returned Alice. "I was christened Alice Seaton, you know, after my godmother, and I will be called Miss Seaton at Lady Sarah's."

"Stuff and nonsense, child!" retorted Selina. "You may call yourself Seaton all the world over, but all the world will know still that you are Alice Dalrymple."

Alice entered upon her new home in London, and gravely told everybody in it that she wished to be called by her second name, Seaton. Lady Sarah laughed, and promised to humour her as often as she could remember to do it.

In December, Colonel Hope had formally adopted his nephew, Gerard. The young man threw up his post in the red-tape office (not at all a wise thing to do), and took up his abode with his uncle. They all went down to the colonel's place in Gloucestershire to spend Christmas, including Frances Chenevix, who almost seemed to have been as much adopted as Gerard, so frequently was she staying with them. Christmas passed; they came to London again, and things went on smoothly and gaily until just before Easter, when a fracas occurred. Gerard Hope contrived in some way to offend the colonel and Lady Sarah so implacably that they discarded him; frequent growls had ended in a quarrel. Gerard was insolent, and the colonel, hot and peppery, turned him out of the house. They went again into Gloucestershire for Easter, Alice with them as companion and Frances as a guest; but not Gerard. In fact, so far as one might judge, he was discarded for ever.

The cause was this: Lady Sarah, detecting the predilection of her sister Frances for the young man, and believing that he was equally attached to her, went out of her way and her pride to offer her to him. Gerard had refused it point blank. No wonder Lady Sarah was angry!

The sweet month of June came round again, and the London season, as I have said, was at its height. Amidst those who were plunging headlong into its vanities was Selina Dalrymple. She had coaxed and begged and prayed her husband to give her just another month or two of it this year, assuring him she should die if he did not. And Oscar, though wincing at the cost, knowing well he could not and ought not to afford it, at length gave in. It appeared that he could deny her nothing. The expenses of the previous season were far more than he had expected, and as yet he had not been able to discharge them all. Apart, this, from his wife's private expenses, of which he as yet remained in ignorance.

It may be questioned, however, whether Selina enjoyed this second season quite as much as she had the last. The visit and the gaiety and the homage were as captivating as ever, but she lived in a kind of terror; for Madame Damereau was pressing for the payment of her account. If that came to Oscar's knowledge, he would not only do to her, she hardly knew what, perhaps even box her ears, but he would be quite certain to carry her forthwith from this delightful London life to that awful prison, Moat Grange, at Netherleigh.

One afternoon, Oscar was turning out of his temporary home in Berkeley Street—for they had the same rooms as last year—when he saw coming towards him a young lady who walked a little lame. It was Alice Dalrymple.

"Ah, Alice!" he cried. "Have you come to London?"

"Yes," she replied. "Lady Sarah is better, and we left Gloucestershire yesterday to join the colonel here: he has been writing for us for more than a week past. Is Selina at home?"

"She is, for a wonder. Waiting for somebody she intends to go out with."

"How is she?"

"I cannot tell you how she is. Rather strange, it seems to me."

"Strange!"

"Take my arm, Alice, and walk with me a few paces. There's something the matter with Selina, and I cannot make it out," continued Mr. Dalrymple. "She acts for all the world as if she had committed some crime. I told her so the other day."

"Acts in what way?" cried Alice.

"She's frightened at her own shadow. When the post used to come in at the Grange she would watch for the boy, dart down the path, and seize the letters, as if she feared I might read the directions of hers. When she was recovering from that fever, and I would take her letters in to her, she more than once became blanched and scared. Often I ask her questions, or address remarks to her, and she is buried in her own thoughts, and does not hear me. She starts and moans in her sleep; twice lately I have awakened in the middle of the night and found her gone from the bed and pacing the dressing-room."

"You alarm me," exclaimed Alice. "What can it be?"

"I can only suppose that her nerves are overwrought with all these follies she is plunged into. It is nothing but turmoil and excitement; turmoil and excitement from day to day. I was a fool to come here again this year, and that's the truth."

"Selina had always led so very quiet a life," murmured Alice.

"Of course she had; and it has been a wonderful change for her; enough to upset the nervous system of a delicate woman. Selina has not been too strong since she had that fever."

"She ought to keep more quiet."

"She ought; but she will not. Before we came up I told her she must not do as she did last year; and I thought she did not mean to. Alice, she is mad after these gay frivolities; worse than she was last summer, I do believe—and that need not be. I wished not to come; I told Selina why—the expense, and other reasons—but she would. She would, Alice. I wonder what it is that chains her mind to this Babel of a city. I hate it. Go you in and see her, Alice. I can't stay now, for I have an appointment."

Mrs. Dalrymple was in her bedroom when Alice entered, dressed, and waiting to go out: dressed with an elegance regardless of expense.

"Good gracious, child, is it you!" she exclaimed.

When the first moments had passed, Alice sat down and looked at her sister: her cheek was thin, and its bloom told more of hectic than of health.

"Selina!" exclaimed Alice, "what is the matter? You are much altered."

"Am I? People do alter. You are altered. You look ill."

"Not more so than usual," replied Alice. "I grow weaker with time But you are ill: I can see it. You look as if you had something preying on your mind."

"Nonsense, Alice. You are fanciful."

"What is it?" persisted Alice.

"If I have, your knowing it would do me no good, and would worry you. And yet," added Mrs. Dalrymple, "I think I will tell you. I have felt lately, Alice, that I must tell some one!"

Alice laid gentle hold of her. "Let us sit down on the sofa, as we used to sit together at the Grange, when we were really sisters. But, Selina, if you have wanted a confidant in any grief, who so fitted to be that as your husband?"

"He!" cried Selina—"he! It is the dread of his knowing it—the anxiety I am in, daily and hourly, to keep it from him—that is wearing me out. Sometimes I say to myself, 'What if I put an end to it all, as Robert did?'"

Alice was accustomed to the random figures of speech her sister was at moments given to using; nevertheless her heart stood still.

"What is it that you have done, Selina?"

"Ruined Oscar."

"Ruined Oscar!"

"And ruined myself, with him," added Selina, in reckless tones, as she took off her bonnet with a jerk, and let it lie in her lap. "I have contracted debts that neither he nor I can pay, thousands upon thousands; and the worry of it, the constant fear is rendering my life a—I will not say what—upon earth."

"Debts! thousands upon thousands!" confusedly uttered Alice.

"It is so."

"How did you contract them? Not as—as—Robert did? Surely that infatuation is not come upon you?"

"No. But that infatuation, as you call it, is in fashion in our circles just now. I could tell you of one young lady, whom you know, who amuses herself with it pretty largely."

"A young lady!"

"She is younger than I am—but she's married," returned Selina: and the young lady in question was the Lady Adela Grubb. "My embarrassment arises from a love of pretty gowns," she added lightly; for it was not possible for Selina Dalrymple to maintain a tragic mood many minutes together. "Damereau's bill for last season was between three and four thousand pounds. It is between four and five thousand now."

Alice Dalrymple felt bewildered. "It is not possible for one person to owe all that for one year, Selina!"

"Not possible?" repeated Mrs. Dalrymple. "Some of my friends spend double—treble—four times what I do."

"And so their example led you on?" cried Alice, presently, waking up from a whirlpool of thought.

"Something led me on. If one is in the world, one must dress."

"No, Selina: not as you have done. Not to ruin. If people have only a small income they dress accordingly."

"And make a sight of themselves. I don't choose to."

"Better that, and have peace of mind," remarked Alice.

"Peace of mind! Oh, I don't know where that is to be found nowadays."

"I hope you will find it, Selina. How much do you say you owe?"

"There's four thousand to Damereau, and—"

"Who is Damereau?"

"Goodness me, Alice; if you never did spend a season in town, you ought to know who she is, without asking. Madame Damereau's the great milliner and dressmaker; every one goes to her."

"I remember now. Lady Sarah has her things elsewhere."

"Then I owe for India shawls, and lace, and jewels, and furs and things. I owe six thousand pounds if I owe a farthing."

"What a sum!" echoed Alice, aghast. "Six thousand pounds!"

"Ay, you may well repeat it! Which of the queens was it who said that when she died the name of Calais would be found engraven on her heart? Mary, I think. Were I to die, those two words, 'six thousand,' would be found engraven on mine. They are never absent from me. I see them written up in figures in my dreams; I see them always; in the ball-room, at the opera, in the park they are buzzing in my ears; when I wake from my troubled sleep they come rushing over me, and I start from my bed to escape them. I am not at all sure that it won't turn out to be seven thousand," candidly added Mrs. Dalrymple.

"You must have dressed in silver and gold," said poor Alice.

"No: only in things that cost it: such things as these," said Mrs. Dalrymple, pulling at her bonnet with both hands in irritation so passionate that it was torn in two.

"Oh, pray! pray!" Alice interposed, but too late to prevent the catastrophe. "Your beautiful bonnet! Selina, it must have cost three or four guineas. What a waste!"

"Tush!" peevishly replied Mrs. Dalrymple, flinging the wrecks to the middle of the room. "A bonnet more or less—what does it matter?"

Alice sat in thought; looking very pained, very perplexed.

"It appears to me that you are on a wrong course altogether, Selina. The past is past; but you might strive to redeem it."

"Strive against a whirlpool," sarcastically responded Selina.

"You are getting deeper into it: by your own admission, you are having new things every day. It is adding fuel to fire."

"I can't go naked."

"But you must have a large stock of dresses by you."

"Do you think I would appear in last year's things? I can't and I won't. You do not understand these matters, Alice."

"Then you ought not to 'appear' at all. You should have stopped at the Grange."

"As good be in a nunnery. Once you have been initiated into the delights of a London season, you can only come back to it. Fancy my stopping at that mouldy old Grange."

"What is to be the end of all this?" lamented Alice.

"Ah, that's it! The End. One does not know, you see, how soon it may come. I'd not so much mind if I could get all the season first. The torment of it is, that Damereau is pressing for payment. She is throwing out hints that she can't supply me any longer on credit—and what on earth am I to do if she won't? What a shame it is that there should be so much worry in the world!"

"The greatest portion of it is of our own creating, Selina. And no worry ought to have the power very seriously to disturb our peace," the younger sister continued, in a whisper.

"Now, Alice, you are going to bring up some of those religious notions of yours! They will be lost upon me. One cannot have one's body in this world and one's heart in the next."

"Oh yes, we can," said Alice, earnestly.

"Well, I don't suppose I am going into the next yet, unless I torment myself out of this one; so don't go on about it," was Selina's graceless reply. But as Alice rose to leave, her mood changed.

"Forgive my fractiousness, Alice; indeed, you would excuse it, if you only knew how bothered and miserable I am. It makes me cross with myself and with other people."

"Ma'am," interrupted Ann, Mrs. Dalrymple's maid, "Lady Burnham is at the door, waiting for you."

"I am not going out today," answered her mistress, rising. "I have changed my mind."

"Oh, my patience!" uttered the maid. "What's this? Why, ma'am, it's never your bonnet?"

No man is a hero to his valet-de-chambre: I fear the same may be said of woman. "Bother the bonnet," was the undignified reply of Mrs. Dalrymple, as she flirted the pieces further away with her foot. Ann humbly followed them to the far-off corner, and there took them into her hands. "Reach me another bonnet," said her mistress; "I think I will go, after all. What's the use of staying indoors?"

"Which bonnet, ma'am?"

"Oh, I don't know! Bring some out."

An array of bonnets, new and costly, were displayed for Mrs. Dalrymple's difficult choice. Alice, to whom all this was as a revelation, took her departure with uplifted hands and a shrinking heart.

Mrs. Dalrymple went downstairs, and took her seat in Lady Burnham's carriage. The latter, an extremely wealthy woman, full of pleasurable excitement, imparted some particulars she had learnt of the marriage festivities about to be held in a family of their acquaintance, to which they were both invited. Lady Burnham was then on her road to Damereau's to order a suitable toilette for it—one that would eclipse everybody's but the bride's. Selina, in listening, forgot her cares: when carried out of herself by the excitement of preparing for these pomps and vanities, she generally did so forget. But only then. In the enacting of the pomps and vanities themselves, when they were before her in all their glory, and she made one of the bedizened crowd, her nightmare would return to her; the skeleton in the closet would at those festive times, be exceeding prominent and bare. The reader may be a philosopher, a grave old F.R.S., very learned in searching out cause and effect, and so be able to account for this. I am not.

Selina's mouth watered as she listened to Lady Burnham's description of what she meant to wear at the wedding, and what she recommended to Selina: and the carriage stopped at Madame Damereau's. Mrs. Dalrymple's orders were quite moderate today—only amounting to about ninety pounds.

Was she quite silly? the reader will ask. Well, not more so than many another thoughtless woman.

Madame Damereau took the order as politely and carefully as though Mrs. Oscar Dalrymple had been made of bank notes and gold. She knew better manners—and better policy, too—than to make any objection before others of her clientèle. But that same evening, when Selina was dressing, she was told that a lady who gave the name of Cooper wished to see her. Selina knew that there was a Mrs. Cooper in the establishment of Madame Damereau, a partner, she fancied, or book-keeper; something of that sort. She had seen her once or twice; a lady-like woman, who had been reduced.

"Let Mrs. Cooper come up here," she said to the maid. And Mrs. Cooper entered the bedroom.

"I come from Madame Damereau's," she began, taking the chair that Selina pointed to. "She hopes—"

"For goodness' sake, speak low!" interrupted Selina, in ill-concealed terror. "Mr. Dalrymple is only in his dressing-room, and I do not wish him to hear all my private affairs. These London walls are thin. She wants money, I suppose."

"She hopes, madam, that you will make it convenient to let her have some," said Mrs. Cooper, sinking her voice to a whisper. "If it were only a few hundred pounds," she said. "That is trifling compared with the whole sum, which amounts now to—"

"Oh, I know what it amounts to; I can guess it near enough," hastily interposed Mrs. Dalrymple. "In the course of a week or two I will see what I can do."

Poor Selina, at her wits' end for excuses, had said "in the course of a week or two" so many times now, that Madame Damereau was tired of hearing the phrase.

Mrs. Cooper hesitated, not much liking her errand. "She bade me say, madam, that she was extremely sorry to cause inconvenience, but that she cannot execute the order you gave today unless she previously receives some money."

"Not execute it!" repeated Selina, with flashing eyes. "What do you mean by saying such a thing to me?"

"Madam, I am but the agent of Madame Damereau. I can only speak as she bids me."

"True," answered Selina, softening; "it is not your fault. But I must have the things. You will get them for me, will you not?" she said, in an accent of entreaty, feeling that she was speaking to a gentlewoman, although one who but held a situation at a milliner's. "Oh, pray use your influence; get her to let me have them."

Mrs. Cooper stood in distress, for hers was one of those refined natures that cannot bear to cause or to witness pain.

"If it depended upon me, indeed you should have them," she answered, "but I have no influence of that sort with Madame Damereau. She would not allow the slightest interference between her and her ladies: were I to attempt it, I might lose my place in her house, and be turned out again to struggle with the world."

"Has it been a harsh world to you?" inquired Selina, pityingly.

"Oh yes," was Mrs. Cooper's answer, "or I should not be where I am now. And I am thankful to be there," she hastily added: "I would not seem ungrateful for the mercy that has followed me in my misfortunes."

"I think misfortunes are the lot of all," spoke Selina. "What can I do to induce Madame Damereau to furnish me with these things?"

"Perhaps you had better call and see her yourself, madam," replied Mrs. Cooper, relapsing into her ostensible position. "I will try and say a word to her tonight that may prepare her. She has a good heart."

"I will see her tomorrow. Thank you," replied Mrs. Dalrymple, ringing for Mrs. Cooper to be shown out.

Selina finished dressing, and went forth to the evening's gaiety with what spirits she had. Once plunged into the gay scene, she forgot care and was merry as the merriest there. Her husband had never seen her face brighter.

On the following day, Selina proceeded to Madame Damereau's at an early hour, before any of the other clientèle would be likely to appear. But the interview, although Mrs. Cooper had said as much as she dared, was not productive of good. Madame had gradually learnt the true position of Oscar Dalrymple, that he was a very poor man, instead of a rich one; she feared she might have trouble over her account, and was obstinate and obdurate. Not exactly insolent: she was never that, to her customers' faces: but she and Mrs. Dalrymple both lost temper, and the latter was impolitic enough to say some cutting things, not only in disparagement of madame's goods, but about the "cheating prices" she had been charged. Madame Damereau's face turned green, and the interview ended by her stating that if some money was not immediately furnished her, she should sue Mr. Dalrymple for the whole. Selina went away sick at heart; for she read determination on the incensed lips of the Frenchwoman.

CHAPTER XIV

LADY ADELA

"How sly Mary has been!"

The above exclamation spoken by Lady Adela Grubb in a sort of resentful tone, as she read a letter while sipping her coffee, caused her husband to look up. He sat at the opposite end of the breakfast-table, attractive with its silver and flowers and its beautiful Worcester china.

"Are you speaking of your sister Mary?" he asked. "What has she done?"

Any answer to this question Lady Adela did not condescend to give. Unless the tossing of the letter across the table to him could be called one—and she did it with a gesture of scorn. The letter, a short one, came from Miss Upton, of Court Netherleigh.

"My DEAR ADELA,

"I have a little business to transact in London tomorrow, and will take luncheon with you at one o'clock, if quite convenient. Tell your husband, with my kind regards, that I hope to see him also—if he can spare an hour from that exacting place of his, Leadenhall Street. So I am to have your sister Mary as a neighbour, after all!

"Your sincere friend,

"MARGERY UPTON."

"Which means, I presume, that Mary is to marry Cleveland," remarked Mr. Grubb, as he read the concluding sentence.

"Stupid thing! I told her, weeks ago, she was flirting with him."

"Nay, not flirting, Adela. Cleveland is not capable of that."

Adela tossed her head. How lovely she looked! fair as the fresh summer morning.

"She was flirting, though. And he would flirt, if he were not too old. Parsons, as a rule, flirt more than laymen. She must be hard up for a husband to take him. He has a houseful of children!"

"I dare say she likes him," said Mr. Grubb.

"Oh, nonsense! One only point can be urged in his favour—that he is a patrician."

"That he is what?" cried Mr. Grubb, who was drinking his coffee at the moment, and did not hear the word.

"A patrician. Not a plebeian."

The offensive stress laid by Adela on the last word, the marked scorn sitting on her lips, brought a flush to her husband's brow. Nothing seemed to afford her so much gratification as to throw out these lance-shafts to Mr. Grubb, on what she was pleased to term his plebeian origin.

"Do you wish for more coffee?" she asked ungraciously.

"No. I have not time for it. I must make the best of my way into the City, if I am to get back to luncheon."

"There is not the least necessity for you to get back," was her slighting remark. "You will not be missed, if you don't come."

"By yourself, no. I am aware of that. But I do not care to be so lacking in common courtesy as to disregard the express wish of Miss Upton."

"She may have expressed it out of mere politeness."

"Miss Upton is not one to express a wish out of mere politeness," replied Mr. Grubb, as he gathered up some papers of his that were by the side of his plate. "Besides, I shall like to see her."

Approaching his wife, who had taken up the Morning Post, he stood over her. "Good-bye, Adela," he said; and bent to kiss her cheek.

"Oh, good-bye," she retorted in curt tones, and jerked her cheek away from his very lips.

He went away with a suppressed sigh. This line of treatment had been dealt out to him by her so long now that he had become inured to it. It was none the less bitter for that.

Adela, dropping the newspaper and picking up a rose from one of the glasses on the breakfast-table, went to the window to see whether it looked very hot, for she wanted to walk to her mother's and hear about Mary's contemplated marriage. She saw her husband cross the square. For some reason he was crossing it on foot, his close carriage slowly following him: on very hot days he rarely used an open one. What a fine, noble-looking man he was! what a face of goodness and beauty was his!—how few could compare with him. At odd moments this would even strike Adela; it struck her now; and a flash of something like pride in him darted into her heart.

Ah! she saw now why he had walked across the square instead of getting into his carriage at the door: her father was advancing towards him. The two met, shook hands, stood for a few moments talking, and then Lord Acorn put his arm within his son-in-law's, and they turned the corner together.

"Papa wants more money of him," thought Adela. "It's rather too bad, I must say. But that Leadenhall Street is just a mine of wealth."

For, now and again, ever since the marriage, Lord Acorn had come with his troubles and embarrassments to Mr. Grubb, who seldom refused to assist him.

As the clock was striking one that day, they sat down to lunch: Miss Upton, who had just arrived, Mr. Grubb, and Lady Adela. Miss Upton never took the meal later if she could help it. Indeed, at home she took it at twelve. Her breakfast hour was eight precisely, and by twelve she was ready for luncheon. Lady Acorn came in as they were sitting down, threw her bonnet on a chair, and sat down with them. Hearing that Miss Upton would be there, she had come, uninvited, to meet her.

"How early you went out, mamma!" cried Adela, in rather an aggrieved tone. For, when she reached Chenevix House that morning, she found her mother and sisters had already left it: so that she had heard no particulars at all about Lady Mary's proposed wedding, not even whether there was certainly to be one, and Adela had her curiosity upon the subject.

"We went shopping," answered Lady Acorn. "One likes to do that before the heat of the day comes on. Do you know that Mr. Cleveland is going to marry again, Margery?" she added abruptly, looking across the table at Miss Upton.

"Yes, I know it. He came to the Court yesterday morning to tell me of it. I think Mary will make him a good wife."

"She has courage," said Mr. Grubb, with a pleasant laugh. "How many children are there? Ten?"

"No. Eight. And they are of all ages; from seven, up to four-and-twenty," added Miss Upton.

Lady Acorn was nodding her head, in emphatic acquiescence to Mr. Grubb's remark. "I told Mary she had the courage of Job, when the thing first came to my ears. Eight children and a poor country Rector! Young women are ready to marry a broomstick when they get to Mary's age, if the chance falls in their way."

"Had Job so much courage, mamma?" put in Adela.

"Courage or patience, or some such virtue. It is not I that would have taken an old widower with a flock of young ones," continued the countess, in her plain-speaking tartness.

"You will get rid of us all in time, mamma," observed Adela.

"It entails trouble enough," was her mother's ungracious rejoinder. "I am quite done over with heat and fatigue now—going about from one place to another after Mary's things. Gowns and bonnets and slips and mantles, and all the rest of it! Girls are so exacting when they are going to marry: they must have this, and they must have that, and Mary is no exception to the rule. One would think she had picked up a duke."

"It is natural they should be," observed Miss Upton.

"But it's not the less ridiculous," retorted the countess. "One thing I must say—that Tom Cleveland is showing himself in desperate haste to take another wife."

"The haste is for his children's sake," said Miss Upton; "be very sure of that, Betsy. 'I must have some one to control and train them; since my poor wife's death the girls have run wild,' he said to me yesterday, when he told me about Mary, and the tears were almost running down his cheeks."

"It is a great charge," spoke Mr. Grubb. "I mean for Lady Mary."

"It is," acquiesced Miss Upton. "But I hope—I think—she will be found equal to it, and will prove a good stepmother. That she understands the responsibility she is undertaking, and has counted the cost, I am sure of, by what she said in a long letter I received from her this morning."

"It is to be hoped she will have no children of her own," struck in Lady Acorn. "Many a woman makes a good stepmother until her own babies come. After that—"

"After that—what?" asked Miss Upton, for Lady Acorn had stopped abruptly.

"After that, she thinks of her own children and not of the first wife's. And sometimes the poor things get hardly dealt by."

"And when is the wedding-day to be?" asked Adela.

"The day after twelve months shall have elapsed since the death of the first Mrs. Cleveland; or in as short a time subsequent to that day as may be convenient to me and the milliners," laughed Lady Acorn.

"That will make it some time in August, mamma?"

"Yes, in August."

"Adela, you must give them a substantial present—something worth having," said Mr. Grubb to his wife.

"Is Damereau to furnish the wedding-dresses?" questioned Adela, ignoring her husband's remark rather too pointedly, and addressing her mother.

"Damereau!" shrieked the countess. "Not if I know it. We have been to plain Mrs. Wilson. Damereau gets dearer every day. She is all very well for those who have a long purse: mine's a short one."

At the close of the luncheon, Miss Upton said she must take her departure: she had commissions to do. A fly waited for her at the door.

"You should use one of Adela's carriages," said Mr. Grubb, as he took her down to it.

"Ah, thank you; I know you and she would lend it to me with hearty goodwill; but I like, you see, to be independent," was Miss Upton's answer. "I have employed the same fly and the same man for years. When I am coming to London, I write to him previously, and he holds himself at my service for the day."

"Is there anything I can do for you?" asked Mr. Grubb, as he placed her comfortably in the closed fly.

"Nothing. Unless you will get in and ride a little way with me. I am going first to a shop in the Strand. Perhaps you can't spare the time."

"Indeed I can," he answered, stepping in and taking the seat facing her. "The Strand will be all in my way to Leadenhall Street."

They had not seen much of one another, and yet they were intimate, for each liked the other. Mr. Grubb had paid one short visit to Court Netherleigh with his wife; it was in the first year of his marriage, and they stayed three days. Miss Upton called on them sometimes when she came to town, perhaps once or twice a-year; and that was all.

"You were saying something to Adela about giving a present to her sister," began Miss Upton, as they ambled along. "I take it that you were sincere."

"Indeed I was. I should like to give them something that will be useful—regardless of cost," he added, with a smile. "Can you suggest anything?"

"I can. A little open-carriage and pony—if you would like to go as far as that. Mary will want it badly. The old pony-carriage used by Mrs. Cleveland all her married life to get about the straggling parish in, is the most worn, ramshackle thing now you ever saw; it will hardly hold together. And the poor pony is on its last legs."

"They shall have a new one. Thank you for telling me," added Mr. Grubb, with a sunny smile.

"And I dare say you wonder why I can't give them this thing myself," resumed Miss Upton; "but the truth is—don't laugh—I am refurnishing the house, and I don't like to do too much. It would look ostentatious, patronizing, and Cleveland would feel it so in his heart. I had a rare battle with him about the furniture, when I told him what I meant to do; I had already, in fact, given orders for it. 'You cannot bring Lady Mary home to that shabby dining and drawing-room of yours,' I said to him yesterday. 'I fear I can't afford to have them renewed,' he answered me, his face taking a long look. 'Of course you can't,' I said, 'whoever heard of a parson who could; I mean to do it myself.' Well, then we had a fight. Mary had seen the walls and the rooms and knew what they were, he maintained. Upon which I cut short the argument by saying the orders were already given, and the workmen ready to go in. I had seen for a month or two past, you must understand, Francis, how matters were going between him and Mary Chenevix."

Miss Upton broke off with a short laugh. "The idea of my calling you Francis!" she exclaimed. "Will you forgive me?"

"Forgive you! Dear Miss Upton, if you only know how pleasant to me the name sounds from your lips!"

"When I think of you it is generally as Francis Grubb, and so it escaped me. Well, then, you will give them this new pony and carriage?"

"I will. And thank you sincerely for suggesting it."

"Does Adela make you a good wife yet?" cried Miss Upton, fixing her keen eyes upon him. And Francis Grubb, at the abrupt query, grew red to the very roots of his waving hair.

"Is she becoming affectionate to you, as a gracious wife should be?" pursued Miss Margery, for he did not answer.

"I do not complain of my wife; please understand that, Miss Upton."

"Quite right of you not to. But I believe I understand rather more than appears on the surface; have understood for some time past. I gave her a lecture when I was last here. I did, indeed; though you may not suppose it."

He smiled. A poor smile at best. Margery Upton leaned forward and put her hand upon his hand, that lay on his knee.

"There is only one thing for it—patience. Bear quietly. Adela used to be a sweet girl! I think she has a good heart, and what evil spirit has taken possession of her I cannot conceive. I think things will work round in time, even as you could desire them."

"Ay!"

"And, for the present, I say, keep up a good heart—and bear. It is my best advice to you."

He took her hand within both his, and pressed it fervently, making no further reply. And just then the fly pulled up in the Strand.

"I have not asked about your mother," said Miss Upton, as he stood at the door to say farewell after getting out.

"She is pretty well, now."

"And your sister? Does she get over that wretched business of Robert Dalrymple's?"

"Of course—in a degree. Time softens most things. But she will never forget him."

He shook hands finally with Miss Upton; he walked on to his house in Leadenhall Street, his step flagging, his heart weary. Entering his own private room, he found two ladies within it. His mother, who was seated in the most easy chair the room afforded; and his sister. Mrs. Lynn was a tall, dignified, upright woman still: her beautiful grey eyes were just like his own, her refined countenance, sickly now, bore yet its marks of unusual intellect.

"Mother!" he exclaimed, in surprise. "How glad I am to see you!"

"I drove up to the Bank upon a little matter of business, and came on to see you after it was transacted," she explained, as he kissed her. "It is unusual to find you out at this time of day, Francis; but the clerks thought you would be in soon, and I waited. I am glad of the rest; the journey has so tired me."

"Why will you not let me do your matters of business for you, mother?" he tenderly asked, as he busied himself to get a glass of wine for her and some biscuits.

"Because so long as I can do things for myself, I like to do them," she answered, "and my old-fashioned chariot is an easy one: I do not care to become quite the incapable old woman before the necessity for it inevitably sets in. And now, how is it with yourself, Francis? Your brow wore a troubled look as you entered."

Never did Francis Grubb give a more genial smile than now. Not even to his mother would he willingly show his care. "It is quite well with me," he laughed; "well and flourishing. Take your wine, mother."

"Your wife?" whispered Mrs. Lynn, in a tone of doubt—of pain. "Is she—more friendly?"

"Oh, we are friendly enough—quite so," he lightly answered, angry with himself for not being able to suppress the flush that rose at the question. "Is that a new dress you have on, Mary? It is marvellously pretty."

"If her child had only lived!" sighed Mrs. Lynn, alluding to Lady Adela.

"Quite new; new on today; and I am very glad you admire it," gaily answered Mary, as she spread out the dress with both hands, and turned herself about on her brother's dull red carpet for inspection. She was as thankful to drown the other subject as he was: she knew, unhappily, more about it than her mother. "I am going out on a visit, so of course I must have some pretty things."

"Going where?"

"To Lawn Cottage, at Netherleigh. Mrs. Dalrymple wants me—she is lonely there. I can only spare her a week, though: it will not do to leave mamma for longer. Alice is at Lady Sarah Hope's, you know, and Selina is in town, the gayest of the gay."

"Rather too gay, I fancy," remarked Mr. Grubb. "Mother," he added, turning from his sister, "I have just left your friend of early life—Miss Upton. She inquired after you."

"Very good of her!" retorted Mrs. Lynn, proudly and stiffly. "I do not care to be spoken to of Margery Upton, as you know, Francis. She—and others—voluntarily severed all connection between us in those early years. It pained me more than you, or any one else, will ever know; but it is over and done with, and I do not willingly recall it, or them, to my memory."

Ah! that separation might have brought keen pain to Mrs. Lynn in early days, but not so cruelly keen as the pain something else was bringing to her son in these later ones. As Francis Grubb, his visitors departed, took his place at his desk, and strove to apply his mind to his business, he found it a difficult task. Twice today had his wife's behaviour to him been remarked upon—by Miss Upton and by his mother. Was it, could it be the fact, that the unhappiness of his home, the miserable relations obtaining between himself and his wife, had become patent to the world? The draught had already been rising to a pretty good height in his cup of bitterness; this would fill it to the brim.

CHAPTER XV

THE DAY OF RECKONING

The hum of the busy London world came floating drowsily in through a bedroom window in Berkeley Street, open to the hot and brilliant summer day, and falling, unnoticed, upon the ears of Mrs. Oscar Dalrymple.

"What an idiot I have been!" soliloquized she. "And what a cat that Damereau is!"

The above pretty speech—not at all suitable for pretty lips—was given vent to by Selina on her return from that morning visit to her milliner, when the latter had wholly refused to listen to reason, and both had lost their courtesy.

Her dainty bonnet tossed on the bed, her little black lace mantle on the back of her low dressing-chair, Selina, who had come straight home, swayed herself backwards and forwards in the said chair, as she mentally ran over the items of the keen words just exchanged between herself and madame, and wondered what in the world she was to do.

"If I had only kept my temper!" she thought, in self-reproach. "It was always a fault of mine to be quick and fiery—like poor Robert. Nothing but that made her so angry. What on earth would become of me if she should do as she says—send the account to Oscar?"

Selina started up at the thought. Calmly equable to a rather remarkable degree in general, she was one of the most restless of human beings when she did give way to excitement. Just as Robert had been.

"If he had but lived!" she cried, tears filling her eyes as her thoughts reverted to her brother, "I'd have taken this trouble to him and he would have settled it. Robert was generous!"

But Selina quite forgot to recall the fact that her brother's income, at the best, would not have been larger than her husband's was. Not quite as large, indeed, for Oscar had his own small patrimony of six or seven hundred a-year in addition. Just now she could not be expected to remember common sense.

The Dalrymples had a distant cousin, a merchant, or cotton-broker, or something of the kind, residing in Liverpool, who was supposed to be fabulously rich. He had quarrelled with the family long ago, and was looked upon as no better than an ill-natured, growling bear. An idea had come into Selina's brain lately—what if she wrote to tell him her position and beg a little money from his rich coffers to set her straight? It came to her again now, as she sat there. But, no that ungenial man was known to hold unseemly debt and extravagance of all kinds in especial abhorrence. He would only write her a condemnatory answer; perhaps even re-enclose her begging letter to Oscar! Selina started from the thought, and put away for ever all notion of aid from Benjamin Dalrymple.

"How is this woman to be pacified?" she resumed, her reflections reverting to Madame Damereau. "What a simpleton I was to provoke her! Two or three hundred pounds might do it for the present. Where am I to get them? If she carries out this dreadful threat and appeals to Oscar, what should I do? What could I do? And all the world would know— Oh!" she shivered, "I must stop that. I must get some from him, if I can. I will try at once. Ugh; what a calamity the want of money is!"

She descended the stairs and entered the dining-room, where her husband was. He sat at the table writing letters, and seemed to be in the midst of business accounts.

"Oscar!"

He looked up. "What is it?"

"Oscar," she said, advancing close to him, "can you, please, let me have a little money?"

"No, that I can't, Selina. I am settling up a few payments now, and can only do it by halves. Others I am writing to put off entirely for the present."

He had bent over his writing again, as if the question, being answered, was done with.

"Oscar, I must have it."

"What money do you mean? Some for housekeeping. I can let you have that."

"No, no: for myself. I want—I want—two hundred pounds," she said, jerking it out. She did not dare to say three; her courage failed her.

He put down the pen and turned towards her in displeasure. "Selina, I told you before we came to town that I could not have these calls made upon me, as I had last year. You know how very small our income is, and you know that your extravagance has already crippled it. The allowance I make you is greater than I can afford. I cannot give you more."

"Oh, Oscar, I must have it," she exclaimed in excitement, terrified at the aspect her situation presented to her, for her mind was apt to be imaginative. "Indeed, I must—even at an inconvenience. Only two hundred pounds!"

"To squander away in folly?"

"No. If it were only to squander away, I might do without it; and I cannot do without this."

Mr. Dalrymple looked keenly at her, and she turned from his gaze. "Let me know what you want it for, that I may judge of the necessity you speak of. If it is not convenient to you to tell me, Selina, you must be satisfied with my refusal."

"Well, then," she said, seeing no help for the avowal, "I owe it."

"Owe it! Owe two hundred pounds! You!"

So utter was his astonishment, so blank his dismay, that Selina's heart failed her. If her owing two hundred pounds thus impressed him, what would become of her when he learnt the whole truth!

"And I am pressed for it," she faintly added. "Please let me have it, Oscar."

"What have you gone in debt for?"

"Various things," she answered, not caring to avow particulars. But he looked steadfastly at her, waiting for the truth. "Dress."

"The compact between us was that you should not run into debt," he said, in severe tones; "you promised to make your allowance do. You have behaved ill to me, Selina."

She bent her head, feeling that she had. Oh, feeling it terribly just then.

"Is this all you owe? All?"

"Y—es." But the falsehood, as falsehoods ought to, left a tremor on her lips.

Without speaking another word, he unsealed a paper in which were enclosed some bank-notes, and handed several to her, to the amount of two hundred pounds. "Understand me well, Selina, this must never occur again," he said, in an impressive tone. "These notes had a different and an urgent destination."

"What a goose I was, not to ask for the other hundred!" was her mental comment, as she escaped from the room. "It is not of the least use offering Damereau two hundred: but she might take three. And where am I to get it?"

Where, indeed? Did the reader ever try when in extremity to borrow a hundred pounds, or what not?—and does he remember how very hopeless a cause it seemed when present before him? Just as it appeared now to Selina Dalrymple.

"I wonder whether Alice could lend it to me?" she cried, swaying her foot helplessly as she sat in the low chair. "It's not in the least likely, but I might ask her. Who's this?"

The "Who's this," applied to a footstep on the stairs. It was her husband's. Some tiresome, troublesome old man of their acquaintance had come up from Netherleigh, and Oscar wanted his wife to help entertain him. Remembering the two hundred pounds just procured from Oscar she did not like to refuse, and went down.

They dined, to accommodate this gentleman, at what Selina called an unearthly hour—four o'clock; and it was evening before she could get to Lady Sarah Hope's. Alice, looking ill, was alone in the drawing-room, having begged to be excused going down to dinner. On a table in the back room lay some of Lady Sarah's jewels; valuable gems. Selina privately wished they were hers. She had to take her departure as she came, for Alice could not help her. A curiously mysterious matter connected with these jewels has to be related. It ought to come in here; but it may be better to defer it, not to interfere with the sequence of events connected with this chapter.

Nothing further could be done that evening, and Selina went to rest betimes—eleven o'clock—disappointing two or three entertainments that were languishing for her presence: but she had no heart that night.

To rest! It was a mockery of the word, for she had become thoroughly frightened. She passed the night turning and tossing from side to side; and when morning came, and she arose, it was with trembling limbs and a fevered brain.

Her whole anxiety was to make up this money, three hundred pounds; hoping that it would prove a stop-gap for the milliner, and stave off that dreaded threat of application to Oscar. What was to come afterwards, and how in the world further stop-gaps would be supplied, she did not now glance at. That evil seemed a hundred miles off, compared with this one.

A faint idea had been looming through her mind; possibly led to by what she had seen at Lady Sarah Hope's. At the commencement it had neither shape nor form, but by midday it had acquired one, and was entertained. She had heard of such things as pledging jewels: she was sure she had heard that even noble ladies, driven to a pinch, so disposed of them. Mrs. Dalrymple locked her bedroom door, reached out her ornaments, and laid them in a heap on the bed.

She began to estimate their value: what they had cost to buy, as nearly as she could remember and judge, amounted to fully five hundred pounds. They were not paid for, but that was nothing. She supposed she might be able to borrow four hundred upon them: and she decided to do it. Some few, others, had belonged to her mother. Then, if that cormorant of a French marchande de modes refused to be pacified with a small sum, she should have a larger one to offer her. Yes, and get the things for the wedding-breakfast besides.

The relief this determination brought to the superficial mind of Selina Dalrymple, few, never reduced to a similar strait, can picture. It almost removed her weight of care. The task of pledging them would not be a pleasant one, but she must go through with it. The glittering trinkets were still upon the bed when some one knocked at the room-door. It was only her maid, come to say that Miss Alice was below. Selina grew scared and terrified; for a troubled conscience sees shadows where no shadows are, and hers whispered that curious eyes, looking on those ornaments, must divine what she meant to do with them. With a hasty hand she threw a dress upon the bed, and then another on the first, and then a heavy one over all, before unbolting the door. The glittering jewels were hidden now.

Oscar Dalrymple was thinking profoundly as he sat over his after-dinner wine—not that he ever took much—and the street-lamps were lighted, when a figure, looking as little like Mrs. Dalrymple as possible, stole out of the house; stole stealthily, and closed the door stealthily behind her, so that neither master nor servant should hear it. She had ransacked her wardrobe for a plain gown and dark shawl, and her straw bonnet might have served as a model for a Quaker's. She had been out in the afternoon, and marked the place she meant to go to. A renowned establishment in its line, and respectable; even Selina knew that. She hurried along the streets, not unlike a criminal; had she been going to rob the warerooms of their jewels, instead of offering some to add to their hidden store, she could not have felt more guilty. When she reached the place she could not make up her mind to enter: she took a turn or two in front, she glanced in at its door, at the window crowded with goods. She had never been in a pawnbroker's in her life, and her ideas of its customers were vague: comprising gentlewomen in distress, gliding in as she was; tipsy men carrying their watches in their hand; poor objects out of work, in dilapidated shirt-sleeves; and half-starved women with pillows and flat-irons. It looked quiet, inside; so far as she could see there did not appear to be a soul. With a desperate effort of resolution she went in.

She stood at the counter, the chief part of the shop being hidden from her. A dark man came forward.

"What can we do for you, ma'am?"

"Are you the master?" inquired Selina.

"No."

"I wish to see him."

Another presently appeared: a respectable-looking, well-dressed man, of good manners.

"I am in temporary need of a little money, and wish to borrow some upon my jewels," began Mrs. Dalrymple, in a hoarse whisper; and she was really so agitated as scarcely to know what she said.

"Are they of value?" he inquired.

"Some hundreds of pounds. I have them with me."

He requested her to walk into a private room, and placed a chair. She sat down and laid the jewels on the table. He examined them in silence, one after another, not speaking until he had gone through the whole.

"What did you wish to borrow on them?"

"As much as I can," replied Mrs. Dalrymple. "I thought about four hundred pounds."

"Four hundred pounds!" echoed the pawnbroker. "Madam, they are not worth, for this purpose, more than a quarter of the money."

She stared at him in astonishment. "They are real."

"Oh yes. Otherwise, they would not, to us, be worth so many pence."

"Many of them are new within twelve months," urged Selina. "Altogether, they cost more than five hundred pounds."

"To buy. But they are not worth much to pledge. The fashion of these ornaments changes with every season: and that, for one thing, diminishes their value."

"What could you lend me on them?"

"One hundred pounds."

"Absurd!" returned Mrs. Dalrymple, her cheeks flushing. "Why, that one set of amethysts alone cost more. I could not let them go for that. One hundred would be of no use to me."

"Madam, it is entirely at your option, and I assure you I do not press it," he answered, with respectful courtesy. "We care little about taking these things in; so many are brought to us now, that our sales are glutted with them."

"You will not be called upon to sell these. I shall redeem them."

The jeweller did not answer. He could have told her that never an article, from a service of gold plate to a pair of boy's boots, was pledged to him yet, but it was quite sure to be redeemed—in intention.

"Are you aware that a great many ladies, even of high degree, now wear false jewellery?" he resumed.

"No, indeed," she returned. "Neither should I believe it."

"Nevertheless, it is so. And the chief reason is the one I have just mentioned: that in the present day the rage for ornaments is so great, and the fashion of them so continually changing, that to be in the fashion, a lady must spend a fortune in ornaments alone. I give you my word, madam, that in the fashionable world a great deal of the jewellery now worn is false; though it may pass, there, unsuspected. And this fact deteriorates from the value of real stones, especially for the purpose of pledging."

He began, as he spoke, to put the articles into their cases again, as if the negotiation were at an end.

"Can you lend me two hundred pounds upon them?" asked Mrs. Dalrymple, after a blank pause.

He shook his head. "I can advance you what I have stated, if you please; not a pound more. And I feel sure you will not be able to obtain more on them anywhere, madam, take them where you will."

"But what am I to do?" returned she, betraying some excitement. Very uselessly: but that room was no stranger to it. The jeweller was firm, and Mrs. Dalrymple gathered up her ornaments, her first feeling of despair lost in anger. She was leaving the room with her parcel when it occurred to her to ask herself, in sober truth, WHAT she was to do—how procure the remainder of the sum necessary to appease Madame Damereau. She turned back, and finally left the shop without her jewels, but with a hundred pounds in her pocket, and her understanding considerably enlightened as to the relative value of a jewel to buy and a jewel to pledge.

Now it happened that, if Mrs. Dalrymple had repented showing her temper to Madame Damereau, that renowned artiste had equally repented showing hers to Mrs. Dalrymple. She feared it might tell against her with her customers, if it came to be known: for she knew how popular Selina was; truth to say, she liked her herself. Madame came to the determination of paying Mrs. Dalrymple a visit, not exactly to apologize, but to soothe away certain words. And to qualify the pressing for some money, which she meant to do (whether she got it or not), she intended to announce that the articles ordered for the wedding festivities would be supplied. "It's only ninety pounds, more or less," thought madame, "and I suppose I shall get the money some time."

She reached Mrs. Dalrymple's in the evening, soon after that lady had departed on her secret expedition to the pawnbroker. Their London lodgings were confined. The dining-room had Mr. Dalrymple in it, so Madame Damereau was shown to the drawing-room, and the maid went hunting about the house for her mistress.

Whilst she was on her useless search, Mr. Dalrymple entered the drawing-room, expecting to find it tenanted by his wife. Instead of that, some strange lady sat there, who rose at his entrance, made him a swimming curtsy, the like of which he had never seen in a ball-room, and threw off some rapid sentences in an unknown tongue.

His perplexed look stopped her. "Ah," she said, changing her language, "Monsieur, I fear, does not speak the French. I have the honour, I believe, of addressing Mr. Dalreemp. I am covered with contrition at intruding at this evening hour, but I know that Mrs. Dalreemp is much out in the day; I thought I might perhaps get speech of her as she was dressing for some soirée."

"Do you wish to see her? Have you seen her?" he asked.

"I wait now to see her," replied madame.

"Another of these milliner people, I suppose," thought Oscar to himself, with not at all a polite word in connection with the supposition. "Selina's mad to have the house beset with them; it's like a swarm of flies. If she comes to town next year may I be shot!"

"Ann! tell your mistress she is wanted," he called out, opening the door.

"I can't find my mistress, sir," said the servant, coming downstairs. "I thought she must be in her own room, but she is not. I am sure she is not gone out, because she said she meant to have a quiet evening at home tonight, and she did not dress."

"She is somewhere about," said Mr. Dalrymple. "Go and look for her."

Madame Damereau had been coming to the rapid conclusion that this was an opportunity she should do injustice to herself to omit using. And as Mr. Dalrymple was about to leave her to herself, she stopped him.

"Sir—pardon me—but now that I have the happiness to see you, I may ask if you will not use your influence with Mrs. Dalreemp to think of my account. She does promise so often, so often, and I get nothing. I have my heavy payments to make, and sometimes I do not know where to find the money: though, if you saw my books, your hairs would bristle, sir, at the sums owing to me."

"You are—?"

"I am Madame Damereau. If Mrs. Dalreemp would but give me a few hundred pounds off her bill, it would be something."

A few hundred pounds! Oscar Dalrymple wondered what she meant. He looked at her for some moments before he spoke.

"What is the amount of my wife's debt to you, madame?"

"Ah, it is— But I cannot tell it you quite exactly: there are recent items. The last note that went in to her was four thousand three hundred and twenty-two pounds."

He had an impassive face, rarely showing emotion. It had probably not been moved to it half-a-dozen times in the course of his life. But now his lips gradually drew into a straight thin line, and a red spot shone in his cheek.

"WHAT did you say? Do you speak of the account?"

"It was four thousand three hundred and twenty-two pounds," equably answered madame, who was not familiar with his countenance. "And there have been a few trifles since, and her last order this week will come to ninety pounds. If you wish for it exactly, sir," added madame, seizing at an idea of hope, "I will have it sent to you when I go home. Mrs. Dalreemp has the details up to very recently."

"Four thousand pounds!" repeated Mr. Dalrymple, sitting down, in a sort of helpless manner. "When could she have contracted it?"

"Last season, sir, chiefly. A little in the winter she had sent down to her, and she has had things this spring: not so many."

He did not say more, save a mutter which madame could not catch. She understood it to be that he would speak to Mrs. Dalrymple. The maid returned, protesting that her mistress was not in the house and must have changed her mind and gone out; and Madame Damereau, thinking she might have gone out for the evening, and that it was of no use waiting, made her adieu to Mr. Dalrymple, with the remarkable curtsy more than once repeated.

He was sitting there still, in the same position, when his wife appeared. She had entered the house stealthily, as she had left it, had taken off her things, and now came into the room ready for tea, as if she had only been upstairs to wash her hands. Scarcely had she reached the middle of the room, when he rose and laid his hand heavily on her shoulder. His face, as she turned to him in alarm, with its drawn aspect, its mingled pallor and hectic, was so changed that she could hardly recognize it for his.

"Oscar, you terrify me!" she cried out.

"What debts are these that you owe?" he asked, from between his parted lips.

Was the dreaded moment come, then! A low moan escaped her.

"Four thousand and some hundred pounds to Damereau, the milliner! How much more to others?"

"Oh, Oscar, if you look and speak like that, you will kill me."

"I ask how much more?" he repeated, passing by her words as the idle wind. "Tell me the truth, or I shall feel tempted to thrust you from my home, and advertise you."

She wished the carpet would open and let her in; she hid her face. Oscar held her, and repeated the question: "How much?"

"Six thousand pounds—in all—about that. Not more, I think."

He released her then with a jerk. Selina began to cry like a school-girl.

"Are you prepared to go out and work for your living, as I must do?" he panted. "I have nothing to keep you on, and shall not have for years. If they throw me into a debtor's prison tomorrow, I cannot help it."

"Oh," shrieked silly Selina, "a prison! I'd go with you."

"I might have expected something of this when I married into your branch of the family," returned Oscar, who, in good truth, was nearly beside himself. "A mania follows it. Your uncle gambled his means away, and then took his own life; your father hampered himself with his brother's debts, and remained poor; your brother followed in his uncle's wake; and now the mania is upon you!"

"Oh, please, Oscar, please!" pleaded Selina, who had no more depth of feeling than a magpie, while Oscar had plenty of it. "I'll never, never go in debt again."

"You shall never have the chance," he answered. And, there and then, Oscar Dalrymple, summoning his household, gave orders for their removal to the Grange. Selina cried her eyes out at having to quit the season and its attractions summarily.

Thus, as a wreathing cloud suddenly appears in the sky, and as suddenly fades sway, had Mrs. Dalrymple, like a bright vision, appeared to the admiring eyes of the London world, and vanished from it.

CHAPTER XVI

THE DIAMOND BRACELET

But, as you have heard, there is something yet to relate of that hot June day, or, rather, of its evening, when poor Selina Dalrymple had applied for help, and unsuccessfully, to her sister Alice.

The great world of London was beginning to think of dinner. In a well-furnished dressing-room, the windows being open for air, and the blinds drawn down to exclude the sun, stood a tall, stately lady, whose maid was giving the last touch to her rich attire. It was Lady Sarah Hope.

"What bracelets, my lady?" asked the maid, taking a small bunch of keys from her pocket.

"Not any, now: it is so very hot. Alice," added Lady Sarah, turning to Alice, who was leaning back on a sofa, "will you put all my bracelets out for me against I come up? I will decide then."

"I put them out, Lady Sarah?" returned Alice. "Yes, certainly."

"If you will be so kind. Hughes, give the key to Miss Seaton." For they did sometimes remember to address Alice by her adopted name.

Lady Sarah left the room, and the maid, Hughes, began taking one of the small keys off the ring. "I have leave to go out, miss," she explained, "which is the reason why my lady has asked you to see to her bracelets. My mother is not well, and wants to see me. This is the key, ma'am."

As Alice took it, Lady Sarah reappeared at the door. "Alice, you may as well bring the bracelet-box down to the back drawing-room," she said. "I shall not care to come up here after dinner: we shall be late as it is."

"What's that about the bracelet-box?" inquired a pretty-looking girl, who had come swiftly out of another apartment.

"Lady Sarah wishes me to bring her bracelets down to the drawing-room, that she may choose which to put on. It was too hot to wear them to dine in, she said."

"Are you not coming in to dinner, Alice?"

"No. I walked out, and it has tired me. I have had some tea instead.".

"I would not be you for all the world, Alice! To possess so little capability of enjoying life."

"Yet, if you were as I am, weak in health and strength, your lot would have been so soothed to you, Frances, that you would not repine at or regret it."

"You mean I should be content," laughed Frances, upon whom the defection of Mr. Gerard Hope earlier in the year did not appear to have made much impression: though perhaps she did not know its particulars. "Well, there is nothing like contentment, the sages tell us. One of my detestable schoolroom copies used to be 'Contentment is happiness.'"

"I can hear the dinner being taken in," said Alice. "You will be late in the drawing-room."

Lady Frances Chenevix turned away to fly down the stairs. Her light, rounded form, her elastic step, all telling of health and enjoyment, presented a marked contrast to that of Alice Dalrymple. Alice's face was indeed strangely beautiful, almost too refined and delicate for the wear and tear of common life, but her figure was weak and stooping, and her gait feeble.

Colonel Hope, thin and spare, with sharp brown eyes and sharp features, sat at the foot of his table. He was beginning to look so shrunk and short, that his friends jokingly told him he must have been smuggled into the army, unless he had since been growing downwards, for surely so little a commander could never expect to be obeyed. No stranger could have believed him at ease in his circumstances, any more than they would have believed him a colonel who had seen hard service in India, for his clothes were frequently threadbare. A black ribbon supplied the place of a gold chain as guard to his watch, and a blue, tin-looking thing of a galvanized ring did duty for any other ring on his finger. Yet he was rich; of fabulous riches, people said; but he was of a close disposition, especially as regarded his personal outlay. In his home and to his wife he was liberal. A good husband; and, putting his crustiness and his crotchets aside, a good man. It was the loss of his two boys that had so tried and changed him. His large property was not entailed: it had been thought his nephew, Gerard Hope, would inherit it, but Gerard had been turned from the house. Lady Sarah remarked that it was too hot to dine; but the colonel, in respect to heat, was a salamander.

Alice meanwhile lay on the sofa for half-an-hour; and then, taking the bracelet-box in her hands, descended to the drawing-rooms. It was intensely hot, she thought; a sultry, breathless heat; and she threw open the back window. Which in truth made it hotter, for the sun gleamed right athwart the leads which stretched themselves beyond the windows over the outbuildings at the back of the row of houses.

Alice sat down near this back window, and began to put out some of the bracelets on the table before it. They were rare and rich: of plain gold, of silver, of pearl, of precious stones. One of them was of gold links, studded with diamonds; it was very valuable, and had been the present of Colonel Hope to his wife on her recent birthday. Another diamond bracelet was there, but it was not so beautiful or so costly as this. When her task was done, Alice passed into the front drawing-room, and put up one of its large windows. Still there was no air in the room.

As she stood at it, a handsome young man, tall and agile, who was walking on the opposite side of the street, caught her eye. He nodded, hesitated, and then crossed the street as if to enter.

"It is Gerard!" muttered Alice, under her breath. "Can he be coming here?" She walked away from the window hastily, and sat down by the bedecked table in the other room.

"Just as I supposed!" exclaimed Gerard Hope, entering, and advancing to Alice with stealthy steps. "When I saw you at the window, the thought struck me that you were alone here, and they at dinner. Thomas happened to be airing himself at the door, so I crossed over, found I was right, and came up. How are you, Alice?"

"Have you come to dinner?" inquired Alice, speaking at random, and angry at her own agitation.

"I come to dinner!" repeated Gerard. "Why, you know they'd as soon sit down with the renowned Mr. Ketch."

"Indeed I know nothing about it: we have been away in Gloucestershire for months, as I dare say you are aware: I was hoping that you and the colonel might have been reconciled. Why did you come in, Gerard? Thomas may tell them."

"Thomas won't. I charged him not to. The idea of your never coming up till June! Some whim of Lady Sarah's, I suppose. Two or three times a-week for the last month have I been marching past this house, wondering when it was going to show signs of life. Frances is here still?"

"Oh yes. She remains here altogether."

"To make up for— Alice, was it not a shame to turn me out?"

"I was extremely sorry for what happened, Mr. Hope, but I knew nothing of the details. Lady Sarah said you had displeased herself and the colonel, and after that she never mentioned your name."

"What a show of smart things you have here, Alice! Are you going to set up a bazaar?"

"They are Lady Sarah's bracelets."

"So they are, I see! This is a gem," added Gerard, taking up the fine diamond bracelet already mentioned. "I don't remember this one."

"It is new. The colonel has just given it to her."

"What did it cost?"

Alice laughed. "Do you think it likely I have heard? I question if Lady Sarah has."

"It never cost a farthing less than two hundred guineas," mused Gerard, turning the bracelet in various directions, that its rich diamonds might give out their gleaming light. "I wish it was mine."

"What should you do with it?" laughed Alice.

"Spout it."

"I do not understand," returned Alice. She really did not.

"I beg your pardon, Alice. I was thinking of the colloquial lingo familiarly applied to such transactions, instead of to whom I was talking. I mean raise money upon it."

"Oh, Mr. Hope!"

"Alice, that's twice you have called me 'Mr. Hope.' I thought I had been 'Gerard' to you for many a year."

"Time changes things; and you seem more like a stranger than you used to," returned Alice, a flush rising to her sensitive face. "But you spoke of raising money: I hope you are not in temporary embarrassment."

"A jolly good thing for me if it turns out only temporary," he rejoined. "Look at my position! Debts hanging over my head—for you may be sure, Alice, all young men, with a limited allowance and large expectations, contract debts—and thrust out of my uncle's home with just the loose cash I had in my pocket, and my clothes sent packing after me."

"Has the colonel stopped your allowance?"

Gerard Hope laid down the bracelet from whence he had taken it, before he replied.

"He stopped it then; it's months ago, you know; and I have not had a shilling since, except from my own resources. I first went upon tick; then I disposed of my watch and chain and all my other little matters of value: and now I am upon tick again."

Alice did not answer. The light tone vexed her.

"Perhaps you don't understand these free terms, Alice," he said, looking fondly at her, "and I hope you may never have occasion to. Frances would: she has lived in their atmosphere."

"Yes, I know what an embarrassed man the earl often is. But I am grieved to hear about yourself. Is the colonel implacable? What was the cause of the quarrel?"

"You know I was to be his heir. Even if more children had come to him, he undertook to provide amply for me. Last autumn he suddenly sent for me to tell me it was his pleasure and Lady Sarah's that I should take up my abode with them. So I did take it up, glad to get into such good quarters; and stopped here like an innocent, unsuspicious lamb, until—when was it, Alice? March? Then the plot came out."

"The plot," exclaimed Alice.

"It was nothing less. They had fixed upon a wife for me; and I was ordered to hold myself in readiness to marry her at any given moment."

"Who was it?" inquired Alice, in a low tone, as she bent her head over the bracelets.

"Never mind," laughed the young man; "it wasn't you. I said I would not have her; and they both, he and Lady Sarah, pulled me and my want of taste to pieces, assuring me I was a monster of ingratitude. It provoked me into confessing that I liked some one else better. And then the colonel turned me out."

Alice looked her sorrow, but she did not express it.

"Of course I saw the imprudence then of having thrown up my place in the red-tape office; but it was done. And since then I have been having a fight with my creditors, putting them off with fair words and promises. But they have grown incredulous, and it has come to dodging. In favour with my uncle, and his acknowledged heir, they would have given me unlimited time and credit, but the breach between us is known, and it makes all the difference. With the value of that at my disposal"—nodding at the bracelet—"I should stop a few pressing personal trifles and go on again for a while. So you see, Alice, a diamond bracelet may be of use to a gentleman, should some genial fortune drop one into his hands."

"I sympathize with you very much," said Alice, "and I would I had it in my power to aid you."

"Thank you for your kind wishes; I know they are genuine. When my uncle sees the name of Gerard Hope figuring in the insolvent list, or amongst the outlaws, he— Hark! Can they be coming up from dinner?"

"Scarcely yet," said Alice, starting up simultaneously with himself, and listening. "But they will not sit long today, because they are going to the opera. Gerard, they must not find you here."

"It might get you turned out as well as myself! No, not if I can help it. Alice!"—suddenly laying his hands upon her shoulders, and gazing down into her eyes—"do you know who it was I had learnt to love, instead of—of the other?"

She gasped for breath, and her colour went and came. "No—no; do not tell me, Gerard."

"Why, no, I had better not, under present circumstances. But when the good time comes—for all their high-roped indignation must and will blow over—then I will; and here's the pledge of it." He bent his head, took one long earnest kiss from her lips; and the next moment was gone.

Agitated almost to sickness, trembling and confused, Alice stole to look after him, terrified lest he might not escape unseen. She crept partly down the stairs, so as to obtain sight of the hall-door, and make sure that he got out in safety. As Gerard drew it quietly open, there stood a lady just about to knock. It was Selina, waiting to exchange a few words with Gerard. He waved his hand towards the staircase. Alice met her, and took her into the front drawing-room.

"I cannot stay to sit down, Alice: I must hasten back to dress, for I am engaged to three or four places tonight. Neither do I wish to horrify Lady Sarah with a visit at this untoward hour. I had a request to make to you, and thought to catch you in your room before you went in to dinner."

"They are alone, and are dining earlier than usual. I was too tired to appear. What can I do for you, Selina?"

Mrs. Oscar Dalrymple had come (as you have already heard) to try that one hopeless task—the borrowing money of her sister.

"I am in pressing need of it, Alice," she said. "Can you lend it me?"

"I wish I could," returned Alice; "I am so very sorry. I sent all I had to poor mamma the day before we came to town. It was only twenty-five pounds."

"That would have been of no use to me: I want more. I thought if you had been misering up your salary, you might have had a hundred pounds, or so, by you."

Alice shook her head. "I should be a long while saving up a hundred pounds, even if dear mamma had no wants. But I send to her what I can spare. Is it for—dresses, and that?"

"Yes," was Selina's laconic answer.

"I wish I had it to give you! Do not be in such a hurry," continued Alice, as her sister was moving to the door. "At least wait one minute while I fetch you a letter I received from mamma this morning, in answer to mine. You will like to read it, for it is full of news of the old place. You can take it home with you, Selina."

Alice left her sister standing in the front-room, and went upstairs. But she was more than one minute away; she was three or four, for she could not at first lay her hand upon the letter. When she returned, her sister advanced to her from the back drawing-room, the folding-doors between the two rooms being, as before, wide open.

"What a fine collection of bracelets, Alice!" she exclaimed, as she took the letter. "Are they spread out for show?"

"No," laughed Alice; "Lady Sarah is going to the opera, and will have no time to spare when she comes up from dinner. She asked me to bring them all down, as she had not decided which to wear."

"I like to dress entirely before dinner on my opera nights."

"Oh, so of course does Lady Sarah," returned Alice, as her sister descended the stairs; "but she said it was too hot to dine in bracelets."

"It is fearfully hot. Good-bye, Alice. Don't ring: I will let myself out."

Alice returned to the front-room and looked from the window, wondering whether her sister had come in her carriage. No. A trifling evening breeze was rising and beginning to move the curtains about. Gentle as it was, it was grateful, and Alice sat down in it. In a very few minutes the ladies came up from dinner.

"Have you the bracelets, Alice. Oh, I see."

Lady Sarah went into the back-room as she spoke, and stood before the table, looking at the bracelets. Alice rose to follow her, when Lady Frances Chenevix caught her by the arm, and began to speak in a covert whisper.

"Who was that at the door just now? It was a visitor's knock. Do you know, Alice, every hour, since we came to town, I have fancied Gerard might be calling. In the country he could not get to us, but here— Was it Gerard?"

"It—it was my sister," carelessly answered Alice. It was not a true answer, for her sister had not knocked, and she did not know who had. But it was the readiest that rose to her lips, and she wished to escape the questioning, for more reasons than one.

"Only your sister," replied Frances, turning to the window with a gesture of disappointment.

"Which have you put on?" inquired Alice, going towards Lady Sarah.

"Those loose, fancy things; they are the coolest. I really am so hot: the soup was that favourite soup of the colonel's, all capsicums and cayenne, and the wine was hot; there had been a mistake about the ice. Gill trusted to the new man, and he did not understand it. It was all hot together. What the house will be tonight, I dread to think of."

Lady Sarah, whilst she spoke, had been putting the bracelets into the jewel-box, with very little care.

"I had better put them straight," remarked Alice, when she reached the table.

"Do not trouble," returned Lady Sarah, shutting down the lid. "You are looking flushed and feverish, Alice; you were wrong to walk so far today. Hughes will set them to rights tomorrow morning; they will do until then. Lock them up, and take possession of the key."

Alice did as she was bid. She locked the case and put the key in her pocket. "Here is the carriage," exclaimed Lady Frances. "Are we to wait for coffee?"

"Coffee in this heat!" retorted Lady Sarah; "it would be adding fuel to fire. We will have some tea when we return. Alice, you must make tea for the colonel; he will not come out without it. He thinks this weather just what it ought to be: rather cold, if anything."

Alice had taken the bracelet-box in her hands as Lady Sarah spoke; when they had departed, she carried it upstairs to its place in Lady Sarah's bedroom. The colonel speedily rose from table, for his wife had laid her commands on him to join them early. Alice helped him to his tea, and as soon as he was gone she went upstairs to bed.

To bed, but not to sleep. Tired as she was, and exhausted in frame, sleep would not come to her. She was living over again her interview with Gerard Hope. She could not, in her conscious heart, affect to misunderstand his implied meaning—that she had been the cause of his rejecting the union proposed to him. It diffused a strange rapture within her; and, though she had not perhaps been wholly blind and unconscious during the period of Gerard's stay with them, and for some time before that, she now kept repeating the words, "Can it be that he loves me? can it be?"

It certainly was so. Love plays strange pranks. There was Gerard Hope—heir to the colonel's fabulous wealth, consciously proud of his handsome person, his height and strength—called home and planted down by the side of a pretty and noble lady on purpose that he might fall in love with her: the Lady Frances Chenevix. And yet, the well-laid project failed: failed because there happened to be another at that young lady's side: a sad, quiet, feeble-framed girl, whose very weakness may have seemed to others to place her beyond the pale of man's love. But love thrives by contrasts; and it was the feeble girl who won the love of the strong man.

Yes; the knowledge diffused a strange rapture within her, Alice Dalrymple, as she lay that night; and she may be excused if, for a brief period, she allowed range to the sweet fantasies it conjured up. For a brief period only. Too soon the depressing consciousness returned to her, that these thoughts of earthly happiness must be subdued: for she, with her confirmed ailments and conspicuous weakness, must never hope to marry, as did other women. She had long known—her mother had prepared her for it—that one so afflicted and frail as she, whose tenure of existence was likely to be short, ought not to become a wife; and it had been her earnest hope to pass through life unloving, in that one sense, and unloved. She had striven to arm herself against the danger, against being thrown into the perils of temptation. Alas! it had come insidiously upon her; all her care had been set at naught; and she knew that she loved Gerard Hope with a deep and fervent love. "It is but another cross," she sighed, "another burden to surmount and subdue, and I will set myself from this night to the task. I have been a coward, shrinking from self-examination; but now that Gerard has spoken out, I can deceive myself no longer. I wish he had spoken more freely, that I might have told him it was useless."

It was only towards morning that Alice dropped asleep: the consequence was that long after her usual hour for rising she was still sleeping. The opening of her door awoke her. It was Lady Sarah's maid who stood there.

"Why, miss; are you not up? Well, I never! I wanted the key of the small jewel-box; but I'd have waited, had I known."

"What do you say you want?" returned Alice, whose ideas were confused; as is often the case on being suddenly awakened.

"The key of the bracelet-box, if you please."

"The key?" repeated Alice. "Oh, I remember," she added, recollection returning to her. "Be at the trouble, will you, Hughes, of taking it out of my pocket: it is on that chair, under my clothes."

The servant came to the pocket, and speedily found the key. "Are you worse than usual, Miss Seaton, this morning," asked she, "or have you overslept yourself?"

"I have overslept myself. Is it late?"

"Between nine and ten. My lady is up, and at breakfast with the Colonel and Lady Frances."

Alice rose the instant the maid left the room, and made haste to dress, vexed with herself for sleeping so long. She was nearly ready when Hughes came in again.

"If ever I saw such confusion as that jewel-case was in!" cried she, in as pert and grumbling a tone as she dared to use. "The bracelets were thrown together without law or order—just as if they had been so much glass and tinsel from the Lowther Arcade."

"It was Lady Sarah," replied Alice. "I would have put them straight, but she told me to leave it for you. I thought she might prefer that you should do it."

"Of course her ladyship is aware there's nobody but myself knows their right places in it," returned Hughes, consequentially. "I could go to that or to the other jewel-box in the dark, ma'am, and take out any one thing my lady wanted, without disturbing the rest."

"I have observed that you have the gift of order," remarked Alice, with a smile. "It is very useful to those who possess it, and saves them much trouble and confusion."

"So it do, ma'am," said Hughes. "But I came to ask you for the diamond bracelet."

"The diamond bracelet!" echoed Alice. "What diamond bracelet! What do you mean, Hughes?"

"It is not in the box."

"The diamond bracelets are both in the box," rejoined Alice.

"The old one is there; not the new one. I thought you might have taken it out to show some one, or to look at yourself, ma'am, for it's just a sight for pleasant eyes."

"I can assure you it is in the case," said Alice. "All are there, except the pair Lady Sarah had on. You must have overlooked it."

"I am a great donkey if I have," grumbled the girl. "It must be at the very bottom, amongst the cotton," she soliloquized, as she returned to Lady Sarah's apartments, "and I have just got to take every individual article out, to get to it. This comes of giving up one's keys to other folks."

Alice entered the breakfast-room, begging pardon for her late appearance. It was readily accorded. Her office in the house was nearly a sinecure. When she had first entered upon it Lady Sarah was ill, and required some one to sit with and read to her: now that she was well again, Alice had little to do.

Breakfast was scarcely over when Alice was called from the room. Hughes stood outside the door.

"Miss Seaton," said she, with a long face, "the diamond bracelet is not in the box. I thought I could not be mistaken."

"But it must be in the box," said Alice.

"But it is not," persisted Hughes, emphasizing the negative. "Can't you believe me, ma'am? I want to know where it is, that I may put it up and lock the box."

Alice Seaton looked at Hughes with a puzzled, dreamy look. She was thinking matters over. Her face soon cleared again.

"Then Lady Sarah must have kept it out when she put in the rest. It was she who returned them to the case; I did not. Perhaps she wore it last night."

"No, miss, that she didn't. She wore only those two—"

"I saw what she had on," interrupted Alice. "But she might also have put on the other, without my noticing. Or she may have kept it out for some other purpose. I will ask her. Wait here an instant, Hughes; for of course you will like to be at a certainty."

"That's cool," thought Hughes, as Alice went into the breakfast-room, and the colonel came out of it, with his Times. "I should have said it was somebody else would like to be at a certainty, instead of me," continued the girl, indulging in soliloquy. "Thank goodness the box wasn't in my charge last night, if anything dreadful has come to pass. My lady don't keep out her bracelets for sport. Miss Seaton has left the key about, that's what she has done, and it's hard to say who hasn't been at it: I knew the box had been ransacked over."

"Lady Sarah," said Alice, "did you wear your new diamond bracelet last night?"

"No."

"Then did you put it into the box with the others?"

"No," repeated Lady Sarah, who was languidly toying with a basket of ferns.

"After you had chosen the bracelets you wished to wear, you put the others into the box yourself," explained Alice, thinking she was not understood. "Did you put in the new one, the diamond, or keep it out?"

"The new one was not there."

Alice stood confounded. "It was lying on the table, at the back of all the rest, Lady Sarah," she presently said. "Next the window."

"I tell you, Alice, it was not there. I don't know that I should have worn it if it had been, but I certainly looked for it. Not seeing it, I supposed you had not put it out; and I did not care sufficiently to ask for it."

Alice felt in a mesh of perplexity; curious thoughts, and very unpleasing ones, were beginning to dawn upon her. "But indeed the bracelet was there when you went to the table," she urged. "I put it there."

"I can assure you that you labour under a mistake, as to its being there when I came up from dinner," answered Lady Sarah. "Why do you ask?"

"Hughes has come to say it is not in the case. She is outside, waiting."

"Outside, now? Let her come in. What's this about my bracelet, Hughes?"

"I don't know, my lady. The bracelet is not in its place, so I asked Miss Seaton for it. She thought your ladyship might have kept it out yesterday evening."

"I neither touched it nor saw it," said Lady Sarah.

"Then we have had thieves at work," spoke Hughes, decisively; who had been making up her mind to that as a fact.

"It must be in the box, Hughes," said Alice. "I laid it out on the table in the back drawing-room; and it is impossible that thieves—as you phrase it—could have come there."

"Oh yes, it is in the box, no doubt," said Lady Sarah, somewhat crossly, for she disliked to be troubled, especially in hot weather. "You have not searched properly, Hughes."

"My lady," answered Hughes, "I can trust my hands and I can trust my eyes, and they have all four been into every hole and crevice of the box."

Lady Frances Chenevix laid down the Morning Post, and advanced. "Is the bracelet really lost?"

"It cannot be lost," returned Lady Sarah. "You are sure you put it out, Alice?"

"I am quite sure of that. It was lying first in the case, and—"

"Yes, it was," interrupted Hughes. "That is its place."

"And was consequently the first that I took out," continued Alice. "I put it on the table; and the others in a semicircle, nearer to me. Why, as a proof that it lay there—"

What was Alice going to add? Was she going to adduce as a proof that Gerard Hope had taken it up and made it a subject of conversation? Recollection came to her in time; she faltered and abruptly broke off. But a faint, horrible dread, to which she would not give a shape, came stealing over her; her face turned white, and she sank on a chair, trembling visibly.

"Now look at Alice!" uttered Frances Chenevix. "She is going into one of her agitation fits."

"Do not agitate yourself, Alice," cried Lady Sarah; "that will do no good. Besides, I feel sure the bracelet is all safe in the case: where else can it be? Fetch the case, Hughes, and I will look for it myself."

Hughes whirled out of the room, inwardly resenting the doubt cast on her eyesight.

"It is so strange," mused Alice, "that you did not see the bracelet when you came up from dinner."

"It was certainly not there to see," returned Lady Sarah. "Perhaps you'll now look for yourself, my lady," cried Hughes, returning with the jewel-box in her hands.

The box was well searched. The bracelet was not there.

"This is very strange, Hughes," exclaimed Lady Sarah.

"It's very ugly also, my lady," answered Hughes, in a lofty tone, "and I'm thankful to the presiding genuses which rules such things, that I was not in charge when it happened. Though maybe, if I had been, it never would have took place, for I can give a guess how it was."

"Then you had better give it," said her mistress, curtly.

"If I do," returned Hughes, "I may offend Miss Seaton."

"No, you will not, Hughes," said Alice. "Say what you please: I have need to wish this cleared up."

"Well, ma'am, if I may speak my thoughts, I think you must have left the key about. And we have strange servants in the house, as my lady knows. There's a kitchen-maid that only entered it when we came up; and there's the new under-butler."

"Hughes, you are wrong," interrupted Alice. "The servants could not have touched the box, for the key was never out of my possession, and you know the lock is a Bramah. I locked the box last night in her ladyship's presence, and the key was not out of my pocket afterwards, until you took it from there this morning."

"The key seems to have had nothing to do with it," interposed Frances. "Alice says she put the diamond bracelet on the table with the rest; Lady Sarah says when she went to the table after dinner the bracelet was not there. Were you in the room all the while, Alice?"

"Not quite. Very nearly. But no one could possibly have gone in without my seeing them. The folding-doors were open."

"It is quite a mystery," cried Lady Sarah.

"It beats conjuring, my lady," said Hughes. "Did any visitor come upstairs, I wonder?"

"I did hear a visitor's knock while we were at dinner," said Lady Sarah. "Don't you remember, Fanny You looked up as if you noticed it."

"Did I?" answered Lady Frances, in a careless tone.

At that moment Thomas happened to enter with a letter; and his mistress put the question to him: Who had knocked?

"Sir George Danvers, my lady," was the ready answer. "When I said the colonel was at dinner, Sir George began to apologize for calling; but I explained that you were dining earlier than usual, because of the opera."

"No one else called?"

"Nobody knocked but Sir George, my lady."

"A covert answer," thought Alice. "But I am glad he is true to Gerard."

"What an untruth!" thought Lady Frances, as she remembered hearing of the visit of Alice's sister: "Thomas's memory must be short." In point of fact, Thomas knew nothing of it.

All the talk—and it was much prolonged—did not tend to throw any light upon the matter; and Alice, unhappy and ill, retired to her own room. The agitation had brought on a nervous and violent headache; she sat down in a low chair, and bent her forehead on her hands. One belief alone possessed her: that the unfortunate Gerard Hope had stolen the bracelet. Do as she would, she could not put it out of her mind: she kept repeating that he was a gentleman, that he was honourable, that he would never place her in so painful a position. Common sense replied that the temptation was suddenly laid before him, and he had confessed his pecuniary difficulties to be great; nay, had he not wished for this very bracelet, that he might make money—

A knock at the chamber-door. Alice lifted her sickly countenance, and bade the intruder enter. It was Lady Frances Chenevix.

"I came to— Alice, how wretched you look! You will torment yourself into a fever."

"Can you wonder at my looking wretched?" returned Alice. "Place yourself in my position, Frances: it must appear to Lady Sarah as if I—I—had made away with the bracelet. I am sure Hughes thinks so."

"Don't you say unorthodox things, Alice. They would rather think that I had done it, of the two, for I have more use for diamond bracelets than you."

"It is kind of you to try to cheer me," sighed Alice.

"Just the thing I came to do. And to have a bit of chat with you as well. If you will let me."

"Of course I will let you."

"I wish to tell you I will not mention that your sister was here last evening. I promise you I will not."

Alice did not immediately reply. The words and their hushed tone caused a new trouble, a fresh thought, to arise within her, one which she had not glanced at. Was it possible that Frances could imagine her sister to be the—

"Lady Frances Chenevix!" burst forth Alice. "You cannot think it! She! my sister!—guilty of a despicable theft! Have you forgotten that she moves in your own position in the world? that our family is scarcely inferior to yours?"

"Alice, I forgive you for so misjudging me, because you are not yourself just now. Of course, your sister cannot be suspected; I know that. But as you did not mention her when they were questioning Thomas, nor did he, I supposed you had some reason for not wishing her visit spoken of."

"Believe me, Selina is not the guilty person," returned Alice. "I have more cause to say so than you think for."

"What do you mean by that?" briskly cried Lady Frances. "You surely have no clue?"

Alice shook her head, and her companion's eagerness was lulled again. "It is well that Thomas was forgetful," remarked Frances. "Was it forgetfulness, Alice; or did you contrive to telegraph to him to be silent?"

"Thomas only spoke truth, as regards Selina: he did not let her in. She came but for a minute, to ask me about a private matter, and said there was no need to tell Lady Sarah she had been."

"Then it is all quite easy; and you and I can keep our own counsel."

Quite easy, possibly, to the mind of Frances Chenevix. But anything but easy to Alice Dalrymple: for the words of Lady Frances had introduced an idea more repulsive, more terrifying even, than that of suspecting Gerard Hope. Her sister acknowledged that she was in need of money, "a hundred pounds, or so;" nay, Alice had only too good cause to know that previously; and she had seen her come from the back room where the jewels lay. Still—she take a bracelet! Selina! It was preposterous.

Preposterous or not, Alice's torment was doubled. Which of the two had been the black sheep? One of them it must have been. Instinct, sisterly relationship, reason, and common sense, all combined to turn the scale against Gerard. But that there should be a doubt at all was not pleasant, and Alice started up impulsively and put her bonnet on.

"Where now!" cried Lady Frances.

"I will go to Selina's and ask her—and ask her—if—she saw any stranger here—any suspicious person in the hall or on the stairs," stammered Alice, making the best excuse she could make.

"But you know you were in or about the drawing-rooms all the time, and no one came into them, suspicious or unsuspicious; so, how will that aid you?"

"True," murmured Alice. "But it will be a relief to go somewhere or do something."

Alice found her sister at home; had disturbed her, in fact, at a very interesting employment, as the reader may remember. In spite of her own emotional preoccupation, Selina instantly detected that something was wrong; for the suspense, illness, and agitation had taken every vestige of colour from Alice's cheeks and lips.

"What can be the matter, Alice?" was her greeting. "You look just like a walking ghost."

"I feel that I do," breathed poor Alice, "and I kept my veil down in the street, lest I might be taken for one and scare the people. A great misfortune has fallen upon me, Selina. You saw those bracelets last night, spread out on the table?"

"Yes."

"They were in my charge, and one of them has been abstracted. It was of great value; gold links, holding diamonds."

"Abstracted!" repeated the elder sister, in both concern and surprise, but certainly without the smallest indications of a guilty knowledge. "How? In what manner?"

"It is a mystery. I only left the room when I met you on the staircase, and when I went upstairs to fetch the letter for you. Directly after you left, Lady Sarah came up from dinner, and the bracelet was not there."

"It is incredible, Alice. And no one else entered the room at all, you say? No servant? no—"

"Not any one," interrupted Alice, determined not to speak of Gerard Hope.

"Then, child, it is simply impossible," was the calm rejoinder. "It must have fallen on the ground; or been mislaid in some way."

"It is hopelessly gone. Do you remember seeing it?"

"I do remember seeing amidst the rest a bracelet set with diamonds; but only on the clasp, I think. It—"

"That was another; that one is safe," interrupted Alice. "The one missing is of fine gold links studded with brilliants. Did you see it?"

"Not that I remember. I was there scarcely a minute, for I had only strolled into the back-room just before you came down. To tell you the truth, Alice, my mind was too fully occupied with other things, to take much notice even of jewels. Do not look so perplexed: it will be all right. Only you and I were in the room, you say; and we could not take it."

"Oh!" exclaimed Alice, clasping her hands, and lifting her white, beseeching face to her sister's, "did you take it? In—in sport; or in— Oh, surely you were not tempted to take it for anything else? Forgive me, Selina! you said you had need of money."

"Alice, are we going to have one of your old scenes of excitement? Strive for calmness. I am sure you do not know what you are implying. My poor child, I would rather help you to jewels than take them from you."

"But look at the mystery."

"It does appear to be a mystery, but it will no doubt be cleared up," was the reply, calm and equable. "Alice, what could you have been dreaming of, to suspect me? Have we not grown up together in our honourable home? You ought to know me, if any one does."

"And you really saw nothing of it!" moaned Alice, with a sobbing of the breath.

"Indeed I did not. In truth, I did not. If I could help you out of your perplexity I would thankfully do it. Shall I return with you and assist you to search for the bracelet?"

"No, thank you. Every search has been made."

"You have not told me what could induce you to suspect me?"

"I think—it was the impossibility of suspecting any one else," breathed poor Alice, with hesitation. "And you told me, you know, Selina, how very badly you wanted money."

"So I do; far more badly than you have any idea of, child. So badly that the thought crossed me for a moment of applying to that dreadfully rich fifteenth cousin of papa's in Liverpool, Benjamin Dalrymple, who estranged himself from us years ago; but I knew he would only growl out a 'No' if I did apply. But not badly enough, Alice, to bring me to stealing a diamond bracelet," emphatically concluded Selina.

Not only was the denial fervent and calm, but Selina's manner and countenance conveyed the impression of truth. Alice left her, inexpressibly relieved; though the conviction, that it must have been Gerard, returned to her in full force. "I wish I could see him!" was her mental exclamation.

And, for once, fortune favoured her wish. As she was dragging her weary limbs along, he came right upon her at the corner of a street.

"I am so thankful!" she exclaimed. "I wanted to see you."

"I think you most want to see a doctor, Alice. How ill you look!"

"I have cause," she returned. "That bracelet has been stolen."

"Which bracelet?" asked Gerard.

"That valuable one. The diamond. It was taken from the room."

"Taken when?" he rejoined, looking her full in the face—as a guilty man would scarcely dare to look.

"Then; or within a few minutes of that time. When Lady Sarah came up from dinner it was not there. She came up almost immediately."

"Who took it?" he repeated, not yet recovering his surprise.

"I don't know," she faintly said. "It was under my charge. No one else was there."

"You do not wish me to understand that you are suspected?" he burst forth with genuine feeling. "Their unjust meanness cannot have gone that length!"

"I trust not, but I am very unhappy. It is true I left the room when you did, but I only lingered outside on the stairs, watching—if I may tell the truth—whether you got out safely, and then I returned to it. Yet when Lady Sarah came up from dinner it was gone."

"And did no one else go into the room?" he repeated. "Did Selina? I met her at the door, and sent her upstairs."

"She went in for a minute. But she would not touch the jewels, Gerard."

"Of course not. She counts as ourselves in this. The bracelet was in the room when I left it—"

"You are sure of that?" interrupted Alice.

"I am. When I reached the door, I turned round to take a last look at you, and the diamonds of that particular bracelet gleamed at me from its place on the table."

"Oh, Gerard! Is this the truth?"

"It is the truth, on my sacred word of honour," he replied, looking at her agitated face and wondering at her words. "Why else should I say it? Good-bye, Alice; I cannot stay another moment, for there's somebody yonder I don't want to meet."

He was off like a shot. But his words and manner had conveyed a conviction of innocence to the mind of Alice, just as those of her sister had done. She stood still, looking after him in her dreamy wonder, and was jostled by the passers-by, mentally asking herself which of the two was the real delinquent? One of them it must have been.

CHAPTER XVII

DRIVEN INTO EXILE

Colonel Hope was striding about his library with impatient steps. He wore a wadded dressing-gown, handsome once, but remarkably shabby now, and he wrapped it closely around him, though the heat of the weather was intense. But Colonel Hope, large as were his coffers, never spent upon himself a superfluous farthing, especially in the way of personal adornment; and Colonel Hope would not have felt too warm cased in sheepskins, for he had spent the best part of his life in India, and was, besides, of a chilly nature.

That same afternoon he had been made acquainted with the unpleasant transaction which had occurred in his house the past evening. The household termed it a mystery; he, a scandalous robbery: and he had written forthwith to the nearest chief police-station, demanding that an officer might be despatched back with the messenger, to investigate it. So there he was, waiting for their return in impatient expectation, and occasionally halting before the window, to look out on the busy London world.

The officer at length came, and was introduced. Lady Sarah joined them, and she proceeded to give him the outline of the case. A valuable diamond bracelet, recently presented to Lady Sarah by her husband, had disappeared in a singular manner. Miss Seaton Dalrymple, the companion to Lady Sarah, had temporary charge of the jewel-box. She had brought it down the previous evening, Thursday, this being Friday, to the back drawing-room, and laid several pairs of bracelets out on a table, ready for Lady Sarah, who was going to the opera, to choose which she would wear when she came up from dinner. Lady Sarah chose a pair, and put, herself, the rest back into the box, which Miss Seaton then locked, and carried to its place upstairs. In the few minutes that the bracelets lay on the table, the most valuable one of all, a diamond, disappeared from it.

"I did not want this to be officially investigated; at least, not so quickly," observed Lady Sarah to the officer. "The colonel wrote for you quite against my wish."

"And so have let the thief get clear off, and put up with the loss!" cried the colonel. "Very fine, my lady."

"You see," added her ladyship, explaining to the officer, "Miss Dalrymple is a young lady of extremely good family, with whom we are intimate. She is of feeble constitution, and this affair has so completely upset her, that I fear she will be laid on a sick bed."

"It won't be my fault, if she is," retorted the colonel, taking the implied reproach to himself. "She'd be as glad to find it out as ourselves. The loss of a diamond bracelet, worth two or three hundred guineas, is not to be hushed up. They are not to be bought every day, Lady Sarah."

The officer was taken to the back drawing-room, whence the bracelet disappeared. It presented nothing peculiar. The folding-doors between it and the front-room stood open, the back window, a large one, looked out upon some flat leads. He seemed to take in the points of the double room at a glance: he examined the latches of the two doors opening to the corridor, he looked next from the front windows and then from the one at the back. From the front ones ordinary ingress was impossible; it was nearly as much so from the back one.

The officer leaned out for some time, but could make nothing of a case; The window was shut in by a balcony that just encircled it, and was not accessible from the leads underneath. The house was one of a row, or terrace, of houses, and they all bore the same features: the leads running along below; the confining balconies to the windows on this floor above. But the windows could not be gained from the leads except by means of a ladder; and the balconies were not at all near each other.

"Nothing to be suspected there," concluded the officer, bringing in his head and shoulders. "I should like, if you please, ma'am, to see Miss Dalrymple."

Lady Sarah went for her, and brought her. A delicate girl, with a transparent skin, looking almost too weak to walk. She was in a visible tremor, and shook as she stood before the police-officer: whose name, it turned out, was Pullet.

But he was a man of pleasant manners and speech, and he hastened to reassure her. "There's nothing to be afraid of, young lady," said he, with a broad smile. "We are not ogres: though I do believe some timid folks look upon us as such. Just please to compose yourself; and tell me as much as you can recollect of this."

"I laid out the bracelets here," began Alice, indicating the table underneath the window. "The diamond bracelet, the one lost, I placed just here," she added, touching the middle of the table at the back, "and the rest I put around it."

"It was worth more than any of the others, I believe, ma'am?"

"Much more," growled the colonel.

The officer nodded to himself and Alice resumed:

"I left the bracelets, and went into the other room and sat down at one of the front windows—"

"With the intervening doors open, I presume?"

"Wide open, as they are now," said Alice. "The other two doors were shut. Lady Sarah came up from dinner almost directly; and then, as it appears, the bracelet was not there."

"You are quite certain of that?"

"I am quite certain," interposed Lady Sarah. "I looked particularly for that bracelet: not seeing it, I supposed Miss Seaton had not laid it out. I chose out a pair, put them on, returned the others to the box, and saw Miss Dalrymple lock it."

"Then your ladyship did not miss the bracelet at that time?" questioned Mr. Pullet.

"I did not miss it in one sense, because I did not know it had been put out," she returned. "I saw it was not there."

"But did you not miss it?" he asked of Alice.

"I only reached the table as Lady Sarah was closing the lid of the box," she answered. "Lady Frances Chenevix had detained me in the front-room."

"My sister," explained Lady Sarah. "She is staying with me, and had come up with me from dinner."

"You say you went and sat in the front-room," resumed the officer to Alice, in a quicker tone than he had used previously; "will you show me where?"

Alice did not stir; she only turned her head towards the front-room, and pointed to a chair a little drawn away from the window. "In that chair," she said. "It stood as it stands now."

The officer looked baffled. "You must have had the back-room full in view from there; both the door and window."

"Quite so," replied Alice. "If you will sit down in it, you will perceive that I had an uninterrupted view, and faced the doors of both rooms."

"I perceive that from here. And you saw no one enter?"

"No one did enter. It was impossible any one could do so without my observing it. Had either of the doors been only quietly unlatched, I must have both heard and seen."

"And yet the bracelet vanished," interposed Colonel Hope. "They must have been confoundedly deep, whoever did it; but thieves are said to possess sleight of hand."

"They are clever enough, some of them," observed the officer.

"Rascally villains! I should like to know how they accomplished this."

"So should I," significantly returned the officer. "At present it appears to me incomprehensible."

There was a pause; the officer seemed to muse; and Alice, happening to look up, saw his eyes stealthily studying her face. It did not tend to reassure her.

"Your servants are trustworthy; they have lived with you some time?" resumed Mr. Pullet, not apparently attaching much importance to what the answer might be.

"Were they all escaped convicts, I don't see that it would throw light on this," retorted Colonel Hope. "If they came into the room to steal the bracelet, Miss Dalrymple must have seen them."

"From the time you put out the bracelets, to that of the ladies coming up from dinner, how long was it?" inquired the officer of Alice.

"I scarcely know," panted she. What with his close looks and his close questions, her breath was growing short. "I did not take particular notice of the lapse of time: I was not well yesterday evening."

"Was it half-an-hour?"

"Yes—I dare say—nearly so.

"Miss Dalrymple," he continued in a brisk tone, "will you have any objection to take an oath before a magistrate—in private, you know—that no person whatever, except yourself, entered either of these rooms during that period?"

Had she been requested to go before a magistrate to testify that she, herself, was the guilty person, it could scarcely have affected her more. Her cheeks grew white, her lips parted, and her eyes assumed a beseeching look of terror. Lady Sarah Hope hastily pushed a chair behind her, and drew her down upon it.

"Really, Alice, you are very foolish to allow yourself to be excited about nothing," she remonstrated: "you would have fallen on the floor in another minute. What harm is there in taking an oath privately, when it is to further the ends of justice?"

The officer's eyes were still keenly fixed on Alice Dalrymple's, and she cowered visibly beneath his gaze. He was puzzled by her evident terror. "Will you assure me, on your sacred word, that no person did enter the room?" he repeated in a low, firm tone; which somehow carried to her the impression that he believed her to be trifling with them.

She looked at him; gasped, and looked again; and then she raised her handkerchief in her hand and wiped her ashy face.

"I think some one did come in," whispered the officer in her ear; "try and recollect who it was." And Alice fell back in hysterics, and was taken from the room.

"Miss Dalrymple has been an invalid for years; she is not strong, like other people," remarked Lady Sarah. "I felt sure we should have a scene of some kind, and that is why I wished the investigation not to be gone into hurriedly."

"Don't you think there are good grounds for an investigation, sir?" testily asked Colonel Hope of the officer.

"I must confess I do think so, colonel," was the reply.

"Of course: you hear, my lady. The difficulty is, how can we obtain the first clue to the mystery?"

"I do not suppose there will be an insuperable difficulty," observed Mr. Pullet. "I believe I have obtained one."

"You are a clever fellow, then," cried the colonel, "if you have obtained it here. What is the clue?"

"Will Lady Sarah allow me to mention it—whatever it may be—without taking offence?" continued the officer, looking at her ladyship.

She bowed her head, wondering much.

"What's the good of standing upon ceremony?" peevishly put in Colonel Hope. "Her ladyship will be as glad as we shall be to get back her bracelet; more glad, one would think. A clue to the thief! Who is it?"

Mr. Pullet smiled. When men have been as long in the police force as he had, they give every word its due significance. "I did not say a clue to the thief, colonel: I said a clue to the mystery."

"Where's the difference?"

"Pardon me, it is perceptible. That the bracelet is gone is a palpable fact: but by whose hands it went is as yet a mystery."

"What do you suspect?"

"I suspect," returned the officer, lowering his voice, "that Miss Dalrymple knows how it went."

There was a silence of surprise; on Lady Sarah's part, of indignation.

"Is it possible that you suspect her?" demanded Colonel Hope.

"No," said the officer, "I do not suspect herself: she appears not to be a suspicious person in any way: but I believe she knows who the delinquent is, and that fear, or some other motive, keeps her silent. Is she on familiar terms with any of the servants?"

"But you cannot know what you are saying!" interrupted Lady Sarah. "Familiar with the servants! Miss Dalrymple is a gentlewoman; she has always moved in good society. Her family is little inferior to mine; and better—better than the colonel's," concluded her ladyship, determined to speak out.

"Madam," said the officer, "you must be aware that in an investigation of this nature we are compelled to put questions which we do not expect to be answered in the affirmative. Colonel Hope will understand what I mean, when I say that we call them 'feelers.' I did not expect to hear that Miss Dalrymple had been on familiar terms with your servants (though it might have been); but that question, being disposed of, will lead me to another. I suspect that some one did enter the room and make free with the bracelet, and that Miss Dalrymple must have been cognizant of it. If a common thief, or an absolute stranger, she would have been the first to give the alarm: if not on too familiar terms with the servants, she would be as little likely to screen them. So we come to the question—whom could it have been?"

"May I inquire why you suspect this of Miss Dalrymple?" coldly demanded Lady Sarah.

"Entirely from her manner; from the agitation she displays."

"Most young ladies, particularly in our class of life, would betray agitation at being brought face to face with a police-officer," urged Lady Sarah.

"My lady," he returned, "we are keen, experienced men: and we should not be fit for the office we hold if we were not. We generally do find lady witnesses betray uneasiness when first exposed to our questions, but in a very short time, often in a few moments, it wears off, and they grow gradually easy. It was not so with Miss Dalrymple. Her agitation, excessive at first, increased visibly, and it ended as you saw. I did not think it the agitation of guilt, but I did think it that of conscious fear. And look at the related facts: that she laid the bracelets there, never left them, no one came in, and yet the most valuable one vanished. We have many extraordinary tales brought before us, but not quite so extraordinary as that."

The colonel nodded approbation. Lady Sarah began to feel uncomfortable.

"I should like to know whether any one called whilst you were at dinner," mused the officer. "Can I see the man who attends to the hall-door?"

"Thomas attends to that," said the colonel, ringing the bell. "There is a side-door, but that is only for the servants and tradespeople."

"I heard Thomas say that Sir George Danvers called whilst we were at dinner," observed Lady Sarah. "No one else. And Sir George did not go upstairs."

The detective smiled. "If he had gone, my lady, it would have made the case no clearer."

"No," laughed Lady Sarah; "poor old Sir George would be puzzled what to do with a diamond bracelet."

"Will you tell me," said the officer, wheeling sharply round upon Thomas when he entered, "who it was that called here yesterday evening, while your master was at dinner? I do not mean Sir George Danvers; the other one."

Thomas visibly hesitated: and that was sufficient for the lynx-eyed officer. "Nobody called but Sir George, sir," he presently said.

The detective stood before the man, staring him full in the face, with a look of amusement. "Think again, my man," quoth he. "Take your time. There was some one else."

The colonel fell into an explosion: reproaching the unfortunate Thomas with having eaten his bread for five years in India, to turn upon the house and its master at last, and act the part of a deceitful, conniving wretch, and let in that swindler—

"He is not a swindler, sir," interrupted Thomas.

"Oh no, not a swindler," roared the colonel; "he only steals diamond bracelets."

"No more than I steal 'em, sir," again spoke Thomas. "He's not capable, sir. It was Mr. Gerard."

The colonel was struck speechless: his rage vanished, and down he sat in a chair, staring at Thomas. Lady Sarah coloured with surprise.

"Now, my man," cried the officer, "why could you not have said it was Mr. Gerard?"

"Because Mr. Gerard asked me not to say he had been, sir. He is not friendly here, just now; and I promised him I would not. And I am sorry to have had to break my word."

"Who is Mr. Gerard, pray?"

"He is my nephew," interposed the checkmated colonel. "Gerard Hope."

"But, as Thomas says, he is no swindler," remarked Lady Sarah: "he is not the thief. You may go, Thomas."

"No, sir," stormed the colonel; "fetch Miss Dalrymple here first. I'll come to the bottom of this. If he has done it, Lady Sarah, I will bring him to trial: though he is Gerard Hope."

Alice came back, leaning on the arm of Lady Frances Chenevix; the latter having been dying with curiosity to come in before.

"So the mystery is out, ma'am," began the colonel, to Miss Dalrymple: "it appears this gentleman was right, and that somebody did come in. And that somebody was the rebellious Mr. Gerard Hope."

Alice was prepared for this, for Thomas had told her Mr. Gerard's visit was known; and she was not so much agitated as before. It was the fear of its being found out, the having to conceal it which had troubled her.

"It is not possible that Gerard can have taken the bracelet," said Lady Sarah.

"No, it is not possible," replied Alice. "And that is why I was unwilling to mention his having come up."

"What did he come for?" thundered the colonel.

"It was not an intentional visit. I believe he only followed the impulse of the moment. He saw me at the front window; and Thomas, it appears, was standing at the door. He ran across, and came up."

"I think you might have said so, Alice," observed Lady Sarah, in a stiff tone.

"Knowing he had been forbidden the house, I did not wish to bring him under the colonel's displeasure," was all the excuse Alice could offer. "It was not my place to tell of it."

"I presume he approached sufficiently near the bracelets to touch them, had he wished?" observed the officer, who of course had now made up his mind upon the business—and upon the thief.

"Y—es," returned Alice, wishing she could have said "No."

"Did you notice the bracelet there, after he was gone?"

"I cannot say I did. I followed him from the room when he left, and then I went into the front-room, so that I had no opportunity of observing the bracelets."

"The doubt is solved," was the mental comment of the detective officer.

The colonel, hot and hasty, sent several servants various ways in search of Gerard Hope. He was speedily found, and brought; coming in with a smile on his frank, good-looking face.

"Take him into custody, officer," was the colonel's impetuous command.

"Hands off, Mr. Officer—if you are an officer," cried Gerard, in the first shock of the surprise, as he glanced at the gentlemanly appearance of the other, who wore plain clothes. "You shall not touch me, unless you can show legal authority. This is a shameful trick. Colonel—excuse me for speaking plainly— as I owe nothing to you, I do not see that you have any right, or power, to bring about my arrest."

The group would have made a fine study: especially Gerard, his head thrown back in defiance, and looking angrily at every one.

"Did you hear me?" cried the colonel.

"I must do my duty," said the police-officer, approaching Gerard. "And for authority—you need not suppose I should act without it."

"Allow me to understand a little, first," remarked Gerard, haughtily eluding the officer. "What is it for? What is the sum total?"

"Two hundred and fifty pounds," growled the colonel. "But if you are thinking to compromise it in that way, young sir, you will find yourself mistaken."

"Oh, no fear," retorted Gerard; "I have not two hundred and fifty pence. Let me see: it must be Dobbs's. A hundred and sixty—how on earth do they slide the expenses up? I did it, sir, to oblige a friend."

"The deuce you did!" echoed the colonel, who understood nothing of the speech except the last sentence. "I never saw a cooler villain in all my experience!"

"He was awfully hard up," went on Gerard, "as much so as I am now; and I did it. I don't deny having done such things on my own account, but from this particular one I did not benefit a shilling."

His calm assurance, and his words, struck them with consternation. You see, he and they were at cross-purposes.

"Dobbs said he'd take care I should be put to no inconvenience—and this comes of it! That's trusting your friends. He vowed to me, this very week, that he had provided for the bill."

"He thinks it is only an affair of debt!" screamed Frances Chenevix. "Oh, Gerard what a relief! We thought you were confessing."

"You are not arrested for debt, sir," explained the officer. "You are apprehended for—in short, it is a case of felony."

"Felony!" echoed Gerard Hope. "Oh, indeed! Could you not make it murder?" he added, with sarcasm.

"Off with him to Marlborough Street, officer," cried the exasperated colonel; "I'll come with you, and prefer the charge. He scoffs at it, does he?"

"Yes, that I do," answered Gerard. "Whatever pitfalls I may have walked into in the way of debt and carelessness, I have not gone in for felony."

"You are accused, sir," said the officer, "of stealing a diamond bracelet."

"Hey!" uttered Gerard, a flash of intelligence rising to his face, as he glanced at Alice. "I might have guessed it was the bracelet affair, if I had had my recollection about me."

"Oh, oh," triumphed the colonel, in mocking jocularity. "So you expected it was the bracelet, did you? We shall have it all out presently."

"I heard of the bracelet's disappearance," said Gerard. "I met Alice when she was out this morning, and she told me it was gone."

"Better make no admissions," whispered the officer in his ear. "They may be used against you."

"Whatever admissions I may make, you are at liberty to use them," haughtily returned Gerard. "Is it possible that you do suspect me of taking the bracelet, uncle?—or is this a joke?"

"Allow me to say a word," panted Alice, stepping forward. "I—I—did not accuse you, Mr. Hope; I would not have mentioned your name in connection with it, because I am sure you are innocent; but when It was discovered that you had called, I could not deny that you were upstairs while the bracelets lay on the table."

"Of course I was. But the idea of my taking one is absurdly preposterous," went on Gerard. "Who accuses me?"

"I do," said Colonel Hope.

"Then I am very sorry it is not somebody else, sir, instead of you."

"Explain. Why?"

"Because they should get a kindly taste of my cane across their shoulders."

"Gerard," interrupted Lady Sarah, "do not treat it in that light way. If you did take the bracelet, say so, and you shall be forgiven. I am sure you must have been put to it terribly hard; only confess it, and the matter shall be hushed up."

"No, it shan't, my lady," cried the colonel. "I will not have him encouraged—I mean, felony compounded."

"It shall," persisted Lady Sarah, "it shall, indeed. The bracelet was mine, and I have a right to do as I please. Believe me, Gerard, I will put up with the loss without a murmur; only confess, and let the worry be done with."

Gerard Hope looked at her: little trace of shame was there in his countenance. "Lady Sarah," he asked in a deeply earnest tone, "can you indeed deem me capable of taking your bracelet?"

"The bracelet was there, sir; and it went; and you can't deny it," cried the colonel.

"The bracelet was there, sure enough," assented Gerard. "I held it in my hand for two or three minutes, and was talking to Alice about it. I told her I wished it was mine—and I said what I should do with it if it was."

"Oh, Mr. Hope, pray say no more," involuntarily interrupted Alice.

"What do you want to screen him for?" impetuously broke forth the colonel, turning upon Alice. "Let him say what he was going to say."

"I do not know why I should not say it," Gerard Hope answered, in his spirit of bravado, which he disdained to check. "I said I should pledge it."

"You'll send off to every pawnbroker's in the metropolis, before the night's over, Mr. Officer," cried the choking colonel, breathless with rage. "This beats everything."

"But I did not take it any the more for having said that," put in Gerard, in a graver tone. "The remark might have been made by any one, from a duke downwards, if reduced to his last shifts, as I am. I said if it were mine: I did not say I would steal it. Nor did I."

"I saw him put it down again," said Alice, in a calm, steady voice.

"Allow me to speak a word, colonel," resumed Lady Sarah, interrupting what her husband was about to say. "Gerard—I cannot believe you guilty; but consider the circumstances. The bracelet was there; you acknowledge it: Alice left the apartment when you did, and went into the front-room, and stayed there with the bracelet in view. Yet when I came up from dinner, it was gone."

The colonel would speak. "So it lies between you and Miss Alice," he put in. "Perhaps you would like us to believe she appropriated it."

"No," answered Gerard, with a flashing eye. "She cannot be doubted. I would rather take the guilt upon myself, than allow her to be suspected. Believe me, Lady Sarah, we are both innocent."

"The bracelet could not have gone without hands to take it, Gerard," replied Lady Sarah. "How else do you account for its disappearance?"

"I believe there must be some misapprehension, some great mistake, in the affair altogether, Lady Sarah. It appears incomprehensible now; but it will be unravelled."

"Ay, and in double-quick time," wrathfully exclaimed the colonel. "You must think you are talking to a pack of idiots, Master Gerard. Here the bracelet was spread temptingly out on a table; you went into the room, being hard up for money, fingered it, wished for it, and both you and the bracelet disappeared. Sir"—turning sharply round to Mr. Pullet—"did a clearer case ever go before a jury!" Gerard Hope bit his lip. "Be more just, colonel," said he. "Your own brother's son steal a bracelet!"

"And I am happy my brother is not alive to know it," rejoined the colonel, in an obstinate tone. "Take him in hand, Mr. Officer: we'll go to Marlborough Street. I'll just change my coat, and—"

"No, no, you will not," cried Lady Sarah, laying hold of the dressing-gown and the colonel in it. "You shall not go; or Gerard, either. Whether he is guilty or not, it must not be brought against him publicly. He bears your name, colonel, and so do I, and it would reflect disgrace on us all."

"Perhaps you are made of money, my lady. If so, you may put up with the loss of a two hundred-and-fifty guinea bracelet. I don't choose to do so."

"Then, colonel, you will and you must. Sir," added Lady Sarah to the detective, "we are obliged to you for your attendance and advice, but it turns out to be a family affair, as you perceive, and we must decline to prosecute. Besides, Mr. Hope may not be guilty."

Alice rose, and stood before Colonel Hope. "Sir, if this charge were preferred against your nephew; if it came to trial; I think it would kill me. You know my unfortunate state of health; the agitation, the excitement of appearing to give evidence would be—I—I cannot continue; I cannot speak of it without terror. I pray you, for my sake, do not prosecute Mr. Gerard."

The colonel was about to storm forth an answer, but her white face, her heaving throat, had some effect upon him. Perhaps, also, he was thinking of his dead brother. "He is so doggedly obstinate, you see, Miss Dalrymple! If he would only confess, and tell where it is, perhaps I'd let him off."

Alice thought some one else was obstinate. "I do not believe he has anything to confess," she deliberately said; "I truly believe that he has not. He could not have taken it, unseen by me: and when we quitted the room, I feel sure the bracelet was left in it."

"It was," said Gerard. "When I left the room, I left the bracelet in it, so help me Heaven!"

"And, now, I shall speak," put in Frances Chenevix. "Colonel, if you press the charge against Gerard, I will go before the magistrate, and proclaim myself the thief. I vow and protest I will; just to save him. And you and Sarah could not prosecute me, you know."

"You do well to stand up for him!" retorted the colonel. "You would not be quite so ready to do it, my Lady Fanny, if you knew something I could tell you."

"Oh yes, I should," returned the young lady, with a vivid blush.

The colonel, beset on all sides, had no choice but to submit; but he did so with an ill grace, and dashed out of the room with Mr. Pullet as fiercely as though he had been charging an enemy at full tilt. "The sentimental apes these women make themselves!" cried he, in his polite way, when he got Mr. Pullet in private. "Is it not a clear case of guilt?"

"In my private opinion, it certainly is," was the reply; "though he carries it off with a high hand. I suppose, colonel, you still wish the bracelet to be searched for?"

"Search in and out, high and low; search everywhere. The rascal! to dare even to enter my house in secret!"

"May I be allowed to inquire, colonel, whether the previous estrangement between you and your nephew had anything to do with money matters?"

"No," said the colonel, turning more crusty at the thoughts called up. "I fixed upon a wife for him, and he wouldn't have her; so I turned him out-of-doors and stopped his allowance."

"Oh," was the only comment of Mr. Pullet.

So Gerard was allowed to go out of the house, a free man.

It was the following week, and Saturday night. Thomas was standing at Colonel Hope's door without his hat, a pastime he much favoured, chatting sociably with an acquaintance, when he perceived Gerard come tearing up the street. Thomas's friend backed against the rails and the spikes, and Thomas himself stood with the door in his hand, ready to touch his hair to Mr. Gerard, as he passed. Instead of passing, however, Gerard cleared the steps at a bound, pulled Thomas with himself inside, shut the door, and double-locked it.

Thomas was surprised in all ways. Not only at Mr. Hope's coming in at all, for the colonel had most solemnly interdicted it, but at the suddenness and strangeness of the action.

"Cleverly done," quoth Gerard, when he could get his breath. "I saw a shark after me, Thomas, and had to make a bolt for it. Your having been at the door saved me."

Thomas turned pale. "Mr. Gerard, you have locked it, and I'll put up the chain, if you order me, but I'm afeard it's going again' the law to keep out them detectives by force of arms."

"What is the man's head running on now?" returned Gerard. "There are no detectives after me: it was only a seedy sheriff's officer. Psha, Thomas! there's no worse crime attaching to me than a slight suspicion of debt."

"I'm sure I trust not, sir: only master will have his own way."

"Is he at home?"

"He is gone to the opera with my lady. The young ladies are upstairs alone. Miss Dalrymple has been ill, sir, ever since the bother of the bracelet, and Lady Frances is staying at home with her."

"I'll go up and see them. If the colonel and my lady are at the opera, we shall be snug and safe."

"Oh, Mr. Gerard, had you better go up, do you think?" the man ventured to remark. "If the colonel should come to hear of it—"

"How can he? You are not going to tell him, and I am sure the young ladies will not. Besides, there's no help for it: I can't go out again for hours yet. And, Thomas, if any demon should knock and ask for me, I am gone to—to—an evening party at Putney: went out, you know, by the other door."

Thomas watched him run up the stairs, and shook his head, thinking deeply. "One can't help liking him, with it all; though where could the bracelet have gone to, if he did not take it?"

The drawing-rooms were empty, and Gerard made his way to a small room that Lady Sarah called her boudoir. There they were: Alice buried in the pillows of an invalid-chair, and Lady Frances careering about the room, apparently practising some new mode of waltzing. She did not see him: Gerard danced up to her, took her hands, and joined in it.

"Oh!" she cried, with a little scream of surprise, "you! Well, I have stayed at home to some purpose. But how could you think of venturing within these sacred and forbidden walls? Do you forget that the colonel threatens us with the terrors of the law, if we suffer you to enter? You are a bold man, Gerard."

"When the cat's away, the mice can play," said Gerard, treating them to a pas seul.

"Mr. Hope!" remonstrated Alice, lifting her feeble voice. "How can you indulge in these light spirits while things are so miserable?"

"Sighing and groaning won't make things better," he answered, sitting down on a sofa near to Alice. "Here's a seat for you, Fanny; come along," he added, pulling Frances to his side. "First and foremost, has anything come to light about that mysterious bracelet?"

"Net yet," sighed Alice. "But I have no rest: I am in hourly fear of it."

"Fear!" uttered Gerard, in astonishment.

Alice winced, and leaned her head upon her hand: she spoke in a low tone.

"You must understand what I mean. The affair has been productive of so much pain and annoyance to me, that I wish it could be ignored for ever."

"Though it left me under a cloud," said Gerard. "You must pardon me, if I cannot agree with you. My constant hope is, that daylight may soon be let in upon it. I assure you I have specially mentioned it in my prayers."

"Pray don't!" reproved Alice.

"I'm sure I have cause to mention it, for it is sending me into exile. That, and other things."

"It is the guilty only who flee, not the innocent," said Frances. "You don't mean what you say, Gerard."

"Don't I! There's a certain boat advertised to steam from London Bridge Wharf tomorrow, wind and weather permitting, and it will steam me with it. I am compelled to fly my country."

"Be serious, and say what you mean."

"Seriously, then, I am over head and ears in debt. You know my uncle stopped my allowance in the spring, and sent me—metaphorically speaking—to the dogs. It got wind; ill news always does get wind; I had a few liabilities, and they have all come down upon me. But for this confounded bracelet affair, there's no doubt the colonel would have settled them, rather than let the name of Hope be dubiously bandied about by the public; he would have expended his ire in growls, and then gone and paid up. But that resource is over now; and I go to take up my abode in some renowned colony for desolate Home subjects, beyond the pale of British lock-ups. Boulogne, or Calais, or Dieppe, or Ostend; I don't know which of the four I shall stay in: and there I may be kept for years."

Neither of the young ladies answered immediately. They saw the facts were difficult, and that Gerard was only making light of it before them.

"How shall you live?" questioned Alice. "You must live there as well as here: you cannot starve."

"I shall just escape the starving. I am possessed of a trifle: enough to keep me on potatoes and salt. Upon my word, it's little more. Perhaps I may get some writing to do for the newspapers? Don't you envy me my prospects?"

"When do you suppose you may return?" inquired Lady Frances. "I ask it seriously, Gerard."

"I know no more than you, Fanny. I have no expectations but from the colonel. Should he never relent, I am caged there for good."

"And so you have ventured here to tell us this; and to bid us good-bye?"

"No; I never thought of venturing here," was the candid answer: "how could I tell that the Bashaw would be at the opera? A shark set on me in the street, and I had to run for my life. Thomas happened to be conveniently at the open door, and I rushed in, and saved myself."

"A shark!" exclaimed Alice, her inexperience taking the words literally—"a shark in the street!" Frances Chenevix laughed.

"One with sharp eyes and nimble feet, Alice, speeding after me with a polite invitation from one of the law lords. He is watching outside now."

"How shall you get away?" wondered Frances.

"If the Bashaw comes home before twelve, Thomas must dispose of me somewhere in the lower regions: Sunday is a free day for us, thank goodness. So please to make the most of me, both of you, for it is the last time you will have the privilege. By the way, Fanny, will you do me a favour? There used to be a little book of mine in the glass book-case in the library; my name in it, and a mottled cover: I wish you would go and find it for me."

Lady Frances left the room with alacrity. Gerard immediately bent over Alice, and his tone changed.

"I have sent her away on purpose. She'll be half-an-hour rummaging, for I have not seen the book there for ages. Alice, one word before we part. You must know that it was for your sake I refused the marriage proposed to me by my uncle: you will not let me go into banishment without a hope; a promise of your love to lighten it."

"Oh, Gerard," she eagerly said, "I am so glad you have spoken: I almost think I must have spoken myself, if you had not. Just look at me?"

"I am looking at you," he fondly answered.

"Then look at my hectic face; my constantly tired limbs; my sickly hands: do they not plainly tell you that the topics you would speak of must be barred topics to me?"

"Why should they be? You will get stronger."

"Never. There is no hope of it. Many years ago, when the illness first came upon me, the doctors said I might grow better with time, but the time has come, and come, and come, and—gone; and it has only left me a more confirmed invalid. To an old age I cannot live; most probably but a few years. Ask yourself, Gerard, if I am one who ought to marry, and leave behind a husband to regret me; perhaps children. No, no."

"You are cruel, Alice."

"The cruelty would be, if I selfishly allowed you to talk of love to me; or, still more selfishly, let you cherish hopes that I would marry. When you hinted at this the other evening, the evening that wretched bracelet was lost, I reproached myself with cowardice, in not answering more plainly than you had spoken. I should have told you, Gerard, as I tell you now, that nothing, no persuasion from even the dearest person on earth, shall ever induce me to marry."

"You dislike me. I see that."

"I did not say so," answered Alice, with a glowing cheek. "I think it very possible that—if I could allow myself ever to dwell on such things—I should like you very much; perhaps better than I could like any one."

"And why will you not?" he persuasively uttered.

"Gerard, I have told you. I am too weak and sickly to be other than I am. It would be a sin, in me, to indulge hopes of it: it would only be deceiving myself and you. No, Gerard, my love and hopes must lie elsewhere."

"Where?" he eagerly asked.

Alice pointed upwards. "I am learning to look upon it as my home," she whispered, "and I must not suffer hindrances to obscure the way. It will be a better home than even your love, Gerard."

Gerard Hope smiled. "Even than my love: Alice, you like me more than you admit. Unsay your words, my dearest, and give me hope."

"Do not vex me," she resumed, in a pained tone; "do not seek to turn me from my duty. I—I—though I scarcely like to speak of these sacred things, Gerard—I have put my hand to the plough: even you cannot turn me back."

He did not answer; he only played with the hand he held between both of his.

"Tell me one thing, Gerard: it will be safe. Was not the dispute about Frances Chenevix?"

He contracted his brow; and nodded.

"And you could refuse her! You must learn to love her, for she would make you a good wife."

"Much chance there is now of my making a wife of any one!"

"Oh, this will blow over in time: I feel it will. Meanwhile—"

"Meanwhile you destroy every hopeful feeling I thought to take with me to cheer me in my exile," was his impatient interruption. "I love you alone, Alice; I have loved you for months, nay years, truly, fervently; and I know that you must have seen that I did."

"Love me still, Gerard," she softly answered; "but not with the love you would give to one of earth: the love you will give—I hope—to Frances Chenevix. Think of me as one rapidly going; soon to be gone."

"Oh, not yet!" he cried in an imploring tone, as if it were to be as she willed.

"Not just yet: I hope to see you return from exile. Let us say farewell while we are alone."

She spoke the last sentence hurriedly, for footsteps were heard. Gerard snatched her to him, and laid his face upon hers.

"What cover did you say the book had?" demanded Frances Chenevix of Gerard, who was then leaning back on the sofa, apparently waiting for her. "A mottled? I cannot see one anything like it."

"No? I am sorry to have given you the trouble, Fanny. It has gone, perhaps, amongst the 'have-beens.'"

"Listen," said Alice, removing her hand from before her face, "I hear a carriage stopping. Can they have come home?"

Frances and Gerard flew into the next room, whence the street could be seen. A carriage had stopped, but not at their house. "It is too early for them yet," said Gerard.

"I am sorry things go so cross just now with you, Gerard," whispered Lady Frances. "You will be very dull over there."

"Ay; fit to hang myself, if you knew all. And the bracelet may turn up, and Lady Sarah be sporting it on her arm again, and I never know that the cloud is off me. No chance that any of you will be at the trouble of writing to a fellow."

"I will," said Frances. "Whether the bracelet turns up, or not, I will write to you sometimes, if you like, Gerard, and give you all the news."

"You are a good girl, Fanny," returned he, in a brighter accent, "and I will send you my address as soon as I possess one. You are not to turn proud, mind, and be off the bargain, if you find it to be in a fish-market, au cinquième."

Frances laughed. "Take care of yourself, Gerard."

He took leave of them, and got out by the aid of Thomas, contriving to elude the shark. And the next day the friendly steamer conveyed him into exile on other shores. The prevalent opinion at Colonel Hope's was, that he paid his expenses with the proceeds of the diamond bracelet.

Perhaps it was not only the "bother of the bracelet" as Thomas phrased it, that was rendering Alice Dalrymple so miserable. That, of course, was bad enough to bear, from its very uncertainty. But she was in trouble about her sister. Selina's debts had become known to the world, and the embarrassment into which they had flung her husband. What with her seven thousand pounds (at least) of debts, and the liabilities cast on Oscar by the two London seasons, he owed a sum of ten thousand pounds.

How was he to pay it? He knew not. That he should be a crippled man for years and years, obliged to live in the nearest possible way, before the debts and their attendant costs, in the shape of interest and expenses, could be worked off, he knew. Selina knew it now, and had the grace to feel repentant. They had shut themselves up at Moat Grange, were "immured in it," Selina called it, every outlay of every kind being cut down.

All these things tried Alice; and would try her more as the days went on. There was no corner on earth to which she could turn for comfort.

In the silent watches of the night, in the broad glare of noonday, one question was ever tormenting her brain—which of the two had taken the bracelet? Impossible though it seemed to suspect either of stealing it, emphatically though they both denied it, common sense told Alice Dalrymple that one of them it must have been.

Once more a year has gone its round, bringing again to London all the stir and bustle of another season. It is a lovely afternoon towards the close of May, and there is some slight commotion in Chenevix House. Only the commotion of an unexpected arrival. Lady Mary Cleveland, with her infant child and its nurse, had come up from Netherleigh on a short visit. The infant, barely four weeks old yet, was a very small and fretful young gentleman, who had chosen to make his appearance in the world two good months before the world expected him.

No one was at home but Lady Grace. She ran down the stairs to welcome her sister.

"My dear Mary! I am so glad to see you! We did not expect you until Monday. You are doubly welcome."

"I thought it would make no difference—my coming a few days earlier, and without warning you," said Lady Mary, as she kissed her elder sister. "I am not very strong, Grace, and Mr. Forth has been anxious that I should have a change. This morning was so warm and fine, and I felt so languid, that he said to me, 'Why not start today?' So he and my husband packed me off, whether I would or no. Where's mamma?"

"Mamma is out somewhere. Gone to see the pictures, I think," added Grace, as Lady Mary turned, of her own accord, into a small, cosy sitting-room that used to belong to the girls, and which they had nicknamed "The Hut." "Harriet is with her."

Lady Mary looked surprised. "Harriet! Are the MacIvors here?"

"Oh dear, yes; staying with us. They came up from Scotland on Monday."

"I am rather sorry I came, then. It may be an inconvenience. And there won't be a bit of quiet in the house."

"It will be no inconvenience at all, Mary—what are you thinking of? You are to have your old room, and the baby the room next it. As to the house, it shall be as quiet as you please. I assure you it is wonderfully changed, in that respect, since all you girls were at home together."

"That time seems ages ago," remarked Lady Mary.

"What light-headed, frivolous girls we were—and how life's cares change us! Fancy our all marrying and leaving you behind!"

"There's Frances also."

"I forgot Frances. She is at Sarah's, I suppose, as usual. She will be marrying next, no doubt. I always thought she would be one of the first to marry, though she is the youngest except Adela. And then it will be your turn, Grace."

Grace slightly shook her head. "It will never be mine, Mary—as I believe. I have settled down into an old maid—and I feel like one. I would rather not marry now; at least, I think so. The time has gone by for it."

"What nonsense you talk! Why, you are only about three or four and thirty, Grace, though you are the eldest. A woman is not too old to marry, at that age."

"Well, I am not anxious to marry," replied Grace. "Papa and mamma should have one of us with them in their old age; and Frances will no doubt marry. It will, I know, be all as God pleases. Morning by morning as I get up, I put myself into His good care, and beseech Him to undertake for me—to use me as He will."

Lady Mary Cleveland smiled. This was all very right, of course—Grace had always had a religious corner in her heart.

"And now tell me all the news of Netherleigh," began Grace, when her sister had taken some refreshment, and the small mite of a baby was asleep, and they were back again in "The Hut," Mary lying on the sofa. "How is Aunt Margery?"

"You have had this room refurnished!" cried Mary, looking about her—at the bright carpet and chintz curtains.

"Yes, this spring. It was so very shabby."

"It is very pretty now. Aunt Margery?—oh, she is fairly well. Not too strong, I fancy. I went to the Court yesterday and had lunch with her. She is my baby's godmother."

"Is she? The baby's christened, then?"

"As if we should bring him away from home if he were not! You will laugh at his old-fashioned name, Grace—Thomas."

"Thomas is a very good name. It is your husband's."

"Yes—and not one of his first wife's children bear it. So I thought it high time this one should."

"Why did your husband not bring you up today?"

"Because he has two funerals this afternoon—people are sure to die at the wrong time," added Lady Mary, quaintly. "And the vicar of the next parish, who is always ready to help him, is away this week."

"And the godfathers?—who are they, Mary?"

"My husband is one of them: he has stood to all his children. The other is Oscar Dalrymple."

"Oscar Dalrymple?" echoed Grace.

"Yes. He is not a general favourite; but Mr. Cleveland likes him. And he thinks he has behaved very well in this wretched business of Selina's. The one we should have preferred to have for godfather, we did not like to ask—if you can understand that apparent contradiction, Gracie?"

"And who was that?" asked Grace, looking up.

"Francis Grubb. He has been so very, very kind to us, and we like and respect him so greatly, above all other men on the face of the earth, that we quite longed to ask him to stand to the poor little waif. On the other hand, he is so wealthy and so generous, that my husband thought it might look like coveting more benefits. And so we fixed on Mr. Dalrymple."

Grace mused.

"I never use my beautiful pony-carriage but I feel grateful to Mr. Grubb," went on Lady Mary. "And look how good he has been in regard to Charles!"

A slight frown at the last word contracted Grace's fair and open brow, as though the name brought her some sort of discomfort. It was smoothed away at once.

"Are the Dalrymples at Moat Grange?" she asked.

"Still there; living like hermits, in the most inexpensive manner possible, with two servants only—or three, I forget which. Two maids, I think it is; and a man who has to do the garden—as much as one man can do of it—and feed the two pigs, and milk the cow, and see to the cocks and hens."

A smile crossed Grace's lips. "Does Selina like that kind of life?"

"Selina has to like it; at any rate, to put up with it, and she does it with a good grace. It is she who has reduced Oscar to poverty; the least she can do is to share in his retirement and retrenchments without murmuring. Oscar is trying to let Moat Grange, but does not seem able to succeed. His own little place, Knutford, was let for a term of years when he came into Moat Grange, so they cannot retire to that."

"It was very sad of Selina to act so," sighed Grace.

"It was unpardonable," corrected Lady Mary. "She knew how limited her husband's income was. Thoughtlessness runs in the Dalrymple family. Poor Mrs. Dalrymple wanted to give up the cottage and the income Oscar allows her, and go out into the world to shift for herself; but Oscar would not hear of it. We respect him for it. Close he may be, rather crabbed in temper; but he has a keen sense of honour. It is said his debts amount to ten thousand pounds."

"Ten thousand pounds!" almost screamed Grace.

"Quite that. Though indeed I should have said Selina's debts, rather than his. Mr. Grubb's sister, Mary Lynn, comes sometimes to Netherleigh, to spend a week with Mrs. Dalrymple—who was to have been Mary's mother-in-law, you know, had things gone straight with Robert. What a sweet girl she is!"

"I have always thought Mary Lynn that, since I knew her."

"Do you see Alice Dalrymple often?" continued Lady Mary.

"Pretty often, except when the Hopes are in Gloucestershire. Alice looks very delicate."

"The colonel is not reconciled to Gerard yet?"

"No; and not likely to be. Poor Gerard is somewhere abroad."

"And that mysterious bracelet of Sarah's—I conclude it has never come to light. Grace," added Lady Mary, dropping her voice, "is it still thought that Gerard helped himself to it?"

Grace shook her head. "The colonel thinks so. And as long as he does he will never forgive him, or take him back to favour."

"Well, I don't know that he could be expected to. Poor Gerard! If he did do it, he must have been reduced to some pitiable strait. And my husband's boy, Charley—do you see much of him, Grace?"

"Oh, we see him now and then," replied Grace, in a tone of constraint.

"Adela has quite taken him up, we find. It is a relief to us, for we feared she might not; might even, we thought, resent having him in the house. How kind Mr. Grubb was over that; how considerately thoughtful!" continued Lady Mary. "None can know how truly good he is?"

"You are right there," acquiesced Grace. "But he does not always find his reward."

"How does Adela behave to him now?" questioned Lady Mary, who had understood the last remark to apply to her sister Adela; and again she dropped her voice as she asked it.

"Just as usual. There's no improvement in her."

The previous summer, when the marriage of Lady Mary Chenevix took place with Mr. Cleveland, he, the Rector, came up the day before it, and stayed at Mr. Grubb's by invitation, to be in readiness for the morrow's ceremony. Mr. Grubb liked the Rector: he had felt deeply sorry for him when he was left a widower with so many children, and was glad he was going to have a new helpmate and they a second mother. That night, as they sat talking together after dinner—Adela being at her mother's, deep in all the wedding paraphernalia—the Rector opened his heart and his sorrows to Mr. Grubb: what a care his children were to him, and what he should do to place his many sons out in life. Charles, the second, was chiefly on his mind now. The eldest son, Harry, was in the army, and getting on well; expected to get his company soon. Charles, who was then twenty years of age, had been intended for the Church, but he had never taken to the idea kindly, and was now evincing a most unconquerable dislike to it. "I cannot force him into it," said the Rector, sadly. "I must find some other opening for him. He must go out and begin to earn a living somehow—I have too many of them at home. I suppose,"—he added, in a hesitating tone of deprecation—"you could not make room for him in Leadenhall Street?" But Mr. Grubb told the Rector that he would gladly make room for him; and, amid the grateful thanks of the Rector, it was decided upon, there and then, Mr. Grubb being most liberal in his arrangements. "I must find him a lodging," said the Rector; "perhaps some family would take him and board him." "No, no; he had better come here," said Mr. Grubb; "provided Adela makes no objection. Strange lodgings are the ruin of many a young fellow—and will be of many more. London lodgings are no true home for young men; they take to going abroad at night out of sheer loneliness, get exposed to the temptations of this most dangerous city, teeming with its specious allurements, and fall helplessly into its evil ways. Your son, Mr. Cleveland, shall come here and be sheltered from the danger, if my wife will have him."

Lady Adela apathetically consented, when the proposal was made to her; the lad might come if he liked, she did not care, was all she answered. And so Charles Cleveland came: and his father believed and declared that no man had ever been so good and generous as Mr. Grubb.

A tall, slender, gentlemanly, dark-eyed, very handsome and somewhat idle young fellow Mr. Charles Cleveland turned out to be. He took well enough to his duties in the counting-house; far better than he had taken to Latin and Greek and theology; and Mr. Grubb was as kind to him as could be; and the more active partner, Mr. Howard, not too severe.

But at the close of winter, when Charles Cleveland had been some months located in Grosvenor Square, Lady Adela began to show herself very foolish. She struck up a flirtation with him. Whether it was done out of sheer ennui at the prolonged cold weather, or in very thoughtlessness, or by way of inventing another source of vexation for her husband, Adela set up a strong flirtation with Charles Cleveland, and the world was already talking of it and laughing at it. The matter, absurd though it was in itself, was vexing Grace Chenevix, and her sister's mention of Charley brought the vexation before her.

"We heard something about Adela last week," spoke Lady Mary, maintaining her low tone, "not at all creditable to her: but we hope it is not true."

Grace Chenevix felt her face flush. She assumed that her sister alluded to what was filling her thoughts, and she would have been glad to be spared speaking of it.

"It is only nonsense, Mary. It comes of sheer idle thoughtlessness on Adela's part, nothing more. Rely upon that."

"I am glad to hear you say so, Grace. But—do you ever go there with her?"

"Go where with her?"

"To Lady Sanely's."

The two sisters gazed at one another. They were at cross-purposes.

"To Lady Sanely's?" exclaimed Grace, in surprise. "I don't go there with Adela; I don't go there at all. Mamma has scarcely any acquaintance with Lady Sanely."

"Then how can you speak so confidently?" returned Mary Cleveland. "Adela may be quite deep in the mischief, for all you know."

"Mary, I do not understand you. You must explain what you mean."

"It is said," whispered Mary, glancing round at the walls, as if to reassure herself no one else was present, "that Adela has taken to gambling. That—"

"To gambling?" gasped Grace.

Lady Mary nodded. "It is said that gambling to a very dangerous extent is carried on at Lady Sanely's and that Adela has been drawn into the snare, and goes there nightly, and plays deeply. How do you think we heard this?"

"Heaven knows!" cried poor Grace, feeling a conviction that it might be true.

"From Harry; my husband's eldest son. He has got his promotion at last, as perhaps you know, and is daily expecting orders to embark for India. He ran down last week to see us, and it was he who mentioned it. My husband told him to be careful; that it could not be true. Harry maintained that it was true, and was, moreover, quite well known. He said he thought Lord Acorn was aware of it—but that Mr. Grubb was not."

"Papa cannot be aware of it," disputed Grace.

"Don't make too sure of it, Grace. Papa does a little in that line himself, you know; he may not look upon it in the dreadful light that you do, or that we people do in a rustic parsonage. Anyway, Harry says there's no mistake about Adela."

"Mr. Grubb ought to be warned—that he may save her."

"It is what my husband says—that Mr. Grubb ought to be told. I hope Adela has enough petty sins on her conscience!"

"This the worst of all. She may ruin her husband, rich though he is."

"As poor Robert Dalrymple ruined himself. Scarcely that, however, in this case, Gracie. Mr. Grubb cannot be brought to ruin blindfold by his wife: and it strikes me he will take very good care, for her sake as well as his own, that she does not bring him to it. But he ought to be told without delay."

Grace Chenevix fell into one of the most unpleasant reveries she had ever experienced. Adela went often to Lady Sanely's; she knew that. Another moment, and Lord Acorn came in.

"Papa," cried Lady Mary, after she had greeted her father, "we were talking of Adela. A rumour reached us at Netherleigh that she was growing too fond of card-playing. It is carried on to a high extent at Lady Sanely's house, we are led to believe, and that Adela is often there, and joining in it."

"Ay, they go in for tolerably high stakes at Lady Sanely's," replied the earl, in his careless, not to say supercilious manner. "Very silly of Adela!"

"It is true then, papa!" gasped Grace.

"True enough," he remarked. "I dare say, though, Adela can take care of her purse-strings, and draw them in when necessary."

"How indifferent papa is!" thought Grace, with a sigh.

She was anything but indifferent. She was thinking what it might be best to do; how save Adela from further folly. After dinner, when the carriage came round to take her mother and Harriet to a small early gathering at old Lady Cust's, and Mary, tired with her day's journey, had retired for the night, Grace suddenly spoke.

"Mamma, I think, if you have no objection, I will go with you in the carriage and let it leave me at Adela's. I should like to sit an hour with her."

"I have no objection," was the answer of Lady Acorn, spoken rather tartly; as usual; for she lived in a chronic state of dissatisfaction with her daughter Adela. "Go, if you like. And just give her a hint to mend her manners, Grace, with regard to that boy."

"That is pure idle pastime," was the mental comment of Grace Chenevix. "This other may be worse."

CHAPTER XIX

FLIRTATION

They stood together in the dusk of the evening, the tempter and the deceived. Really it is not too much so to designate them. She, one of the fairest of earth's fair daughters, leaned in a listless attitude against the window-frame, looking out on the square. Perhaps, listening: for a woman of misery, with three children round her, was singing her doleful ditty there, and gazing up at the noble mansion as if she hoped some poor mite might be dropped to her from its superfluity of wealth. The children were thin and haggard, with that sharp, pinching look of age in their faces so unsuited to childhood, and which never comes but from famine and long-continued wretchedness. The mother—she was little more than a girl—made a halt opposite the window: her eye had caught the beautiful face enshrined there amidst the curtains, and she sang out louder and more piteously than ever.

"Now I think that's real—no imposture—none of those made-up cases that the Mendicity Society look up and expose."

The remark came from a young man, who was likewise looking out, a very good-looking fellow of prepossessing countenance. There was an air of tenderness in his manner as he spoke, implying tenderness of heart for her who stood by him. And the Lady Adela roused herself, and carelessly asked, "What's real?" For her mind and thoughts had been dwelling on invisible and absent things, and the poverty and the singing had remained to her as though they had not been.

"That poor wretch there, and those famished children. That one—the boy—looks as if he had not tasted food for a week. See how he fixes his eyes up here! I am sure they are famished."

"Oh, Charles, don't talk so! Street beggars ought not to be allowed to bring the sight of their misery here. It makes one shiver. They should confine themselves to the City, and similar low parts."

"What's that about the City," inquired Mr. Grubb, who had entered and caught the last words; while the young man, Charley Cleveland, moving listlessly towards a distant window, stealthily threw a shilling from it and then quitted the room.

"Street beggars," answered Adela. "I say they ought not to be allowed out of the City, exposing their rags and their wretchedness to us! It is too bad."

"The City is much obliged to you," said her husband, in a marked manner, as if implying that he belonged to it. And the Lady Adela shrugged her shoulders in very French fashion, the gesture betraying contempt for the speaker and his words.

"Adela," he said, quietly drawing her to a sofa and sitting down beside her, "I have long wanted a few minutes' serious talk with you; and I have put it off from day to day, for the subject is full of pain to me, as it ought to be to you. Of shame, I had almost said."

She turned her lovely eyes upon him. He could see the hard and defiant expression they took, even in the twilight gloom.

"You may spare yourself the trouble of a lecture—if that is what you intend. It will do me no good."

"Whether it will do you good or not, you must hear it. Your behaviour—"

She interrupted him, humming a merry tune.

"Adela, listen to me," he resumed; and perhaps it was the first time she had heard from him so peremptory a tone. "Your behaviour is not what it ought to be; it is not wise or seemly; and you must alter it."

"So you have told me ever since we were married, all the four years and odd months," she said, with a half-playful, half-mocking laugh.

"Of your behaviour to me I have told you so repeatedly and uselessly that I have now dropped the subject for ever. What I would speak of is your behaviour to young Cleveland. The world is beginning to notice it; and, Adela, what is objectionable in it shall be discontinued."

"There is nothing objectionable—except in your imagination."

"There is: and you know it, Adela. You may treat me as you like; I cannot, unfortunately, alter that; but I will guard you from being talked about. As to Cleveland—"

"Charley," she broke in, turning her head to look for him; "Charley, do you hear my husband? He would like to— I thought Charley was here."

"Had he been here, I should not have spoken," was Mr. Grubb's reply, signs of mortification on his refined and sensitive lips.

"Is your rôle going to be that of a jealous husband at last?"

"No," he replied. "You have striven, with unnecessary endeavour, to deaden the love for you which once filled my heart; if that love has not turned to gall and bitterness, it is not your fault. This is not a case for jealousy, Adela. You must know that. I jealous of a schoolboy!"

"What is it a case of, then?"

"Your fair reputation. That shall be cared for in the eyes of the world."

"There is no necessity for your caring for it," she retorted. "My reputation—and your honour—are perfectly safe in my own keeping. There lives not a man who could bring disgrace upon me. You are out of your senses, Mr. Grubb."

"That my honour is safe, I do not doubt," he returned, drawing himself slightly up. "Forgive me, if my words could have borne any other construction. I speak only of your reputation for folly—frivolity. The world is laughing at you: and I do not choose that it shall laugh."

A shade of annoyance flashed into her pretty face. "The world is nothing to me. It had better laugh at itself."

"Perfectly true. But I must take care it does not laugh at you. Your mother spoke to me today about Charles Cleveland. She called you a child, Adela; and she said, if I did not interfere and put a stop to it, she should."

"Let my mother mind her own affairs," was Adela's answer, full of resentment. "She can dictate to the two who are left to her, but not to the rest of us. When we married, we passed out of her control."

"Surely not. Your mother is always your mother."

"Pray where did you see her? Has it come to secret meetings, in which my conduct is discussed?"

"Nonsense, Adela! Lady Acorn came to see me in Leadenhall Street, but upon other matters."

"And so you got up a nice little mare's-nest between you! That I was too fond of Charles Cleveland, and ought to be put in irons for it!"

"That you were too free with him, Adela," corrected her husband. "That your manners with him, chiefly in this your own house, were losing that reserve which ought to temper them, though he is but a boy. It was she who said the world was laughing at you."

"And what did you say?" asked Lady Adela, with an ill-concealed sneer.

"I said nothing," he replied, a sort of sadness in his tone. "I could have said that the subject had for some little time been to me a source of annoyance; and I might have added that if I had refrained from remonstrance, it was because remonstrance from me to my wife had ever been worse than useless."

"That's true enough, sir. Then why attempt it now?"

"For your own sake. And in years to come, when time shall have brought to you sense and feeling, you will thank me for being more careful of your fair fame than you seem inclined to be yourself. I do not wish to pursue the subject, Adela; let the hint I have given you avail. Be more circumspect in your manners to young Cleveland. You know perfectly well that you are pursuing this senseless flirtation with him for one sole end—to vex me: you really care no more for him than for the wind that passes. But society, you see, not being behind the scenes, may be apt to attribute other motives to you. Change your tactics; be true to yourself; and then—"

"And then? Well?"

"I shall not be called upon to interpose my authority. To do so would be against my inclination and Charles Cleveland's interests."

"Your authority?" she retorted, in a blaze of scorn—for if there was one thing that put out Lady Adela more than another it was to be lectured: and she certainly did not like to be told that the world was laughing at her. "Have I ever altered my manners for any authority you could bring to bear?—do you suppose that I shall alter them now? Go and preach to your people in the City, if you must preach somewhere."

"Lady Grace Chenevix," interrupted the groom of the chambers, throwing wide the door.

"You are all in the dark!" exclaimed Grace. "I took the chance of finding you at home, Adela. Mamma and Harriet are gone to the Dowager Cust's."

"I am glad you came, Grace," said Mr. Grubb, ringing for lights. "I wanted to look in at the club for half-an-hour: you will stay with Lady Adela."

"Grace," to his sister-in-law, "Lady Adela" to his wife: what did that tell? Anyway, it told that he had been provoked almost beyond bearing.

"Mary came up this afternoon, taking us by surprise," began Grace, as Mr. Grubb left the room, and the man retired after lighting the wax-lights. "She does not seem strong; and the baby is such a poor little thing—"

"Pray are you a party to this conspiracy between my mother and him?" unceremoniously interposed Adela, with a motion of her hand towards the door by which her husband had disappeared, to indicate whom she meant; and the words were the first she had condescended to speak to her sister since her entrance.

"Conspiracy! I don't know of any," answered Grace, wondering what was coming.

"Had you been a few moments earlier, you would have found him holding forth about Charley Cleveland. And he said my mother went to him in the City today to put him up to it."

"Oh, if you mean about Charley Cleveland, I was going to speak to you of it myself. You are getting quite absurd about him, Adela. Or he is about you. It was said at Brookes's the other day that Charley Cleveland was losing his head for Lady Adela Grubb."

Lady Adela laughed. "Who said it, Gracie?"

"Oh, I don't know; a lot of them were together. Captain Foster, and John Cust, and Lord Deerham, and Booby Charteris, and others. It seems Charley was a little overcome the previous evening. He and his brother had been dining with the Guards, very freely, and afterwards they went to—I forget the place—somewhere that young men go to of an evening, and Charley finished himself up with brandy and cigars; and then he managed to hiccup out, that the only angel living upon earth was Lady Adela Grubb."

"And that's all!" she said lightly—"that Charley called me an angel! I told him it was a mare's-nest."

"No; it is not all," quickly answered Lady Grace. "It might be all, if it were not for your folly. I have seen Charley hold your hand in his; I have seen him kiss it; I have seen him bend forward and whisper to you until his hair has all but touched yours. It is very bad, Adela."

"It is very amusing; it serves to pass away the time," laughed Adela. "And, pray, Grace, how came you to know so much of what they say and do at their clubs?"

"That's one of the annoying parts of it. Colonel Hope heard it; he was present. He went home, shocked and scared, to tell Sarah; and Sarah came yesterday morning and told mamma."

"Shocked and scared too? I should like to have seen Sarah's long face!"

"You should have seen mamma's. No wonder she went down to your husband. But that is not all yet, Adela. One of them, I think it was Lord Deerham—whoever it was, had dined here a night or two before—told the others that you flirted with Charley desperately before your husband's eyes, and that while you showed favour to one you snubbed the other."

"And it's true," coolly avowed Adela. "I like Charley Cleveland, and I choose to flirt with him. But if you strait-coated people think I have any wrong liking for him, you err woefully. Grace, all this is but idle talk. I shall never compromise myself by so much as a hazardous word, for Charley, or for any one else. I have just told him so."

"Pleasant! the necessity for such an assertion to one's lord and master!"

"I never loved any one in my life; and I'm sure I am not going to begin now. Not even Captain Stanley—though I did have a passing liking for him. Perhaps you will be surprised to hear, Grace, that there were odd moments in my life during the first year or two after my marriage, when I was nearer loving Francis Grubb than I had been of loving any one—only that I had set out by steeling my heart against him."

Grace gazed at her sister wonderingly.

"But that's all past: and of love I feel none for any mortal man, and don't mean to feel it. But I like amusement—and I am amusing myself with Charley Cleveland."

"You have no right to do it, Adela. What is but sport to you, as it seems, may be death to him."

"That is his look-out," laughed Adela. "My private belief is, if you care to know it, that my husband was thinking as much of Charley as of me when he took upon himself to lecture me just now. Of the consequences to Charley's vulnerable and boyish heart; though he did put it upon me and on what the world might say."

"How grievously you must try your husband!" exclaimed Grace.

"He's used to it."

"You provoking woman! You'll never go to heaven, I should say, if only for your treatment of him. Adela, you made your vows before Heaven to love and honour him: how do you fulfil them?"

"I heard the other day you had turned Methodist: Bessy Cust came in and said it. I am sorry I contradicted it," cried the provoking Adela.

"You cannot set the world at defiance."

"I don't mean to. As to Charley dancing attendance on me, or kissing my hand—what harm is there in it?"

"That may be according to one's own notion of 'harm.' Even the most trifling approach to flirting is entirely unseemly in a married woman."

"Are you quite a competent judge—not being married yourself?" rejoined Adela. "See here, Grace—if you never flirt more with any one than Charley flirts with me, you won't hurt."

"I am afraid he has learnt to love you, Adela."

"Then more silly, he, for his pains. Why, I am oceans of years older than Charley is. He ought to think of me as his grandmother."

"Can't you be serious, child? I want you to see the thing in its proper—or, rather, improper—light. When it comes to a man, other than your husband, kissing you, it is time—

"Who said Charley kissed me?" retorted Adela, in a blaze of anger. "He has never done such a thing—never dared to attempt it. I said he kissed my hand sometimes—and then it has generally had a glove upon it."

"Well, well, whatever the nonsense may be, you must give it up, Adela. There can be no objection on your part to doing so, as you say you do not care for Charles Cleveland."

"Incorrect, Lady Grace. I do care for him; I enjoy his friendship amazingly. What I said was, that I did not love him. That would be too absurd."

"Call it flirtation, don't call it friendship," wrathfully retorted Grace. "And he must be devoid of brains as a calf, to attach himself to you, if he has done it. I hope nothing of this will reach the ears of Mary or of his father. They would not believe him capable of such folly. From this hour, Adela, you must give it up."

"Just what Mr. Grubb has been good enough to tell me; but 'must' is a word I do not understand," lightly rejoined Adela. "Neither you nor he will make me break off my flirtation with Charles Cleveland. I shall go into it all the more to spite you."

"If I were Francis Grubb I should beat you, Adela."

"If!" laughingly echoed Lady Adela. "If you were Francis Grubb, you would do as he does. Why, Gracie, girl, he loves me passionately still, for all his assumed indifference. Do you think there are never moments when he betrays it? He is jealous of Charley; that's what he is, in spite of his dignified denial— and oh, the fun it is to me to have made him so!"

"Adela," said Grace, sadly, "does it never occur to you that this behaviour may tire your husband out?— that his love and his patience may give way at last?"

"I wish they would!" cried the provoking girl, little seeing or caring, in her reckless humour, what the wish might imply. "I wish he would go his way and let me go mine, and give me hundreds of thousands a-year for my own share. He should have the dull rooms in the house and I the bright ones, and we would only meet at dinner on state occasions, when the world and his wife came to us."

Lady Grace felt downright angry. She wondered whether Adela spoke in her heart's true sincerity.

"There's no fear of it, Gracie: don't look at me like that. My husband would no more part company with me, whatsoever I might do, than he would part with his soul. He loves me too well."

"It is a positive disgrace to have one's married sister's name coupled with a flirtation," grumbled Grace: for the Lady Acorn, whatever might be her failings as to tongue and temper, had brought her daughters up to the purest and best of notions. "That reverend man, Dr. Short—I cannot think how it came to his ears—hinted at it today in talking with mamma when they met at the picture-galleries. He—"

"There it is!" shouted Adela, in glee; "the murder's out! So it is you who have been putting mamma up to complain to Mr. Grubb! You are setting your cap at that sanctimonious Dr. Short, and you fear he won't see it if you have a naughty sister given to flirting. Oh, Gracie!"

"You are wrong; you know you are wrong. How frivolous you are, Adela! Dr. Short is going to be married to Miss Greatlands."

"Well, there's something of the sort in the wind, I know. If it's not the Reverend Dr. Short, it's the Reverend Dr. Long; so don't shake your head at me, Gracie."

Dancing across the room, Adela rang the bell. "My carriage," she said to the servant.

"It has been waiting some time, my lady."

"Where are you going?" asked Grace, surprised:

"To Lady Sanely's."

"To Lady Sanely's," echoed the elder sister. Then, after a pause, "Your husband did not know you were going there?"

"Do you suppose I tell him of my engagements? What next, I wonder?"

"Oh, Adela!" uttered Grace, rising from her seat—and there was a piercing sound of grief in her tone, deeper than any which had characterized it throughout the interview—"do not say you are going there! Another rumour is rife about you; worse than that half-nonsensical one about Charles Cleveland; one likely to have a far graver effect on your welfare and happiness."

"I—I do not understand," repeated Adela; but her tone, in spite of its display of haughtiness, betrayed that she did understand, and it struck terror to the heart of her sister. "I think you are all beside yourselves today!"

Grace, greatly agitated, clasped the other's arm as she was turning away. "It is said, Adela—I have heard it, and papa has confirmed it—it is rumoured that you have become addicted to a—a—dangerous vice. Oh, forgive me, Adela! Is it so? You shall not go until you have answered me."

The rich colour in Lady Adela's cheeks had faded to paleness; her eyes dropped; she could not look her sister in the face. From this, her manner of receiving the accusation, it might be seen how much more real was this trouble, than the half-nonsensical one, as Grace had called it, connected with Charles Cleveland.

"Vice!" she vaguely repeated.

"That of gaming," spoke Grace, her own voice unsteady in its deep emotion. "That you play deeply, night by night, at Lady Sanely's."

"What strong words you use!" gasped Adela, resentfully. "Vice! Just because I may take a hand at cards now and then!"

"Oh, my poor sister, my dear sister, you do not know what it may lead to!" pleaded Grace. "You shall not go forth to Lady Sanely's this night—do not! do not! Break through this dreadful chain at once—before it be too late."

Angry at hearing this amusement of hers had become known at home, vexed and embarrassed at being pressed, almost by force, to stay away from its fascinations, Adela flung her sister's arm from her and moved forward with an impatient gesture of passion. They were near a table, and her own hand, or that of Grace, neither well knew which, caught in a beautiful inkstand, and turned it over. The ink was scattered on the light carpet: an ugly, dark blotch.

What cared Adela? If the costly carpet was spoiled, his money might purchase another. She moved on to her dressing-room, caused her maid, waiting there, to envelop her in her evening mantle, and then swept down to her carriage.

That Lady Adela did not care for Charles Cleveland was perfectly true. She would have laughed at the very idea; she regarded him but as a pleasant-mannered boy: nevertheless, partly to while away the time, which sometimes hung heavily on her hands, partly because she hoped it would vex her husband, whom she but lived to annoy, she had plunged into the flirtation.

It was something more on Charley's part. For, while Adela cared not for him, beyond the passing amusement of the moment, would not have given to him a regretful thought had he suddenly been removed from her sight for ever, he had grown to love her to idolatry. It is a strong expression, but in this case justifiable. Almost as the sun is to the world, bringing to it light and heat, life to flowers, perfection to the corn, so had Lady Adela become to him. In her presence he could alone be said to live; his heart then was at rest, feeding on its own fulness of happiness, and there he could thankfully have lived and died, and never asked for change: when obliged to be absent from her, a miserable void was his, a feverish yearning for the hour that should bring him to her again. Surely this was most reprehensible on his part—to have become attached, in this senseless manner, to a married woman! Reprehensible? Hear what one says of another love; he who knew so much about love himself—Lord Byron:

"Why did she love him? Curious fool, be still:
Is human love the growth of human will?"

Could the fault have lain with Lady Adela? Most undoubtedly. She, not casting a thought to the effect it might have upon his heart, and secure in her own supreme indifference, purposely threw out the bait of her beauty and her manifold attractions, and so led him on to love—a love as true and impassioned as was ever felt by man. What did he promise himself by it?—what did he think could come of it? Nothing. He was not capable of cherishing towards her a dishonourable thought, he had never addressed to her a disloyal word. It was not in the nature of Charles Cleveland to do anything of the kind; he was single-minded, single-hearted, chivalrously honourable. He thought of her as being all that was good and beautiful: to him she seemed to be without fault, sweet and pure as an angel. To conceal his deep love for her was beyond his power; eye, tone, manner, tacitly and unconsciously betrayed it. And Lady Adela, to give her her due, did not encourage him to more.

And so, while poor Charley was living on in his fool's paradise, wishing for nothing, looking for nothing, beyond the exquisite sense of bliss her daily presence brought him, supremely content could he have lived on it for ever, Lady Adela already found the affair was growing rather monotonous. The chances were that had her husband and Grace not spoken to her, she would very speedily have thrown off Charley and his allegiance. Adela had no special pursuit whence to draw daily satisfaction. No home (the French would better express it by the word ménage) to keep up and contrive for; the hand of wealth was at work, and all was provided for her to satiety; she had no children to train and love; she had no husband whom it was a delight to her to yield to, to please and cherish: worse than all, she had (let us say as yet) no sense of responsibility to a higher Being, for time and talents wasted.

A woman cannot be truly happy (or a man either) unless she possesses some aim in life, some daily source of occupation, be it work or be it pleasure, to contrive, and act, and live for. Without it she becomes a vapid, weary, discontented being, full of vague longings for she knows not what. One of two results is pretty sure to follow—mischief or misery. Lady Adela was too young and pretty to be miserable, therefore she turned to mischief.

Chance brought her an introduction to the Countess of Sanely, with whom the Chenevix family had no previous acquaintance, and who had a reputation for loving high card-playing and for encouraging it at her house: she and Adela grew intimate, and Adela was drawn into the disastrous pursuit. At first she liked it well enough; it was fascinating, it was new: and now, when perhaps she was beginning to be a little afraid and would fain have retreated, she did not see her way clear to do so: for she owed money that she could not pay.

Lady Grace Chenevix, unceremoniously left alone in her sister's drawing-room, rang the bell. It was to tell them to attend to the ink. The carriage was not coming for her till eleven o'clock, and it was now but half-past ten. Hers were not very pleasant thoughts with which to get through the solitary half-hour. Mr. Grubb came in, and inquired for his wife. Grace said she had gone out.

"What, and left you alone! Where's she gone to?"

"To Lady Sanely's."

"Who are these Sanelys, Grace?" he inquired as he sat down. "Adela passes four or five nights a-week there. The other evening I took up my hat to accompany her, and she would not have it. What sort of people are they?"

"Four or five nights a-week," mechanically repeated Grace, passing over his question. "And at what time does she get home?"

"At all hours. Sometimes very late."

Grace sat communing with herself. Should she impart this matter of uneasiness to Mr. Grubb, or should she be silent, and let things take their chance; which of the two courses would be more conducive to the interests of Adela; for she was indeed most anxious for her. She looked up at him, at his noble countenance, betraying commanding sense and intellect—surely to impart the truth to such a man was to make a confidant of one able to do for her sister all that could be done. Mr. Cleveland and Mary both said he ought to hear it without delay. And Grace's resolution was taken.

"Mr. Grubb," she said, her voice somewhat unsteady, "Adela is your wife and my sister; we have both, therefore, her true welfare at heart. I have been deliberating whether I should speak to you upon a subject which—which—gives me uneasiness, and I believe I ought to do so."

"Stay, Grace," he interrupted. "If it is—about—Cleveland, I would rather not enter upon it. Lady Acorn spoke to me today, and I have given a hint to Adela."

"Oh no, it is not that. She goes on in a silly way with him, but there's no harm in it, only thoughtlessness. I am sure of it."

He nodded his head, in acquiescence, and began pacing the room.

"It is of her intimacy with Lady Sanely that I would speak; these frequent visits there. Do you know what they say?"

"No," he replied, assuming great indifference, his thoughts apparently directed to placing his feet on one particular portion of the pattern of the carpet, and to nothing else.

"They say—they do say"—Grace faltered, hesitated: she hated to do this, and the question flashed across her, could she still avoid it?

"Say what?" said Mr. Grubb, carelessly.

"That play to an incredible extent is carried on there. And that Adela has been induced to join in it."

His assumed indifference was forgotten now, and the carpet might have been patternless for all he knew of it. He had stopped right under the chandelier, its flood of light illumining his countenance as he looked long and hard at Grace, as one in a maze.

Much that had been inexplicable in his wife's conduct for some little time past was rendered clear now. Her feverish restlessness on the evenings she was going to Lady Sanely's; her coming home at all hours, jaded, sick, out of spirits, yet unable to sleep; her extraordinary demands for money, latterly to an extent which had puzzled and almost terrified him. But he had never yet refused it to her.

"It must be put a stop to somehow," said Grace.

"It must," he answered, resuming his walk, and drawing a deep breath. "What's all this wet on the carpet?"

"An accident this evening. Some ink was thrown down: my fault, I believe. At any cost, any sacrifice," continued Lady Grace. "If the habit should get hold of Adela, there is nothing but unhappiness before her—perhaps ruin."

"Any cost, any sacrifice, that I can make, shall be made," repeated Mr. Grubb. "But Adela will listen to no remonstrance from me. You know that, Grace."

"You must—stop the supplies," suggested Grace, dropping her voice to a confidential whisper. "Has she had much of late?"

"Yes."

"More than her allowance? Perhaps not, as that is so liberal."

"Her allowance!" half laughed her husband, not a happy laugh. "It has been, to what she has drawn of me, as a silver coin in a purse of gold."

Grace clasped her hands. "And you let her have it! Did you suspect nothing?"

"Not of this nature. I suspected that she might be buying costly things—after the reckless fashion of Selina Dalrymple. Or else that—forgive me, Grace, I would rather not say more."

"Nay," said Grace, rising to put her hand on his arm and meeting his earnest glance, "let there be entire confidence between us; keep nothing back."

"Well, Grace, I fancied she might be lending it to your mother."

"No, no; my mother has not borrowed from her lately. Oh, how can we save her! This is an insinuating vice that gains upon its votaries, they say, like the eating of opium."

"Your carriage, my lady," interrupted a servant, entering the room. And Grace caught up her mantle.

"Must you go, Grace? It is scarcely eleven."

"Yes. If mamma does not have the carriage to the minute, she won't cease scolding for days, and it must take me home first. Dear Mr. Grubb, turn this over in your mind," she whispered, "and see what you can do. Use your influence with her, and be firm."

"My influence, did you say?" And there was a touch of sarcasm in his tone, mingled with a grief painful to hear. "What has my influence with her ever been, Grace?"

"I know, I know," she cried, wringing his hand, and turning from him towards the stairs, that he might not see the tears gathering in her eyes. Tears of sympathy with his wrongs, and partly, perhaps, of regret: for she was thinking of that curious misapprehension, years ago, when she had been led to believe that it was herself who was his chosen bride. "I would not have treated him so," her heart murmured; "I would have made his life a happy one, as he deserves it should be."

He gained upon her fast steps; and, drawing her arm within his, led her downstairs, and placed her in the carriage.

"Dear Mr. Grubb," she whispered, as he clasped her hands, "do not let what I have been obliged to say render you harsh with poor Adela. Different days may be in store for you both; she may yet be the mother of your children, when happiness in each other would surely follow. Do not be unkind to her."

"Unkind to Adela! No, Grace. Separation, rather than unkindness."

"Separation!" gasped Grace, the ominous word affrighting her.

"I have thought sometimes that it may come to it. A man cannot patiently endure contumely for ever, Grace."

He withdrew his hand from hers, and turned back into his desolate home. Grace sank back in the carriage, with a mental prayer.

"God keep him; God comfort him, and help him to bear!"

CHAPTER XX

A PRESENT OF COFFEE

It was two o'clock when Lady Adela returned home. She ran lightly upstairs and into the drawing-room, throwing off her mantle as she came in. A tray of refreshments stood on a side-table.

Mr. Grubb rose from his chair. "It is very late, Adela."

"Late! Not at all. I wish to goodness you wouldn't sit up for me!"

She went to the table and stood looking at the decanters, as if deliberating what she should take, murmuring something about being "frightfully thirsty."

"What shall I give you?" he asked.

"Nothing," was the ungracious answer, most ungraciously spoken. And she poured out a tumbler of weak sherry-and-water, and drank it; a second, and drank that also. Then, without taking any notice of him, she went up to her chamber. Anything more pointedly, stingingly contemptuous than her behaviour to her husband now, and for some time past, has never been exhibited by mortal woman.

Mr. Grubb rang for the servants to put out the wax-lights, and went up in his turn. There was no sleep for him that night, whatever there might have been for her. He knew not how to act, how to arrest this new pursuit of hers; he scarcely knew even how to open the matter to her. She appeared to be asleep when he rose in the morning and passed into his dressing-room. She herself soon afforded him the opportunity.

He was seated at his solitary breakfast, a meal his wife rarely condescended to take with him, when her maid entered, bringing a message from her lady—that she wished to see him before he left for the City. Master Charley Cleveland, usually his breakfast companion, had not made his appearance at home since the previous night.

"Is your lady up, Darvy?"

"Oh dear yes, sir, and at breakfast in her dressing-room."

He went up to it. How very lovely she looked, sitting there at her coffee, in her embroidered white dress and pink ribbons, and the delicate lace cap shading her sweet features. She had risen thus early to get money from him; he knew that, before she asked for it.

"You wished to see me, Lady Adela."

"I want some money," she said in a light, flippant kind of tone, as if it were the sole purpose of Mr. Grubb's existence to supply her demands.

"Impossible," he rejoined. "You had two hundred pounds from me the day before yesterday."

"I must have two hundred more this morning. I want it."

"What is it that you are doing with all this money? It has much puzzled me."

"Oh—making a purse for myself," she answered saucily.

"You can trust to me to do that for you. I cannot continue to supply you, Adela."

"But I must have it," she retorted, raising her voice, and speaking as if he were the very dirt under her feet. "I will have it."

"No," he replied calmly, but with firm resolution in his tone. "I shall give you no more until your allowance is due."

She looked up, quite a furious expression on her lovely face.

"Not give it me! Why, what do you suppose I married you for?"

"Adela!" came his reproof, almost whispered.

"I would not have taken you but for your money; you know that. They promised me at home that I should have unlimited command of it; and I will."

"You have had unlimited command," he observed, and there was no irritation suffered to appear in his tone, whatever may have been his inward pain. "It is for your own sake I must discontinue to supply it."

"You are intelligible!" was her scornful rejoinder: for, in good truth, this refusal was making havoc of her temper.

"All that you can need in every way shall be yours, Adela. Purchase what you like, order what you like; I will pay the bills without a murmur. But I will not give you money to waste, as you have latterly wasted it, at Lady Sanely's."

She rose from her seat, pale with anger. "First Charles Cleveland, then Lady Sanely: what else am I to be lectured upon? How dare you presume to interfere with my pursuits?"

"I should ill be fulfilling my duty to you, or my love either, Adela, what is left of it, if I did not interfere."

"I will not listen, Mr. Grubb: if you attempt to preach to me, as you did last night, I will run away. Sit down and write me a cheque for the money."

"There is no necessity for me to repeat my refusal, Adela. Until I have reason to believe that this new liking for PLAY has left you, you should draw my blood from me, sooner than money to pursue it. But remember," he impressively added, "that I say this in all kindness."

She looked at him, her delicate throat working, her breath growing short with passion.

"Will you give me the cheque?"

"I will not. Anything more, Adela, for I am late?"

There was no answer in words, but she suddenly raised the cup, which chanced to be in her hand and was half full of coffee and flung it at him. It struck him on the chin, the coffee falling upon his clothes.

It was a moment of embarrassment for them both. He looked steadfastly at her, with a calm, despairing sorrow, and then quitted the room. Lady Adela, her senses returning, sank back in her chair; and in the reaction of her inexcusable passion, she sobbed aloud.

It was quite a violent fit of sobbing: and she smothered her head up that he should not hear. She did feel ashamed of herself, felt even a little honest shame at her general treatment of him. As her sobs subsided, she heard him in his dressing-room, changing his things, and she wished she had not done it. But she must have the money; that, and more; and without it, she should be in a frightful dilemma, and might have her name posted up as a card-playing defaulter in the drawing-rooms of society. So she determined to have another battle for it with her husband, and she dried the tears on her fair young face, and opened his dressing-room door quite humbly, so to say, and went into it.

It was empty. Mr. Grubb's movements had been rapid, and he was already gone. He had put out of sight the stained things taken off, removed all traces of them. Was she not sensible even of this? Did she not know that he was thus cautious for her own sake—that no scandal might be given to the servants? Not she. With his disappearance, and the consequent failure of her hope, all her resentment was returning. Her foot kicked against something on the floor, and she stooped to pick it up. It was her husband's cheque-book, which he must have unconsciously dropped when transferring things from one pocket to another.

Was a demon just then at Lady Adela's side?—what else could have impelled her?—what else whispered to her of a way to supply the money she wanted? Once only a momentary hesitation crossed her; but she drove it away, and carried the cheques to her writing-table and used one of them.

She drew it for five hundred pounds, a heavy sum, and she boldly signed it "Grubb and Howard." For it happened to be the cheque-book of the firm, not of her husband's private account. She was clever at drawing, clever at imitating styles of writing—not that she had ever turned her talent to its present use, or thought so to turn it—and the signature, when finished, looked very like her husband's own. Then she carried back the cheque-book, and laid it on the floor where she found it.

Some time after all this was accomplished, she was passing downstairs, deliberating upon whether she could dare to go to the bank herself to get the cheque cashed, when Charles Cleveland came in, and bounded up the stairs.

"Where did Mr. Grubb breakfast this morning?" he inquired, apparently in a desperate hurry, as they shook hands, and turned into one of the sitting-rooms, Charley devouring her with his eyes all the time. Little blame to him either, for she was looking most lovely: the excitement, arising from what she had done, glowing in her cheeks like a sweet blush rose.

"What a question! He breakfasted at home."

"Yes, yes, dear Lady Adela. I meant in which room." For Mr. Grubb sometimes breakfasted in the regular breakfast-room, and sometimes in his library.

"I really don't know, and don't care," returned Adela, connecting the question somehow, in her own mind, with the present of coffee he had received. "His breakfasting is a matter of indifference to me. And pray, Mr. Charley, where did you breakfast this morning?—and what became of you last night? Have you been making a night of it with the owls and the bats?"

"I went to my brother's. Harry had some fellows with him, and we, as you express it, dear Lady Adela, made a night of it. That is, we broke up so late that I would not disturb your house by returning here: Harry gave me a sofa, and I went direct from him to Leadenhall Street this morning."

"And what have you come back for?"

"For Mr. Grubb's cheque-book. He has missed it, and thinks he must have left it on the breakfast-table."

"Charley," she said, "I was just wanting you. Will you do me a favour?"

"I will do everything you wish," he answered, his tones literally trembling with tenderness.

"I want you to go to the bank in Lombard Street, and got me a cheque cashed. Mr. Grubb gave it me this morning, and I am in a hurry for the money, for I expect people here every minute with some accounts. It is not crossed. Take a cab, and go at once."

"I will. I can leave the cheque-book in Leadenhall Street first."

"No, you must not wait to find the cheque-book. I will look for it whilst you are gone. You will not be many minutes, I am sure, and I tell you I am all impatience."

Charley Cleveland hesitated. "I scarcely know what to say," he replied, dubiously, to this. "Mr. Grubb is waiting for the cheque-book. This is Saturday, you know."

"What if it is?"

"We are always so busy on Saturdays."

"Very well, Charles," she returned in hurt, resentful tones. "If you like Mr. Grubb better than you do me, you will oblige him first. You would be there and back in no time."

"Dearest Lady Adela! Like Mr. Grubb better than— Well, I will do it, though I dare say I shall get into a row. Have the cheque-book ready, that I may not lose a moment when I get back." And Adela nodded assent.

"A confounded row, too," he muttered to himself, as he tore down the stairs, and into the cab; "but I will go through a thundercloud full of rows for her." Charley gave a concise word to the driver, and away dashed the cab towards Lombard Street, at a pace which terrified the road generally, and greatly astonished the apple-stalls.

He was back in an incredibly short space of time, and paid the notes over to her. "Have you found the cheque-book?" he asked then.

"I declare I never thought about it," was Lady Adela's reply. "But he breakfasted in the library, I hear. Perhaps you will find it there."

He rushed into the library. And there, on the table, was the missing cheque-book. Oh, wary Lady Adela!

She followed him into the room. "Charley," she whispered, "don't say you have been out for me—no need to say you have seen me. The fact is, that staid husband of mine had a grumbling fit upon him last night, and accused me of talking and laughing too much with the world in general and Mr. Charles Cleveland in particular. If they find fault with you for loitering, say you were detained on some matter of your own."

He nodded in the affirmative. But a red vermilion was stealing over his face, dyeing it to the very roots of his hair, and his heart's pulses were rising high. For surely in that last speech she meant to imply that she loved him. And Master Charles felt his brain turn round as it had never turned before, and he bent that flushed face down upon her hand, and left on it an impassioned, though very respectful kiss, by way of adieu.

"What a young goose he is!" thought Adela.

Very ill at ease, that day, was the Lady Adela. Reckless though she might be as to her husband's good opinion, implicitly secure though she felt that he would hush up the matter and shield her from consequences, she could not help being dissatisfied with what she had done. Suppose exposure came?—she would not like that. She had written Mr. Howard's name, as well as her husband's! She lost herself in a reverie, her mind running from one ugly point to another. Try as she would, she could not drive the thoughts away, and by the afternoon she had become seriously uneasy. Was such a case ever known as that of a wife being brought to trial for— "Whatever possesses me to dwell upon such things?" she mentally queried, starting up in anger with herself. "Rather order the carriage and go and pay my last night's losses."

From Lady Sanely's she went to her mother's, intending to stay and dine there. Somehow she was already beginning to shrink from meeting her husband's face. However, she found they were all engaged to dine at Colonel Hope's, including her sister Mary. So Adela had to return home: but she took care not to do it until close upon the dinner hour.

Mr. Grubb and Charles Cleveland were both at table. Neither of them alluded to the unpleasant topic uppermost in her mind, so she concluded that as yet nothing had come out. Mr. Grubb was very silent— the result no doubt of the coffee in the morning.

"I am going to Netherleigh tomorrow morning, sir," observed Charles; "shall try to get there in time for church. My father has written to ask me. Could you allow me to remain for Monday also? Harry means to run down that day, to say good-bye."

"Monday?" considered Mr. Grubb. "Yes, I suppose you can. There's nothing particular that you will be required for on Monday, that I know of. You may stay."

"Thank you, sir."

"When does your brother leave?"

"I think on Tuesday morning."

Accordingly, on the following morning, Sunday, Charley left the house to go to Netherleigh. Mr. Grubb went to church, as usual; Adela made excuse—said her head ached. When he returned home at one o'clock, he found she had gone to her mother's; and, without saying to him with your leave, or by your leave, without, in fact, giving him any intimation whatever, she remained at Chenevix House for the rest of the day.

On the Monday, Mr. Grubb went to business at the customary hour, but returned early in the afternoon to attend some public meeting in Westminster, connected with politics. Influential people— Conservatives: who were called Tories then—had for some time past been soliciting him to go into Parliament; he had not quite made up his mind yet whether he would, or not.

He and his wife dined alone. Lord and Lady Kindon, with whom they were intimate, were to have dined with them; but only a few minutes before the time of sitting down, a note came to say they had received ill news of one of their children, who was at school at Twickenham, and had to hasten thither. Adela was tryingly cross and contrary at table: she had not wished to be alone with her husband, lest he should have found out what she had done, and begin upon it. So, after the first few minutes, the meal proceeded nearly in silence. She did not fear the explosion quite as much as she did at first: each hour, as it went on smoothly, helped to make her uneasiness less.

But she was not to escape long. Just as the servants were quitting the room, leaving the wine on the table, one of them came back again.

"Mr. Howard has called, sir. He says he would not disturb you at this hour, but he must see you on a matter of pressing business."

"Pressing business!" echoed Mr. Grubb. "Show Mr. Howard in. A chair, Richard, and glasses."

The stiff and stern old man entered, bowing to Lady Adela. His iron-grey hair looked greyer than usual, and his black coat rusty. Rusty coats are worn by more than one millionaire.

"Why, Howard, this is quite an event for you! Why did you not come in time for dinner? Sit down. Anything new? Anything happened?"

"Why, yes," replied Mr. Howard, who was a slow-speaking man, giving one the idea that the bump of caution must be large on his head. "Thank you, port."

"What is it?" inquired the senior partner.

"I will enter upon the matter presently," replied James Howard, deliberately sipping his wine. By which answer Mr. Grubb of course understood that he would only speak when they were alone.

Lady Adela swallowed her strawberries and left her seat so quickly that Mr. Grubb could hardly get to the door in time to open it, and she went up to the drawing-room. She felt sure, as sure as though she could read his very thoughts, that "that horrid Howard" had come about the cheque. She did not care so much that her husband should find it out; he might do his best and his worst, and the worst from him she did not dread greatly; but that that old ogre should know it, perhaps take steps—oh, that was quite another thing. Could he take steps?—would the law justify it? Adela did not know; but she began to give the reins to her imagination, and cowered in terror.

As she thus sat, her ears painfully alive to every sound, a cab rattled into the square, and stopped at the door. It brought Charles Cleveland. Charley had just come up from Netherleigh; the train was late, and he was in a desperate hurry to get into his dress-clothes, to attend a "spread"—it was what Charley called it—given by his brother. Adela ran out, and arrested him as he was making for his room, three stairs at a time.

"Charley, I want to speak to you—just for a moment. What mortal haste you are in!"

To be invited thus into the drawing-room by her, to meet her again after this temporary absence, was to him as light breaking in upon darkness. "Oh, Charles," she added, giving him both her hands, in the moment's agitation, "surely some good fairy sent you! I am in distress."

"Can I soothe it?" he asked, wondering at her emotion, and retaining her hands in his. "Can I do anything for you?"

"I am in sore need of a friend—to—to shelter me," she continued. "Great, desperate need!"

"Can I be that friend? Suffer me, if you can. Suffer me to be, Lady Adela. Dear! dear! what can have happened?"

"But it may bring danger upon you, difficulty, even disgrace. I believe I ought not to ask it of you."

"Danger and difficulty would be welcome, borne for you," returned Charley, in his loyalty. "Believe that, Lady Adela."

He could not imagine what was amiss, and he caught somewhat of her agitation. That she was in real trouble, nay, in terror, was all too plain. For a moment the thought occurred—was Mr. Grubb angry with her on his account? Oh, what a privilege it appeared to him, foolish but honest-hearted fellow, to be asked to shield her!

"I will trust you," she cried, her emotion increasing. "That cheque— but oh, Charles, do not you think ill of me! It was done in a moment of irritation."

"Say on, dear Lady Adela."

"That cheque—he did not give it me. I had asked for money, and he refused. I wanted it badly; and I was angry with him: so I drew out the cheque."

Charley felt all at sea: not comprehending in the least. She saw it: and was forced to go on with her painful explanation. The colour was coming and going in her cheek; now white as a lily, now rose-red.

"That cheque you cashed for me on Saturday morning, Charley. Mr. Grubb did not draw it. Mr. Howard's name was signed as well as his; and—and he is with my husband in the dining-room, and I am frightened to death."

There was a momentary pause. Charley understood now; and saw all the difficulty of the matter, as she had lightly called it. But his honest love for her was working strongly in his heart, and he formed a hasty, chivalrous resolve to shield her if he could. Had she not appealed to him?

"I want you not to say that it was from me you had the cheque, Charley."

"I never will say it. Rely upon me."

"They cannot do anything to me, I suppose; or to anyone else," she went on. "It is the exposure that would drive me wild. I could not bear that even that old Howard should know it was I. Oh, Charles, what can be done?"

"Be at ease, Lady Adela. You shall never repent your confidence. Not a breath of suspicion shall come near you. I will shield you; I am proud to do it: shield you, if need be, with my life. You little know how valueless that life would be without your society, dear Lady Adela."

"Now, Charles, hold your tongue. You must not take to say such things to me. They are not right—and are all nonsense besides. What would Mr. Grubb think?"

"Forgive me," murmured Charley, all repentance. "I did not mean to say aught that was disloyal to him or you, Lady Adela: I could not be capable of it, now, or ever. And I will keep my word—to shield you through this trouble. I repeat it. I swear it."

He wrung her hand in token of good-faith, and escaped to prepare for his engagement. She sat down, somewhat reassured, but not at all easy in her conscience. The world just now seemed rather hard to the Lady Adela.

CHAPTER XXI

GIVEN INTO CUSTODY

They sat at the well-spread dessert-table in Grosvenor Square, those two gentlemen, the sole partners of almost the wealthiest house in London; keen, honourable, first-rate men of business, yet presenting somewhat of a contrast in themselves. He at the table head, Francis Grubb, was fine and stately, wearing in his countenance, in its expression of form and feature, the impress of true nobility—nature's nobility, not that of the peerage—and young yet. James Howard, who might be called the chief partner, so far as work and constant, regular attendance in the City went, though he did not receive anything like an equal share of the profits, was an elderly man, high-shouldered, his face hard and stern, his hair iron-grey, and his black coat rusty. Mr. Howard had walked up from his house in Russell Square this evening to confer with his chief upon some matter of business. It a little surprised Mr. Grubb: for, with them, business discussions were always confined to their legitimate province—the City.

The Lady Adela, Mr. Grubb's rebellious but very charming wife, quitted the room speedily, leaving them to the discussion that Mr. Howard had intimated he wished for. But Mr. Howard did not show himself in any haste to enter upon it. He sat on, surveying abstractedly the glittering table before him, with its rich cut glass, its silver, its china, and its sweet flowers, talking—abstractedly also—of the passing topics of the day, more particularly of a political meeting which had taken place that afternoon. Mr. Grubb was a Conservative; he a Liberal; or, as it was more often styled in those days, Tory and Whig.

"What news is it that you have brought me, Howard?" began Mr. Grubb, at last, breaking a pause of silence.

"Ay—my news," returned Mr. Howard, as though recalled to the thought. "Did you draw a cheque on Saturday morning, before leaving home, in favour of self, and get it cashed at Glyn's?"

Mr. Grubb threw his thoughts back on Saturday morning. The reminiscence was unpleasant. The scene which had taken place with his wife was painful to him, disgraceful to her. He had drawn no cheque.

"No," he answered, thinking a great deal more of that scene than of Mr. Howard's question.

"A cheque for five hundred pounds, in favour of self?" continued Mr. Howard, slowly sipping his port wine.

"I don't draw at Glyn's in favour of self. You know that, Howard, as well as I do." Messrs. Glyn and Co. were the bankers of the firm; Coutts and Co. the private bankers of Mr. Grubb.

"Just so. Therefore, upon the fact coming to our notice this afternoon that such a cheque had been drawn and paid, I stepped over to Glyn's and made inquiries."

"How did it come to your notice?"

"This way. John Strasfield had all the cheques drawn last week sent to him for the usual purpose of verification—he has his own ways of doing his business, you know. In looking over them he was rather struck with this cheque, because it was drawn to self. Self, too; not selves. After regarding it for a minute or two, another thought struck him—that the signature was not quite like yours. So he brought the cheque to me. I don't think you signed it."

Mr. Grubb rose and closed the door, which he had left ajar after opening it for Lady Adela, the evening being very warm. John Strasfield was their confidential cashier in Leadenhall Street.

"If it is your signature, your hand must have been nervous when you wrote it," continued Mr. Howard, "rendering the letters less decided than usual."

That Mr. Grubb had been nervous on Saturday morning he was quite conscious of; though not, he believed, to the extent of making his hand unsteady. But he had not drawn any cheque.

"It was drawn in favour of self, you say. Was it signed with my private signature, Francis C. C. Grubb?"

"No; with the firm's signature, Grubb and Howard. Glyn's people suspected nothing wrong, and cashed it."

"Who presented the cheque?"

"Charles Cleveland. And he received the money."

"Charles Cleveland!" repeated Mr. Grubb, in surprise, his whole attention fully aroused now. "There is some mystery about this."

"So it seemed to me," answered the elder man. "Cleveland stayed out of town today—by your leave, I think you said."

"Yes, he asked me on Saturday to let him have today; he was going down to Netherleigh: his elder brother, Captain Cleveland, meant to run down there to say good-bye, Charles will be back tonight, I suppose. But—I don't understand about this cheque."

"I'm sure I don't," said Mr. Howard. "Except that Charles Cleveland got it cashed."

"Where did Charles Cleveland procure the cheque?" asked Mr. Grubb, his head all in a puzzle. "Who drew the cheque? Where's the money? Howard, there must be some mistake in your information."

"It was Saturday morning that you left the cheque-book at home, and sent Cleveland for it, if you remember," said Mr. Howard, quietly.

"Ah, to be sure it was; I do remember. A long while he was gone."

"You asked him what made him so long: I chanced to be in your room at the moment: and he said he had been doing a little errand for himself. Well, during the period of his absence, that is, somewhere between ten and half-past eleven, the cheque was presented by him at Glyn's, and cashed. What does it all say?" concluded Mr. Howard.

Francis Grubb looked a little bewildered. No clear idea upon the point was suggesting itself to his mind.

"I thought young Cleveland was given to improvident habits," resumed Mr. Howard, "but I never suspected he was one to help himself to money in this way; to—"

"He cannot have done it," interrupted Mr. Grubb, earnestly decisive. "It is quite impossible. Charles Cleveland is foolish and silly enough, just as boys will be, for he is no better than a boy; but he is honest and honourable."

"Are you aware that he spends a great deal of money?"

"I think he does. I said so to him last week. It was that pouring wet day, Wednesday I think, and I told him he might go down to Leadenhall Street with me in the carriage, if he liked. I took the opportunity of speaking to him about his expenditure, telling him it was a great deal easier to get into debt than to get out of it."

"Which he had found out for himself, I expect," grumbled Mr. Howard. "How did he receive it?"

"As ingenuously as you could wish. Blushed like a school-girl. He confessed that he had been spending too much money lately, and laid it chiefly to the score of his brother's being in London. Captain Cleveland's comrades are rather an extravagant set; the allowance that he gets from his uncle is good;

and Charles has been led into expense through mixing with them. The very moment his brother left, he said, he should draw in and spend next to nothing."

Mr. Howard smiled grimly. "One evening, strolling out after my dinner, I chanced to meet my young gentleman, came full upon him as he was turning out of a florist's, a big bouquet of white flowers in his hand. 'You must have given a guinea for that, young sir,' I said to him, and he did not deny it; just leaped into a cab and was off. I don't suppose those flowers were presented to Captain Cleveland or to any of his comrades."

Mr. Grubb knitted his brow. He had not the slightest doubt they were intended for his wife. What a silly fellow that Charley was!

"He may get into debt; I feel sure he is in debt; but he would not commit forgery—or help himself to money that was not his. I tell you, Howard, the thing is impossible."

"He presented the cheque and received the money," dryly remarked Mr. Howard. "What has he done with it?"

"But no one, not oven a madman, would go to work in this barefaced way," contended his more generous-minded partner, "conscious that it must bring immediate detection and punishment upon his head."

"Detection, yes; punishment does not necessarily follow. That, he may be already safe from."

"How do you mean?"

"Suppose you inquire what clothes he took with him," suggested Mr. Howard. "My impression is that he's off. Gone. The Netherleigh tale may have been only a blind."

Mr. Grubb rose and rang the bell, staggered nearly out of his senses; and, until it was answered, not another word was spoken. Each gentleman was busy with his own thoughts.

"Richard," began the master to his servant, "when Mr. Charles Cleveland left for the country yesterday morning, did he take much luggage with him?"

"I don't think he took any, sir; unless it was his small portmanteau."

"Did you happen to hear him say whether he intended to make a long stay?"

"I did not hear him say anything, sir: he went out early, to catch the first train. But Mr. Cleveland is back."

"Back!" echoed Mr. Howard, surprised into the interference.

"Yes, sir, just now, and went out again as soon as he had dressed. He is gone to dine at the Army and Navy."

"Then no elucidation can now take place until morning," observed Mr. Grubb, as the servant withdrew. "When he has gone out lately on these dining bouts he does not get home till late, sometimes not at all. But rely upon it, Howard, this matter will be cleared up satisfactorily, so far as he is concerned. Though what the mystery attending the cheque can be, I am not able to imagine."

"I'm sure I am not, looking at it from your point of view," returned the elder man. "See here: you come down to Leadenhall Street on Saturday morning, and find you have left the cheque-book of the firm at home here. You send Charles Cleveland for it, telling him to take a cab and to make haste. After being away three or four times as long as he need be, he comes back with the cheque-book, having found it, he says, where you had told him it probably would be found—in the room where you breakfasted. He does not account for his delay, except by the excuse that he was doing an errand for himself, and begs pardon for it. Well and good. Today we find that a cheque has been abstracted from that same cheque-book, filled in for five hundred pounds, and was cashed by Cleveland himself; all during this same interval on Saturday morning when he declines to account for his time. What do you make of it?"

Put thus plainly before him, Mr. Grubb did not know what to make of it, and his faith in Charles Cleveland began to waver. The most confiding mind cannot fight altogether against palpable facts. Mr. Howard opened his pocketbook, took the cheque in question from it, and laid it, open, before his senior partner.

"This is not Cleveland's writing," remarked Mr. Grubb.

"Of course not. It is an imitation of yours. That is, not his ordinary handwriting. He has done it pretty cleverly. Glyn's were deceived. Not but that I consider Glyn's clerk was incautious not to see the difference between 'self' and 'selves.' He says he did not notice the word at all: but he ought to have noticed it."

"It is a singular affair altogether," observed Mr. Grubb, in a musing tone. "To begin with, my bringing home the cheque-book at all was singular. You were not in the City on Friday, you know, Howard, and—"

"I couldn't come when I was ill," grunted out Mr. Howard.

"My dear, good old friend, do you suppose I thought you could?" answered Mr. Grubb, checking a laugh. "I was going to say that, as you were absent, I signed the cheques on Friday, and the book lay on my desk. It happened that my private cheque-book also lay there. When I left, I put the firm's cheque-book in my pocket by mistake, and locked up the other; meaning, of course, to do just the contrary. But for this carelessness on my part, Charles Cleveland would not have had the opportunity of—Good Heavens! what a blow this will be for his father! We must hush it up!"

"Hush it up!" cried out the other and sterner man of business. "Not if I know it. That's just like you, Francis Grubb! Your uncle Francis, my many years' friend, used to accuse you, you know, of having a soft place in your heart."

"I am thinking of that good man, with his many cares, the Rector of Netherleigh."

"And I am thinking of his son's bold, barefaced iniquity. Be you very sure of one thing, sir—Glyn's won't hush it up; they are the wrong people to do it. Neither must you. A pretty example it would be! No, thank you, no more wine! I have had my quantum."

"Well, well, we shall see, Howard. I cannot understand it yet."

When Mr. Grubb got upstairs that night, he found his wife gone out, leaving no message for him. She never did leave any. Darvy thought her lady had gone to the opera. Mr. Grubb followed, and found her there. The box was full, and there was little room for him. He said nothing to her of what had occurred: he meant to keep it from her if he could, to save her pain; and from all others, for the Honourable and Reverend Mr. Cleveland's sake.

Mr. Grubb sat down to breakfast the next morning alone. Lady Adela had not risen; Charles Cleveland did not make his appearance.

"Does Mr. Charles Cleveland know I am at breakfast, Hilson?" he inquired of the butler, who was in attendance.

"Mr. Charles Cleveland left word—I beg your pardon, sir, I forgot to mention it—that he has gone out to breakfast with his brother, Captain Cleveland, who sails today for India. He went out between six and seven."

"He came home last night, then?"

"Yes, sir; about one o'clock."

Mr. Grubb glanced over the letters waiting beside his plate, some for himself, some for Lady Adela. Amidst the former was one from his sister, written the previous day. Her mother (who had been seriously ill for some time) was much worse, she said, and she begged her brother to come down, if possible, in the morning.

It chanced that Mr. Grubb had made one or two appointments for people to see him that morning at his house; so that it was eleven o'clock when he reached Leadenhall Street.

"Well, where is he?" began Mr. Howard, without ceremony of greeting.

"Where's who?" asked Mr. Grubb.

"Charles Cleveland."

"What—is he not come yet?" returned Mr. Grubb, whose thoughts had been elsewhere.

"Not yet. I don't think he means to come."

To be late, or in any other way inattentive to his duties, had not been one of Charley's sins. Therefore his absence was the more remarkable. Mr. Grubb started for Blackheath, almost endorsing Mr. Howard's opinion that the delinquent had embarked with his brother for India; or for some other place not speedily accessible to officers of justice.

Twelve o'clock was striking by St. Paul's when Charley bustled in; hot, and out of breath. He was told that Mr. Howard wanted him.

"I beg your pardon, sir, for being so late," he panted, addressing himself to that gentleman, when he reached his private room, "especially after my holiday of yesterday. I went early this morning to Woolwich, and on board ship with my brother, intending to be back by business hours; but, what with one delay and another, I was unable to get up till now."

"It is not business-like at all, sir," growled the old merchant. "But—stay a bit, Mr. Cleveland; we have a few questions to put to you."

Charles glanced round. In his hurry, he had seen no one but Mr. Howard. His eye now fell on a little man, who sat in a corner. Charley knew him to be connected with Messrs. Glyn's house; and he knew that the time was at hand when he would have need of all his presence of mind and his energies. It chanced that this gentleman had just called to enquire if anything had come to light about the mysterious cheque.

"You presented a cheque for five hundred pounds at Glyn's on Saturday morning, and received the amount in notes," began Mr. Howard, to Charles. "From whom did you get that cheque?"

No reply.

"Purporting to be drawn and signed by Mr. Grubb. I ask from whom you received it?"

"I decline to answer," Charles said at length, speaking with hesitation, in spite of his preparation for firmness.

"Do you deny having presented the cheque?"

"No. I do not deny that."

"Do you deny having received the money for it?" interposed the gentleman from the bank.

"Nor that, either. I acknowledge to having received five hundred pounds. It would be worse than folly to deny it," continued Charles to him, in a sort of calm desperation, "since your clerk could prove the contrary."

"But did you know what you were laying yourself open to?" cried Mr. Howard, evidently in a marvel of astonishment, for he took these admissions of Charles's to be tantamount to an absolute acknowledgment of his guilt.

"I know now, sir."

"Will you refund the money?" asked Mr. Howard, dropping his voice; for that stern man of business had been going over the affair half the night as he lay in bed, and concluded to give the reckless young fellow a chance. Truth to say, Mr. Howard's bark was always worse than his bite. "Out of consideration for your family, connected, as it is, with that of the head of our firm, we are willing to be lenient; and if you will confess, and refund—"

"I cannot refund, and I must decline to answer any more questions," interrupted Charles, fast relapsing into agitation.

Mr. Howard stared at him. "Do you understand, young man, what it is that you would bring upon your head? In point of fact, we are laying ourselves open to, I hardly know what penalty of law, in making you this offer; but Mr. Grubb is anxious it should be hushed up for your father's sake—whom every one respects. If you decline it; if you set me at defiance, as it seems to me you wish to do; I shall have no resource but to give you into custody."

"I beg to state that the matter is not in our hands yet," spoke up the banker to Charles. "If it were, we could not make you any such offer. Though of course we can fully understand and appreciate the motives that actuate your principals, with whom the affair at present wholly rests. It would be a terrible blow to fall on the Cleveland family; and every one must wish to save them from it."

"I—I am very sorry," gasped Charles, feeling all this to his heart's core. "Unfortunately—"

"The matter is not known beyond ourselves," interposed Mr. Howard again, indicating himself and the banker; "and it need not be. But it is solely out of consideration for your family, you understand, that we offer to hush it up. Will you explain?"

"I cannot. Unfortunately, I cannot, sir. It is not in my power?"

"Then I give you in charge at once."

"I can't help it," said poor Charles, passing his hand over his hot brow.

Mr. Howard, very hard, very uncompromising when deliberately provoked, was as good as his word. And Charles Cleveland was given into custody for forgery.

CHAPTER XXII

"THAT IT MAY BE WELL WITH US IN AFTER-LIFE"

It was all over and done with long before Mr. Grubb got up from Blackheath in the afternoon. He felt terribly vexed. Vexed for Charles himself, terribly vexed for Charles's family, vexed on his own score. To his refined and sensitive mind, it almost seemed that he had violated the sacred laws of hospitality, for Charles had been staying, as a guest, in his house.

The first thing he did was to hasten to the prison to which Charles had been conveyed, preparatory to his examination on the morrow. The young man was in his cell, sitting on the edge of his narrow bed, and looking very downhearted. The entrance of Mr. Grubb seemed to bring to him a sudden flash of hope. He started up.

"Oh, sir," he exclaimed, in high excitement, "will you not look over this one error? My father will replace the money—I am sure he will, rather than suffer this public disgrace to fall upon the family. Do not force the shame upon him. And—and there's my brother—just embarked—what will he do? Oh, Mr. Grubb, if you will but have mercy!

"Charles—don't excite yourself like this—I have come here to offer you the mercy," spoke Mr. Grubb; and his considerate manner, his voice of music, were just like a healing balm. "I have come straight from Mr. Howard to renew the offer he made you. It is not yet too late: we will make things right tomorrow: there will be no prosecutor, you understand. Will you give me, myself only, the particulars you denied to Mr. Howard?"

Just for one eager moment the wish flashed across Charles's mind that he might tell the truth to this good man. Was he not Adela's husband, and would he not excuse her in his love? The next, he saw how futile was the wish. Could he be the one to betray her?—and to her husband? Shame upon him for the thought! He had vowed to her to hold her harmless, and he would do so for her sake.

"To me it appears that there is a mystery in the affair which I cannot fathom," continued Mr. Grubb. "Your conduct in it is perfectly incomprehensible. It may be better for you to confide in me, Charles."

"I cannot, sir. I wish I could."

"What if I tell you that, in spite of appearances, I do not myself believe you guilty?"

A bright, eager flush, a glance as of mutual understanding illumined for a moment Charley's face. It seemed to say that just, honourable natures know and trust in each other's innocence, no matter what may be the surrounding signs of guilt. But the transient expression faded away to sadness, and Mr. Grubb was in doubt whether it had really been there.

"I can explain nothing," said the prisoner. "I can only thank you, sir, for this proof of confidence, and implore your clemency on the ground of compassion alone."

"Charles Cleveland, this won't do. You are either guilty or innocent. Which is it?"

"Guilty, of course," said Charley, in his desperation. For if he said "innocent," the next rejoinder would be, "Then who is guilty?" And he could not answer that, or any other close question.

"Did you do this vile thing of your own accord; or were you induced to do it by another?" pursued Mr. Grubb, his head running upon Charley's debts and Charley's fast companions.

"I—I—pray do not ask me more, sir! It is a wretched business, and I must suffer for it."

"Am I to understand that you wholly refuse to confide in me?—refuse to be helped? I would be your true friend."

"I must refuse," gasped poor Charley. "I have nothing to tell. I did present the cheque at Glyn's, and I drew the money. And—and I hope you will forgive me, sir, for I am very miserable."

"Is all the money spent?"

"I—I have not as much as a shilling of it. If I had, I'd give it back. It's too late."

Nothing better than this could Mr. Grubb wring from the unfortunate prisoner. And he left him believing he was guilty. He left in rather an angry mood, too, for he thought Charles was bearing out Mr. Howard's report, and showing himself defiantly, ungratefully obstinate. That he had been in some most pressing and perhaps dangerous difficulty on the Saturday morning, and had used these desperate means to extricate himself, must be, he concluded, the fact. A great deal of his compassion for Charles melted away; the young man seemed hardened.

In the morning the case was taken before the magistrates. It was heard in private. The influential house, Grubb and Howard, could have commanded a greater concession than that. One magistrate only sat, a very pliable one, Sir Turtle Kite. The case was only slightly gone into, the prosecutors asking for a remand until the following week: they wished to trace out more particulars, also wished to trace the notes. Then the prisoner would be brought up again; and meanwhile he was consigned to that awful place, Newgate.

In spite of all efforts to keep it secret, the affair partially got wind. Not, however, in its true details. All kinds of exaggerated rumours and surmises ran the round of the clubs. But for the recent sojourn of Captain Cleveland in London, Charley might have remained quite an obscure individual, as regarded the fashionable world. But he had been a great deal with his brother, and was known and liked everywhere.

What a commotion arose! Charles Cleveland in Newgate on a charge of robbery, or forgery, or what not! Charley Cleveland, the popular—Charley Cleveland, the grandson of an earl gathered to his fathers, and nephew of one who stood in his shoes—Charley Cleveland, the out-and-out good fellow, who was wont to scare the blue-devils away from every one—Charley Cleveland, who, in defiance of his improvidence and his shallow pocket, was known to be of the nicest honour amongst the honourable!

"The thing's altogether preposterous," stuttered John Cust, who had a natural stammer. "If Charley had drawn the money he would have had the money, and I know that on Saturday afternoon he had not a rap, for he borrowed three sovs. of me to take him down to Brighton—"

"Netherleigh, Cust."

"Netherleigh, then. What put Brighton in my head, I wonder? Fancy he went to try to get some money out of his governor."

"Which he did," added Lord Deerham. "A five-pound note."

"And paid me back the three sovs. on the Monday night, when he came to his brother's spread at the Rag and Famish," continued John Cust. "Gammon! Charley has not been making free with any one's name."

"But he acknowledges to having drawn the money," squeaked Booby Charteris. "A thousand pounds, they say."

"You may take that in yourself, Booby. We don't."

"But the Lord Mayor—"

"Lord Mayor be hanged! If he swears till he's black in the face that Charley did it, I know he didn't. There."

"'Twasn't the Lord Mayor. Some other of those City bigwigs."

"Anyway, he is in Newgate. It's said, too, that it is Grubb and Howard who have sent him there."

"Did he rob their cash-box?"

"Do they accuse him of it, you mean, Booby. As if Charley would do such a thing!"

"Let us go down to Newgate, and have a smoke with him," cried Charteris, who had so small a share of brains and so very small a voice as to have acquired the nickname of Booby. "It may cheer the young fellow up, under the present alarming state of things."

"As if they'd admit us inside Newgate, or a smoke either!" retorted John Cust. "There's only one thing more difficult than getting into Newgate, and that is, if you are in, getting out again. Don't forget that, Booby."

"Couldn't some of us go and punch a few heads down there, beginning with old Howard's?" again proposed Booby. "I don't say Grubb's."

"Grubb has had nothing to do with bringing the charge; you may rely upon that," said Lord Deerham. "Grubb's a gentleman. You shut up, Booby."

Ah! it was all very well for these idle, foolish young men to express their sympathy with the prisoner in their idle, foolish way: but, what of the distress of those connected with him?

Thomas Cleveland, Honourable and Reverend, heard from his wife, who was still staying at her mother's, that something was amiss, and came up from Netherleigh to find his son incarcerated in Newgate, and accused of forgery. Down he went to the prison at once, and obtained admission. Charley looked, in that short period, greatly changed. His dress was neglected, his hair unkempt, and his face haggard. Charley, the fastidious!

Mr. Cleveland was overcome beyond control, and sobbed aloud. He was a venerable-looking man of nearly sixty years now, and had always been a fond father. Charley was little less affected.

"Why did you not kill me when you last came down, Charles?" he moaned out in his perplexity and anguish. "Better have put me out of this world of pain than bring this misery upon me. Oh, my boy! my boy! you were your mother's favourite: how can you so have disgraced her memory?"

"I would I had been put out of the world, rather than be the curse to you I have proved," writhed Charley, wishing Newgate would yawn asunder and engulph him. "Oh, don't—father, don't!" he implored, as Mr. Cleveland's sobs echoed through the cell. "If it will be a consolation to you to know it, I will avow to you that I am not guilty," he added, the sight of his father's affliction momentarily outweighing his precaution. "By all your care of me, by your present grief, by the memory of my dead mother, I swear to you that I am not guilty."

Mr. Cleveland looked up, and his heart leaped within him. He knew Charles was speaking truth. It was impossible to mistake that earnest tone.

"Thank God!" he murmured. "But what, then, is this I hear, about your declining to make a defence?" he presently asked. "I am told you have as good as acknowledged your guilt." Charles hung his head, and relapsed into prudence again.

"My boy, answer me. How came you to accept—as it were—the charge, if you are innocent?"

"For your private comfort I have said this, dear father, but it must remain between us as if it had not been spoken. The world must still, and always, believe me guilty."

"But why?—why? What mystery is this?"

"Do not ask me, sir. Believe that you have not a son more free from the guilt of this crime than I am. Nevertheless, I must pay the penalty, for I cannot defend myself."

Mr. Cleveland thought this about the most extraordinary thing he had ever met with. Nothing more could be got out of Charles; nevertheless, he did believe in his innocence. From Newgate he went on to Leadenhall Street, to see the gentlemen who had brought this charge, and found only one of them in: Mr. Grubb.

"You are not more pained at the affair than I am," said the latter, closing the door of his private room, "and certainly not more astonished."

"Oh, Mr. Grubb," cried the clergyman, "could you not have hushed this wretched disgrace up, for all our sakes?—or at least made more inquiries before taking these extreme steps? You who have shown so much true friendship for me!"

"I would have hushed it up. I wished to hush it up altogether. I would have paid the money over and over again out of my own pocket, rather than it should have become known, even to Mr. Howard. It was he, however, who brought the tidings of it to me."

"And Mr. Howard would not?"

"Mr. Howard would. At first he seemed inclined to be hard. Thorough business men look upon these things with a stern eye. However, he knew my wishes, and came to. He was the first to speak to Charles. He asked him to acknowledge the truth to him, and he would forgive it. Charles refused; set him, so to say, at defiance; told him, I believe, to do his best and his worst; and Mr. Howard gave him into custody."

"It is very strange."

"When I found what had happened—I had been out of town that day—I went at once to Charles. I told him that I could not believe him guilty, and I entreated him to tell me the circumstances of the case, which looked to me then, and look still, unaccountably mysterious—"

"And he would not?" interrupted Mr. Cleveland, recalling how Charles had just met a similar request from himself.

"He would not tell me a word: told me he would not. I said I could even then set matters straight, and would get his release on the morrow, and nothing about it should ever transpire. He thanked me, but said he had nothing to tell; was, in fact, guilty. I could only think he must be guilty, and left him with that impression on my mind."

"It is altogether very strange," repeated Mr. Cleveland, in a musing tone, as he sat stroking his face and thinking. "Will you state the particulars to me, as far as you are cognizant of them. I asked Charles to do so, but he would not."

"It occurred on Saturday morning," began Mr. Grubb. "When I reached the City, here, I found I had not got with me the cheque-book of the firm, which I had taken away by mistake the previous evening; and I sent Charles home to look for it. He was a long while gone, but brought it when he came. During the period of his absence one of the cheques was abstracted, filled up for five hundred pounds, and—"

"Filled up by whom?"

"The writing was an imitation of mine. Charles presented it at Glyn's, and got it cashed. All this he acknowledges to; but he refuses to say what he did with the money."

"Mr. Grubb," cried the agitated father, "appearances are against him—were never, I perceive, more strongly against any one; but, before Heaven I believe him to be innocent."

Mr. Grubb made no reply.

"He has assured me of his innocence by the memory of his dead mother; and innocent I am sure he must be. He stated in the same breath that he should avow it to no one else, but submit to the penalty of the crime just as though he had committed it. As to what he did with the money—he could not have used it for himself. On that very Saturday afternoon he had to borrow money to bring him down to Netherleigh the next morning. John Cust lent it him."

"It is very singular," acknowledged Mr. Grubb.

"Charles confessed as much to me at Netherleigh—that he had borrowed the money from Cust to get down with; three pounds, I think it was. I gave him a five-pound note, and a lecture with it. He promised to be more cautious for the future, and said that after Harry left he should not have occasion to spend much—which is true. But now, what I would like to know is this—if he drew that money, that five hundred pounds, where is it? How came it that the next hour, so to say, he had none in his pocket?"

Mr. Grubb certainly could not answer, and remained silent.

"Has he been made the instrument of another?" returned Mr. Cleveland. "Was be imposed upon by any one?—sent to cash a cheque that he himself thought was a genuine and proper cheque?"

"That is scarcely likely. Were it the case, what objection could he have to declare it? My opinion is—I am sorry to have to give it—that Charles had got into some desperate money trouble, and used desperate remedies to extricate himself."

"What more desperate trouble could he be in than this?"

"True. But he may have hoped we should be lenient. Even now," added Mr. Grubb, his voice trembling with the concern he felt; "we might be able to save him if he would only disclose the truth. Mr. Howard absolutely refuses to quash the matter unless he does so: and I think he is right."

"But Charles won't disclose it; he won't," bewailed the clergyman, taking the other's hand in token of his gratitude. "Look here, my dear friend," he added, after a pause of thought, "can Charles be keeping silence to screen some one?"

"To screen some one? How?"

"That he did this thing willingly, with his eyes open, I never will believe. It is not in a Cleveland's nature to commit a crime. Moreover, I repeat to you that he has just assured me of his innocence by the memory of his dead mother. No, no; whatever may be the facts, Charles was not wilfully guilty. I could stake my life upon it. In cashing that cheque he must have been made the innocent tool of another, whom he won't betray out of some chivalrous feeling of honour."

"But no one had possession of the cheque-book but Charles," reasoned Mr. Grubb. "He found it in the breakfast-room where I had left it. My servants are honest; they would not touch it. Moreover, it was Charles himself who presented the cheque for payment, and got the money."

Mr. Cleveland rubbed his grey hair back with a look of perplexity; hair that was getting scanty now. Look at the case in what way he would, it presented contradictions and difficulties that seemed to be insuperable.

"You are staying at Lord Acorn's, I suppose?" remarked Mr. Grubb, when the clergyman rose to leave.

"Until Saturday. I can't run away from London and leave my boy in Newgate. Heaven be with you! I know you'll do for him what you can."

The whole of the after-part of this day certain words spoken by the unhappy father haunted Francis Grubb. In cashing that cheque he must have been made the innocent tool of another, whom he won't betray, out of some chivalrous feeling of honour. An idea had been presented to him which he might never have taken up of himself; a painful idea; and, do what he would, he could not drive it away. It intruded itself into his business; it followed him home to dinner; and it worried him while he ate it. He had not found Lady Adela at home. She was dining out somewhere. Certainly, Mr. Grubb's domestic life was not a very sociable one. After dinner, he went to his club.

It was eleven o'clock before he got home; later than he meant to be, but he did not expect his wife to be there yet. The butler, a trustworthy, semi-confidential servant, who had entered the service of the uncle, Francis Grubb, when his present master was a boy, and who had become greatly attached to him, came to the drawing-room to see if anything was wanted.

"Is Lady Adela in?" asked his master.

"No, sir. Her ladyship came in not long ago, for a minute or two, and went out again."

"Stay a minute, Hilson," cried Mr. Grubb, as the man was turning away. "Shut the door. Carry your memory back to last Saturday. Did you happen to see Mr. Charles Cleveland come in that morning?"

"Yes, sir: I was at the front-door, talking to one of Lady Acorn's servants, who had brought a parcel for my lady. Mr. Cleveland jumped out of the cab he was in, and ran past me all in a hurry, saying he had come to look for something the master had left behind him."

"Did he go at once to the room where I breakfasted?"

"No, sir. My lady chanced to be descending the stairs at the moment; Mr. Cleveland asked her where Mr. Grubb had breakfasted, and she turned with him into the small room. In a minute or two, it could not have been more, he came running out again, leaped into the cab, and went away in it at a great rate. That was the first time, sir."

Mr. Grubb lifted his eyes. "The first time! What do you mean?"

"Mr. Charles Cleveland came back again, sir. Not directly; half-an-hour or three-quarters later it may have been, perhaps more, I had not taken particular note of the time. I was in the hall then, watching John clean the lamp—he has done it slovenly of late. The front-door was rung and knocked at as if it was going to be knocked down. I opened it, and Mr. Charles Cleveland rushed past me up to the drawing-room. I never hardly saw anybody in a greater hurry than he seemed to be. He came down again directly, my lady with him, and they went into the breakfast-room. He then ran out to the cab, and drove away at a fiercer rate than before."

"Was it the same cab?"

"Oh yes, sir. Taking both times together, he was not in the house three minutes."

"Not long enough to—" Mr. Grubb checked himself, and remained silent.

"Not long enough to have drawn a false cheque, sir, when the handwriting has to be studied—as we have been saying below," put in the butler, following too closely his master's thoughts.

Mr. Grubb felt disagreeably startled. "Hilson! what are you saying? Who has talked of this below?"

"Only Darvy, sir. She got to know of it this morning, through— Well, sir, I believe through a letter that my lady gave her to read."

"But how was that?" questioned Mr. Grubb, in a displeased tone.

"It was through a mistake of my lady's, sir," replied Alison, dropping his voice. "She had meant to give Darvy a note from Madame Damereau, about the trimming of a dress; instead of that, she gave her one from Lady Grace. Darvy has been uneasy ever since, and she spoke in confidence to me."

"Why uneasy?"

"Well, sir, Darvy thinks it an unpleasant thing to have happened, especially for us upper servants. The cheque must have been torn out and filled in by somebody."

"Nonsense," interposed Mr. Grubb. "Take care you do not speak of this, Hilson; and caution Darvy."

"No fear of me, sir; you know that. I told Darvy she must have misunderstood Lady Grace's note, and that she must hold her tongue; and I am sure she will. She was very sorry to have read it. She asked my lady's instructions as to the dress, and my lady tossed the note to her, saying she would find them there. Darvy read on to the very end, expecting to come to them. That's how it was, sir."

Mr. Grubb remained on alone, deep in painful thought, his head bent on his hand. His vague suspicions were strengthening—strengthening terribly.

And what of Lady Adela? This could not have been a good time for her—as the children say. Made aware that morning by Grace's letter that Charles was taken into custody, she was seized with terror; and perhaps it was not so much carelessness as utter bewilderment that caused the stupid error of handing the wrong letter to Darvy. Adela saw her father in the course of the day. Too anxious to remain passive, she went out to hear what she could at Lord Acorn's, putting to him a cautious word of inquiry. Lord Acorn made light of the whole business—he did not yet know the particulars. Charley would soon be released, he carelessly said; Grubb would take care of that. As to a little fright, or a short incarceration, it would do Master Charley good—he had been going the pace of late. And this opinion of her father's so completely reassured Lady Adela, that her fears of consequences to Charley subsided: she returned home, took up her visiting, and was her own saucy self again.

She came in early tonight, before twelve o'clock, looking cross: Her husband rose from his chair, and smoothed his troubled face.

"Where have you been, Adela?"

"At Lady Sanely's:" and the tone of defiance audible in Lady Adela's answer arose from the consciousness that he had forbidden her to go there. The dissatisfied face she brought back with her, and the early hour of her return, seemed to say that she had not met with much pleasure there this evening. Perhaps she had staked, and lost, all the money she had taken; or, perhaps play was not going on that night.

She threw herself into a chair, eating a biscuit she had caught up from a plate on the table, and let her mantle fall from her shoulders. How very pretty she looked! Her dress was white lace, trimmed about with small blush roses; her cheeks were a lovely flush; a pearl necklace, of priceless value, lay on her fair neck, bracelets to match encircled her slender arms: one of the many magnificent gifts of her fond husband.

"Don't shut the door," cried Adela, tartly, for he had crossed the room to do it. "I'm sure it's hot enough."

"Ah, but I want to say a few words to you," he replied, as he closed it. And the Lady Adela, divining by a subtle instinct which penetrates to us all at odd moments, one cannot tell how or wherefore, that the subject of his "few words" was to be Charley's trouble, and not her transgression as to Lady Sanely's, armed herself for reprisal. Adela never felt sure afterwards that she had not been wicked enough to put up a hasty prayer for aid. Aid to be firm in disguising the truth: aid to blind him as to her share in the past Saturday's exploit, and to strengthen the accusation against Charley. Rising from her seat, she crossed to the nearest window and threw it open, as if needing a breath of the soft midnight air.

"This is a sad business about Charles Cleveland, Adela. I find you know of it."

"Yes," she answered, fanning away a moth that was floating in, attracted by the light. "I hope you are satisfied with your work. You had a paltry spite against him, and you have cast him into Newgate to gratify it."

"Adela, you know better."

"It is enough to ruin his prospects for life. It would ruin some people's—they who are without influential connections. Of course Charley will soon be on his legs again, and laugh at his paltry enemies."

Mr. Grubb put his hand, almost caressingly, on his wife's arm, and caused her to turn her face to him. "Will you tell me what you know of this, my dear?"

"Tell you what I know of it!—how should I know anything of it?" she retorted, flirting her costly fan. "Poor Charley may have meant to borrow the money for a day or two—I don't accuse him; I only say it may have been so—and then to have replaced it: but you and that old kangaroo of a partner of yours have prevented his doing it. To gratify your own revenge you seized upon him before he had time to act, and threw him into that place of crime where men are hung from—Newgate. You did it to bring disgrace upon my family, through my sister Mary."

He did not reply to this; he was accustomed to her unjust accusations.

"Adela," he said, dropping his voice to a whisper, "were you wholly ignorant of this business? Who drew the cheque?"

She turned round with a start, defiance in her eyes.

"Adela, my wife," he whispered, gently laying both hands upon her shoulders in his earnestness, "if you had anything to do with this business, if Charles Cleveland was not the guilty party, acknowledge it now. Confide in me for once. I will avert consequences from him and suspicion from you. The secret shall be buried in my breast, and I will never revert to it."

Oh, what possessed her that she did not respond to this loving appeal in time? Was it pure fright that prevented her? Shame?—Shame to have to confess to her guilt? Any way, she steeled her heart against it. Her lovely features had grown white, and her eyes fell before his. Presently she raised them, flashing with indignation, her tone, her words, as haughty as you please.

"Mr. Grubb, how dare you offer me this insult?"

"Do not meet me in this way, Adela. I am asking you a solemn question; remember that there is One above Who will hear and register your answer. Were you the principal in this transaction, and was

Cleveland but your agent? Do not fear to trust me—your husband: you shall have my free forgiveness, now, beforehand, my shelter, my protection. Only tell me the truth, as you wish it to be well with us both in after-life."

Again she cowered before his gaze, and again recovered herself. Could it be that her better angel was prompting her to the truthful path?

"What can possibly have induced you to put such a question to me?"

"It is an idea that has forced itself upon my mind. Without some such explanation the affair is to me an utter mystery. If Charles Cleveland—"

"And don't you think you ought to be ashamed of yourself!" she interrupted. "I rob a bank! I steal a cheque! Has it come to this—that you suspect me?"

"Forgive me, Adela, if I am wrong. Be it how it may, you should meet me differently. Oh, my wife, let there be perfect confidence between us at this moment, on this subject. Tell me the truth, as before Heaven!"

"Am I in the habit of telling you untruths? I thought the truths I tell you were generally a little too plain to be pleasant," she added, in her bravado. "None but a mean-spirited man could so suspect his wife."

"This is all you have to say to me, Adela—your definite answer?"

"Definite enough," she retorted, with a nervous sob, between a laugh and a cry; for, what with fear and discomfort, she was becoming slightly hysterical.

"I am bound to believe you, Adela," he said, the tears in her eyes disarming his latent doubts. "I do believe you. But—"

"And now that you have had your say, listen to me," she interrupted, choking down all better feelings and speaking with contemptuous anger. "Never speak on the subject to me again if you would keep up the semblance of peace between us. My spirit is being dangerously aroused against you, Mr. Grubb; not only for this injustice to me, but for your barbarous treatment of poor Charles Cleveland."

Once more, he knew not why or wherefore, something like a doubt returned to Mr. Grubb's mind. He held her before him.

"It has been the truth, Adela?—as I hope, and pray, and trust! I ask it you once again—that it may be well with us in after-life."

"Would I trouble myself to tell a falsehood about it to you! Do you think I have no feeling—that I should bear such distrust? And if you would recompense me for this mauvais quart d'heure, you will release that poor fellow tomorrow—for his father's sake."

She flung her husband's arm away and quitted the room, leaving him to his feelings. Few can imagine them—torn, outraged, thrown back upon his generous heart. But she had certainly managed to dispel his doubts of herself. No guilty woman, as he believed, could have faced it out as she did.

"It must have been Cleveland's own act and deed, and no other person's," he mentally concluded. "What madness could have come over the lad?"

CHAPTER XXIII

One of the most able counsellors of the day, Mr. Serjeant Mowham, chanced to be intimately acquainted with the Rector of Netherleigh; and the unhappy father despatched him to Newgate, in a friendly, not in a legal capacity, to see what he could do with or for the prisoner.

He could not do much. The old saying, "Tell your whole case to your lawyer and your doctor," is essential advice, but Charles Cleveland would tell nothing, neither truth nor falsehood. In vain Serjeant Mowham protested, with tears in his eyes (a stock of which, so the Bar affirmed, he kept in readiness), that he was working in the dark, working for pure friendship's sake, and that without some clue or hint to go upon, no defence that had a chance of success could be made, even though his advocate before the judge told all the untruths that ever advocate's tongue gave utterance to. The prisoner was immovable, and Serjeant Mowham in despair.

How matters really would have ended, and whether Mr. Howard would have allowed it to come to trial, cannot be said, had not fortune been kinder to Charles than he was to himself.

One morning, when the days before the prisoner's second examination were growing few, the Earl of Acorn had a slice of luck. He had backed a certain horse at a provincial race meeting, and the horse won. Amongst other moneys that changed hands was a fifty-pound note. An hour after the earl received it he made his way into his drawing-room in haste, where sat his daughters, Grace, and Mary Cleveland; the latter with her infant on her lap.

"Mary," cried the earl, "what were the numbers of the notes paid over to Charles Cleveland at Glyn's? I partly remember them, but not quite."

"My husband has the numbers," answered Lady Mary. "But the thing has given me by far too much worry, papa, for me to retain them in my head. I am not sure I ever heard them."

"I have them," interrupted Grace. "I copied them the other day. There was no knowing, I thought, but it might prove useful."

"Quite right, Gracie, girl," said the earl. "Let's see them: 'A/Y 3, 0, 2, 5, 5,'" continued Lord Acorn, reading one of the numbers which Lady Grace laid before him. "I thought so. One of these notes has just been paid to me, Mary, by young Waterware."

"Where did he get it?" eagerly inquired Grace.

"I did not ask him. It was only since I left him that I noticed the number. I'll get it out of him by-and-by."

"At once, at once, sir," urged Mary. "Oh, papa, do go to him. I feel sure Charles is not guilty."

"No impatience, Mary. Where the deuce am I to pick up Waterware at this time of day? I might as well look for a needle in a bottle of hay. Tonight I shall know where to find him."

Chance, however, favoured the earl. In strolling up St. James's Street in the afternoon, he met Lord Waterware.

"I say, Waterware," he began, linking his arm in that of the younger peer, "where did you get that fifty-pound note you gave me this morning?"

"Where did I get it? Let's see. Oh, from Nile. He was owing me a hundred pounds, and paid me yesterday. That fifty, two twenties, and a ten. Why? It's not forged, I suppose," cried the young nobleman, with a yawn.

"Not exactly. Wish I had a handful of them. Good-day. I'm going on to Nile's."

Colonel Nile, though addicted to playing a little at cards for what he called amusement, and sometimes did it for tolerably high stakes, was a very different man from those other men mentioned in this history—Colonel Haughton and Mr. Piggott, who had led Robert Dalrymple to his ruin. They were professed gamblers, and had disappeared from good society long ago. Colonel Nile was a popular member of it, liked and respected.

Lord Acorn found him at home, walking about in a flowery dressing-gown. He was a middle-aged man and a bachelor, and well off.

"The fifty-pound note I paid over to Waterware," cautiously repeated Colonel Nile, somewhat surprised at the question, and wondering whether random young Waterware had got into any scrape. "Why do you want to know where I got it?"

"Because it is one of the notes that Charley Cleveland is in trouble for: the first of them that has been traced. You must give me the information, Nile, or I shall apply for it publicly."

"Oh, I have no objection in the world," cried the colonel, determined to afford all that was in his power, and so wash his hands of any unpleasantness that might turn up. "I received it at Lady Sanely's loo table, from— Egad! from your own daughter, Lady Adela."

"From Lady Adela!" echoed the surprised listener.

"From Lady Adela, and nobody else," repeated Colonel Nile. "She paid another fifty to the old Dowager Beck the same evening."

Lord Acorn stared. "But surely they don't play as high as that there!"

"Don't they, though! and higher too. To tell you the truth, Acorn, it's getting a little too high for prudent people. I, for one, mean to draw in. Old Mother Sanely lives but for cards, and she'd stake her head if it were loose. She has the deuce's own luck, though."

With a mental word, sharp and short, given to his daughter Adela for allowing herself to be mixed up in company and amusement such as this, Lord Acorn brought his attention back to the present moment. "Adela gave another fifty-pound note to Lady Beck, you say, the same evening! Do you happen to know its number?"

"Not I," retorted the colonel, who was not altogether pleased at the question. "I don't make it my business to pry into notes that do not concern me."

"How long is it ago?"

"I hardly know. Nearly a week, I suppose. It is four or five days since I was first confined to the house with this incipient gout. I think it was the night before that—Saturday night."

Lord Acorn proceeded straight to Lady Beck's; and, with much trouble and persuasion, she was induced to exhibit the note spoken of by Colonel Nile, which was still in her possession, for, like the colonel, she had been ill for some days, so had had no opportunity of playing it away. The old dowager was verging on her dotage, and could not, at first, be convinced that the earl was not going to take law proceedings against her for winning money of his daughter. He soothed her, copied the number by stealth, went home, and compared it with Lady Grace's pocketbook. It was another of the notes!

"What do you think of it, Grace?" cried the earl, in perplexity. "Can Cleveland have been owing money to Adela?"

"I should imagine not," replied Lady Grace.

"To think she should be such a little fool as to frequent a place where they play like that!"

"But, papa, you knew of it."

"I did not know old Sanely went in for those ruinous stakes. Five pounds, or so, in a night to risk—I thought no worse than that."

Grace understood now. She had deemed her father indifferent. He was then looking at it from one point of view; she from another.

"It wears a singular appearance," mused the earl. "To tell you the truth, Grace, I don't like the fact of these notes being traced to Adela. It looks—after the rumour of the absurd flirtation they carried on— almost as if she and Cleveland had gone snacks in the spoil. What now, Gracie? Are you going to fly?"

For Lady Grace Chenevix had bounded from her chair in sudden agitation, her arms lifted as if to ward off some dread fear. "Sir! father! the thing has become clear to me. That I should not have suspected it before!—knowing what I did know."

"Child," he cried, gazing at her in amazement, "what is the matter with you?"

"Adela did this. I see it all. She drew the cheque. Charles Cleveland was only her instrument; and, in his infatuated attachment he has taken the guilt on himself, to shield her. Well may he have asserted his innocence to his father! Well may his conduct have appeared to us all so incomprehensible!"

"Why, Grace, you are mad!" gasped the earl. "Accuse your sister of—of—forgery! Do you reflect on the meaning of your words?"

"Father, do not look so sternly at me. I feel sure I am right. I assure you it is as if scales had fallen from my eyes, for I see it perfectly clearly. Adela wanted money for play: she had been drawn in, far deeper than any one suspected, sir, at Lady Sanely's gaming-table. It was Mr. Grubb's intention to refuse her further funds: no doubt he did refuse them: and then—"

"How do you know it was his intention?"

"Oh, papa, I do know it; never mind how, now; I say that Mr. Grubb must have refused her; and she, when this cheque-book fell into her hands—"

"Don't continue, Grace," sharply interposed Lord Acorn; "you make my blood run cold. You must prove what you assert, or retract it. If—it—is proved"—the earl drew a long breath—"Cleveland must be extricated. What a thundering fool the fellow must be?"

"Let me have time to think," said Grace, putting her hand to her head. "Extricated of course he must be, for I know it is true, but—if possible—without exposing Adela."

With the last words, Grace sank back in her chair and burst into a storm of sobs. Lord Acorn was little less moved. They spoke together further, and agreed not to tell Mary Cleveland, in spite of her state of impatience, that Lord Acorn had traced the numbers of the two notes.

Lady Grace decided to confide all to Mr. Grubb. It could not be kept from him long; and she wanted to bespeak his clemency for Adela. So in the evening she proceeded to his house, tolerably sure that her sister would be out somewhere or other. But she found Mr. Grubb also out: at his club, Hilson thought. Grace dismissed her carriage, went up to the drawing-room, and wrote a word to Mr. Grubb, asking him to come home. The thought crossed her, that perhaps it was not quite the thing to do, but Lady Grace Chenevix was not the one to stand upon formal ceremony.

He returned at once, looking rather anxious. "Anything the matter, Grace? Anything amiss with Adela? She's not ill?"

"She is at the opera, I fancy; very well, no doubt." And then she sat down and imparted her suspicions— just an allusion to them—that her poor sister was the culprit.

"Grace," he whispered, "I don't mind telling you that the same fear haunted me, and I spoke to her. She indignantly denied it."

"Two of the notes have been traced," murmured Grace.

"Traced!"

"Paid away by Adela at Lady Sanely's."

There was a dead silence. Lady Grace Chenevix did not raise her eyelids, for she felt keenly the pain of avowal. An ominous shade of despair overspread his face.

"Grace, Grace," he broke forth in anguish, "what is it you are saying?"

"One of them, for fifty pounds, came into my father's hands today, and he has traced it back to Adela," continued Grace, striving to keep down the signs of her pain. "Another of them she paid the same evening to the Dowager Beck. Papa knows of this; he found it out today. What inference can we draw but that Adela— You know what I would say."

"Could she descend to this?" he groaned. "To be a party with Charles Cleveland in—"

"Charles was no party to it," interrupted Grace, warmly; "he must have been her instrument, nothing more. Rely upon that. Whatever may be his follies, he is the soul of honour. And it must be from some chivalrous sense of honour, of noblesse oblige, you understand, that he is continuing to shield her now the matter has come out. What is to be done? Charles Cleveland must not be tried as a felon."

"Heaven forbid!—if he be indeed innocent. But, Grace," thoughtfully added Mr. Grubb, "I cannot but think you are mistaken. Were Adela guilty, she would have acknowledged it to me when I assured her in all tenderness that I would forgive, shield, and protect her."

Grace answered by a despairing gesture. "She would not confess to you for very shame, I fear. Dear Mr. Grubb, what is to be done? We have to save Adela's good name as well as his. You must see Charles, and get the truth from him."

"I would rather get it from Adela."

"If you can. I doubt it. Having denied it once, she will never confess now."

Lady Grace had reason. Mr. Grubb spoke to his wife the following morning. He said that two of the notes had been traced to her possession; and that, for her own sake, she had better explain, while grace was yet held out to her. But he spoke very coolly, without the smallest sign of endearment or tenderness; nay, there was a suspicion of contempt in his tone, and that put Adela's spirit up.

What answered she? Was she quite blind, quite foolish? She persisted in her denial, called him by a scornful name, haughtily ordered him to be silent, and finally marched out of his presence, declaring she would not re-enter it until he could finally drop all allusion to the subject.

With a half-curse on his lips—he, so temperate and sweet-tempered a man!—Mr. Grubb went straight to Newgate, and obtained an interview with the prisoner. It came to nothing satisfactory; Charles was harder in his obstinacy than ever. From thence Mr. Grubb drove back to the West End, to Chenevix House. Some morning visitors were there, and Lady Mary Cleveland was exhibiting her baby to them. Mr. Grubb admired with the rest, and then made a sign to Grace. She followed him into the next room.

"I don't see what is to be done," he began. "Adela will not hear a word, will not admit anything, and I can make nothing of Charles Cleveland. Upon my mentioning Adela—of course, only in hints; I could not accuse my wife outright to him—he interrupted me with a request that I would not introduce Lady Adela's name into so painful a matter; that he had brought the disgrace upon himself, and was prepared to pay for it. I think he may have lent the two notes to Adela. It would be only one hundred pounds out of the five. I cannot believe, if my wife were guilty, that Cleveland would take the penalty upon himself. Transportation for life, or whatever the sentence incurred may be, is no light matter, Grace."

Grace shuddered. "Do not let him incur the risk of it."

"I would rather cut off my right hand than punish a man unjustly, were he my greatest enemy. But unless I can get at the truth of this matter, and find proof that your view of it is correct, I shall have no plea, to my partner, to my bankers, or to my own conscience, for hushing it up; and the law must take its course."

"Alas! alas!" murmured Lady Grace.

"You seem to overlook my feelings in this affair, Grace," he whispered, a deep hue dyeing his cheeks. "That she may have had something to do with it, her paying away the notes proves: and to find the wife of your bosom thus in league with another— You don't know what it is, Grace."

"I can imagine it," she answered, the tears standing in her eyes, as she rose to answer his adieu. "Believe me, you have, and always have had, my deepest and truest sympathy; but Adela is my sister; what more can I say?"

Grace sat on, alone. The murmur of voices came to her from the adjacent room, but she heeded it not. She leaned her head upon her hand, and debated with herself. It was imperative that the real facts of the case should be brought to light; for if Charles Cleveland were permitted to stand his trial, perhaps to suffer the penalty of transportation, and it came out, later, that he was innocent, and her sister the guilty party, what a fearful position would be that of Adela!

Could Charley not be brought to confess through stratagem, mentally debated Grace. Suppose he were led to believe that Adela, to save him, had declared the truth, then he might speak. It was surely a good idea. Grace weighed it, in all its bearings, and thought the end would justify the means. But to whom entrust so delicate a mission? Not to Mr. Cleveland, he would betray it all to Charles at the first sentence; not Mr. Grubb; his high sense of honour would never let him intimate that Adela had confessed what she had not; not to Lady Mary, for her only idea of Newgate was that it was a place overflowing with infectious fevers, which she should inevitably bring home to baby. Lord Acorn? Somehow Grace could not ask him. Who next? Who else was there? Herself? Yes, and Grace felt that none were more fitted for the task than she was—she who had the subject so much at heart. And she resolved to go.

But she could not go alone to Newgate. Her mother ought to be with her. Now the matter, relative to the tracing of the notes to Adela, had been kept from Lady Acorn. Grace disclosed it to her in the emergency, and made her the confidante of what she meant to do.

Lady Acorn sat aghast. For once in her life she was terrified to silence and meekness. Grace obtained her consent, and the time for the expedition was fixed. Not that Lady Acorn relished it.

"If it be as you and your father believe, Grace, Master Charley Cleveland deserves the soundest shaking man ever had yet," cried she, when speech returned to her.

"Ah, mamma! Then what must Adela deserve?"

"To be in Newgate herself," tartly responded Lady Acorn.

CHAPTER XXIV

A DISAGREEABLE EXPEDITION

It was Monday morning. Charles Cleveland sat on his iron bedstead in his dreary cell in Newgate: of which cell he had become heartily tired by this time: chewing there in solitude the cud of his reflections, which came crowding one upon another. None of them were agreeable, as may be imagined, but pressing itself upon him more keenly than all, was the sensation of deep, dark disappointment. Above the discomfort of his present position, above the sense of shame endured, above the hard, degrading life that loomed for him in the future, he felt the neglect of Lady Adela. She, for whom he was bearing all the misery and disgrace in this dreadful dungeon, had never, by letter or by message, sought to convey a ray of sympathy to cheer him. The neglect, the indifference may have been unavoidable, but it told not the less bitterly on the spirit of the prisoner.

A noise at his cell door. The heavy key was turning in the lock, and the prisoner looked up eagerly—a visit was such a break in his dreary day. Two ladies were entering, and his heart beat wildly—wildly; for in the appearance of one he discerned some resemblance to Lady Adela's. Had she come to see him! and he had been so ungratefully blaming her! But the lady raised her veil, and he was recalled to his sober senses. It was only Grace Chenevix.

"So, Charles, an awful scrape you have brought yourself into, through your flirting nonsense with Adela!" began the Countess of Acorn, as she followed her daughter in.

"Now, mamma, dear mamma," implored Grace, in a whisper, "if you interfere, you will ruin all."

"Ruin all! much obliged to you, Grace! I think he has ruined himself," retorted the countess, in a shrill tone. Never famous for a sweet temper or a silent tongue, Lady Acorn was not improved by the trouble that had fallen on them, or by this distasteful expedition which she had been forced, so to say, to take this morning, for she could not allow Grace to come alone. The unhappy prisoner would reap the full benefit of her acrimony.

"I wonder you can look us in the face," she went on to him. "Had any one told me I should sometime walk through Newgate attended by turnkeys, I should have said it was a libel. We came down in a hack cab. I wouldn't have brought the servants here for the world."

"I shall ever feel grateful to you," breathed Charles.

"Oh, never mind about gratitude," unceremoniously interrupted Lady Acorn; "there's no time for it. Let us say what we have to say, Grace, and be gone. I'm all in a tremor, lest those men with keys should come and lock me up. Of course, Charles, you know it has all come out."

Charles looked up sharply.

"Which is more luck than you could have expected," added the countess, while Grace sat on thorns, lest some unlucky admission of her mother's should ruin all, as she had just phrased it, and unable to get a word in edgeways. "Of all brainless simpletons you are the worst. If Adela chose (like the thoughtless, wicked girl she is, though she is my daughter) to write her husband's name to a cheque, was that any reason why you should go hotheaded to work, and make believe you did it? Mr. Grubb is not your husband, and you have no right to his money. Things that the law will permit a wife to do with impunity, you might be run up to the drop for."

"Who has been saying this?" breathed the prisoner, bewildered with the torrent of words, and their signification. "Surely not Lady Adela."

"Charles," interposed Grace, and her quiet tones, after those of the countess, sounded like the lulling of a storm, "there is no necessity for further mystery, or for your continuing to assume the guilt; which, as my mother says, was an unwise step on your part—"

"I did not say unwise," sharply interrupted the countess; "call things by their right names, Lady Grace. It was insanity, and nobody but an idiot would have done it. That's what I said."

"The circumstances are known to us now," went on Grace, speaking quietly. "Poor Adela, at her wits' end for money, drew the cheque, and sent you to cash it. And then, terrified at what she had done, persuaded you to assume the responsibility."

"She did not persuade me," explained Charles, falling completely into the snare, and believing every word that was spoken, yet still anxious to excuse Lady Adela. "I volunteered to bear it. And I would do as much again."

"Charles—mamma, pray let me speak for a minute—had you been present when Adela wrote the cheque, you would been doubly to blame. She—"

Charles shook his head. "I was not present."

"She, poor thing, was excited at the moment, and incapable of reflection, but you ought to have recalled her to reason, and refused to aid in it—for her own sake."

"And of course I should," eagerly answered Mr. Charles, "had I known there was anything wrong about it. She brought me the cheque, ready filled in—"

"When you went up from the City for the cheque-book, on the Saturday morning. Yes, we know all."

"I declare I thought it was Mr. Grubb's writing, if ever I saw his writing in my life. I was not likely to have any other thought—how could I have? And I never recalled the matter to my mind, or knew anything more about it, till the Monday night, when I came up from Netherleigh: as I suppose Lady Adela has told you, if she has told you the rest."

"And then you undertook to shield her," interposed Lady Acorn, "and a glorious mess you have made of it between you. Grace, how you worry! you can speak when I have done. What she did would have been hushed up by her husband for all our sakes, but what you did was a very different matter. And the disgrace you have gratuitously brought upon yourself may yet be blazoned forth to every corner of the United Kingdom."

"And these are all the thanks I get," remarked Charles, striving to speak lightly.

"What other thanks would you like?" remarked the countess. "A service of plate presented to you? You deserve a testimonial, don't you, for having run your head into a noose of this dangerous kind for any woman! And for Adela, of all others, who cares for no one on earth but her blessed self. Not she."

"My mother is right," said Lady Grace, "and it may be as well, Charles, that you should know it. Adela has never cared for you in any way, except as an amusing boy, who could talk nonsense to her when she chose to condescend to listen. If you have thought anything else—"

"I never had a disloyal thought to Lady Adela," interrupted Charles, warmly. "Or to her husband—who has always been so kind to me. I would have warded all such—all ill—from her with my life."

"And nicely she has repaid you!" commented Lady Acorn. "Do you suppose she would have confessed this herself?—no, we found it out. She would have let you suffer, and never said 'Thank you.' I tell you this, Master Charley; and I hope you will let it prove to you what the smiles of a heartless butterfly of a married woman are worth."

He bit his dry and fevered lips with mortification—fevered for her. And Lady Acorn, after bestowing a few more unpalatable truths upon the unhappy prisoner, took her daughter's arm and hurried away, glad to escape from the place and the interview.

"A capital success we have had, Gracie," she cried, when they were outside the stone walls, "but it is all thanks to me. You would have beat about the bush, and palavered, and hesitated, and done no good. I got it out of him nicely—like the green sea-gull that the boy is. But, Grace, my child"—and Lady Acorn's voice for once grew hushed and solemn—"what in the world will be done with Adela?"

It was a painful scene, that in which they brought it home to Lady Adela. When Lady Acorn carried to her husband the news of Charles's unconscious avowal, he was struck almost dumb with consternation. The worst conclusion he had come to, in regard to some of the notes being traced to his daughter, was that she had but borrowed money from Charles Cleveland. Innocently? Yes; he could not and would not think she had any knowledge of how Charles became possessed of the notes. Lord Acorn, in spite of his perpetual embarrassments, and his not altogether straightforward shifts to evade them, possessed the true sense of honour that generally belongs to his order. He possessed it especially in regard to woman; and to find that his most favoured and favourite daughter had been guilty of theft; of—of— He could not pursue the thought, as he sank down with his pain.

"We had better go to her, and hear what she has to plead in excuse, and—and—ascertain how far her peculations have gone," he said presently to his wife. "Perhaps there are more of them. Poor Grubb!"

So they went to Grosvenor Square, arm-in-arm, but sick at heart, and found Lady Adela alone. She was toying with a golden bird in a golden cage; gold at any rate in colour; a recent purchase. Her afternoon dress of muslin had golden-hued sprigs upon it, and there was much gilding of mirrors and other ornaments in the room, the taste of that day. A gay scene altogether, and Adela the gayest and prettiest object in it.

She was not quite as heartless, though, as appeared on the surface, or as Lady Acorn judged her to be. Adela was growing frightened. She was beginning to realize what it was she had done, and to wonder, in much self-torment, what would come of it. That Mr. Grubb would release Charles Cleveland she had not at first entertained the smallest doubt, or that the affair would be entirely hushed up. Charles would be true to her, never disclose her name, and there it would end. With this fond expectation she had buoyed herself up. But as the days went on, and Charles was still kept in Newgate, soon to be brought up for another examination preparatory to committal for trial, she grew alarmed. For the past day or two her uneasiness had been intolerable. Could she have saved Charles and his good name by confessing the truth, and run away for ever from the sight of men, she would have done it thankfully; but to take the guilt upon herself, and such debasing guilt, and remain before the world!—this was utterly repugnant, not to say impossible, to the proud heart of Lady Adela.

It was so unusual to see her father and mother come in together, and to see them both with solemn faces, that Adela's heart leaped, as the saying runs, into her mouth. Still, it might not portend any adverse meaning, and she rallied her courage.

"I want to make him sing," she cried, turning on them her bright and smiling face. "Did you ever see so beautiful a colour, papa? I hope he is not too beautiful to sing."

But there was no answering smile on the faces of either father or mother, only an increased solemnity. Lord Acorn, waving his hand towards the bird as if he would, wave off a too frivolous toy, touched her arm and pointed to a chair.

"Sit down, Adela."

She turned as white as death. Lady Acorn opened her lips to begin, a great wrath evidently upon them, but her lord and master imperatively waved his hand to her for silence, as he had just waved away the frivolous bird, and addressed his daughter.

"What is to become of you, Adela?"

She neither spoke nor moved. She sat back in an armchair, with her white and terror-stricken face. Her teeth began to chatter.

"How came you to do it?" he continued.

"To—to—do what?" she gasped.

"To do what!" screamed out Lady Acorn, utterly unable to control her tongue and her reproaches longer—"why, to rifle your husband's cheque-book of a cheque, and fill it in, and forge the firm's signature, and despatch that unsuspicious baby, Charles Cleveland, to cash it."

"Who—who says I did that?" asked Adela, making one last, hopeless, desperate effort to defend herself.

"Who—"

"Betsy, if you can't let me speak, you had better go away for a few minutes," cried Lord Acorn, arresting a fresh burst of eloquence from his wife. "That you did do this thing, Adela, is known now; some of the notes have been traced to you, all the particulars have been traced, and Charles Cleveland has confessed to them. Any denial you could attempt would be more idle than the chirping of that bird."

"Charles has confessed to them?" she whispered, taken aback by this blow. Nothing, save his confession, could have brought it absolutely home to her.

"Did you set up a fantastic hope that he would keep silence to the end, and go to his hanging to save you?" demanded Lady Acorn, defying her lord's wish to have the whole ball to himself. "Proofs came out against you, Madam Adela, as your father says; they were carried to Charles Cleveland, and he could but admit the truth."

"Why did you do this terrible thing? That my daughter whom I have so loved, should be capable of sullying herself with such disgrace!" broke off Lord Acorn, with a wail. In good truth, it had been a blow to him, and one he had never bargained for. To play a little at Lady Sanely's for amusement, was one thing; he had, so to say, winked at that; but to gamble and to steal money to pay her gambling debts, was quite another. "Adela, I could almost wish I had died before hearing of it."

Adela burst into tears. "I wanted the money so badly," she sobbed, hiding her face with her trembling hands. "I owed it—a great deal—to people at Lady Sanely's. I was at my wits' end, and Mr. Grubb would not give me any more. Oh, papa, forgive me! Can't it be hushed up?"

"Did you help yourself to more than that?" asked Lord Acorn.

"I do not understand," she faltered, not catching his meaning.

"Have you drawn or used any other false cheque?"

"Oh no, no; only that. Papa, won't you forgive me?"

He shook his head. No, he felt that he could not. "My forgiveness may not be of vital consequence to you, one way or the other, Adela," he remarked, with a groan, that he drowned by coughing. "The termination of this affair does not lie with me."

"It lies with my husband," she said in a low tone. "He will hush it up."

"It does not lie with him, Adela," sternly spoke Lord Acorn. "Had it been one of his private cheques, had you used his name only, it might in a great degree have rested with him—unless the bankers had taken it up."

"But you borrowed old Mr. Howard's name as well," struck in Lady Acorn; "and, if he pleases to be stern and obstinate, he can just place you where Charles Cleveland is, and you would have to stand your trial in the face and eyes of the world. A pretty disgrace for us all! A frightful calamity!"

Adela looked from one to the other, her face changing pitiably; now white as snow with fear, now hectic with emotion and shame.

"Mr. Grubb has full power in Leadenhall Street," she pleaded. "He will take care to shield me."

"Are you sure of that?" quietly asked her father. "Has your conduct to him been such—I don't allude to this one pitiable instance, I speak of your treatment of him generally—has it been such that you can assume he will inevitably go out of his way to shield you, right or wrong?"

In spite of the miserable shame that filled her, a passing flush of triumph crossed her face. Ay! and her heart. What though she had persistently done her best to estrange her husband, with her provoking ways and her scornful contumely, very conscious felt she that she was all in all to him still. Why, had he not begged of her to confide this thing to him, and he would make it straight and guard her from exposure?

"I have nothing to fear from him, papa; I know it. It will be all right."

"How can you assert this in barefaced confidence, you wicked child?" groaned Lady Acorn. "I would not—no, I would not be so brazen for the world."

"Adela, don't deceive yourself with vain expectations; it may be harder for you in the end," interposed her father, once more making a deprecatory motion towards the place where his wife's tongue lay. "You are assuming a surety which you have no right to feel; better look the truth sternly in the face."

"I am his wife, papa," she faintly urged. "He will be sure to shelter me."

"He may be able to shelter you from exposure; I doubt not but that he will do it, so far as he can, for his own sake as well as for yours; for all our sakes, indeed. But—"

"A few years ago you might have been hanged," struck in Lady Acorn. "Hanged outside Newgate. I can remember the time when death was the penalty for forgery. Dr. Dodd was hung for it. How would you have liked that?"

Adela did not say how she would have liked it. She was passing her hands nervously across her face, as if to keep down its pallor. As to Lord Acorn, he despaired of being allowed to finish any argument he might begin, and paced the room restlessly.

"But, though your husband may shield you from public exposure, it is too much to hope that he will absolve you from consequences, and I think you will have to face and bear them," recommenced Lord Acorn, talking while he walked. "Had my wife served me as you have served Grubb, I should have put her away from me for ever; and I tell it you, Adela, before her as she stands there, though she is your mother."

"And served me right, too," commented Lady Acorn.

"How do you mean, papa?" gasped Adela.

"My meaning ought to be plain enough," was Lord Acorn's angry reproof. "Are you wilfully shutting your eyes to the nature of the offence you have sullied yourself with?—its degradation?—its sin?" he sharply questioned. "There's hardly a worse in our criminal code, that I know of, except murder."

"But I do not understand," she faintly reiterated. "If my husband absolves me, who else—"

"He may absolve you so far as the general public goes, shield you from that penalty," was the impatient interruption; "but not from your offence to himself. In my judgment, you must not look for that."

Adela did not answer. She glanced at her father questioningly, with an imploring look.

"A man has put his wife away from him for a much less cause than this," continued Lord Acorn. "And your husband, I fancy, must have been already pretty nigh tired out. What has your conduct been to him, Adela, ever since your marriage?"

She bent her head, her face flushing. To be taken to task by her father was a bitter pill, in addition to all the other discomfort.

"It has been shameful!" emphatically pronounced Lord Acorn. "For my part, I marvel that Grubb has borne it. But that I make it a rule not to interfere with my daughters, once they have left my roof for that of a husband, I should not have borne it tamely for him; and that I now tell you, Adela. One or two hints that I have given you from time to time you have disregarded."

"He has borne with her and indulged her to the top of her bent, when he ought to have taken her by the shoulders and shaken her insolence out of her," nodded the mother.

"Had you been a loving wife, Adela, things might have a better chance of going well with you," pursued her father, with another motion of the hand. "But, remembering what your treatment of your husband has persistently been, you can have no plea for praying leniency of him now, or he much inclination to accord it."

Lady Adela would have liked to give her head a saucy toss. She knew better; her father could not judge of her husband as she could. "Francis can't beat me," she thought. "He can lecture me, and will; and I must bear it meekly for once, under the circumstances."

She looked up at her father.

"My husband is very fond of me, in spite of all," she whispered.

"Yes; he is fond of you," returned Lord Acorn, with emotion. "Too fond. His behaviour to you proves that. Why, how much money have you had of him, drawn from him by your wiles, beyond your large legitimate allowance?"

Adela did not answer. "Has he spoken of it?" she asked, the question occurring to her.

"No, he has not spoken of it; he is not the man to speak of it. I gather so much from your sisters: they talk of it among themselves. One might have thought that your husband's kindness to you would have won your regard, had nothing else done it. It strikes me all that will be over now," concluded Lord Acorn.

Adela answered by a sobbing sigh.

"You have been on the wrong tack for some time now," he resumed, as an afterthought. "Who but a silly-minded woman would have made herself ridiculous, as you have, by flirting with a boy like Charles Cleveland? Do—"

"Oh, papa! You cannot think for a moment I meant anything!" she exclaimed, her cheeks flushing hotly.

"Except to vex your husband. Do you think your foolishness—I could call it by a harsher name—did not give sorrow to myself and your mother? We had deemed you sensible, honourable, open as the day: not the hard-hearted, frivolous woman you have turned out to be. Well, Adela, people generally have to reap what they sow: and I fear your harvest will not be a pleasant one."

She pressed her trembling hands together.

"Where are you going?" inquired Lady Acorn, as her husband took his hat up.

"To Leadenhall Street—to Grubb. Some one must apprise him of this dreadful truth; and I suppose it falls to me to do it—and a most distressing task it is. Would you have allowed young Cleveland to stand his trial?—to have suffered the penalty of the crime?" broke off Lord Acorn to his daughter.

"It would never have come to that, papa."

"But it would have come to that; it was coming to it. I ask, would you have allowed an innocent lad to be sent over the seas for you?"

Adela shuddered. "I must have spoken then," was her faint answer.

Lord Acorn, jumping into a cab, proceeded to Leadenhall Street, to make this wretched confession to his son-in-law. Had he been making it of himself, he would have felt it less. He was, however, spared the task. Mr. Grubb was not in the City, and Mr. Grubb already knew the truth.

It chanced that, close upon the departure of Lady Acorn and her daughter Grace from Charles Cleveland's cell that morning, Serjeant Mowham was shown into it: and the reader may as well be reminded that the learned serjeant had not taken up Charles's case in his professional capacity, but simply as an anxious friend. Without going into details, Charles told him that the truth had now come out, his innocence was made apparent to those concerned, and he hoped he should soon see the last of the precious walls he was incarcerated within. Away rushed Serjeant Mowham to Leadenhall Street, asking an explanation of Messrs. Grubb and Howard; and very much surprised did he feel at finding those gentlemen knew nothing.

"I am positive it is a fact," persisted the serjeant to them. "One cannot mistake Charley's changed tones and looks. Some evidence that exculpates him has turned up, rely upon it, and I thought, of course, you must know what it was. Lady Acorn and one of her daughters went out from him just before I got there."

Mr. Grubb felt curious; rather uneasy. If Charles Cleveland was exonerated, who had been the culprit?

"I shall go and see him at once," he said to Mr. Howard.

And now Charles Cleveland fell into another error. Never supposing but that Mr. Grubb must know at least as much as Lady Acorn knew, he unconsciously betrayed all. In his eagerness to show his kind patron he was not quite the ungrateful wretch he appeared to be, he betrayed it.

"I never thought of such a thing, sir, as that it was not your cheque—I mean your own signature," he pleaded. "I wouldn't have done such a thing for all the world—and after all your goodness to me for so many months! It was only when I came up from Netherleigh on the Monday evening I found there was something wrong with it."

"You heard it from Lady Adela," spoke Mr. Grubb, quietly accepting the mistake.

"Yes. She told me how it was. Mr. Howard was with you then in the dining-room, and his coming had frightened her. She seemed in dreadful distress, and I promised to shield her as far as I could."

"You should have confided the truth to me," interrupted Mr. Grubb. "All trouble might have been avoided."

"But how could I?—and after my voluntary promise to Lady Adela! What would you have thought of me, sir, had I shifted the blame from myself to lay it upon her?" added Charley, lifting his ingenuous, honest eyes to his master's.

Mr. Grubb did not say what he should have thought. Charles rather misinterpreted the silence: he fancied Mr. Grubb must be angry with him.

"Of course it has been a heavy blow to me, the being accused of such a thing, and to have had to accept the accusation, and to lie here in Newgate, with no prospect before me but transportation; but I ask you what else I could do, sir? I could not clear myself at the expense of Lady Adela."

Mr. Grubb did not answer this appeal. Telling Charles that steps should be taken for his release, and enjoining him to absolute silence as regarded Lady Adela's name, he returned to Leadenhall Street, and held a private conference with his partner.

What passed at it was known only to themselves, or how far Francis Grubb found it necessary to speak of his wife. Mr. Howard noticed one thing—that the young man (young, as compared with himself) looked at moments utterly bewildered; once or twice he talked at random. The following morning was the one fixed for Charles's second examination before Sir Turtle Kite, when, that worthy alderman being satisfied, he must of course be released.

Barely was the conference over and this resolution fixed upon, when a most urgent summons came to Mr. Grubb from Blackheath—his mother was supposed to be dying. He started off without the loss of a moment. And when, some time later, the Earl of Acorn arrived, he found only Mr. Howard, and learnt from him that Charles would be discharged on the following morning.

Just for a moment we must return to Adela. When Lady Acorn left her—after exhausting her whole vocabulary in the art of scolding, and waiting to drink some tea she asked for, for her lips were parched—Adela buried her face on the gold-coloured satin sofa-cushion, and indulged her repentance to her heart's content. It was sincere—and bitter. Were the time to come over again—oh, that it could!—far rather would she cut off her right hand than do what she had done; she would die, rather than do such a thing again. It was altogether a dreadful prospect yet—at least, it might be. What if they would not exonerate Charley without inculpating her? Not her husband; she did not fear him; old Howard, and the bankers, and those aldermen on the bench? How should she meet it? where should she run to? what would the world say of her? Lady Adela started from the cushion affrighted. Her lips were more parched than her mother's had been, and she rang for some tea on her own score.

She sat back in her chair after drinking it, her pretty hands lying listless on her pretty dress, and tried to think matters out. As soon as her husband came home she would throw herself upon his bosom and confess all, and plead for mercy with tears and kisses as she had never pleaded before, and give him her word never to touch another card, and whisper that in future she would be his dear wife. He would not refuse to forgive her; no fear of that; he would tell her not to be naughty again, and make all things right. She would tell him that she might have loved him from the first, for it was the truth, but that she steeled her heart and her temper against him, because of his name and of his being a City man; and she would tell him that she could and should love him from henceforth, that the past was past, and they would be as happy together as the day was long.

A yearning impatience grew upon her for his return as she sat and thought thus. What hour was it? Surely he was at home sometimes earlier than this!

As she turned her head to look at the timepiece on the marble console, Hilson came in, a note on his small silver salver.

"One of the clerks brought it up from Leadenhall Street, my lady," he remarked, as he held it out to her. "He said there was no answer."

It was not her husband's writing, and Lady Adela opened it with trembling fingers. Had some now and dreadful phase turned up in this unhappy business? The fear, that it had, flashed through her.

"DEAR MADAM,

"Mr. Grubb has been sent for to his mother, who is dangerously ill. He requested me to drop you a line to say he should probably remain at Blackheath for the night. I therefore do so, and despatch it to you by a clerk.

"Your obedient servant,

"JAMES HOWARD."

"So I can't do it," she cried, thinking of all she had been planning out, something like resentment making itself heard in her disappointed heart. "What a wretched evening it will be!"

Wretched enough. She did not venture to go to Chenevix House whilst lying under its wrathful displeasure; she had not the face to show herself elsewhere in this uncertainty and trouble.

"I wish," she burst forth, with a petulant tap of her black satin slipper on the carpet, "I wish that tiresome Mrs. Lynn would get well! Or else die, and have done with it."

The Lady Adela was not altogether in an entirely penitential frame of mind yet.

CHAPTER XXV

What a delightful world this might be if all our fond plans and hopes could only be fulfilled! if no adverse influence crept in to frustrate them!

Never a doubt had crossed the mind of those concerned for the welfare of Charles Cleveland, that he would be set at liberty on Tuesday, the day following the one above spoken of.

It was not to be. Charles was brought up, as previously, for private examination before Alderman Sir Turtle Kite. No evidence was offered; on the contrary, a legal gentleman, one Mr. Primerly, the noted solicitor for the house of Grubb and Howard, intimated that there was none to offer—the charge had been a mistake altogether.

Sir Turtle Kite was a little man, as broad as he was long, with a smiling round face and shiny bald head, the best-hearted, easiest-natured, and pleasantest-tempered of all the bench of aldermen. He would fain have been lenient to the worst offender; added to which, he knew about as much of the law as he did of the new comet, just then spreading its tail in the heavens. Therefore, unconsciously lacking the acumen to make an able administrator of justice, Sir Turtle, as a natural sequence, was especially fond of sitting to administer it. Latterly he had sat daily, and generally alone, much gout and dyspepsia prevailing just then amidst his brother-aldermen. The Lord Mayor of the year was a bon vivant, and gave a civic dinner five days in the week. Certain recent judicial decisions of Sir Turtle's, mild as usual, had been called in question by the newspapers; and one of them sharply attacked him in a leading article, asking why he did not discharge every prisoner brought before him, and regale him with luncheon.

Reading this article at breakfast, Sir Turtle came forth to the magisterial bench this day, Tuesday, smarting under its castigation. And, to the utter surprise of every one in the private justice-room, he declined to release the prisoner, Charles Cleveland. Rubbing his bald head, and making the best little speech he could—he was no orator—Sir Turtle talked of the fatal effects that might arise from the miscarriage of justice, and his resolve to uphold it in all its integrity.

Mr. Grubb was not present. Mr. Howard, who was, stared with astonishment, having always known the benevolent little alderman to be as pliant as a bit of cap-paper. James Howard said what he dared; as much as it was expedient to say, against the alderman's decision; but to no purpose. Sir Turtle, trying to put the wisdom of an owl into his round face, demanded to know, if the prisoner was not guilty, who was? This not being satisfactorily explained, he remanded the prisoner to the following morning, when he would probably be committed for trial. And, with this consolatory decision, Charles was conveyed back to his lodgings in Newgate.

Mr. Howard, somewhat put out by the contretemps, and by the alderman's rejection of his declared testimony that the prisoner was innocent, wrote a note to Lord Acorn with the news, and sent it to Chenevix House by hand. He had promised to notify the release of Charles, when that should be accomplished. But he had to notify a very different fact.

"Bless my heart!" exclaimed Lord Acorn, when he opened the note late in the afternoon, for he (also relieved of his worst fears) had been out gadding. "This is a dreadful thing!"

"What is the matter?" cried his wife, who was sitting there with Grace. "One would think the world was coming to an end, to look at your face."

The earl's face just then was considerably lengthened. He stood twirling his whiskers, and gazing at James Howard's very plain handwriting.

"They won't release Cleveland, Howard writes me," said the earl. "Things have taken a cross turn."

Grace closed her book and clasped her hands. Lady Acorn threw down her knitting, and inquired who would not release him.

"The magistrate who has sat to hear the case," replied Lord Acorn. "Sir—what's the odd name?—Turtle Kite. He refuses, absolutely, to release Charles, until the true culprit shall be brought before him—seems to think it is a trick, Howard says."

"Good Heavens!" cried Lady Grace, foreseeing more dire consequences than she would have liked to speak of. "What will become of Charles? What of Adela? Oh, papa! they cannot compel her to appear, can they?—to take Charles's place?"

"I don't know what they can do," gloomily responded the earl. "Hang these aldermen! What right have they to turn obstinate, when a prisoner's innocence is vouched for?"

"And where is the prisoner?" cried my lady.

"Taken back to Newgate. Is to be brought up again tomorrow, to be committed for trial. Well, this is a pretty kettle of fish!"

Grace bit her pale and trembling lips. "Was Mr. Grubb at the examination, papa?"

"No. Grubb's at Blackheath. Has not been up, Howard says, since he went down yesterday. What on earth is to be done?"

"The best thing to do is for you to go to Blackheath and see Mr. Grubb," promptly cried the countess. "If Adela were a child, I should beat her. Bringing all this worry and disgrace upon us!"

"I couldn't go there and be back for the dinner," cried he.

For they were engaged that evening to a state dinner at a duke's.

"Bother dinner!" irascibly retorted Lady Acorn. "If this affair can't be stopped, Adela will have to be smuggled over to the Continent, and stay in hiding there. If it is not stopped, and her name has to appear, we shall never be able to show our faces at a dinner-table again."

Lord Acorn wore a perplexed brow. Look at the affair in what light they would, it seemed to present nothing but difficulty. Once Charles Cleveland was committed for trial, what would be the end of it? He could not be allowed to stand his trial—and what might not that involve for Adela?

Lord Acorn, hating personal trouble of all kinds, especially trouble so disagreeable as this, betook himself—not to Blackheath, as enjoined by his wife, but to the City. He would see Mr. Howard first, and hear what his opinion was. Jumping out of the cab which had conveyed him to Leadenhall Street, he jumped against Serjeant Mowham.

"No good your going up," cried the serjeant. "Howard has left, and Grubb seems to be nowhere today."

"Have you heard about poor Charley?" asked Lord Acorn.

"Of course I have; that has brought me here. Primerly came to my chambers on other business, and told me what had happened. I came down here at once to catch one of the partners—or both of them—and see if there's anything to be done."

"What can be done?" returned Lord Acorn.

"Be shot if I know," said the serjeant. "It will be a serious thing for Charley, mind you, if he does get committed for trial—as Sir Turtle Kite has promised."

"What an ill-conditioned, revengeful man that Sir Turtle Kite must be!"

"There you are wrong, my lord. He is just the contrary: one of the sunniest-natured little men you can picture, and about as able upon the bench as my old wig would be if you stuck it there. The newspapers have been going in to him lately for his leniency, so I suppose he thinks he must make an example of somebody. One of the papers had a bantering article this morning, suggesting that Sir Turtle should open a luncheon-room at the court, and treat the delinquents who appeared before him to bottled stout and oysters. That article, I suspect, is the cause of his turning crusty today. Look here," added the serjeant, lowering his voice and catching hold of the other's button-hole, "what is there at the bottom of all this matter? Who was it that Charley made himself a scapegoat for? Do you know?"

As it chanced, they were jostled just then by some one of the many passers-by in the busy street—nearly pushed off the causeway. Lord Acorn, forgetting his usual superlative equanimity, allowed himself to be put out by it, and so evaded an answer.

"Nobody does know, that I can find out," said the serjeant, returning to the charge, and facing Lord Acorn, with whom he had long been on intimate terms: "and Charley makes a mystery of it. I suspect it was some one of those wild blades he has been hand-in-glove with lately—and that he won't betray him."

"Ah, yes, no doubt," carelessly assented Lord Acorn, his face wearing a deeper tinge than ordinary. "I wonder where Howard is? Charley must be saved."

"It will be of no use your seeing Howard, Lord Acorn—except for any odds and ends of information he might afford you. The affair is out of his hands now."

"But it can't be out of Mr. Grubb's!"

"Indeed it is. It is in Sir Turtle Kite's."

"Could one do any good with him?"

Serjeant Mowham laughed. "I can't say, one way or the other. You might try, perhaps. Don't say, though, that I recommended it."

The peer smoothed his brow, smooth enough before to all appearance. How often do these smiling brows hide a heavy load of perplexity within!

"As for me, I must be off," added the serjeant. "I've a consultation on for five o'clock at my chambers, and I believe five has struck."

He bustled away, leaving Lord Acorn in the crowd. Thought is quick. That nobleman was saying to himself, "What if I do see Sir Turtle?—who knows but I might come over him by persuasion? Wonder where he is to be found?"

He glanced up and down Leadenhall Street, at its houses on this side and on that, as if, haply, he might discern the name. During this survey he found himself subjected to an increased amount of jostling, and became aware that the clerks were pouring out of the offices of Grubb and Howard.

"Oh—ah," began Lord Acorn, addressing a young man who was nearly the last, all his nonchalance of manner in full force again, "can you tell me where Sir Turtle Kite is to be found?"

"Sir Turtle Kite, sir?" replied the young clerk, civilly. "I think—I'm not quite sure—but I think his place is somewhere down by the river. Here—Aitcheson"—stopping an older clerk—"where is Sir Turtle Kite's place? This gentleman is asking."

"Tooley Street—forget the number—can't mistake it," replied the other, who seemed in a great hurry to get away, and threw back the words as he went.

"Tooley Street," repeated Lord Acorn, by way of impressing the name on his mind. "Some commercial stronghold, I apprehend. What business is he?"

"He's a tallow-merchant, sir."

"Ah—thank you—a tallow-merchant," repeated his lordship, with a deprecatory shrug of the shoulders at the objectionable word, tallow. "Thank you very much." And the young man, who was of good breeding, lifted his hat and walked away.

Lord Acorn had as much notion in which direction he must look for Tooley Street as he might have had in looking for the way to the North Pole. Making another inquiry, this time of a policeman, the road was pointed out to him, and the information given that it was "not far." That, at least, was the policeman's opinion.

So Lord Acorn, whose cab had been dismissed at first, and who liked walking, for he was a lithe, active man for his age, at length reached Tooley Street, and began a pilgrimage up and down its narrow confines, which seemed to be choked up with cumbersome drays and trolleys. Presently he discovered a huge pile of dark buildings, all along the wide face of which was posted the name of the firm: "Turtle Kite, Tanner, Rex, and Co." The goal at last!

Wondering within himself how Sir Turtle Kite, or any other person possessing rational instincts and ordinary lungs, could exist in such an atmosphere of dirt and turmoil, Lord Acorn looked about for the entrance. There was none to be seen: and he was beginning seriously to speculate whether Turtle Kite, Tanner, Rex, and Co. entered the building by means of a rope-ladder affixed to one of the little square holes that served for windows, when a man, who had the appearance of a porter, came out of a narrow, dark entry.

"Is there any entrance to this building, my man?"

"Entrance is up here, sir; waggon-entrance on t'other side."

"Oh—ah—you belong to it, I perceive. Do you happen to know whether Sir Turtle Kite is in?"

"There's nobody in at all, sir; warehouses is shut for the evening," returned the porter. "Sir Turtle don't come here much hisself now; he leaves things mostly to Tanner and Rex. They'll both be here tomorrow morning, sir. Watchman's coming on presently."

"Ah, yes, no doubt," assented Lord Acorn, in his suave way. "Then Sir Turtle does not live here, I presume."

The porter checked a laugh at the notion. "Sir Turtle lives at Brixton, sir. Leastways, it's between Brixton and Clapham. Rosemary Lodge, sir—a rare beautiful place it is."

Brixton now! To Lord Acorn's dismayed mind it seemed that he might almost as well start for the moon; and for a few seconds he hesitated. But—having undertaken this adventurous expedition—adventurous in more ways than one—he must carry it through for his unhappy daughter's sake.

"Do you fancy Sir Turtle is likely to be at home now, at—ah, Rosemary House—if I go there, my man?"

"Most likely, sir. He is mostly at home earlier than this. Sir Turtle is very fond of his garden and greenhouses, you see, and makes haste home to 'em. He's got no wife nor child. But it's Rosemary Lodge, sir; not Rosemary House."

"Ah, yes, thank you—Rosemary Lodge," repeated his lordship, dropping a shilling into the porter's hand, and hailing the first cab he met.

"Rosemary Lodge, Brixton," said he to the driver.

"Yes, sir. What part of Brixton?"

"Don't know at all," said his lordship. "Never was at Brixton in my life."

"Brixton's a straggling sort of place, you see, sir. I might be driving you about—"

"It is between Brixton and Clapham," interrupted the earl. "Rosemary Lodge: Sir Turtle Kite's."

"Oh, come, the name's something," said the man, as he drove off.

Rosemary Lodge was not difficult to find, once the locality was reached. It was a large and very pretty white villa, painted glass borders surrounding its windows, and it stood in the midst of a spacious lawn dotted with beds of bright flowers. Walking round the gravel-drive, Lord Acorn rang at the door, which was speedily opened by a man in chocolate-coloured livery.

"Is Sir Turtle Kite at home?"

"Yes, sir; but he is at dinner; just sat down to it."

"At dinner!" echoed Lord Acorn. "I want to see him very particularly."

"Well, sir, Sir Turtle does not much like to be disturbed at his dinner," hesitated the man. "Perhaps you could wait?—or call again?"

"Look here," said Lord Acorn, hunting in his pocket for his card-case, a bright idea seizing him, "you shall ask Sir Turtle to allow me to go into the dining-room to him, and I'll say the few words I have to say while he dines. I suppose he is alone! I won't disturb him from it. Deuce take it!" muttered his lordship, finding he had not his card-case with him. "You must take in my name: Lord Acorn."

This colloquy took place in the hall. At that moment another serving-man came out of the dining-room—his master wanted to know what the stir was. Lord Acorn caught a glimpse of a well-spread table, and of a round, good-humoured face above it. "Announce me," he rapidly said: and the servant did so.

"Lord Acorn."

Up rose Sir Turtle, his beaming countenance looking its surprise, his napkin tucked into his uppermost button-hole. Lord Acorn, a fascinating mannered man as any living, entered upon his courtly apology, his short explanation, and offered his hand. In two minutes his lordship was seated at the dinner-table, regaling himself with real turtle soup, served out of a silver tureen; he and his host laughing and talking together as freely as though they were friends of years.

"It is so very good of you to ask me to partake of your dinner in this impromptu way, Sir Turtle," remarked his lordship. "I should have lost mine. We were to have dined—I and my wife—with the Duke of Dunford this evening, but I could not have got back for it. As to my business, the little matter I have come down to you to speak of, I won't trouble you with that until dinner's over."

"Quite right, my lord," said the knight. "Never unite eating and business together when it can be avoided. As to your lordship's partaking of my dinner, such as it is, the obligation lies on my side, and I think it very condescending of you."

Sir Turtle Kite, knight, alderman, and tallow-merchant, held the same reverence for dukes and lords that many another Sir Turtle holds, and his round face and his little bald head shone again with the honour of having the Earl of Acorn as a guest. But he need not have disparaged his dinner by saying "such as it is!" Lord Acorn had rarely sat down to a better. The knight liked to dine well, and he had a rare good cook.

"As rich as Croesus, I know: these City men always are," thought Lord Acorn. "And he is as genial a little man as one could wish to meet, and not objectionable in any way," mentally added his lordship, as the dinner went on.

It was not until the wine was on the table, and the servants were gone, that Lord Acorn entered upon and explained the subject which had brought him. He spoke rather lightly, interspersing praises of the wines, which for excellence matched the dishes. One bottle of choice claret, brought up specially for his lordship to taste, was truly of rare quality.

"It would be so very dreadful a thing if this honest-minded, chivalrous young fellow were to be compelled to stand a trial," continued the earl, confidentially, as he sipped the claret. "Painful to your generous heart, I am quite sure, Sir Turtle, as well as to mine and Mr. Grubb's."

"Of course it would, my lord."

"And I thought I would come to you myself and privately explain. By allowing this young fellow to be released tomorrow, you will be doing a righteous and a generous act."

Sir Turtle nodded. "But what a young fool the lad must be to have allowed the world to think him guilty!" he remarked. "Who is it that he is screening, do you say, my lord? Some unfortunate acquaintance of his, who had got into a mess? Was the fellow also staying at Grubb's?"

Lord Acorn coughed. "Yes: the culprit was staying in Grosvenor Square at the time. He, the true criminal, is out of the law's reach now, and can't be caught," added the Earl, drawing upon his invention. "And we wish to keep his name quiet, and give him another chance. But that the prisoner, who has been twice before you, is innocent as the day, I give you my solemn word of honour. I hope you will release him, dear Sir Turtle."

"I will," assented Sir Turtle. "There's my hand upon it. And those libellous newspapers may go and be—hanged."

Perhaps the word "hanged" was not exactly the one Sir Turtle rapped out in his zeal. But he was not before his own magisterial bench just then. Lord Acorn clasped the hand warmly. He had taken quite a fancy to the genial little alderman, and he felt inexpressibly grateful.

"I do thank you; I thank you truly—for the young fellow's sake. What claret this is, to be sure! Not equal to the port, you say? I have a bin of very good port myself, and if you will dine with me tomorrow, Sir Turtle, you shall taste it. Seven o'clock, sharp. Come a little before it. I shall be glad to see you."

Sir Turtle Kite, in his gratification, hardly knew whether he stood on his head or his heels. He had never, to his recollection, been bidden to an earl's dinner-table before, and was profuse in thanks.

"I'll ask Grubb to join us," said Lord Acorn. "You know him?"

"Ay, we all know Grubb. What a charming young man he is! Young compared with you and me, my lord—especially with me," added Sir Turtle. "So honourable, so good, and so prosperous!"

Lord Acorn made quite an evening of it: looking at the greenhouses, and the pinery, and the growing melons, with all the rest of the horticultural treasures at Rosemary Lodge, and went back to town on the top of a West-end omnibus.

CHAPTER XXVI

INFATUATION

Midnight. Pacing her chamber in her light dressing-robe, its open sleeves thrown back from her restless hands, as if for coolness, was the Lady Adela. Throughout the whole business she had never been so terrified as now, had never before realized her dangerous position in all its fulness. Her heart and her brow were alike beating with fever heat.

On the Monday evening, for we must go back a day, after receiving the news that her husband would probably not be home, as conveyed to her by note from Mr. Howard, Adela did not spend quite the solitary hours she had anticipated. Grace came to her: and though rather given to calling Grace an "old lecturer," Adela was heartily glad to see her now. The evening's solitude had only intensified her fears, and dismal doubts chased each other through her mind.

Ever thoughtful and kind, though she did condemn Adela, Grace came to bring her the tidings that Charles Cleveland would be discharged on the morrow—for Lord Acorn, on his return from that afternoon's interview with Mr. Howard, in Leadenhall Street, had spoken of the release as an assured fact. The more bitter the condemnation by her father and mother of Adela, and it really was bitter, the greater need, thought Grace, that some one should stand by her: and here she was, with her cheering news. And the relief it brought no pen can express. Adela forgot her fears; ay, and her repentance. She became her own light-headed self again, and provoked Grace by her saucy words. In the great revulsion of feeling she almost forgot her trouble; nay, resented it.

"What a shame!—to frighten me as papa and mamma did this afternoon! I thought old Howard would not be quite a bear; and I knew my husband had all power in his hand—if he chose to exercise it."

"Any way, Adela, he has exercised it. You have a husband in a thousand. I do hope you will show your gratitude by behaving to him well in future."

"I dare say! I did think of—what do you suppose I thought of doing, Gracie? That if he proved obdurate, as papa hinted, I would win him over by saying, 'Let us kiss and be friends.'"

"If you could have so won him."

"If!" retorted Adela, a mocking smile on her pretty lips. "You do think he yet cares for me a little, Gracie; but you do not know how much. I believe—now don't you start away at my irreverence!—that he loves me better than Heaven. I shall not do it now."

"Do what?" asked Grace.

"Kiss and be friends. Neither the one nor the other. I shall abuse him instead; reproach him for having stood out so long about that poor wretched Charley: and I shall hold him at arm's-length, as before. The time has not come for me to be reconciled to him."

"You do not mean it, Adela! You cannot be so wicked."

"Not mean it! You will see. So will he. Tra-la-la-la! Oh, what a horrible nightmare it has been!—and what a mercy to awaken from it!"

She laid hold of her pretty gold-sprigged muslin dress with both hands; she had not changed it; and waltzed across the room and back again. Grace wondered whether she could be growing really heartless; she was not born so: but of course it must be a glad relief.

The old proverb, "when the devil was sick," no doubt so well known to the reader that it need not be quoted, is exemplified very often indeed in our everyday life. With the removal of the danger, Adela no longer remembered it had been there, only too willingly did she thrust it away from her. She passed a good night, and the next day was seen driving gaily in the Park and elsewhere with her friend the young Lady Cust—who was just as frivolous as herself.

Evening came: Tuesday evening, please remember. Mr. Grubb did not come home: neither had Adela heard from him: she supposed him to be still at Blackheath, and sat down to dinner alone. She wondered whither Charley had betaken himself off on his release: and whether he would be likely to call upon her. She hoped not: her cheeks would take a tinge of shame at facing him. Suppose he were to come in that evening!

Charley did not come. But Frances Chenevix did. Frances, very downright, very outspoken, had been honestly indignant with Adela for the part she had played, she had not scrupled to tell her so, and they had quarrelled. Therefore Adela was not much pleased to see her. She found that Frances had been dining at home, and had ordered the carriage round here on her way back to Lady Sarah Hope's. It was about nine o'clock.

"Is your husband at home?" she inquired of Adela, without any circumlocution, when she entered the drawing-room.

"No. He has not been home since yesterday morning. I expect he is at Blackheath with that wavering old mother of his, dying today and well tomorrow," listlessly added Adela.

"Had he been at home I should have sent him round to the mother and Grace; they are so frightfully uneasy."

"The mother?" repeated Adela. "Is she back already from the Dunfords'?"

"She has not been to the Dunfords'," said Frances. "I suppose you know of the dreadful turn affairs have taken with Charles Cleveland?"

Something like a drop of iced water seemed to trickle down Adela's back. "I know nothing—I have heard nothing," she gasped. "Is Charles not set at liberty?"

"Good gracious, no! And he is not going to be. The city magistrates won't do it; they will commit him for trial."

It was as if a whole pailful of cold water were pouring down now. "Oh, Frances, it cannot be true!"

"It is too true. Mr. Howard wrote this afternoon to tell papa that Charles was remanded back to prison, and would be committed in the morning. Papa went off at once to see about it, and mamma sent an excuse to the Dunfords. I was to have dined quietly with Grace and Mary this evening; and I heard all this when I arrived."

"And—is papa not back yet?" again gasped Adela.

"No; and mamma can hardly contain herself for uneasiness. For, of course, you see what this implies?"

Adela was not sure whether she saw it or not. She only gazed at her sister.

"It means that either Charles must suffer, or you, Adela, so far as can be gathered from present aspects. And the question at home is—can they allow him to suffer, even if he be willing, and the truth does not transpire in other ways?"

"To—suffer?" hesitated Adela.

"To stand his trial."

"Why does not Mr. Grubb stop all this?" angrily flashed Adela, in her sick tremor.

"Mr. Grubb would no doubt be only too glad to do it—and Mr. Howard also would be now, but it is out of their hands. Once a magistrate turns adverse, it is all up. Charley's lawyer impressed upon the magistrate, one Sir Turtle Kite, that his client was not the individual who was guilty: very well, said Sir Turtle, bring forward the individual who was guilty, and he would release Charley; not before. Adela, we have not seen the mother cry often, but she sobbed tonight."

Suddenly, violently, almost as though she had caught the infection from the words, Adela burst into a storm of sobs. The revulsion from terror to ease had told upon her feelings the previous night, but not as that of ease to terror was telling this. What now of her boastful, saucy avowals to Grace?

Leaving her sister to digest the ill-starred news, Frances departed; she could not keep the carriage longer, as It was wanted by Lady Sarah. Adela sat up till past eleven, and then, shivering inwardly, went to her room, but she was too uneasy to go to bed. Dismissing her maid, she put on a dressing-gown—as was told at the beginning of the chapter—and so prepared to pass the wretched night. Now pacing the carpet in an agony, now gazing eagerly from the open window at every cab that rattled across the square, lest happily it might bring her husband. She could see no refuge anywhere but in him.

The intelligent reader has of course discerned that it was on this same evening Lord Acorn was at Rosemary Lodge, making things right with Sir Turtle Kite. About eleven o'clock the earl got home, bringing with him his glad tidings. Lady Acorn, relieved of her fears, took up her temper again, and was more wrathfully bitter against Adela than ever. But Adela knew nothing of all this.

With the morning, Wednesday, Sir Turtle Kite appeared on the magisterial bench, and the prisoner, Charles Cleveland, was brought before him. As before, the proceedings were heard in private. Mr. Grubb was present; had come up specially from Blackheath. He assured Sir Turtle that the prisoner was wholly innocent, had been made the unconscious dupe of another: upon which Sir Turtle, in a learned speech that even his own legal clerk could make neither head nor tail of, discharged the prisoner, and graciously informed him he left the court "without a stain upon his character."

Charles looked half-dazed amidst the sea of faces around him: he made his way to Mr. Grubb. "I thank you with my whole heart, sir," he whispered deprecatingly. "I shall never forget your kindness."

"Let it be a warning to you for all your future life," was the grave, kind answer.

The question flashed through Charley's mind—where was he to go? That he had forfeited his post at Grubb and Howard's, and his residence in Mr. Grubb's house, went without saying. At that moment Lord Acorn advanced from some dark region of the outer passage.

"You are going down to Netherleigh this afternoon with your father, Charles," said he. "But you can come home with me first and get some lunch. Wait a minute. I want to speak to Mr. Grubb."

Mr. Grubb appeared to have vanished. Lord Acorn could not see him anywhere. He wrote a line in pencil, asking him to dine with him that day at seven o'clock, sent it to Leadenhall Street, and got into a cab with Charley.

"Oh," said the Countess of Acorn, when she saw the ex-prisoner arrive, "so you are here, young man! It is more than I expected."

"And more than I did—since yesterday," confessed he.

"Pray what name do you give to that devoted chivalry of yours, Charley?—the taking of another's sins upon your own shoulders?" whispered Frances Chenevix, who happened to be at her father's. In fact, Colonel Hope and Lady Sarah, outwardly anxious, and inwardly scandalized at the whole affair, beginning with Adela and ending with Charley, had despatched her to Chenevix House for any news there might be.

"I don't know," answered Charley. "Perhaps you might call it infatuation."

"That was just it," nodded Frances. "Don't you go and be an idiot again. That is my mother's best name for you."

Charles nodded assentingly. He saw the past in its true light now. He was a changed man. His confinement and reflections in prison, combined with the prospect of being condemned as a felon, from which he had then seen no chance of escape except by his own confession, which he had persistently resolved not to make, had added years to his experience in life. He was a light-hearted, light-headed boy when he entered Newgate; he came out of it older and graver than his years.

More severely than for aught else did he blame himself for having responded in ever so slight a degree to the ridiculous flirtation commenced by Lady Adela; and for having fallen into worshipping her almost as he might have worshipped an angel; and he thanked God in his heart, now, that he had never been betrayed into offering her a disrespectful look or word. She belonged to her husband; not to him; and to be disloyal to either of them Charley would have regarded as the most consummate folly or sin.

Was he cured of that infatuation? Ay, he was. The heartless conduct of Lady Adela, in leaving him to bear the brunt of the crime and the disgrace that came of it, without giving heed or aid, had helped to cure him. He had not wished that she should sacrifice her good name to save his, though the whole sin lay with her; but he did think she might have offered him one little word of sympathy. He lay languishing within the walls of that awful prison for her sake, and she had never conveyed to him, by note or message, so much as the intimation, I am sorry for you. Charles Cleveland could not know that Adela had been afraid to do it; afraid lest the smallest notice on her part should lead to the betrayal of herself. What she would have done, what they would all have done, had he really been committed to take his trial, she does not know to this day. However, to him her silence had appeared to be heartless indifference; and that, combined with his own danger and his prolonged reflection, had served to change and cure him.

"I am very thankful, Charles," breathed Grace, and the tears stood in her eyes as she took his hand. "No one knows what trouble this has been to me."

"I have more cause to be thankful than you, Grace; and I think I am," he answered. "It has been to me a life's lesson."

"Ay. You will not fall into mischief again, Charley?" she said, almost entreatingly. "You will not lose your wits for a married woman, as you did for Adela?"

"If ever again I get trapped by any woman, married or single, all courtly smiles one day, when she wants to amuse herself and serve her turn, and all careless neglect the next, like a confounded weathercock, I'll give you leave to transport me to a penal settlement in earnest," was Charley's wrathful interruption, the sense of his wrongs pressing upon him sorely. "But let me thank you, Grace," he added, his tone changing to one of deep feeling, "for all your care and concern for me."

Charles could not eat any lunch, though the table was well spread. In spite of his release from the great danger, he was altogether miserable. Lady Acorn talked at him; Lady Frances, taking matters lightly, after her custom, joked and laughed, and handed him all the sweets upon the table, one dish after another. It was all one to Charley: and perhaps he felt that he merited Lady Acorn's reproaches more than he did the offered sweets. He had not yet seen his father and his stepmother. For the past two or three days they had been staying with their relative, the Earl of Cleveland; a confirmed invalid, who lived in seclusion a few miles out of London.

They all departed for Netherleigh in the course of the afternoon: the Rector, Lady Mary and the baby; Charles joining them at the railway-station. What was to become of him in future? It was a question he seriously put to himself. Surely he had bought experience, if any young man ever had in this world; an experience that would leave behind it its lasting and bitter pain.

Seven o'clock—nay, some fifteen minutes before it—brought Sir Turtle Kite to the Earl of Acorn's. Sir Turtle enjoyed the visit and the dinner immensely—though he frankly avowed his opinion that his own port wine was the best. For once the earl's wife made herself gracious; tart though she might be at other times, she knew something of gratitude; and Grace, who made the fourth at table, could not keep her heart's thankfulness out of her manner—for where should they all have been without Sir Turtle?

But Mr. Grubb did not make his appearance. Neither had Lord Acorn heard from him.

CHAPTER XXVII

SEPARATION

Pacing his library at Chenevix House, in almost the same perturbation that was tormenting his mind when we first met him in this history, strode the Earl of Acorn. The cause of disquiet was not the same. Then it had arisen from a want of cash; now it was the trouble connected with his daughter Adela.

By the mantelpiece, erect and noble as ever, but with a countenance full of pain, stood Mr. Grubb. He could scarcely speak without betraying his emotion. Lord Acorn was agitated also—which was a great deal to say of him.

Mr. Grubb had come this morning to inform Lord Acorn of the separation he had resolved upon; and to submit its terms for his approval. Never, he said, would he live with his wife again. After what had passed recently, and after the years of penance he had endured with her, he could only put her away from him.

"And, egad, it is what I should do myself," thought the earl. But he did not say so. He said just the opposite.

"Must this be, Grubb? Cannot she and you make it up—or something?"

"Never again," was the decisive answer. "Could you, looking at matters impartially, wish me to do it? Though, as her father, perhaps it is too much to expect you to exercise an impartial judgment," considerately added Mr. Grubb.

"I don't excuse her; mind that, Grubb. And I acknowledge—I'll be shot if I can help saying it—that some men would have put her away before this. She has behaved ill to you; no doubt of it; but she is young and light-headed, and will gain sense with time. Can't there be some modification?"

"Not any," spoke Mr. Grubb. "The pain this decision has caused me no one will ever know, but there has not been one moment's wavering in my mind as regards its absolute necessity. Lord Acorn, I think you cannot blame me. Imagine yourself in my place, and then see whether you do."

"I don't, I don't, looking at it from your point of view," said the earl. "I am thinking of Adela, and the blow it will be to her."

"A blow?—to be rid of me? Surely not. It is what she has been wishing for years."

"In talk. Girls will talk—silly minxes! To be put away by you, Grubb, and from her home, is quite another thing."

"She must care for my home as little as she cares for me. She has already taken the initiative, and left it."

Lord Acorn wheeled round on his heel in surprise. "Left your home, Grubb? What do you mean?"

Mr. Grubb looked surprised in his turn. "Did you not know it? Is she not here?"

"She is certainly not here, and I did not know it. Confound these silly women! She has run away, I suppose, to hide herself from—"

"From the law," Lord Acorn would have said; but he did not end the sentence. He asked Mr. Grubb when she went, and how, and if he had any idea where she was. Mr. Grubb had not any idea, and related all he knew; he had supposed her to be at Chenevix House.

Heaven alone knew, or ever would know, the terrible shock, the blow the discovery of his wife's treachery brought to Mr. Grubb. That she should have been capable of robbing him, of forging his name and his partner's, of obtaining the money, all in so imprudent, so barefaced a manner, and of using it to pay her gaming debts, would alone have filled him with a dismay to shrink from. But that she should have allowed the guilt and the punishment to fall upon another; and that she should have impudently denied her own guilt to himself, and flung back with scorn his entreaties for her confidence and the offer he made to shield her in all tenderness, shook his soul to the centre.

From the hour of his enlightenment he was a changed man. That which the insults, the scorn of years, had failed to effect on his heart, was accomplished now. His consideration for his wife had turned to sternness; his love to righteous anger. Never again would he bear her contumely; no longer should his home be hers. This most fatal action of hers—the crime she had committed, and the innocent tool she had made of Charles Cleveland—afforded Mr. Grubb the justification for extreme measures, which he might otherwise have lacked. During the hours he spent by his mother's sick-bed, he formed and matured his plans. Not with Lady Adela would he enter on the negotiations for their separation, but with her father and mother. She must return to them; must live under their protection and guidance, as she did before her marriage; she was not yet old enough or wise enough to be trusted alone.

And Mr. Grubb came up from Blackheath to make known his decision to Lord Acorn. It was the morning following the day of Charles's release and of Sir Turtle Kite's dinner at Chenevix House.

Mrs. Lynn's illness had been a dangerous one. For many hours it had not been known whether she would live or die. On the Tuesday evening, Mr. Howard went to Blackheath, carrying with him the tidings of the obduracy of Sir Turtle Kite: in consequence of which, Mr. Grubb came up on the Wednesday to attend the examination. His mother was then a shade better, but he returned to her the instant the examination was over and Charles released.

On the Thursday morning, Mr. Grubb again came up, as just stated, to confer with Lord Acorn. On his way he called at his own home in Grosvenor Square, intending to acquaint his wife with his decision— that they must separate—but not to enter into details with her. Hilson looked very glad to see his master, and feelingly inquired after Mrs. Lynn. Better, answered Mr. Grubb; she might recover now.

"Ask Lady Adela if she will be good enough to come to me here," he added to the butler, as he turned into his library.

"Her ladyship is not at home, sir," promptly replied Hilson.

"Not at home!" and Mr. Grubb could not altogether keep his surprise out of his tone. "She has gone out early."

"My lady left home yesterday morning, sir, before breakfast. Darvy, I believe, carried a cup of tea to her room."

"But she returned, I suppose?"

"No, sir, not since."

"Where is her ladyship gone? Do you know?"

"Not at all, sir. Darvy was mysterious over it. She heard her lady say this was no longer any home for her; she told me that much. John was sent to fetch a cab, and her ladyship and Darvy went away in it, with a carpet bag."

"She must be at Lord Acorn's," remarked Mr. Grubb; a conclusion he had rapidly come to. Hilson agreed with it.

"No doubt, sir. My lady may have felt lonely here without you."

Mr. Grubb went straight to Chenevix House. Not to see Adela, but to enter on his business with Lord Acorn. And then, as you find, he learnt that she was not there.

"Stay a moment," said Lord Acorn, a recollection occurring to him. "Adela was at Colonel Hope's yesterday: I remember Frances said so. She must be staying there. That's it."

"Probably so," was Mr. Grubb's cold assent. "She has, I say, taken the initiative in the matter."

He sat down as he spoke, motioning Lord Acorn to the seat on the other side of the small table between them, and took a paper from his pocketbook on which he had pencilled a few notes, as to the terms of separation.

Terms that were wonderfully liberal in their pecuniary aspect. Lord Acorn heard the amount of the sum he proposed to allow his wife annually with a thrill of generous admiration. Oh, what a fool Adela has been! thought he. Why could she not have made herself a loving helpmeet to this noble-minded man, whose every instinct is good and great?

"Are you satisfied with the amount, Lord Acorn?"

"Quite."

"It will be paid to you; not to herself," continued Mr. Grubb. "As a matter of course, her home must be with you and her mother. The allowance that you may deem suitable for herself personally you will be good enough to pay to her out of it, as you and she may arrange. I do not interfere with details. She had better have her own separate carriage and horses."

Lord Acorn nodded in silence. He knew why he was to be the recipient of the income, instead of Adela—that she might not have the means at her disposal to lose herself in future at Lady Sanely's. That had been the leading source of this last dangerous episode.

"I hope you will take care of her," cried Mr. Grubb, as he rose, and pressed Lord Acorn's hand in parting.

"To the best of my power. Ah, Grubb I—I can't grumble, of course; no, neither at the step nor the proposed arrangements—but, if you could but see your way to condone the past; to receive her back!"

"Never again," was the quiet answer. "Darvy can attend to the removal of her things from Grosvenor Square."

Mr. Grubb walked back to his own home with slow and thoughtful steps, his heart filled with the bitterness of disappointed hopes. It is no light matter for a man to part for ever with the wife of his bosom; to say to her, "Your road lies that way from henceforth; mine this." Especially a wife who had been loved as Francis Grubb had loved his.

That Adela had run away from his home, abandoned it and him, he entertained not the slightest doubt. She had been tacitly demonstrating to him for years that she wished to be rid of him—indeed, not always tacitly—and now she had accomplished it. This impression did not lead to Mr. Grubb's decision to put her away; it had, and could have had, nothing to do with that: but it tended to deaden any small regret he may have felt.

It was a wrong impression, however. Lady Adela had not run away from Grosvenor Square to be quit of her husband; she had left it under fear.

When Frances Chenevix quitted her the night already told of, Tuesday, leaving her with the dread news that the magistrates would not release Charley, unless they produced the true culprit, herself, in his stead, Adela's worst fears were aroused. She passed a wretched night, now pacing her chamber, now tossing on her sleepless bed. She saw the matter now in its true colours, all its deadly peril, its shameful sin. Throwing herself on her knees, she raised her hands in prayerful agony, beseeching the Most High to spare them both—herself from exposure, the innocent young fellow, who had been made her tool, from punishment—and she took a solemn oath never again to be tempted to play.

Whether the prayer soothed her spirit, or whether the natural reaction that follows upon violent emotion set in, certain it was that a sort of calm stole over Adela. Her head lay on the bed, her arms were outstretched, and by-and-by she slept. If, indeed, it could be called sleep.

For she still seemed to be conscious of the peril that awaited her and a sort of dream, that was half reality, began weaving its threads in her brain.

She thought she was in that, her own chamber, and kneeling down by the bed, as she was, in fact, kneeling. She seemed to be endeavouring to hide and could not. Suddenly, a faint noise arose in the street, and she appeared to rise from her knees, and go to the window to peep out. There she saw two fierce-looking men, whom she knew instinctively to be officers of justice come to apprehend her, mounted on horses. Each horse had a red lantern fixed above its head, from which bright red rays radiated on all sides. As she looked, the rays flashed upwards and discovered her. "There she is!" called out a voice that she knew to be Charles Cleveland's, and in the fright and horror she awoke. Her whole frame shook with terror, and several minutes passed before she could understand that it was not reality.

The peril existed, all too surely. What if Charles, to save himself, avowed the truth, that it was she who was guilty, and was already piloting those dread officers of justice to her house? Nay, and if he did not avow it, others must. How could she, she herself, allow him to stand in her place to suffer for her, now that it had come to this?

The dream had struck to her nerves. Ensuing upon the natural fear, it had created a perfect terror. The horrible red lights seemed yet to flash upon her face: and a lively dread set in that the officers might be, there and then, on their way westward, to secure her. This fear tormented her throughout the rest of the livelong night; and by the morning it had grown into a desperate belief, a reality, a living agony. There was only one step that could save her—flight.

With the first sounds of stir in the house, she rang for Darvy. That damsel, fearing illness, threw on a few garments, and ran to her lady's room. To her intense astonishment, there stood Lady Adela, up and dressed, her eyes wild and her cheeks hectic.

"I want to go away somewhere, Darvy," she said, her lively imagination picturing to herself, with increased certainty and increased terror, the capturing officers drawing nearer and nearer. "Will you pack up a few things, and have a cab called?"

"Name o' goodness!" uttered Darvy, who was three-parts Welsh, and was privately wondering whether her lady had gone suddenly demented. "And what's it all for, my lady?—and where is it you want to go?"

"Anywhere; this house is no longer a home for me. At least—there, don't stand staring, but do as I tell you," broke off Lady Adela, saying anything that came uppermost in her perplexity and fear. "Put up a few things for me in haste, and get a cab."

"Am I to attend you, my lady?" asked the bewildered woman.

"No—yes—no. Yes, perhaps you had better," finally decided Lady Adela, in grievous uncertainty. "Don't lose a moment."

Darvy obeyed orders, believing nevertheless that somebody's head was turned. She got herself ready, packed a carpet bag, had the thought to take her lady a cup of tea, exchanging a little private conference with her crony, the butler, while she made it, and ordered the cab. Then she and Lady Adela came down and entered it, neither of them having the slightest notion for what quarter of the wide world she was bound.

"Where to?" asked John of Darvy, as she followed her mistress into the cab.

"Where to, my lady?" demanded Darvy, in turn. "Anywhere. Tell him to drive on," responded Lady Adela.

"Tell him to drive straight on," said Darvy to John.

"Where can I go?—where shall I be safe?" thought Adela to herself, as they went along. "I wonder—I wonder if Sarah would take me in?" came the next thought. "They"—the "they" applying to the legal thief-catchers—"would never think of looking for me there. Sarah is angry with me, I know, but she won't refuse to hide me. Darvy, direct the man to Colonel Hope's."

This last sensible injunction was a wonderful relief to Darvy's troubled mind. And to Colonel Hope's they went.

Lady Sarah "took her in," and Adela hid herself away in the bedroom of her sister Frances. Truth to say, they were in much anxiety themselves, the colonel included, as to what trouble and exposure might not be falling upon Adela. They did not refuse to shelter her, but they let her know tacitly how utterly they condemned her conduct. Lady Sarah was coldly distant in manner; the colonel would not see her at all.

Before the day was over—it was in the afternoon—Grace came to them with the truth—that Charles Cleveland was released and had gone to Netherleigh. Adela, perhaps not altogether entirely reassured about herself, said she would stay at the colonel's another night, if permitted: and she did so.

That was the explanation of Adela's absence from home. She had left the house in fear; not voluntarily to quit it or her husband. Her husband, however, not knowing this, took the opposite view, and dwelt upon it as he walked away from Lord Acorn's in the summer sun. Not that, one way or the other, it would make any difference to him.

Entering his house, Mr. Grubb went straight upstairs to his dressing-room, intending to change the coat he wore for a lighter one. The bedroom door came first. He opened that, intending to pass across it, when he came face to face with his wife.

Just for a moment he was taken by surprise, having supposed the room to be empty. She had returned from Lady Sarah's, and was standing at the dressing-glass, doing something to her hair, her bonnet evidently just taken off. She wore a quiet dress of black silk—the one she had gone away in.

That frequent saying, "the devil was sick," was alluded to a few pages back. It might again be quoted. Lady Adela, when she thought the trouble had not passed and her heart was softened, had mentally rehearsed once more a little scene of tenderness, to be enacted when she next met her husband. She met him now; and she turned back to the looking-glass without speaking a word.

She now knew that the danger was over; over for good. Charley was discharged, scathless; her own name had been kept silent and sacred—and there was an end of it.

She turned back to the glass, after looking round to see who it was that had come in, saying not a word. Possibly she anticipated a lecture, and deemed it the wisest plan to keep silent—who knew? Not Mr. Grubb. She gave him neither word nor smile, neither tear nor kiss.

He walked across the room, and stood at the window nearest the dressing-table, turning to face her. Could she not have said good-morning?—could she not have asked him how he had been these three days, and what the news was from Blackheath? She appeared to be too much occupied with her lovely hair.

"I must request you to give me your attention for a few minutes, Lady Adela."

There was something in the proud, distant tone, in the formality of the address, that caused her to glance at him quickly. She did not like his face. It was stern, impassive, as she had never before seen it.

"Yes," she answered, quite timidly.

In the same cold tone, with the same unbending countenance, Mr. Grubb in a few concise words informed her of the resolution he had taken. He could never allow her to inhabit the same house with himself again; her father and mother would receive her back in her maiden home. The arrangements connected with this step had been settled between himself and Lord Acorn: and he should be glad if she made it convenient to leave Grosvenor Square that day.

Intense astonishment, gradually giving place to dismay, kept her silent. The comb dropped from her hand. "Anything but this," beat the refrain in her heart; "anything but this." For Lady Adela, so alive to the good opinion of the world, would almost rather have preferred death than that she should be publicly put away by her husband.

"You have no right to do this," she stammered, her face ashy pale.

"No right! After what has passed? Ask your father whether I possess the right, or not," he added, his voice stern with indignation. "But for my clemency, you might have taken the place from which Charles Cleveland has been released."

"Is that the reason?" she asked.

"It has afforded the justification for the step. Following on the course of treatment you have dealt out to me for years—"

"I have been very wrong," she interrupted. "I meant to have told you so. I have not behaved as—as—I ought to behave for a long while; I acknowledge it. Won't you forgive me?"

"No," he answered—and his voice had no relenting in it.

"I will try and do better; I will indeed," she reiterated: not daring now to offer the caresses her imagination had planned out. "Oh, you must forgive me; you must not put me away!"

"Lady Adela, but a few days ago, it was my turn to make supplication to you; I did so more than once. I told you I would protect, forgive, shield you. I prayed you, almost as solemnly as I pray to Heaven, to trust me—your husband—as you wished it to be well with us in our future life. Do you remember how you met that prayer?—how you answered me?"

Yes, she did. And her face flushed painfully at the remembrance.

"As you rejected me, so must I reject you."

"Not to separation!"

"Separation will be only too welcome to you. Have you not been telling me as much for years?"

"But not in earnest; not to mean it really. I will give up play—I have given it up; believe that. A man may not reject his wife," she continued in agitation.

"He may—when he has sufficient reason for it. Look at the wife you have been to me; the shameful treatment you have persistently dealt to me. I speak not now of this recent act of disgrace, by which you hazarded your own good name and mine—I will not trust myself to speak of it—but of the past. Few men would have borne with you as I have borne. I loved you with a true and tender love: how have you repaid me?"

"Let us start afresh," she said, imploringly, putting up her hands. Indeed this was a most terrible moment for her.

"It may not be," he coldly rejoined. "My resolution has been deliberately taken, and I cannot change it upon impulse."

"I had meant to pray you to forgive me—for this and all the past—I had indeed. I had meant to say that I would be different—would try to love you."

"Too late."

"In a little while, then," she panted, her face working with emotion, tears starting to her eyes. "You will take me back later! In a week or two."

"Neither now nor later. My feelings were long, long outraged, and I bore with you, hoping for better things. But in this last fearful act, and more especially in the circumstances attending it, you have broken all allegiance, you have deliberately thrown off my protection. Lady Adela, I shall never live under the same roof with you again."

She laid her hand upon her palpitating heart. He crossed the room with the last words, and quietly left it. A faint cry of distress seemed to be sounding in his ear: "Mercy! mercy" as he closed the door. Descending the stairs with a deliberate step, he caught up his hat in the hall, and went out. And Adela, the usually indifferent, fell to the ground in a storm of anguished tears.

CHAPTER XXVIII

ON THE WAY FROM BLACKHEATH

Strolling hither and thither, just as his steps led him, for in truth he had no purpose just then, so intense was his mental distress, Mr. Grubb found himself somehow in Jermyn Street. He was passing the

Cavendish Hotel, his eyes nowhere, when a hand was laid upon his arm. A little lady in a close bonnet and black veil, standing at the hotel entrance, had arrested him.

"Were you going to pass me, Francis Grubb?"

"Miss Upton!" he exclaimed, coming with an effort, out of his wilderness, and clasping her offered hand. "I did not see you; I was buried in thought."

"In deep thought, as it seemed to me," rejoined Miss Upton, regarding his face with a meaning look. "Come upstairs to my sitting-room."

"Are you staying here?" he asked.

"Only until tomorrow afternoon. I came from home this morning. Sit down and take lunch with me," she added, removing her bonnet. "It is ready, you perceive. I told them to have it on the table by one o'clock. They are punctual, and so am I."

"You have been out?"

"Only to Chenevix House. I came up on business of my own, but I wanted to see the Acorns, so I drove there at once, after reporting myself here to the hotel people, to whom I wrote yesterday to secure my rooms. No meat! Why, what do you live upon?"

Something like a faint smile parted his lips. "Thank you—no, not today. I have no appetite."

"Try," she kindly whispered, leaning forward and laying her hand for a moment upon his. "Other men have had to bear as much before you."

So, then, she knew it! A vivid red dyed his brow. How painful it was, this allusion to it, even from her.

"You have heard it?" he breathed.

"I heard of the trouble about the cheque last week from the Rector, during a flying visit he had to pay Netherleigh. The man was in terrible distress, hardly knowing whether his son was guilty or not guilty. A little further news dropped out later, and yesterday Charles was brought home by his father and stepmother; his name cleared, but some one else's mentioned."

She paused a moment. Mr. Grubb said nothing.

"When I reached Lady Acorn's this morning, she was alone—and in a state, not of temper, but of real, genuine distress," continued Miss Upton. "I told her I had come to hear the whole truth about this miserable business, and she told me all, from beginning to end. She is full of wrath and bitterness: and who can wonder?"

"Against me?"

"Against you! No. Against Adela. She did not spare her daughter in the recital. She said that Mr. Grubb—you—were at that moment with Lord Acorn, negotiating, she believed, the articles of a separation. Was it so?"

"Yes. They are arranged."

"Alas! I have long foreseen that it might come to it. Before there was any notion of this last terrible offence of hers, I thought the day of retribution must surely come, unless she mended her ways. But we will say no more, now. Adela is my god-daughter, and I will do what I can for her, though I would rather have seen her in her grave."

He lifted his eyes to the earnest face.

"I would, indeed. Far rather would I have seen her in her grave than what she is—a heartless woman. You have been to her a husband in a thousand, and this is how she has requited you. And now, tell me—if you don't mind telling tales out of school—how Acorn is going on: for I expect you know. Fighting shy of his debts, as usual?"

In spite of the mental pain that pressed so heavily upon him, Mr. Grubb could not forbear a smile, her tone was so quaint. "Just now his lordship is flourishing," replied he, his voice assuming a lightness he did not feel. "He had a slice of luck at the Derby: won, it is said, between ten and twelve thousand pounds."

Miss Upton lifted her hands. "What a sum of money to win, or to lose! He might have lost it, I suppose, as easily as gained it: and then where would he have been? How can men do these things lightly? How much does he owe you?"

The question was put abruptly. A faint colour tinged Mr. Grubb's face. He hesitated.

"You do not care to say," quickly spoke Miss Upton. "Quite right of you, no doubt. I conclude you feel pretty secure, having taken his bonds on Court Netherleigh—whenever it shall fall in."

"I have not taken any bonds on Court Netherleigh. Believe that, Miss Upton."

"Do you mean to say that he has not offered you bonds on it, as security for your loans?"

"He has offered them over and over again. But I have never taken them. In the first place, it would have been no true security. Court Netherleigh is not his, and there exists, of course, a possibility that it may never be his: for he—is older than its present possessor," concluded Mr. Grubb, his eyes meeting Miss Upton's. "No; for what I have lent Lord Acorn, I possess no security beyond his acknowledgment."

"Ah," shortly commented Miss Upton. "I told you once, you know, that you were safe in letting him borrow money on the Netherleigh estate. But I did not mean to imply that I sanctioned your doing so; certainly not to help him to any extent."

"I have not helped him to any great extent. At least, not to more than I can afford to lose with equanimity. I have never advanced to him a sum, large or small, but in the full consciousness that it would probably never be returned."

Miss Upton nodded her approval, and passed to another topic. "Will you tell me how your mother is?" she asked. "I hear she is so ill as to be in danger, and that you have been afraid to leave her."

"She was in danger three or four days ago, and I was sent for in haste. But the danger has passed, and she is tolerably well again—excepting for weakness. My mother has had several of these attacks now, and it seems to me, that each one is more severe than the last. They are connected with the heart."

"Ay, we must all have some affliction or other as we draw near to the close of life; some reminder, more or less ominous in itself, that God will soon be calling us to that better world where there is neither sickness nor death," she remarked, dreamily. "She is going—and I am going—and yet—"

"Not you, surely, dear Miss Upton!" he interrupted, struck with the words.

She looked at him for a moment, saw his concern, and smiled.

"Are we not all going?" she asked—"some sooner, some later. And yet, I was about to say, what a short time ago it seems since I and Catherine Grant were girls together: dear friends and companions! How much I should like to see her!"

"Would you really like to do so? Would you care to go to Blackheath?"

"I should. But I don't know how to get there. When one comes to be close upon sixty years of age, and not strong, these short railway journeys try one mightily. I know they try me."

"Dear Miss Upton, you can go to Blackheath without the slightest exertion or trouble. My carriage will take you to my mother's door, and bring you back to this. Shall it do so?"

"Without trouble, you say? Then I will go this afternoon. No time like the present. I had meant to do two or three errands for myself, and told the fly to be here at three o'clock, but Annis shall do them for me."

"The carriage shall be here instead. Will you have it open or shut?"

"Open in going. Closed in returning, if it be at all late. Catherine and I will have a great deal to say to each other; once we meet, we shall not be in haste to part. That is, if she does not cherish too much resentment to speak to me at all. Of course, you will accompany me?"

"Of course I will," he answered: and hastened away to give the necessary orders. Not to his house; he did not go near that; and did not intend to do so, until fully assured that Lady Adela had left It; he went direct to the stables.

At three o'clock the carriage stood before the door of the hotel. Its master stood waiting for it, and Miss Upton came out, followed by her maid Annis, who was departing to do the errands. Mr. Grubb handed Miss Upton into the carriage, and they drove to Blackheath.

"Catherine!"

"Margery!"

The names simultaneously broke from their lips when the early friends met; they who had lived estranged for the better part of their lives. Mrs. Lynn was in what she called her invalid sitting-room, one that opened from her bed-chamber, and which she occupied when she was too ill to go downstairs. She was lying on a sofa near the open window—from which window there was to be seen so fair a landscape—but she rose when Miss Upton entered.

They sat on the sofa side by side, hand clasping hand. Grievances were forgotten, estrangement was at an end. Miss Upton had taken off her bonnet and mantle, and looked as much at home as though she had lived there for years. They fell to talking of the old days. Francis remained below with his sister.

"I did not expect to see you again, Margery, on this side the grave," spoke Mrs. Lynn. "Not so very long ago, I should have declined a visit from you had you proffered it. It is only when sickness has subdued the spirit that we lay aside old animosities."

"And therefore towards the end of life sickness comes to us. I said so this afternoon to your son. We quarrel and fight and take vengeance on one another in our hotheaded days: but when the blood chills with years and the world is fading from us, we see what our crooked ways have been worth."

"You were all very bitter with me for marrying Christopher Grubb, Margery; and you took care to let me know it. Uncle Francis—as we used to call Sir Francis Netherleigh, though without the slightest right to do so—was the most bitter of all."

"Just as Elizabeth Acorn's girls call me 'aunt' in these later years," remarked Miss Upton. "Yes, Uncle Francis was very angry. He thought you had thrown yourself away."

"Elizabeth Acorn has never condescended to take the slightest notice of me. Although my son has married her daughter, she has never given him the smallest intimation that she remembers we were friends in early life."

"Betsy always had her crotchets; they don't diminish with age," returned Miss Upton. "She may be called a disappointed woman; and disappointment seldom renders any one more genial."

Mrs. Lynn did not understand. "Disappointed in what way?"

"In her husband. Not in himself, but in his circumstances. When Betsy married him, it was to enter, as she supposed, upon a career of unlimited wealth and splendour. Instead of that, she found him to be the most reckless of men as regards money, spending all before him, and her life has been one of almost incessant embarrassment. You little know what shifts she has been sometimes put to. It has soured her, Catherine. What a noble man your son is," added the speaker, after a brief pause. "One in a thousand."

"And what a miserable mistake he made in wedding Adela Chenevix!" returned Mrs. Lynn, with emotion. "She makes him the most wretched wife. He does not open his lips to me, he never will do it; but I can see what a blighted life his is—and I hear others speak of it. I cannot help thinking that he is in some especial trouble with her at the present moment, or why does he remain down here, now that I am better?"

"So they have not thought well to tell his mother," reflected Margery Upton. Neither would she tell her.

"You are happy in your children, Catherine. Of your son the world may be proud—and is. As to your daughter, she is one of the sweetest girls I know."

"Yes, I am truly happy in my children," assented Mrs. Lynn. "It is a wonderful consolation. But happiness does not attend them. Francis we have spoken of. And poor Mary lost her betrothed husband, Robert Dalrymple, by a dreadful fate, as you know. She will never marry."

"Ah, that was a cruel business. Poor Robert! If he had only brought his troubles to me, I would have saved him."

"The singular thing is, that he did not take them to Francis," quickly spoke Mrs. Lynn. "Francis had the power to help him, equally with yourself, and he had the will. The very last day of Robert's life; at least, I think it was the last, he was with Francis in Grosvenor Square, and I believe Francis then offered to help him—or as good as offered to do so."

Margery Upton sighed. It was an unprofitable subject; a gloomy reminiscence. "Let us leave it, Catherine," she said. "Did you give your son the name of Francis in remembrance of Francis Netherleigh?"

"Indeed I did not. Sir Francis Netherleigh had wounded me too greatly for me to wish to retain any remembrance of him. Francis was named after his uncle and his father."

"Were you surprised at Netherleigh's being left to me?" resumed Miss Upton, breaking a pause of silence.

"Not at all. I thought it the most natural thing for Sir Francis to do. I had married, and was discarded; Betsy Cleveland had also married; her husband was a nobleman; mine was rich; and we neither of us needed Netherleigh. It was not likely he would leave it to either of us. You, on the contrary, continued to live with him as his niece—his child—and you had no fortune. It was a just bequest, Margery, in my judgment. It never occurred to me to think of it in any other light."

"Betsy Acorn has never forgiven me for having inherited it—or forgiven Uncle Francis for leaving it to me. I have wondered at odd moments whether you felt about it as she did."

"I?" returned Mrs. Lynn, in surprise. "Never. Sir Francis did right in leaving it to you. And, now, tell me a little about yourself, Margery. Are you in good health? You do not look strong."

We will leave them to themselves. It was a pleasant, and yet partly a sad meeting; and perhaps each opened her heart to the other in more confidential intercourse than had ever been exchanged between them before.

"Won't you come down and stay with me, and see the old place again, Catherine?" spoke entreatingly the mistress of Court Netherleigh, in parting.

"Never again, Margery. I would willingly come to you; I should like to see the dear old spot; but I shall never be able to go another day's journey from this, my home. Not very long now, and I shall be carried from it."

Twilight was advancing, when the carriage came round to take Miss Upton back to London. Lovely sunset colours lingered in the west; a few light clouds floated across the sky; the crescent moon shone with a pale silvery light.

Lost, no doubt, in thoughts of the past interview, Margery Upton sat in silence, leaning back in her corner of the carriage. Mr. Grubb did not break it. So far as could be seen, he was wholly occupied with the beauties of the sky. At least a mile of the way was thus passed. Presently she glanced at him, and noted his outward, dreamy gaze. How this trouble of his had troubled her, she did not care to tell. He had her warmest sympathy.

"Do not let this crush you," she suddenly cried, leaning towards him. "Do not let the world see that it has subdued you; don't give her that triumph. God can never mean that the life of a good and noble Christian man, as you are, should be blighted. Yes, I know," she continued, interrupting some words he spoke, "troubles come to all, and it is on the best of us, as I believe, that they fall most heavily; on God's chosen few."

He laid his other hand upon hers, and kept it there.

"It is, you know, through tribulation that we enter into the Kingdom," she continued, softly; "and tribulation takes various shapes and forms, as may be best suited to our true welfare. The cruelest pain that the world knows may be fraught with guidance to the gate of Eternity: which, otherwise, we might have missed."

He could but give a silent assent.

"Accept this trial, Francis. Bear it like a man, and you will in time live it down. Make no change in your manner of living; do not give up your home or establishment: no, nor your visitors: continue all that as before. It is my best advice to you."

"It is the best advice you could give," he answered, with emotion. "Thank you for all your sympathy, dear Miss Upton. Thank you ever."

She drew back to her corner, and he looked out at the night again. Thus nearly another mile was passed.

"Did you find my mother much changed?" he said by-and-bye. "Should you have known her again?"

"Known her again!"—returned Miss Upton, with a brief smile. "I knew whom I was going to see, and therefore I could trace the features I was once familiar with. We were girls when we parted, young and blooming; now we are old women verging on the grave. Catherine retains her remarkable eyes, undimmed, unclouded. They are beautiful as ever; beautiful as yours."

Francis Grubb had heard so much of his eyes all his life, remarkable eyes, in truth, as Miss Upton called them, and very beautiful, that the allusion fell unheeded, if not unheard, on his ear. Something else in the words laid more hold upon him.

"Not verging on the grave yet, I trust: you. My dear mother will not, I fear, be spared long to us; but she has an incurable disease. Such is not your case, dear Miss Upton; and you should not talk so. You are young yet, as compared with many people. As, in fact, is my mother."

Margery Upton touched his arm, that he should look at her. "How do you know that I have not an incurable disease? Why should not such a thing come to me, as well as to your mother?"

Something in the tone, the earnest look, struck on him with fear. "It cannot be!" he slowly whispered.

"It is. I am dying, Francis. Dying slowly but surely. The probability is that I shall go before your mother goes."

He remembered how worn and weary he had thought her looking for some time past; how especially so on this same morning when she stopped him at the door of the Cavendish. He recalled a sentence, a word, that had fallen from her now and then, seeming to imply that she saw the close of life drawing near. Yet still, with all this presenting itself to him in a sudden mental effort, he could only reiterate: "It cannot be; it cannot be!"

"It is," she repeated. "I have suspected it for some time. I know it now."

A lump seemed to rise in his throat. How truly he esteemed and valued this good lady he never quite realized until this morning. She resumed.

"I know my friends, the few who consider they have a right to concern themselves about me, wonder that I should have come up to town so much more frequently during the past few months than I was wont to come. What I come for is to see my physician, Dr. Stair. I live too far off to expect him to come to me; and the journey does me no harm. I have an appointment with him tomorrow at eleven: after that, I return home."

"Is it the heart?" he asked, drawing a deep breath.

"No: but it is a disorder none the less fatal than some of those diseases that attack the heart. It is about two years ago—perhaps not quite so much," she broke off, "since I began to fear I was not well. I let it go on for a little time; Frost, our local doctor, did not seem to make much out of it; and then I came up to Dr. Stair. He is a straightforward man, and he plainly said he did not like my symptoms, but he thought he could subdue them and set me right. I grew better for a time; the malady seemed to have been checked, though it did not entirely leave me. Latterly it has returned with increased force; and—I know my fate."

The disclosure brought to him the keenest pain. "If I could only avert it!" he cried out, in his sorrow; "if I could only ward it off you!"

"No one on earth can do that. For myself, I am quite resigned; resting, and content to rest, in God's good hands."

"And, how long—"

"How long will it be before the end comes, you would ask," she said, for he did not conclude the sentence. "That I do not know. I mean to put the question to Dr. Stair tomorrow, and I am sure he will answer it to the best of his belief. It may be pretty near."

"Do you suffer pain?"

"Always; more or less. That will grow worse, I suppose, before it is over."

"Alas! alas!" he mentally breathed. "Should not your friends be made acquainted with this, Miss Upton?"

"My chief friends are acquainted with it. I have no very close friends. The Rector of Netherleigh is the closest, and he has known of it for some time. That is, he knows I am suffering from a disorder that I shall probably never get the better of. Your mother knows it, for I told her this evening; and now you know it. My faithful maid Annis knows a little—Frost and Dr. Stair most of all. No one else knows of it in the wide world: and I do not wish that any one should know."

"Is it right? Right to them?"

"Why, what other friends have I? Lady Acorn, you may say. She has never been as a friend to me. Your mother and I, had opportunity permitted, might have been the truest and dearest friends, but I and Betsy Acorn, never. She and I do not assimilate. Time enough to proclaim my condition to the world when I become so ill that it cannot be concealed."

She fell into a reverie; and they scarcely exchanged another word for the rest of the way.

"You will not speak of this to the Acorns," she said to him, as the carriage stopped at the hotel.

"Certainly not, as you do not wish it. Or to any one else."

"It would only give a fillip to Lord Acorn's extravagance. With the prospect of coming into Court Netherleigh close at hand, he would increase his debts thick and threefold."

Francis Grubb nodded assent; he knew how true it was: he shook her hand with a lingering pressure, and watched her up the stairs. Then, dismissing his carriage, he walked through the lighted streets to Charing-Cross Station on his way back to Blackheath.

It may be that he shunned his home lest his wife should still be in it. He need not have feared. Within an hour of his departure from it at midday, while she was still in the depth of the bewilderment which the blow had brought her, Lord Acorn arrived. His errand was to take her away with him; and to take her peremptorily. He did not say to her, "Will you put on your bonnet and come with me, Adela:" he said, curtly, "Come."

"I cannot leave my home in this dreadful way, papa," she gasped, voice and hands alike trembling. "I cannot leave it for ever."

"You will," he coldly answered. "You must. You have no alternative. I am come to remove you from it."

"No, no," she pleaded. "Oh, papa, have mercy! Papa, papa!"

"You should have made that prayer to your husband, Adela—while the time to do it yet remained to you."

She clasped her hands in bitter repentance. "He will forgive me yet; I know he will. He may let me—"

"Never," interrupted Lord Acorn. "You may put that notion out of your mind for good, Adela. Francis Grubb will never forgive you, or receive you back while life shall last."

She moaned faintly.

"And you have only yourself to thank for it. Put your things on, as I bid you," he sternly added. "This is waste of time. And send your maid to me for instructions."

And thus Adela was removed from her husband's house overwhelmed with shame and remorse.

CHAPTER XXIX

A DREARY LIFE

In the light of the late but genial autumn sunshine lay Court Netherleigh. September was quickly passing. It was summer weather when we last met the reader; it is getting on for winter now.

In that favourite room of Miss Upton's where we first saw her—Miss Margery's room, as it is called in the household—she sits today, shivering near a blazing fire, a bright cashmere shawl worn over her purple silk gown, a simple cap of rich white lace shading her shrunken features. Her malady is making steady progress, and she always feels cold.

The small, pretty room has been renewed, but its old colours are retained. The glass-doors, that used to stand open when the sun shone or the air was balmy, are closed today, for the faintest breath of wind chills the invalid. On the table at her elbow lies a book of devotion half closed, her spectacles resting between the leaves; one of those books that the gay and busy world turn from as being so gloomy, and that bring comfort so great to those who are leaving it. Miss Upton sits back in her chair, looking up at the blue heavens, where she is so soon to be.

"I cannot help wishing sometimes," she began in low dreamy tones, "that more decided revelation of what heaven will be had been vouchsafed to us. I mean as to our own state there, our work, and occupations. Though I suppose that all work—work, as we call it here—will be as rest there. We know that we shall be in a state of happiness beyond conception; but we know not precisely of what it will consist."

"I suppose we were not meant to know," replied the young lady to whom she spoke, who sat apart on the green satin sofa, her elbow resting on one arm of it, her delicate hand shading her face. The tone of her voice was weary and depressed, the other hand lay listless on her muslin dress. "Time enough for that, perhaps, when we get there—those who do get there."

"Don't be irreverent," came the quick reproof.

"Irreverent! I did not mean to be so, Aunt Margery."

"You used to be irreverent enough, Lady Adela. As the world knows."

"Ay. Things have changed for me."

It was indeed the Lady Adela sitting there. But she was altered in looks almost as much as Miss Margery. The once careless, saucy, haughty girl had grown sad, her manner utterly spiritless, the once blooming face was pale and thin. Only yesterday had she come to Court Netherleigh, following on a communication from Lady Acorn.

"I can do nothing with her; she is utterly self-willed and obstinate; I shall send her to you for a little while, Margery," wrote Lady Acorn to Miss Upton: and Margery Upton had replied that she might come.

That a wave of trouble had swept over Lady Adela, leaving desolation and despair behind it, was all too visible. To be put away by her husband in the face and eyes of her own family and of the world, was to her proud spirit the very bitterest blow possible to be inflicted on it; a cruel mortification, that she would never quite lose the sting of as long as life lasted.

On the very day the separation was decided upon, not an hour after Mr. Grubb left her in her chamber after apprising her of it, Lord Acorn, as you have read, came to the house, and took her from it without ceremony. His usual débonnaire indifference had given place to a sternness, against which there could be no thought of rebellion.

She took up her abode at Chenevix House that day, and Darvy followed with the possessions that belonged to her. She was not kindly received, or warmly treated. No, she had given too serious offence for that. Her mother did not spare her in the matter of reproach; her father was calmly bitter; Grace was cold. Lady Sarah Hope ran away to the country to avoid her, taking her sister Frances and Alice Dalrymple; and Lady Sarah made no scruple of letting it be known at her father's why she had gone.

Lord and Lady Acorn might have their personal failings, the one be too lavish of money, the other of temper, but they had at least brought up their daughters to be good and honourable women, instilling into them strict principles; and the blow was a sharp one. They deemed it right and just not to spare her who had inflicted it—inflicted it in wanton wilfulness—and they let her pain come home to her. It all told upon Adela.

The world turned upon her a cold shoulder. Rumours of the separation between Mr. and Lady Adela Grubb soon grew into certainty; and the world wanted to know the cause of it. For, after all, the true and immediate cause, that terrible crime she had allowed herself to commit, never transpired. The very few cognizant of it buried the secret within their own bosoms for her good name's sake. No clue transpiring as to this, people fell back upon the other and only cause known, more or less, to them—her long-maintained cavalier treatment of her husband. Mr. Grubb must have come to his senses at last, reasoned society, and sent her home to her mother to be taught better manners. And society considered that he had done righteously.

So the world, taking up other people's business according to custom, turned its back upon her. Which was, to say the least of it, inconsistent. For now, had the Lady Adela been suspected of any grave social crime; one, let us say, involving fears of having to appear before the Judge of the Divorce Court, society would have shaken hands with her as usual, so long as public proceedings remained in abeyance: what every one may privately see or suspect goes for nothing. This other offence was lighter, it did not involve those fatal extremes; this was more as though she were being punished as a naughty child; consequently the world thought fit to let its opinion be known, and to deal out a meed of censure on its own immaculate score.

But it told, I say, on Lady Adela. Told cruelly. Cast off by her husband for good and aye; tacitly reproached daily and hourly by her parents; rejected by her sisters, as though she might tarnish them if brought into too close contact, and looked askance at by society; Lady Adela drank the cup of repentance to the dregs.

If she could, if she could only undo her work—if that one fatal morning, when she found the cheque-book lying on the floor of her husband's dressing-room, had never been numbered in the calendar of the past! She was for ever wishing this fruitless wish. For ever wishing that her treatment of her husband had been different in the time before that one temptation set in.

No more invitations came for her from the gay world. Not that she would have accepted them. For the short time the Chenevix family remained in town after the outbreak, cards would come in, bidding Lord and Lady Acorn and their daughter Grace to this entertainment or to that; but never a one came for Lady Adela Grubb. She might have passed out of existence for all the notice taken of her. Mr. Grubb had suggested to her father that she should have her own carriage. She did not set one up; she would have had no use for it, had it been set up for her.

They went to their seat in Oxfordshire, carrying her with them. Lord Acorn returned to town in a day or two: Grace went on to Colonel Hope's place near Cheltenham, to stay with her sisters, Sarah and Frances. This left Adela and Lady Acorn alone; and her ladyship very nearly drove the girl wild with her tartness. She would have driven her quite wild had Adela's spirit been what it once was; but it was altogether subdued.

"Mamma," said Adela to her one day, after some mutual bickering, "do you want me to die?"

"Don't talk like a simpleton," retorted Lady Acorn.

"I think I shall die—if I have to lead this life much longer."

"You are as much likely to die as I am. What do you mean?"

"I mean what I say. I think I must—must kill myself, or something. Take a dose of opium, perhaps."

"You wicked girl! Running on in that false manner! Whatever your life may be, you have brought it upon yourself."

"Yes," thought Adela, "there lies the sting."

"What's the matter with the life?" tartly resumed her mother.

"It is so weary. And there's no hope left in it."

"It would not be weary if you chose to exert yourself. Get music—books—work. Look at Grace, how busy she is when we are staying here, with her sick-clubs, and her poor cottagers, and her schools."

Lady Adela turned up her pretty nose. "Sick-clubs and schools! Yes, that suits Grace."

"At all events, it keeps her from being dull. What do you do all day long! Just sit with your head bent on your hand, or mope about the rooms like one demented! It gives me the fidgets to look at you! You should rouse yourself, Adela."

"Rouse myself to what?" she faintly asked. "There's nothing to rouse myself to."

"Make something: some interest for yourself. No life is open to you now except a quiet one. Even were it possible that you could wish for any other, I and your father would take care you did not enter on it. But quiet lives may be made full of interest, if we will; a great deal more so than noisy ones."

Good advice, no doubt: perhaps the only advice now open to Lady Adela. She did not profit by it. The weary time went on, and she grew more weary day by day. Lady Acorn called her obstinate; sometimes Adela retaliated. At last, the countess, losing all patience, wrote to Miss Upton to say she should send her for a little change to Court Netherleigh; for she was quite unaware of the critical state of Miss Upton's health.

And this was the first time, this morning when we see Miss Upton and Adela sitting together, that any special conversation had been held between them. The previous day had been one of Miss Margery's "bad days," when she was confined to the sofa in her chamber, and she had only been able to see Adela for a minute or two, to bid her welcome. Miss Upton criticizing Adela's appearance by the morning light, found her looking ill, but she quite believed her to be just as graceless as ever.

"Things change for all of us, Adela," observed she, continuing the conversation. "They have changed most especially for you."

Lady Adela raised her face, something like defiance on it. Was the miserable past to be recalled to her here, as well as at home?—was she going to be for ever lectured upon its fruits, as her mother lectured her? She was wretched enough herself about it, Heaven knew, and would undo it if she could; but that was no reason why all the world should be incessantly casting it in her teeth. She answered sharply.

"The past is over, Aunt Margery, and the less said about it the better. To be told of it will do me no good."

Aunt Margery did not like the tone. Could this mistaken girl—she really looked but as a girl—be extenuating the past, and her own conduct in it?

"Do you know what I said, Adela, when the news reached me of all you had done, and I thought of the consequences it might involve? I said—and I spoke truly—that I would rather have seen you in your grave."

"Said it to mamma, I suppose?"

"No. I tried to excuse you to her. I said it to your husband."

"Oh—to him," said Adela, assuming an indifference she did not feel.

"And I am not sure but death might have been a happier fate for you than this that you have brought upon yourself—disgrace, the neglect of the world, and a dreary, purposeless life."

It might have been. Adela felt it so to her heart's core. She bit her lips to conceal their trembling.

"All the same, Aunt Margery, he was harsher than he need have been."

"Who was?"

"Mr. Grubb."

"Do you think so, Adela—remembering your long course of scorn and cruelty? My only wonder was that he had not emancipated himself from it long before."

Adela flushed, and began to tap her foot on the carpet in incipient rebellion. Of all things, she hated to be reminded of that mistake of the long-continued years. Miss Margery noted the signs.

"Child, I do not wish to pain you unnecessarily: but, as the topic has come up, I cannot allow you to mistake my opinion. You had a prince of a husband; a man of rare merit: he has, I truly believe, scarcely his equal in the world—"

"I know you always thought him perfection," interrupted Adela.

"I found him so. As near perfection as mortal man may be here."

"Including his name," she put in, with a touch of her old sauciness.

Miss Upton replied not in words: she simply looked at her. It was a long, steady, and very peculiar look, one that Adela did not understand, and it passed away with a half-smile.

"For true nobility of mind," resumed Miss Margery, "for uprightness of life, for goodness of heart, who is like him? Look at his generosity to all and every one. Recall one slight recent act of his—what he did for that fantastically foolish lad, Charles Cleveland. Most men, provoked as Mr. Grubb had been by you, and in a degree also by Charles, would have abandoned him to his fate. Not he. That is not his way. When the poor Rector was fretting himself to discover what was next to be done with Charles, and the young fellow was mooning about Netherleigh, his hands in his pockets, trying to make up his mind to go and enlist, for he saw no other opening for him, there came a letter to the Rector from Mr. Grubb. He had interested himself with his correspondents in Calcutta—I'm not sure but it is a branch of his own house—and had obtained Charles a place, out there, at just double the salary he enjoyed here."

"And Charley is half-way over the seas on his voyage to it," lightly remarked Adela. "Charley was only a goose, Aunt Margery."

"You cannot say that of your husband," sharply returned Miss Margery, not approving the tone. "Unless it was in his love for you. Your husband was fond of you to folly; he indulged your every whim; he would have made your life happy as a dream of Paradise. And how did you requite him?"

No answer. The rebellious tapping of the foot had ceased.

"It has been a sad, cruel business altogether," sighed Miss Upton: "both for him and for you. It has blighted his life; taken all the sunshine out of it. And what has it done for yours?"

What indeed? Adela pushed back her pretty brown hair with both hands from her feverish forehead.

"Any way, the blight does not seem to have sensibly affected him, Aunt Margery. One hears of him here, there, and everywhere. You can't take up a newspaper but you see his name reiterated in it—Grubb, Grubb, Grubb!"

She put a great amount of scorn into the name. Miss Upton sighed.

"I am grieved to see you in this frame of mind, Adela."

"I am only saying what's true, Aunt Margery. I'm sure one would think he had taken the whole business of the world upon his shoulders. He is being asked to stand for some county or other now."

"Yes; he is playing an active part in the world," assented Miss Margery. "All honour to him that it is so! Do you suppose that one, wise and conscientious as he is, would put aside his duties to God and man because his heart has been well-nigh broken by a heartless wife? Rather would he be the more earnest in fulfilling them. Occupation will enable him to forget the past sooner and more effectually than anything else would."

"To forget me, I suppose you mean, Aunt Margery."

"Would you wish him to remember you, Adela—and what you have been to him? I tell you, child, that my whole heart aches for your husband: it ached long before you left him; while—I must say it—it was full of resentment against you. I am very sorry for you, Adela; you are my god-daughter, and I will try my best, whilst you stay with me, to soothe your wounds and reconcile you to this inevitable change. It has tried you: I see that, in spite of your pretended carelessness; you appear to me to be anything but strong."

"I am not strong, Aunt Margery. And if I fade away into the grave, I don't suppose any one will miss me or regret me."

"The best thing for her, perhaps, poor child—to be removed from this blighted life to the bright and beautiful life above! And her husband, released from his trammels, would then probably find that comfort in a second wife which he missed in her. Who knows but this may be God's purpose? He is over all."

Was Margery Upton aware that these words were spoken in a murmur—not merely thought? Probably not. They reached Adela: and a curious pang shot through her heart.

The butler came into the room at the moment, bringing a message to his mistress. One of her tenants had called, and wished very much to be allowed a short interview with her. And Miss Upton, who was still able to attend at times to worldly matters, quitted the room at once.

A faint cry escaped Lady Adela as the door closed. She turned her face upon the sofa-cushion, and burst into a flood of distressing tears.

CHAPTER XXX

LAST WORDS

December was in, and winter weather lay on the earth. Court Netherleigh looked out on a lovely view, rare as a scene from fairyland. Snow clung to the branches of the trees in feathery beauty; icicles sparkled in the sun. A new and strange world might have replaced the old one.

Margery Upton lay on the sofa in her dressing-room. She was able to get into it most days, but she had given up going downstairs now. During the months that had gone on since the autumn and the time of Lady Adela's sojourn, the fatal disease which had fastened on Miss Upton had made its persistent though partly imperceptible ravages, and her condition was now no longer a secret; though few people suspected how very near the end might be. In her warm dressing-gown of soft violet silk, for she remained loyal to her favourite colour, and her lace cap shading her face, she lay between the fireplace and the window, gazing at the snowy landscape. She did not look very ill, and Grace Chenevix might be excused for the hopeful thought, now crossing her mind, that perhaps after all Aunt Margery would rally. Grace had come down to spend a few days with her. She sat on the other side the hearthrug, tatting, the small ivory shuttle passing rapidly through her fingers.

"You do not have this beautiful scene in London, Grace," observed Miss Upton.

"Not often, Aunt Margery. Now and then, once, say, in four or five winters, the trees in the park look lovely. Of course we never see so beautiful a prospect as this is in its completeness."

"I wonder if our scenery in the next world will be much more beautiful—or if it will even be anything like this?" came the dreamy remark from the invalid. "Ah, Grace, I suppose I shall soon know now."

Lady Grace checked a sigh. She thought it best to be cheerful. The shuttle had to be threaded again, and she got up to reach the ball of thread.

"Who was your letter from this morning, Gracie? Annis said you had one: from 'foreign parts,' she took care to inform me."

Grace smiled. "Yes, I had, Aunt Margery; I had forgotten it for the moment. It was from Harriet. They are still in Switzerland, and mean to stay there."

"I thought they were to go to Rome for Christmas."

"But Adela objects to it so much, Harriet says; so they intend to remain where they are, in the desolate old château. They have made it as air-tight as they can, and keep up large wood fires. Adela shrinks from meeting the world, and Rome is unusually full of English."

"How is Adela?"

"Just the same. Worse, if anything; more sad, more spiritless. Harriet begins to fear she will become really ill; she seems to have a sort of low fever upon her."

"Poor girl!" sighed Miss Upton. "How she has blighted her life! I had a letter, too, this morning," she resumed, "from Mrs. Lynn. She is very ill; thinks she cannot last much longer—Francis told me so last week. I wonder"—in a half-whisper—"which of us will go first, she or I?"

"Was Mr. Grubb here last week, Aunt Margery?"

"For a few hours. I like him to come to me sometimes; he is a great favourite of mine. Grace, do you know what I have often wished—that that old story, that he proposed for you, had been fact instead of misapprehension. With you he would have found the happiness he missed with Adela."

A flush passed over Grace's fair, placid face. She bent her head.

"Marriages are said, you know, to be made in heaven," she remarked, looking up with a smile; "so I conclude that all must have been right. Were the years to come over again, Adela would act very differently. She—oh, Aunt Margery, the snowy sprays are disappearing!"

"Ay; the sun has come out, and the snow melts. Few pleasant things last long in this world, child; something or other comes to mar them. But I thought you meant to go to Moat Grange this morning, Grace. You should start at once; it has struck eleven."

"I said I should like to see Selina, and to call on Mrs. Dalrymple on the way."

"Well, do so. Selina will receive you with open arms. She must be amazingly lonely, shut up in that dreary house from year's end to year's end. They see no company."

Grace put her tatting into its little basket, and rose. "Are you sure you shall not feel dull at being left, Aunt Margery?" she stayed to ask.

"I never feel dull, Grace."

Barely had Grace started on her walk, when the maid came to the dressing-room to say the Rector had called. "Will you see him, ma'am?" she inquired.

"Yes, Annis, I wish to see him," was Miss Upton's reply, as she rose from her recumbent position on the sofa and sat down upon it. Annis folded a grey shawl over her mistress's knees, put a footstool under her feet, and sent up Mr. Cleveland.

After a short time given to subjects of more vital importance, Miss Upton began to talk of her worldly affairs, induced to it possibly by a question of the Rector's as to whether all things were settled.

"You mean my will, I suppose," she answered, slightly smiling. "Yes, it is settled and done with. Will you be surprised to hear that I made my will within a month of coming into this estate, and that it has never been altered?"

"Indeed!" he remarked.

"I added a codicil to it last year, specifying the legacies I wish to bequeath; but the substance of the will, with its bequest, Court Netherleigh, remains unchanged."

Mr. Cleveland opened his lips to speak, and closed them again. In the impulse of the moment, he was about to say, "To whom have you left it?" But he remembered that it was a question he could not properly put.

"You were about to ask me who it is that will inherit this property, and you do not like to do so," she said, nodding to him pleasantly. "Well—"

"I beg your pardon," he interrupted. "The thought did arise to me, and I almost forgot myself."

"And very natural that it should arise to you. I am about to tell you all about it. I meant to do so before my death: as well now as any other time."

"Have you left it to Lord Acorn?"

"No; that I have not," she replied, in quick, decisive tones, as if the very suggestion did not please her. "Lord Acorn and his wife have chosen to entertain the notion; though they have not had any warranty for it from me, but the contrary: understand me, please, the contrary. Court Netherleigh is willed to Francis Grubb."

Mr. Cleveland's surprise was so great that for the moment he could only gaze at the speaker. He doubted if he heard correctly.

"To Francis Grubb!" he exclaimed.

"Yes; to him, and no other. I see how surprised you are. The world will feel surprise also."

"But Mr. Grubb is so rich!—he does not want Court Netherleigh," debated the Rector: not that he had any wish to cavil with the decree; he simply spoke out the thought that occurred to him.

"Were Mr. Grubb in possession of all the wealth of the Indies, he would still inherit Court Netherleigh," said she, looking across at her listener.

"I see. He is a favourite of yours; and most deservedly so."

"Cast your thoughts outwards, Mr. Cleveland, to the circle known to you and to me," she continued: "can you point out one single individual who has any abstract right to succeed to Court Netherleigh?"

"No, I cannot," he said, after a pause. "It is only because I have been accustomed to think it would become Lord Acorn's that I feel surprise."

"Lord Acorn would only make ducks-and-drakes of it; we all know that. And, to return to the subject of right, or claim, he does not possess so much of that as does Mr. Grubb."

Mr. Cleveland waited. He could not quite understand.

"Listen," said Miss Upton. "We three girls—you know whom I mean—were the only relatives Sir Francis Netherleigh had in the world. The other two married; I was left; and, after my mother's death, I came to live here. One day, during his fatal illness—it was the very last day he ever came downstairs—he bade me put aside my work and listen to him. It was a lovely summer afternoon, and we were sitting in the blue drawing-room, at the open window, he in his easy-chair. Uncle Francis—as we three girls had always called him, though, as you know, he was no uncle of ours—began speaking to me for the first time of his approaching death. I burst into tears, and that did not please him: he could be impatient at times. 'I want you to listen to me rationally, not to cry,' he said; 'and you must have known for some time that I was going.' So I dried my tears as well as I could, and he went on to tell me that it was I who would succeed to Court Netherleigh. I was indeed surprised! I could not believe it; just as you did not believe me now, when I told you I had bequeathed it to Francis Grubb; and I said something about not taking it—that I was not of sufficient consequence to be the mistress of Court Netherleigh. That put him out—little things had done so of late—and he testily asked me who else there was to take it. 'I have neither son nor nephew, more's the pity,' he went on, 'no relative of any kind, except you three girls. Had Catherine Grant not married she would have had Court Netherleigh,' he continued, 'but she put herself beyond the pale of society. Betsy Cleveland has done the same; and there is only you.' He then passed on to say how he should wish the place to be kept up. 'And to whom am I to leave it?' I said to him in turn, feeling greatly perplexed; 'I shall not know what to do with it.' 'That is chiefly what I want to talk to you about,' he answered. 'Perhaps you will marry, and have a son—' 'No; I shall never marry—never!' I interrupted. For I had had my little romance in early life," broke off Miss Upton, looking at the Rector, "and that kind of thing had closed for me. You have heard something of it, I fancy?"

Mr. Cleveland nodded: and she resumed.

"Uncle Francis saw I was in earnest; that no heir to Court Netherleigh would ever spring from me. 'In that case,' he said, 'I must suggest some one else,' and there he came to a pause. 'There's Lord Acorn,' I ventured to say, 'Betsy's husband—' 'Hold your tongue, unless you can talk sense!' he called out in anger. 'Would I allow Court Netherleigh to fall into the hands of a spendthrift? If George Acorn came into the property tomorrow, by the end of the year there would be nothing left of it: every acre would be mortgaged away. I charge you,' he solemnly added, 'not to allow George Acorn, or that son of his, little Denne, or any other son he may hereafter have, ever to come into Court Netherleigh. You understand, Margery, I forbid it. Putting aside Acorn's spendthrift nature, which would be an insurmountable barrier, and I dare say his son inherits it, I should not care for a peer to own the property; rather some one who will take the name of Netherleigh, and in whom the baronetcy may perhaps be revived.' You now see," added Miss Upton, glancing at the earnest face of the Rector, "why I am debarred, even though it had been my wish, from bequeathing Court Netherleigh to Lord Acorn."

"I do indeed."

"To go back to my uncle. 'Failing children of your own,' he continued, 'there is only one I can name as your successor—there's no other person living to name—and that is the little son of Catherine Grubb.' 'Catherine's son!' I interrupted, in very astonishment. 'Yes; why not?' he answered. 'She offended me; but he has not; and I hear, for I have made inquiries through Pencot, that he is a noble little lad: his name, too, is Francis—Pencot has obtained all necessary information. In the years to come, when he shall be a good man—for Pencot tells me no pains are being spared to make him that—perhaps also a great one, he may come here and reign as my successor, a second Sir Francis Netherleigh. In any case, he must take the name with the property; it must be made a condition: do not forget that.' I promised that I would not forget it, but I could not get over the surprise I felt. This boy was the son of Christopher Grubb; and it was to him, to his calling, so much objection had been raised in the family."

"It does appear rather contradictory on the face of it," agreed Mr. Cleveland.

"Yes. Uncle Francis saw what was in my mind. 'Were the past to come over again,' he observed, 'I might be less harsh with Catherine, more tolerant to him.' 'But Mr. Grubb is in trade, is a merchant, just as he was then,' I returned, wonderingly. 'When our days in this world draw to their close, and we stand on the threshold of another, ideas change,' returned my uncle. 'We see then that the inordinate value we have set on worldly distinctions may have been, to say the least of it, exaggerated; whilst the principles of right and justice become more weighty. What little right or claim there is in the matter, with regard to a successor to Court Netherleigh, lay with Catherine Grant. I have had to substitute you, Margery, for her; but it is right that her son should come in after you. I also find that Mr. Grubb's business is of a high standing, altogether different from the ideas we formed of it.'"

"How did any right lie with Catherine Grant—more than with you or Elizabeth Cleveland?" asked the Rector.

"In this way: Catherine Grant was the most nearly related to Sir Francis. Her mother was his first cousin, whereas my mother and Betsy's mother were only second cousins. Catherine also was the eldest of the three, by about a year. So you perceive he spoke with reason—the right of succession, if any right existed, lay with her."

Mr. Cleveland nodded.

"'After you come into possession here, do not lose time in making your will,' he continued. 'Tomorrow I will write down a few particulars to guide you, which you can, at the proper time, show to Pencot. The lad's name, Francis Grubb, will be put in as your successor, and when he comes here, in later years, he must change it to Francis Netherleigh.' 'But,' I rejoined, 'suppose the little boy should grow up a bad man, a man of evil repute, what then?' 'Then,' he said, striking his hand emphatically upon the elbow of his chair, 'I charge you to destroy your first will, and make a fresh one. Look out in the world for yourself, and choose a worthy successor—not any one of the Acorns, mind, I have interdicted that; some gentleman of fair and estimable character, who will do his duty earnestly to God and to his neighbour, and who will take my name. Not the baronetcy. Unless he were of blood relationship to me, though ever so remote, no plea would exist for petitioning for that. But I think better things of this little boy in question,' he added quickly; 'instinct whispers that he will be found worthy.' As he is," emphatically concluded Miss Upton. "And I intend him to be, and hope he will be, a second Sir Francis Netherleigh. I have put things in train for it."

Miss Upton paused a moment, as if lost in the past.

"It is a singular coincidence, not unlike a link in a chain," she went on, dreamily, "that the present Prime Minister should be an old habitué of Court Netherleigh; many a week in his boyhood did he pass here with Uncle Francis, who was very kind to him. He has continued his friendship with me unto this day; coming down to visit me occasionally. I made a confidant of him during his last visit, telling him what I am now telling you, and I asked him to get this accomplished. He promised faithfully to do so, for our old friendship's sake, and in remembrance of his obligations to Uncle Francis, who had been a substantial friend to him. It would not be difficult, he said, Mr. Grubb assenting—whom, by the way, he esteems greatly. Therefore, you will, I hope, at no very prolonged period after my death, see him reigning here, Sir Francis Netherleigh."

"Has Mr. Grubb assented?" asked the Rector.

Miss Upton shook her head and smiled. "Mr. Grubb knows nothing whatever about the matter. He has no more idea that he will inherit Court Netherleigh than I had that I should inherit it before that revelation to me by Uncle Francis. He will know nothing until I am dead. I have written him a farewell letter, which will then reach him, explaining all things; just as I have written out a statement for the world, disclosing the commands laid upon me by Uncle Francis, lest I should be accused of caprice, and possibly—Mr. Grubb of cupidity."

"You are content to leave him your successor?"

"More than content. I look around, and ask myself who else is so worthy. After Uncle Francis's death, I was not content. No, I confess it: Catherine had offended all our prejudices, and her child shared them in my mind. But I never thought of disputing the charge laid upon me, and my will was made in the boy's favour. From time to time, as the years passed on, Mr. Pencot brought me reports of him—that he was growing up all that could be wished for. Still, I could not quite put away my prejudice; and whether I should have sought to make acquaintance with him, had chance not brought it about, I cannot say. I met him first at a railway-station."

"Indeed?" cried Mr. Cleveland, who had never heard of that day's meeting.

"I was going down to Cheltenham with Annis and Marcus, and our train came to grief near Reading; the passengers had to get out whilst the damage, something to an axle, was tinkered up. Francis Grubb was coming up from the Acorns' place in Oxfordshire: it was during the time he was making love to Adela, and the accident to my train stopped his. I was sitting by the wayside disconsolately enough on my little wooden bonnet-box, when one of the nicest-looking and grandest men, for a young man, I ever saw, came up and politely asked if he could be of any service to me. My heart, so to say, went out to him at once, his manner was so winning, his countenance so good and noble. Something in his eyes struck me as familiar—you know how beautiful they are—when in another moment my own eyes fell on the name on his hand-bag, 'C. Grubb.' Then I remembered the eyes; they were Catherine's; and I knew that I saw before me her son and my heir."

"And your silent prejudice against him ceased from that time," laughed the Rector.

"Entirely. I have learnt to love him, to be proud of him. Catherine cannot feel more pride in her son than I feel in him. But I have never given him the slightest hint that he will inherit Court Netherleigh. Not that I have never felt tempted to do so. When Adela has jeered at his name, in her contemptuous way, it has been on the tip of my tongue more than once to say to her: He will bear a better sometime. And I have told himself once—or twice—that he was quite safe in letting Acorn borrow money on Court Netherleigh. He is safe, you see, seeing that it is he himself who will come into it: though, of course, he took it to mean that Acorn would do so."

Mr. Cleveland drew a long breath. These matters had surprised him, but in his heart of hearts he felt thankful that the rich demesnes would become Francis Grubb's and not thriftless George Acorn's.

"Never a word of this abroad until I am gone, my old friend," she enjoined, "not even to your wife; you understand that?"

"I understand it perfectly, dear Miss Upton, and will observe it."

"You will not have long to wait."

CHAPTER XXXI

IN THE OLD CHÂTEAU

A draughty old château in Switzerland. Not that it need have been draughty, for it lay at the foot of a mountain, sheltered from the east winds. But the doors did not fit, and the windows rattled, after the custom of most old châteaux: and so the winter air crept in. It stood in a secluded spot quite out of the beaten tracks of travellers; and it looked upon one of the most glorious prospects that even this favoured land of lovely scenery can boast.

That prospect in part, and in part the very moderate rent asked for the house, had induced Sir Sandy MacIvor to take it for the autumn months. The MacIvors, though descended from half the kings of Scotland, could not boast of anything very great in the shape of income. Sir Sandy's was but small, and he and his wife, Lady Harriet, formerly Harriet Chenevix, had some trouble to make both ends meet. The little baronet was fond of quoting the old saying that he had to cut his coat according to his cloth. Therefore, when Lady Adela went to them for a prolonged stay, the very ample allowance made for her to Sir Sandy was most welcome.

Upon the close of Adela's short visit to Court Netherleigh in the autumn, she returned to her mother. The visit had not been productive of any good result as regarded her cheerfulness of mind and manner; for her life seemed only to grow more dreary. Lady Acorn did not approve of this, and took care daily to let Adela know she did not, dealing out to her sundry reproaches. One day when Adela was unusually low-spirited, the countess made use of a threat—that she should be transported to that gloomy Swiss fastness the MacIvors had settled themselves in, and stop there until she mended her manners.

A chance word, spoken at hazard, sometimes bears fruit. Adela, a faint light rising in her eyes as she heard this, lifted her voice eagerly. "Mother, let me go; send me there as soon as you please," she said. "It will at least be better for me there than here, for I shall be out of the world."

"Out of the world!" snapped Lady Acorn. "You can't be much more out of it than you are down here in Oxfordshire."

"Yes, I can. The neighbours, those who are at their places, come in to see us, and papa sometimes brings people home from town. Let me go to Harriet."

It was speedily decided. Lady Acorn, severe though she was with Adela, had her welfare at heart, and she thought a thorough change might be beneficial to her. An old friend, who chanced to be going abroad, took charge of Lady Adela to Geneva: Sir Sandy MacIvor and his wife met her there, and took her back with them to the château.

That was in October. Adela found the château as isolated as she could well desire, and therefore she was pleased with it; and she told Sir Sandy and Harriet she was glad to have come.

They had never thought of staying in this château for the winter; they meant to go to Rome early in December. But as that month approached, Adela evinced a great dislike to move. She would not go to Rome to encounter the English there, she told them; she would stay where she was. It a little perplexed the MacIvors; Adela had now grown so weak and low-spirited that they did not like to cross her or to insist upon it that she must go; neither did they care to give her up as their inmate, for her money was of consequence to them.

"What if we make up our minds to stay here for the winter, Harriet?" at length said Sir Sandy, who was as easy-tempered, genial-hearted a little laird as could be met with in or out of Scotland: though he stood only five feet high in his shoes, and nothing could be seen of his face except his small retroussé nose standing out of the mass of bright yellow hair which adorned it.

"It will be so cold," grumbled Harriet. "Think of all these draughts."

"They won't hurt," said the laird, who was bred to such things, his paternal stronghold in the Highlands not being altogether air-tight. "I'll nail some list over the cracks, and we'll lay in a good stock of wood and keep up grand fires. I think we might be comfortable, Harriet. It must be as you decide, of course, dear; but Adela can't be left here alone, and if we say she must go with us to Rome, she may fret herself into a fever."

"She is doing that as it is," returned Harriet. "We might stay here, of course—and we should get the place for an old song during the cold months. Perhaps we had better do so. Yet I should like to have been in Rome for the Christmas festivities, and for the carnival later."

"We will go next Christmas instead," said Sir Sandy.

As they had no children, they were not tied to their Scottish home, and could lay their plans freely. It was decided to remain in the château for the winter, and Sir Sandy began hammering at the doors and windows.

So they settled down contentedly enough; and, cold though it was, in spite of the list and the hissing wood fires, which certainly gave out more sparks than heat, Sir Sandy and his wife made the best of it.

It was more than could be said of Lady Adela. She not only did not make the best of things, but did not try to do so. Not that she complained of the cold, or the heat, or appeared to feel either. All seemed as one to her.

Her room was large; its great old-fashioned sofa and its heavy fauteuils were covered with amber velvet. Uncomfortable-looking furniture stood about—mahogany tables and consoles with cold white marble tops. The walls of the room were papered with a running landscape, representing green plains, rivers, blue mountains, sombre pine-trees, castles, and picturesque peasants at work in a vineyard. In a recess, shut off with heavy curtains, stood the bed; it was, in fact, a bedroom and sitting-room combined, as is so frequently the case on the Continent.

In a dress of black silk and crape, worn for Margery Upton, who had died the day after Christmas-Day, Lady Adela sat in this room near the crackling wood fire. January was wearing away. She leaned back in the great yellow armchair in listless apathy, her wasted hands lying on her lap, a warm cashmere shawl drawn round her, and two scarlet spots on her once blooming-cheeks. The low fever, that, as predicted by Lady Harriet weeks and weeks ago, she was fretting herself into, had all too surely attacked her. And she had not seemed in the least to care whether or not she died of it.

"If I die, will my death be sudden?" she one day startled the Swiss doctor by asking him.

"You will not die, you will get well," replied Monsieur Le Brun. "If you will only be reasonable, be it understood, and second our efforts to make you so, by wishing for it yourself," he added.

"I do wish it," she murmured; though her tone was apathetical enough. "But I said to you, 'If I die,'—and I want the question answered, sir. Would there be time to send for any friends from England that I may wish to see?"

"Ample time, miladi."

"Harriet," she whispered to her sister that same night, "mind you send for Mr. Grubb when I get into that state that I cannot recover—if I do get into it. Will you?"

"What next!" retorted Harriet. "Who says you will not recover?"

"I could not die in peace without seeing my husband—without asking for his forgiveness," pleaded the poor invalid, bitter tears of regret for the past slowly coursing down her cheeks. "You will be sure to send in time, won't you, Harriet?"

"Yes, yes, I promise it," answered Harriet, humouring the fancy; and she set herself to kiss and soothe her sister.

Lady Harriet MacIvor, who resembled her mother more than any of the rest, both in person and quickness of temper, had been tart enough with Adela before the illness declared itself, freely avowing that she had no patience with people who fretted themselves ill; but when the fever had really come she became a tender and efficient nurse.

The sickness and danger had passed—though of danger there had not perhaps been very much—and Adela was up again. With the passing, Lady Harriet resumed again her tendency to set the world and its pilgrims right, especially Adela. January was now drawing to a close.

The fever had left her very weak. In fact, it had not yet wholly taken itself away. She would lie back in the large easy-chair, utterly inert, day after day, recalling dreams of the past. Thinking of the luxurious home she had lost, one that might have been all brightness; picturing what she would do to render it so, were the opportunity still hers.

For hours she would lose herself in recollections of the child she had lost; the little boy, George. A rush of fever would pass through her veins as she recalled her behaviour at its baptism: her scornful rejection of her husband's name, Francis; her unseemly interruption from her bed to the clergyman that the name should be George. How she yearned after the little child now! Had he lived—why surely her husband would not have put her away from him! A man may not, and does not, put away the mother of his child; it could never have been. Would he have kept the child—or she? No, no; with that precious, living tie between them, he could not have thrust his wife from him. Thus she would lie, tormenting herself with deceitful fantasies that could never be, and wake with a shudder to the miserable reality.

Sufficient of the fever lingered yet to tinge with hectic her white face, and to heat her trembling hands. But for one thought Adela would not have cared whether she died or lived—at least, she told herself so in her misery; and that thought was that, if she died, her husband might take another wife. A wife who would give him back what she herself had not given—love for love. Since Miss Upton, perhaps unwittingly, had breathed that suggestion, it had not left Adela night or day.

How bitterly she regretted the past none knew, or ever would know. During these weeks of illness, before the fever and since, she had had leisure to dwell upon her conduct; to repent of it; to pray to Heaven for pardon for it. The approach of possible death, the presence of hopeless misery, had brought Adela to that Refuge which she had never sought or found before, an ever-merciful God. Never again, even were it possible that she should once more mingle with the world, could she be the frivolous, heartless, unchristian woman she had been. Nothing in a small way had ever surprised Lady Harriet so much, as to find Adela take out her Bible and Prayer-book, and keep them near her.

She sat today, buried as usual in the past, the bitter anguish of remembrance rending her soul. We are told in Holy Writ that the heart of man is deceitful and desperately wicked. The heart of woman is undoubtedly contradictory. When Adela was Mr. Grubb's wife, she had done her best to scorn and despise him, to persuade herself she hated him: now that he was lost to her for ever, she had grown to love him, passionately as ever man was loved by woman. The very fact that relations between them could never be renewed only fostered this love. For Lady Adela knew better than to deceive herself with vain hopes; she knew that to cherish them would be the veriest mockery; that when Francis Grubb threw her off, it was for ever.

Many a moment did she spend now, regretting that she had not died in the fever. It would at least have brought about a last interview; for Harriet would have kept her word and sent for him.

"Better for me to die than live," she murmured to herself, lifting her fevered hand. "I could have died happily, with his forgiveness on my lips. Whereas, to live is nothing but pain; weariness—and who knows how many years my life will last?"

Darvy came in; a tumbler in her hand containing an egg beaten up with wine and milk. Darvy did not choose to abandon her mistress in her sickness and misfortunes, but Darvy considered herself the most ill-used lady's-maid that fate ever produced. Buried alive in this dismal place in a foreign country, where the companions with whom she consorted, the other domestics, spoke a language that was barbarous and unintelligible, Darvy wondered when it would end.

"I don't want it," said Adela, turning away.

"But Lady Harriet says you must take it, my lady. You'll never get your strength up, if you refuse nourishment."

"I don't care to get my strength up. If you brought me some wine and water, Darvy, instead, I could take that. Or some tea—or lemonade. I am always thirsty."

"And what good is there in tea or lemonade?" returned Darvy, who ventured to contend now as she never had when her lady was in health, coaxing her also sometimes as if she were a child. "Lady Harriet said if you would not take this from me, my lady, she should have to come herself. And she does not want to come; she's busy."

To hear that Harriet was busy seemed something new. "What is she busy about?" languidly asked Adela.

"Talking," answered Darvy. "Some English traveller has turned out of his way to call on her and Sir Sandy, my lady, and he is giving them all the home news."

"Oh," was the indifferent comment of Lady Adela. Home news was nothing to her now. And, to put an end to Darvy's importunity, she drank the refreshment without further objection.

Margery Upton had died and was buried; and her will, when it became known, created a nine-days' wonder in London. Amidst those assembled to hear its reading, the mourners, who had just returned from the churchyard, none was more utterly astonished than Mr. Grubb. Never in his whole life had such an idea—that he would be the inheritor of Court Netherleigh—occurred to him. Miss Upton's statement of why it was left to him, as explained by her by word of mouth to Mr. Cleveland, was read out after the will; and Francis Grubb found a private letter, written by her to himself, put into his hand.

Lord Acorn was similarly astonished. Intensely so. But, in his débonnaire manner, he carried it off with easy indifference, and did not let his mortification appear. Perhaps he had not in his heart felt so sure of Court Netherleigh as he had allowed the world to think: Miss Upton's warnings might not have been quite lost upon him. Failing himself, he would rather Francis Grubb had it than any one; there might be no trouble about those overdue bonds; though Lord Acorn, always sanguine, had not allowed himself to dream of such a catastrophe as this.

Perhaps the most unwelcome minor item in the affair to Lord Acorn was having to carry the news home to his wife. It was evening when he arrived there. He and Mr. Grubb had travelled up together: for the easy-natured peer did not intend to show the cold shoulder to his son-in-law because he had supplanted him.

"Will you give me a bit of dinner, Frank?" asked the earl, as they got into a cab together at the terminus, only too willing to put off the mauvais quart d'heure with my lady as long as might be.

"I will give it to you, and welcome, if there is any to be had," smiled Mr. Grubb. "I left no orders for dinner today, not knowing when I should be back."

Alighting in Grosvenor Square, they found dinner prepared. Afterwards Lord Acorn went home. His wife, attired in one of Madame Damereau's best black silk gowns, garnished with a crape apron, was sitting in the small drawing-room, all impatience.

"Well, you are late," cried she. "What can have kept you until now?"

"It is only ten o'clock," replied the earl, drawing a chair to the fire. "At work, Gracie!" he added, turning to his daughter, who sat at the table, busy with her tatting.

"Only ten o'clock!" snapped the countess. "I expected you at five or six. And now—how are things left? I suppose we have Court Netherleigh?"

"Well, no; we have not," quietly replied Lord Acorn.

"Not!"

"Not at all. Grubb is made the heir. He has Court Netherleigh—and is to take the name."

Lady Acorn's face, in its petrified astonishment, its righteous indignation, would have made a model for a painter. Not for a couple of minutes did she speak, voice and words alike failed her.

"The deceitful wretch!" broke from her at length. "To play the sneak with Margery in that way!"

"Don't waste your words, Betsy. Grubb knew nothing about it: is more surprised than you are. Court Netherleigh was willed to him when Margery first came into it; when he was a young lad. She only carried out the directions of Sir Francis Netherleigh."

Lady Acorn was beginning to breathe again. But she was not the less angry.

"I don't care. It is no better than a swindle. How deceitful Margery must have been!"

"She kept counsel—if you mean that. As to being deceitful—no, I don't see it. She never did, or would, admit that the estate would come to us: discouraged the idea, in fact."

"All the same, it is a frightful blow. We were reckoning on it. Was no one in her confidence?"

"No one whatever except the old lawyer, Pencot. Two or three weeks before she died she disclosed all to Cleveland in a confidential interview. As it is not ourselves, I am heartily glad it's Grubb."

"What has she done with all her accumulated money?" tartly went on her ladyship. "She must have saved a heap of it, living in the quiet way she did!"

"Yes, there is a pretty good lot of that," equably replied the earl. "It is left to one and another; legacies here, legacies there. I don't come in for one."

"No! What a shame!"

"You do, though," resumed Lord Acorn, stretching out his boots to catch the warmth of the fire. "You get ten thousand pounds."

The words were to the countess as a very sop in the pan. Her fiery face became a little calmer.

"Are you sure?" she asked.

"Quite sure," nodded the earl. "You don't get it, though, without conditions. Only the interest for life; the sum itself then goes to Grace, here. I congratulate you, Gracie, my dear."

Grace let fall her shuttle; her colour rose. "Oh, papa! And—what do my sisters have?" she added, ever, in her unselfishness, thinking of others.

"Mary, Harriet, and Frances have a thousand pounds each; Sarah and Adela only some trinkets as a remembrance. I suppose Margery thought they were well married, and did not require money."

"And, papa, who else comes in?" asked Grace, glancing across at her mother, who sat beating her foot on the carpet.

"Who else? Let me see. Thomas Cleveland has two thousand pounds. And Mrs. Dalrymple, the elder, has a thousand. And several of Margery's servants are provided for. And I think that's about all I remember."

"The furniture at Court Netherleigh?" interrupted Lady Acorn. "Who takes that?"

"Grubb; he takes everything belonging to the house and estate; everything that was Sir Francis Netherleigh's. He is left residuary legatee. Margery Upton has only willed away what was her own of right."

"As if he wanted it!" grumbled Lady Acorn.

"The less one needs things, the more one gets them, as it seems to me. The baronetcy is to be renewed in him, Betsy."

"The baronetcy! In him!"

"Sir Francis wished it. There won't be much delay in the matter, either. Margery Upton put things in train for it before she died."

Lady Acorn could only reply by a stare; and there ensued a pause.

"The idiot that little minx Adela has shown herself!" was her final comment. "Court Netherleigh, it seems, would have been hers."

The little minx Adela, wasting away with fever in her Swiss abode, knew nothing of all this, and cared less. The barest items of news concerning it came to the MacIvors; Grace wrote to Harriet to say that Court Netherleigh had been willed to Mr. Grubb, not to her father; but in that first letter she gave no details. That much was told to Adela. She aroused herself sufficiently to ask who had Court Netherleigh, and was told that Margery Upton had left it to Mr. Grubb.

"I knew he was a favourite of hers," was all the comment she made; and, but for the sudden flush, Lady Harriet might have thought the news was perfectly indifferent to her: and she made no further allusion to it, then or afterwards.

But of the particulars, I say, Sir Sandy and Lady Harriet remained in ignorance, for Grace did not write again. No one else wrote. And their extreme surprise at Mr. Grubb's inheritance had become a thing of the past, when one day a traveller, recently from England, found them out and their old château. It was Captain Frederick Cust, brother to the John Cust who stuttered. The Custs and the Acorns had always been very intimate; the young Cust lads, there were six of them, and the Ladies Chenevix had played and quarrelled together as boys and girls. Captain Cust knew all about the Court Netherleigh inheritance, and supplied the information lacking, until then, to Sir Sandy and Lady Harriet MacIvor. No wonder Darvy had said that Lady Harriet was too busy to go upstairs: she was as fond of talking as her mother.

And so, the abuse they had been mutually lavishing upon Mr. Grubb in private for these two or three past weeks they found to be unmerited. He was the lucky inheritor, it is true, but through no complicity of his own.

"You might have known that," said Captain Cast, upon Lady Harriet's candidly avowing this. "Grubb is the most honourable man living; he would not do an underhand deed to be made king of England tomorrow. I am surprised you could think it of him for a moment, Harriet."

"Be quiet, Fred," she retorted. "It was not an unnatural thought. The best of men will stretch a point when such a property as Court Netherleigh is in question."

"Grubb would not. And he could have bought such a place any day had he a mind to do it."

"And he is to take up the baronetcy! You are sure that is true?"

"Sure and certain. And I wish him joy with all my heart! There's not one of us in the social world but would welcome him into our order with drums and trumpets."

Lady Harriet laughed. "You are just the goose you used to be, Fred."

"No doubt," assented Captain Frederick. "Where's the use of being anything better in such a silly world as this? Your wife has always paid me compliments, MacIvor, since the time we were in pinafores."

"Just as she does me," nodded little Sir Sandy. "And how is Mr. Grubb?—I liked him, too, captain. Does he still keep up that big establishment in Grosvenor Square all for himself?"

"Yes. Why shouldn't he? He is rich enough to keep up ten of them. By the way, he is a member of Parliament now—do you know it? They've returned him for Wheatshire."

And thus the conversation continued. But we need not follow it.

After Captain Cust left at night, for he stayed the day with them, Lady Harriet sat in silent thought, apparently weighing some matter in her mind.

"Sandy," she said at length, looking across at him, "I don't think I shall tell Adela anything about this—I mean that her husband is to take the baronetcy. It will be better not."

"Why?" asked Sir Sandy.

"It will bring her past folly home to her so severely. It may bring all the fever back again."

"As you please, of course, dear. But she did not seem to care at all when told he had inherited Netherleigh."

"That's all you know about it, Sandy!" retorted Lady Harriet. "I saw—all the light in her eyes and the flush in her cheeks. I tell you, sir, she is in love with her husband now, though she may never have been before, and it will try her too greatly, in her weak state. Her chief bone of contention in the old days was his name; that's removed now. And she has forfeited that lovely place, Court Netherleigh!"

"You know best, my dear. Perhaps it will be kinder not to tell her. But you will have to caution Darvy, and those about her: this is news that will not rest in a nutshell. Though," remarked Sir Sandy, after a pause, "with all deference to your superior judgment, Harriet, I do not think she can care much more for her husband now than she cared of old."

"Listen, Sandy," was the whispered answer. "Yesterday evening at dusk I went softly up to Adela's room, and peeped in to see whether she was dozing. She sat in the firelight, her head bent over that little old photograph she has of Mr. Grubb. Suddenly she gave a little cry, and began raining tears and kisses upon it."

CHAPTER XXXII

ADELA STARTLED

In a small "apartement" in the Champs Elysées, so small, indeed, that the whole of it could almost have been put into the salon of the château in Switzerland, and in its small drawing-room sat Lady Harriet MacIvor and Monsieur le Docteur Féron. Lady Adela sat in it also; but she went for nobody now. It was a lovely April day; the sun shone through the crimson draperies of the window, the flowers were budding, the trees were already green.

Monsieur le Docteur Féron and Lady Harriet were talking partly to, partly at Adela. Inert, listless, dispirited, she paid little or no attention to either of them, or to anything they might choose to say: life and its interests seemed to be no longer of moment to her.

When we saw her in January she was recovering from the low fever. But she did not grow strong. The fever subsided, but the weakness and listlessness remained. Do what they would, the MacIvors could not rouse her from her apathy. Sir Sandy tried reasoning and amusement; Lady Harriet alternately soothed and ridiculed; Darvy, even, ventured now and again on a good scolding. It was all one.

That exposé the previous summer, when she was put away by her husband, seemed to have changed Adela's very nature. At first her mood was resentful; then it became repentant: that was succeeded by one of heart-sickening remorse. Remorse for her own line of conduct during the past years. With the low fever in Switzerland, she began to think of serious things. The awakening to the responsibilities that lie upon us to remember and prepare for a future and better state—an awakening that comes to us all sooner or later, in a greater or a less degree—came to Lady Adela. She saw what her past life had been, all its mocking contempt for what was good, its supreme indifference, its intense selfishness. Night by night, on her bended knees, amid sobs and bitter tears, she besought forgiveness of the Most High. Her cheeks turned red with shame whenever she thought of her kind and good husband, and of how she had requited him. Lady Harriet was right too in her surmise—that Adela had now grown to love her husband. How full of contradictions this human heart of ours is, experience shows us more surely day by day. When she could have indulged that love, she threw it contemptuously from her; now that the time had gone by for indulging it, it was becoming something like idolatry.

Adela did not grow strong; perhaps, with this distressed frame of mind, much improvement was not to be looked for. At length the MacIvors grew alarmed, and resolved to take her to Paris for change and for better advice. Contrary to expectation, Adela made no objection; it seemed as though she no longer cared a straw where she went, or what became of her. "If we offered to box her up in a coffin and bury her for good and all, I don't believe she'd say no," said Lady Harriet one day to the laird. To Paris they went, reaching it during March, and Monsieur le Docteur Féron was at once called in, a man of great repute amongst the English. It was now April, and Monsieur le Docteur, with all his skill, had done nothing.

"But truly there's no reason in it, miladi," he was saying this fine day to Lady Harriet, in English, the language he generally chose to use with his patients, however perfectly they might speak his own. "Miladi Adela has nothing grave amiss with her; absolutely nothing. I assert that to sit as she does has no reason, no common sense in it."

"As I tell her continually," rejoined Lady Harriet, inwardly smiling at his quaint phrases.

"What illness she has, rests on the nerves," proceeded the doctor. "A little on the mind. The earliest day I saw her I asked whether she did have one great shock, or trouble: you remember, do you not, madame?"

"But—good gracious!—one ought not to give way for ever to any shock or trouble—even if one has had such a thing," remonstrated Lady Harriet.

"As I say. Can anything be more clear? Miladi has nothing to make her ill, and yet miladi sits there, ill, day after day. You hear, madame?" turning to Adela.

"Oh yes, I hear," she gently answered, lifting her wan but still lovely face for a moment and then letting it droop again.

"And it is time to end this state of things," resumed the doctor to Lady Harriet. "It must be finished, madame."

"It ought to be," acquiesced Lady Harriet. "But if she does not end it herself, how are we to do it?"

"You go out, madame, with monsieur, your husband, into a little society: is it not so?" spoke the doctor, after a pause of consideration, during which he stroked his face with his gloved hand.

"Of course we do, Monsieur Féron; we are not hermits, and Paris is gay just now," quickly answered Lady Harriet. "We go to the Blunts' tonight."

"Then take her at once also; take her with you. That may be tried. If it has no result, truly I shall not know what to propose. Drugs are hopeless in a case like this," added the doctor, as he made two elaborate bows, one to each lady, and went out.

"Now, Adela, you hear," began Lady Harriet, the moment the door closed, and her voice was sternly resolute. "We have tried everything, and now we shall try this. You go with us to Mrs. Blunt's tonight."

She did not refuse—wonderful to be able to say it. She folded her hands upon her chest and sighed in resignation: too worn out to combat longer: or, perhaps, too apathetical.

"What is it, Harriet? Not a dinner-party?"

"Oh dear, no. An evening party: a crowd, I dare say. Music, I think. And now I shall go and talk to Darvy about what you are to wear," concluded Lady Harriet, escaping from the room lest there should come a tardy opposition. But no, Adela never made it. It seemed to her that she was quite worn out with it all; with the antagonism and the preaching, and the doctors and Harriet; wearied to death. Darvy dressed her plainly enough; a black net robe with black trimmings; and Lady Adela quietly submitted, saying neither yes nor no.

"Don't let me be announced, Harriet," pleaded Adela, as they were going along. "No one cares to hear my name now. I can creep in after you and Sir Sandy."

Mr. and Mrs. Blunt's house was small and their company large. Lady Harriet expected a crowd, and she met with it. Adela, unannounced according to her wish, shook hands with Mrs. Blunt, and escaped into a small recess at the end of the further reception-room. It was draped off by crimson-and-gold curtains, and she sat down, thankful to be alone. She turned giddy: the noise, the lights, the crowd unnerved her. It was so long now since she had mingled in anything of the sort.

She sat on, and began thinking when the last time had been. It came into her memory with a rush. The last time she had made one in these large gatherings was at her own home in Grosvenor Square, not very many days before she finally left it. Ay, and the attendant circumstances also came back to her, even to the words which had passed between herself and her husband. In the bitter contempt she cherished for him, she had not chosen to inform him of the assembly she purposed having, but had sent out the cards unknown to him. He knew nothing about it until the night arrived and he came home to dinner.

"What is the awning up for?" he asked of Hilson, wondering a little.

"My lady has an assembly tonight, sir," was the answer.

"A large one?"

"Yes, sir."

Mr. Grubb knitted his brow, and went on to his wife. It was not the fact of the assembly that vexed him: it was that she had not thought it worth her while to inform him of it. Darvy was putting the finishing touches to her hair. How well she remembered it now; every minute particular came back to her: where she sat in the room—not at the dressing-glass as usual, but before the open window, for it was intensely hot. Her robe was of costly white lace, adorned with pearls. Pearls that he had given her.

"What is this, Adela?" he had asked. "I hear you have a large assembly tonight."

"Well?" she retorted.

"Could you not have told me?"

"I did not see any especial necessity for telling you."

"I might have had an engagement. In fact, I have one. I ought to go to one of the hotels tonight to see a gentleman who has come over from India on business."

"You can go," was her scornful reply to this. "Your presence is not needed here; it is not at all necessary to the success of the evening."

"There is one, at any rate, who would not miss me," had been his reply as he left her, to go to his room to dress for dinner. Yes, it all came back vividly tonight.

She bent her face on her hand as she recalled this, hiding it in very shame that she could have been so wicked. Lady Sarah Hope had once told her the devil had got possession of her. "Not only the devil," moaned Adela now, "but all his myrmidons."

A lady was beginning to sing. She had a sweet and powerful voice, and she chose a song Mr. Grubb used to be particularly fond of—"Robin Adair."

Adela looked beyond the draperies at the crowd, gathering itself up for a momentary stillness, and disposed herself to listen. Her thoughts were full of Mr. Grubb, as the verses went on. Every word came home to her aching heart.

"But him I loved so well
Still in my heart doth dwell—
Oh, I shall ne'er forget
Robin Adair."

Applause ensued. It was much better deserved than that usually accorded in these cases. A minute later, and some one called out "Hush!" for the lady had consented to sing again. The noise subsided into silence; the singer was turning over the leaves of her music-book.

To this silence there arose an interruption. Mr. Blunt's English butler appeared, announcing a late guest:

"Sir Francis Netherleigh."

The man had a low, sonorous voice, and every syllable penetrated to Lady Adela's ear. The name struck on the chords of her memory. Sir Francis Netherleigh! Why, he had been dead many a year. Could another Sir Francis Netherleigh be in existence? What did it mean?—for it must be remembered that all such news had been kept and was still kept from her. Lady Adela gazed out from her obscure vantage-ground.

Not for a minute or two did she see anything: the company was dense. Then, threading his way through the line made for him, advanced a man of noble form and face, the form and face of him she had once called husband.

He was in evening-dress, and in mourning. He seemed to be making direct for the recess, and for Adela; and she shrank behind the draperies to conceal herself.

For a moment all things seemed to be in a mist, inwardly and outwardly. What brought Mr. Grubb there—and who was the Sir Francis Netherleigh that had been announced, and where was he?

Not to Adela had he been advancing, neither did he see her. Mrs. Blunt chanced to be standing before the recess; it was to her he was making his way.

"How do you do, Sir Francis?" she warmly exclaimed, meeting his hand. "It is so good of you to come: my husband feared you would not be able to spare the time."

"I thought so also when I spoke to him this afternoon," was the answer, given in the earnest pleasant tones Adela remembered so well. "My stay in Paris is but for a few hours this time. Where is Mr. Blunt?"

"I saw him close by a minute ago. Ah, there he is. John," called Mrs. Blunt, "here is Sir Francis Netherleigh."

They moved towards the fireplace; the crowd closed behind them, hiding them from sight, and Adela breathed again. So then, he was Sir Francis Netherleigh! How had it all come about?

Gathering her shawl around her, she escaped from the recess and glided through the room with bent head. In the outer room, opening to the corridor and the staircase, she came upon her sister.

"Harriet, I must go," she feverishly uttered. "I can't stay here."

"Oh, indeed!" said Lady Harriet. "Well—I don't know."

"If there's no carriage waiting, I can have a coach. Or I can walk. It will do me no harm. I shall find my way through the streets."

She ran down the stairs. Harriet felt obliged to follow her. "Will you call up Sir Sandy MacIvor's carriage," asked Lady Harriet of the servants standing below. "Adela, do wait an instant! One would think the house was on fire."

"I must get away," was the eager, terrified interruption, and Adela bore onwards to the outer door.

The carriage was called, and came up. In point of fact, Sir Sandy and his wife had privately agreed to keep it waiting, in case Adela should turn faint in the unusual scene and have to leave. In the porte cochère they encountered a lady who was only then arriving.

"What, going already!" she exclaimed.

"Yes," replied Lady Harriet; "and I wish you would just tell Sir Sandy for me: you will be sure to see him somewhere in the rooms. Say my sister does not feel well, and we have gone home."

They passed out to the carriage and were soon bowling along the streets. Adela drew into her corner, cowering and shivering.

"Did you see him?" she gasped.

"Oh yes, I saw him," grumblingly responded Lady Harriet, who was not very pleased at having to quit the gay scene in this summary fashion. "I am sure Sandy will conclude we have been spirited away, unless Mrs. Seymour finds him. A fine flurry he'll be in."

"Harriet, what did it mean? They called him Sir Francis Netherleigh."

"He is Sir Francis Netherleigh."

"Since when? Why did you not tell me?"

"He has been Francis Netherleigh since Aunt Margery died: the name came to him with the property. He has been Sir Francis since—oh, for about six weeks now. The old Uncle Francis wished the baronetcy to be revived in him, and his wishes have been carried out."

Adela paused, apparently revolving the information. "Then his name is no longer Grubb?"

"In one sense, no. For all social uses that name has passed from him."

"Why did you never tell me this?" repeated Adela.

"From the uncertainty as to whether you would care to hear it, Adela. We decided to say nothing until you were stronger."

A second pause of thought. "If he has succeeded to the name, why, so have I. Have I not? Though he puts me away from himself, Harriet, he cannot take from me his name."

"Of course you have succeeded to it."

Pause the third. "Then I ought to have been announced tonight as Lady Adela Netherleigh!"

"Had you been announced at all. You solved the difficulty, you know, by telling me you would not be announced—you would creep in after me and Sandy."

"What difficulty?"

"Well, had you heard yourself called Netherleigh, you would have wanted to know, there and then, the why and the wherefore. It might have created a small commotion."

Pause the fourth. "Who is he in mourning for? Aunt Margery?"

"And also for his mother. Mrs. Lynn lived just long enough to see him take up the baronetcy. I think it must have gratified her—that her son should be the one to succeed at last. She would have had Court Netherleigh in the old days, Adela, had she not displeased Uncle Francis by her marriage, not Margery Upton. He told Margery so when he was dying."

"The world seems full of changes," sighed Adela.

"It always was, and always will be. But I fancy the right mostly comes uppermost in the end," added Lady Harriet. "Where is Mary Lynn, you ask? She lives with Sir Francis, in Grosvenor Square; the house's mistress."

Adela ceased her questioning. Amidst the many items for reflection suggested to her by the news, was this: that the once-hated name of Grubb had been suppressed for ever. There flashed across her a reminiscence of a day in the past autumn, when she was last staying at Court Netherleigh. She had been giving some scorn to the name, after her all-frequent custom, and Miss Upton had answered it with a peculiar look. Adela did not then understand the look: she did now. That expressive look, had she been able to read it, might have told her that Mr. Grubb would not long retain the name. Adela shrank closer into the corner of the carriage and pressed her hands upon her burning eyes. Foolish, infatuated woman that she had been!

"Did you notice how noble he looked tonight?" she murmured, after awhile.

"He always did look noble, Adela. Here we are."

The carriage drew up. As Lady Harriet, after getting out herself, turned to give her hand to Adela, still weak enough to require especial care, she did not find it responded to.

"Are you asleep, Adela? Come. We are at home."

"I beg your pardon," was the meek answer.

She had only been waiting to stem the torrent of tears flowing forth. Lady Harriet saw them glistening on her wasted cheeks by the light of the carriage-lamps. Bitter tears, telling of a breaking heart.

"Sandy," observed Lady Harriet to her husband that night, "I do not see that a further stay here will be of any use to Adela. We may as well be making preparations for our journey to the Highlands."

"Just as you please," acquiesced Sir Sandy. "I, you know, would rather be in the Highlands than anywhere else. Fix your own time."

"Then we will start next week," decided Lady Harriet. But we must revert for a few moments to Sir Francis Netherleigh before closing the chapter.

His stay in Paris, a matter of business having taken him there, was limited to some four-and-twenty hours. Upon reaching Calais on his return homewards, he found one of the worst gales blowing that Calais had ever known, and he was greeted with the news that not a boat could leave the harbour. All he could do was to go to an hotel, Dessin's, and make himself comfortable until the morrow. Late in the afternoon he strolled out to take a look at the raging sea, and found it was with difficulty he could struggle against the wind. In returning, he was blown against a gentleman, or the gentleman against him; the two laughed, began an apology, and then simultaneously shook hands—for it was Gerard Hope. Sir Francis Netherleigh's heart went out in compassion; Gerard was looking so thin and careworn.

"Come to my hotel and dine with me, Gerard," he said impulsively. And Gerard went.

After dinner, they left the table d'hôte for a private room, to which a bottle of choice claret was ordered. Talking together of past times, the subject of the lost bracelet came up. Sir Francis, listening attentively to what Gerard said, looking at him keenly as he said it, drew the absolute conclusion that Gerard was not the thief: he was quick at distinguishing truth from falsehood.

"Gerard," he quietly asked, "why have you remained so long abroad? It bears a look, you see, to some people, that you are afraid to come back and face the charge."

"It's not that," returned Gerard. "What I can't face is my body of creditors. They would pretty soon lay hold of me, if I went over. As to the other affair, what could I do in it? Nothing. My uncle will never believe me not guilty; and I could not prove that I am innocent."

"Fill your glass, Gerard. How much do you owe?"

"Well, it must be as much, I'm afraid, as five hundred pounds."

"Is that all?" spoke Sir Francis, rather slightingly.

Gerard laughed. "Not much to many a man; but a very great deal to a poor one. I don't know that I should be much better off at home than here," he added in a thoughtful tone. "So long as that bracelet affair lies in doubt, the world will look askance at me: and I expect it will never be cleared up."

"It was a most singular thing, quite a mystery, as Lady Sarah always calls it. I suppose you have no suspicion yourself, Gerard, as to the culprit."

"Why, yes, I have, unfortunately."

Sir Francis caught at the words. "Who was it?"

Gerard Hope's pale face, so much paler than of yore, turned red. But that he had been in a reverie he would not have made the unguarded admission.

"I am sorry to have said so much, Sir Francis," he avowed hastily. "It is true that a doubt lies on my mind; but I ought not to have spoken of it."

"Nay, but you may trust me, Gerard."

"I don't like to," hesitated Gerard. "It was of a lady. And perhaps I was mistaken."

"Not Alice herself," cried Sir Francis, jestingly.

"No, no. I—think—Alice—holds—the—same—suspicion," he added, with a pause between each word.

"You had better trust me, Gerard. No harm shall come of it, to you or to her; I promise you that."

"I thought," breathed Gerard, "it was Selina Dalrymple."

"Selina Dalrymple!" echoed Sir Francis, utterly surprised. "Since when have you thought that?"

"Ever since."

"But why?"

"Well, partly because no one but myself and Selina went into the room; and I know that it was not I who took it. And partly because her visit to the house that evening was kept secret. Her name, as I dare say you know, was never spoken of at all in connection with the matter. Alice did not say she had been there, and of course I did not."

"But how do you know she was there?"

"I opened the door to her. As I left that back-room where the jewels lay upon the table, I looked round to speak to Alice, and I saw that self-same glistening bracelet lying on the table behind the others. I did not return into the room at all; what I had to say to Alice I said with the door in my hand. Upon opening the front-door, to let myself out, there stood Selina Dalrymple, about to ring. She asked for Alice, and ran upstairs to her quietly, as if she did not want to be heard. That Selina went into the room where the jewels were and admired them, Alice casually said to me when we met in the street next day. But her visit was never spoken of in the house, as far as I know."

Sir Francis made no remark. Gerard went on.

"In the first blush of the loss, I should as soon have suspected myself as Selina Dalrymple; sooner perhaps: but when it came to be asserted at the investigation that no other person whatever had been in the room than myself, excepting Alice, I could not see the reason of that assertion, and the doubt flashed upon me. For one thing"—Gerard dropped his voice—"we learnt how terribly hard-up poor Selina was just then. Worse than I was."

"I am very sorry to have heard this, Gerard," said Sir Francis, perceiving at once how grave were the grounds for suspicion. "Poor Selina, indeed! It must never transpire; it would kill Oscar. At heart, he is fond of her as ever."

"Of course it must not transpire," assented Gerard. "I have never breathed it, until now, to mortal man. But it has made things harder for me, you see."

"It was said at the time, I remember, that you denied the theft in a half-hearted manner. Lady Sarah herself told me that. This suspicion trammelled you?"

"To be sure it did. I vowed to them I did not take the bracelet, but in my fear of directing doubts to Selina, I was not as emphatic as I might have been. I felt just as you express it, Sir Francis—trammelled. And I fear," went on Gerard, after a pause, "that this same suspicion has been making havoc with poor Alice's heart and health. When I receive a letter from Frances, as I do now and then, she is sure to lament over Alice's low spirits and her increasing illness."

Francis Netherleigh sat thinking. "It seems to me, Gerard," he presently said, "that you are being punished unjustly. You ought to return to England."

"Ah, but I can't," answered Gerard, shaking his head. "The sharks would be on to me. Before I could turn round I should be lodged in the Queen's Bench."

"No, no; not if they saw you wished to pay them later, and that there was a fair probability of your doing so."

"My wish is good enough. As to the probability—it is nowhere."

"Creditors are not as hard as they are sometimes represented, Gerard. I can assure you of that. I have always found them reasonable."

Gerard laughed outright. "I dare say you have, Sir Francis. It would be an odd creditor that would be hard to you."

"Ah, but I meant when I have dealt with them for other people," replied Sir Francis, joining in the laugh.

"And if I did get back to London, I should have nothing to live upon," resumed Gerard. "The pittance that I half starve upon in these cheap places, I might wholly starve upon there. I often wish I could get employed as a clerk; no one but myself knows how thankful I should be. But with this other thing hanging over my head, who'd give me a recommendation, and who'd take me without one!"

"Well, well, we will see, Gerard. It is a long lane that has no turning."

They talked yet further, and then Gerard said good-night. And in the morning Sir Francis Netherleigh heard the welcome tidings that the wind had gone down sufficiently to allow the mail-packet to venture out. So he went in her to England.

CHAPTER XXXIII

DESPAIR

The year had gone on, and the season was at its height. In the breakfast-room at Sir Francis Netherleigh's house in Grosvenor Square sat his sister, waiting to pour out the coffee. Ah, how different things were from what they had been in his wife's time! Then he had to wait upon himself at breakfast, often to take it alone; now he always found his sister down before him.

Mary Lynn was good-looking as ever, her wonderful grey eyes, as Miss Upton used to call them, were not a whit less beautiful; but the mirth of early days had given place to a calm, sad seriousness. It could be seen that some great sorrow had passed over her heart and left its traces there for ever. Just now, as she laid down a letter she had been reading, her face wore an especial air of sadness, somewhat of perplexity. Sir Francis entered.

"I have a letter from Netherleigh, Francis, from Alice Dalrymple," began Mary, after they had said good-morning. "Mrs. Dalrymple has met with an accident, and—but I will read you what she says," she broke off, taking up the letter.

"'Selina was driving mamma in a borrowed pony-chaise yesterday; the pony took fright at a passing caravan—a huge thing, Selina says, covered with brooms and baskets and shining tins—ran away, and overturned the chaise. Selina was not hurt, she never is; but mamma has received, it is feared, some internal injury. She asks if you will come down to her, dear Mary. Lose no time; you know how she values you!'"

"Selina was driving carelessly, I expect," observed Sir Francis.

"Of course I will go down. But it cannot be today, Francis?"

"Not very well," he answered, as he took his cup of coffee from her hand. "What should I do with the crowd, coming here tonight, without a hostess to receive them?"

For Sir Francis Netherleigh had bidden the great world to his house that evening. Such invitations from him were rare. This was the first he had given since his wife's departure and his mother's death.

"True," observed Mary, in answer. "And you also expect that gentleman and his wife, who are just home from India, to lunch here today. Then I will write to Alice, and tell her I cannot be with her until tomorrow. Her mother is not so ill, I trust, as to make a day's delay of moment. Perhaps you will go down with me, Francis?"

"If I can. I know I am wanted at Court Netherleigh."

"That is settled, then. And now tell me, will the Hopes also be here at luncheon?"

"Yes, I asked them last night to meet the Didnums. As I told you, Mary, the Hopes and the Didnums were great friends out in India."

Although Francis Netherleigh had put away his wife, the intimate relations that had existed between himself and her family had not been interrupted. He was sometimes at Lord Acorn's and at Colonel Hope's, and they were often with him. Mr. Didnum, the head of a great mercantile house in Calcutta, in constant correspondence with that of Christopher Grubb and Son in London, was an old friend of Colonel Hope, and they were now about to meet at luncheon in Grosvenor Square.

Breakfast over, Sir Francis Netherleigh went to Leadenhall Street as usual, returning in time to receive his visitors.

Frances Chenevix, staying with her sister, Lady Sarah Hope, made one of the party. "I don't know whether I am expected or whether I am not, but I shall go," she remarked to Lady Sarah, in her careless fashion. And she went, and was warmly welcomed. Every one liked gay-hearted Frances Chenevix.

The luncheon had been over some little time, and they were all talking together with interest, when a telegram was brought in for Miss Lynn. It proved to be from the Rector of Netherleigh, the Reverend Thomas Cleveland.

"Mrs. Dalrymple has undergone an operation, and is in a very exhausted condition. Come to her at once. I am sending also to Leadenhall Street to your brother. She is asking for him."

Such a message creates confusion. Sir Francis looked to ascertain at what time they were likely to find a train to carry them to Netherleigh, and found they could just catch one if they started at once. A servant was sent for the fleetest-looking cab he could find; there was no time to get the carriage round.

Mary Lynn was already seated in the cab, and Sir Francis was shaking hands with Colonel Hope, who had come out to the door, when he remembered the guests bidden to his house that night. It caused him to pause.

"You must stay and receive them for me, colonel: be host in my place, and your wife hostess, if she will be so good," he hastily decided. "Explain to every one how it is: dying wishes must be attended to, you know: and my getting back is, I dare say, out of the question."

"All right," answered Colonel Hope. "Don't wait, or you will lose your train."

The colonel returned indoors, went back to the dining-room and told his wife what was required of them. Lady Sarah stared in perplexity.

"Receive the people tonight in his place! Why, we cannot do so, colonel. Did you forget that we dine with those people at Hounslow? It's hard to say at what time we shall get back."

Colonel Hope looked a little perplexed too. "I did forget it," he said in his solemn way. "What is to be done?"

"Let mamma be here early and receive them," suggested Lady Frances. "I will help her."

It was an excellent solution of the difficulty. Mr. and Mrs. Didnum took their departure; and Lady Sarah Hope, accompanied by Frances, entered her carriage and ordered it to Chenevix House. The colonel walked away to his club.

Lady Acorn was alone when they entered. She listened to the news her daughters told her of her son-in-law's being summoned away, and of the request that she would take his place that night, and receive his guests.

"I suppose I must," said she, in her tart way; "but I shall have to get round to Grosvenor Square at an inconveniently early hour. Something is sure to happen when you want things to go particularly smoothly. And now—who do you suppose is here?" continued Lady Acorn.

"How can we tell, mamma?" cried Frances, before Sarah had time to speak. "Mary?"

"No; Adela."

"Adela!"

The countess nodded. "She and MacIvor arrived here this morning by the Scotch mail. Sandy had an unexpected summons to London, from the lawyers who are acting for him in the action about that small property he lays claim to; and when he was starting from home, nothing would do for Adela, it seems, but she must accompany him."

"Has Harriet come also?" asked Lady Sarah.

"No. Sandy goes back in a day or two."

"And Adela? Does she return with him?"

"I don't know. Sir Sandy says she seems miserable with them, and he thinks she will be miserable everywhere."

"Where is she?" asked Frances.

"Upstairs somewhere: Grace is with her. Grace pities and soothes her just as though she were a martyr—instead of a silly woman who has wilfully blighted her own happiness in life, and entailed no end of anxiety on us all."

After their short stay in Paris in the spring, where we last saw Lady Adela, the MacIvors went straight to Scotland, avoiding London and the cost that would have attended a London season, which they could ill afford. Adela also shrank from that; she would have left them had they sojourned in the metropolis. They took up their abode in the Highlands, in the old castle that was the paternal stronghold of the MacIvors, which was utterly bleak, dull, and remote; and, here, for the past three months, Adela had been slowly dying of remorse.

No wonder. Her mind, her whole being, so to say, was filled with the image of her husband; with the longing only to see him; with the bitter, unavailing remorse for the past. That one solitary sight of him, in Paris at Mrs. Blunt's, had revived within her the pain and excitement, which had been previously subsiding into a sort of dull apathy. The château in Switzerland had been, as a residence, lonely and wearisome; it was nothing, in those respects, compared with this old castle of Sir Sandy's. At least, Adela, found it so. In fact, she did not know what she wanted. She shrank from even the bare suggestion of publicity, and she shrank from solitude. She felt herself in the position of one whose whole interest in life has departed while yet a long life lies before her: the saddest of all sad positions, and the most rare.

Was it to continue so for ever and for ever? Yes, she would wail out in answer, when asking herself the question: at least, as long as time should last. For there could be no change in it. She had forfeited all possibility of that. The lone, miserable woman that she was now, must she remain to the end.

She wondered sometimes whether any one ever died of repentance and regret. Existence was becoming all but unendurable. When she opened her weary eyelids to the dawn of a new day she would moan out a faint prayer that God in His compassion would help her to get through it, and would bury her face in the pillow, wishing she could so bury herself and her misery.

It must not be thought she was encouraged in this state of mind. Lady Harriet MacIvor had become intolerably cross about it long ago, openly telling Adela she had no patience with her. From her Adela received no sympathy whatever. Look where she would, not a gleam of brightness shone for her. Sick at heart, fainting in spirit, it seemed to Adela that any change would be welcome; and when Sir Sandy received a letter one morning, telling him his presence was needed in London, and he announced his intention of starting that same day, Adela said she should go with him.

Lady Harriet did not oppose it. In truth, it brought her relief. Adela was becoming more of a responsibility day by day; and she had held some anxious conferences with her husband as to the expediency of their resigning charge of her.

"It is the best thing that could have happened, Sandy," she said to him in private. "Take her over to mamma, and tell her everything. I think they had better keep her themselves for a time."

Hence the unexpected irruption of the travellers at Chenevix House. Lady Acorn was not pleased. Not that she was sorry to see Adela once more; but she had lived in a chronic state of anger with her since the separation, and the accounts written to her from time to time by her daughter Harriet in no way diminished it.

After the briefest interview with her mother, Adela escaped to the chamber assigned her; the one she used to occupy. This left Sir Sandy free to open the budget his wife had charged him with, and to say that for the present he and Harriet would rather not continue to have the responsibility of Adela. Lady Acorn, as she listened, audibly wished Adela was a child again, that she might "have the nonsense shaken out of her."

Lady Sarah Hope raised her condemnatory shoulders, as her mother related this. She had never had the slightest sympathy with the trouble Adela had brought upon herself, or with the remorse it entailed.

"Will you see her, Sarah?" asked Lady Acorn.

"No; I would rather not. At least, not today. I must be going shortly."

Poor Adela! True, she had been guilty of grievous offences, but they had brought their punishment. As we sow, so do we generally reap. This return to her mother's home seemed to bring back all the past sin, all the present anguish, in colours tenfold more vivid.

Kneeling on the floor in the bedroom, her hands clasped round Grace's knees as she sat, Adela sobbed out her repentance, her hopeless longings for the life and the husband she had thrown away.

"Poor child!" sighed Grace, her own tears falling as she stroked with a gentle hand her unhappy sister's hair, "your sorrow is, I see, hard to bear. If I only knew how to comfort you!"

No answer.

"Still, Adela, although he is yet, in one sense of the word, your husband, it is not well for you to indulge these thoughts; these regrets. Were there even the most distant hope that things between you would alter, it would be different; but I fear there is none."

"I know it," bewailed Adela. "What he did, he did for ever."

"Then you should no longer, for your own peace' sake, dwell upon his memory. Try and forget him. It seems curious advice, Adela, but I have none better to give."

"I cannot forget him. My dreams by night, my thoughts by day, are of him, of him alone. If I could only be with him for just one week of reconciliation, to show him how I would, if possible, atone to him, to let him see that my repentance is lasting, though he put me away again at the week's end, it would be something. Oh, Grace, you don't know what my remorse is—how hard a cross I have to bear."

She knelt there in her bitter distress. Not much less distressing was it to Grace. By dint of coaxing, Adela was at length partially calmed, and lay back, half-exhausted, in an easy-chair.

At lunch-time, for this had occurred in the morning, she refused to go down, or to take anything. In the afternoon, when Grace was back again, Darvy brought up a cup of chocolate and some toast. Whilst languidly taking this, Adela abruptly renewed the subject: the only one, as she truly said, that ever occupied her mind.

"Do you see him often, Grace?"

"Rather often," replied Grace, knowing that the question must refer to Sir Francis.

"He is friendly with you, then?"

"Quite so. The friendship has never been interrupted. We are going to his house tonight," she added, perhaps incautiously.

"To Grosvenor Square?" cried Adela.

"Yes. I think it is the first entertainment he has given since you left it. Half London will be there."

"If I could only go!" exclaimed Adela, a light rising in her eye, a flush to her pale cheek. Grace looked at her in surprise; she had forfeited the right ever to enter there. Grace made no comment, and a pause ensued.

"Did you read the speech he made last Thursday night to the Commons?" resumed Adela, in a low tone.

"Yes. Every one was talking of it. Did you read it, Adela?—in Scotland?"

Grace received no answer. Sir Sandy below could have told her that Adela used to seize upon the Times, when it arrived, with feverish interest, to see whether any speech of her husband's was reported in it. If so, Sir Sandy's belief was that she learnt it by heart, so long did she keep the paper.

The chocolate finished, she lay back in the chair, her eyes looking into vacancy, her listless hands folded before her. Grace, sitting opposite, ostensibly occupied with some work, for she was rarely idle, had leisure to note her sister's countenance. It was much changed. Worn, wan, and weary it looked, but there was no special appearance now of ill health.

"You are much better, are you not, Adela?"

"Oh, I am very well," was the languid answer.

"Do you like Scotland?"

"I don't know."

Grace thought she was tired after the night journey, and resolved to leave her to silence; but an interruption occurred. Frances came in.

And, that Frances Chenevix could be melancholy for more than a minute at any time, was not to be expected. In spite of Adela's evidently subdued state of mind, she, after a few staid sentences, ran off at a gay tangent.

"What do you think, Grace?" she began. "We had very nearly lost our party tonight—one, Adela, that your whilom husband gives. He and his sister have been telegraphed for this afternoon to Netherleigh. Poor Mrs. Dalrymple has met with some serious accident; there has been an operation, and the result is, I suppose, uncertain. They have both started by train, and therefore cannot be at home to receive the people tonight."

"Is the party put off, then?" questioned Grace.

"No, there was not time to do it: how could he send round to all the world and his wife? It is to take place without him, mamma playing host in his absence."

"I wonder what Mrs. Dalrymple could want with him?"

"Just what I wondered, Grace. Mamma thinks it must be to speak to him about her affairs. He is her executor, I believe: not, poor woman, that she has much to leave."

Adela had listened to this in silence: an eager look was dawning on her face.

"Do you mean to say, Frances, that he—that my husband—will not be there at all?—in his own house?"

"To be sure I mean it, Adela. He cannot be in two places at once, here and Netherleigh. He and Mary Lynn have only now started on their way there. I tell mamma that whilst she plays host I shall play hostess. Won't it be fun!"

"Grace," began Adela very quietly, after her sisters had left, for Lady Sarah, thinking better of it, came up to see her for a moment, "I shall go with you tonight."

"Go—where did you say?" questioned Grace, in doubt.

"To my husband's house."

Grace dropped her work in consternation. "You cannot mean it, Adela."

"I do mean it. I shall go."

"Oh, Adela, pray consider what you are saying. Go there. Why, you know that you must not do so."

"It was my house once," said Adela, in agitation.

"But it is yours no longer. Pray consider. Of all people in the world, you must not attempt to enter it. It would be unseemly."

Adela burst into tears. "If you knew—if you knew how I long for a sight of it, Gracie," she gasped, "you would not deny me. Only just one little look at it, Grace! What can it matter? He is not there."

How Grace would have contrived to combat this wish, cannot be told: but Lady Acorn came in. In answer to her questioning as to what Adela was crying about now, Grace thought it well to tell her.

"Oh," said the countess, receiving the affair lightly, for she did not suppose Adela could be serious. "Go there, would you! What would the world say, I wonder, if they met Lady Adela Netherleigh at that house? Don't be silly, child."

What indeed! Adela sighed and said no more. Yet, she did so want to go. Lying back in her chair, her thoughts busy with the past and present, the longing took a terrible hold upon her.

She dressed, but did not go down to dinner, refusing that meal as she had refused luncheon. Lady Acorn went straight from the dinner-table to Grosvenor Square, calling on her way at Colonel Hope's for her daughter Frances, as had been arranged. Grace, who did not care to leave Adela alone for too long an evening, would go later with Sir Sandy. She hastened to dress, not having done so before dinner, and then went to her sister's room to remain with her to the last moment.

But when Grace got there, she found, to her dismay, that Adela was prepared to go also. Her fan lay on the table, her gloves beside it.

"Adela, indeed you must not go!" decisively spoke Grace. "Only think how—I said it this afternoon—unseemly it will be."

"If you only knew how I am yearning for it," came the piteous reiteration, and Adela entwined her wasted arms entreatingly about her sister. "My own home once, Gracie, my own home once! I seem to be dying for a sight of it."

Never had Grace felt so perplexed, rarely so distressed. "Adela, I dare not sanction it; dare not take you. What would be said and thought? Mamma—"

"You need not take me; I don't wish to get you into trouble with mamma. Darvy can tell them to get a cab. Grace, you have no right to oppose me," went on Adela, in low, firm tones; "what right can you have? My husband will not be there, and I must see my old home. It may be the last time I shall have the chance of it."

Sir Sandy's step was heard outside in the corridor, passing to his chamber. Grace opened the door, and told him of the trouble. He put his little head inside and said a few words to Adela in his mild way, begging her not to attempt to go; and then went on to his room.

"I must go, Gracie; I must go! Grace, don't look harshly at me, for I am very miserable."

What was Grace to do? A little more combating, and she yielded in very helplessness. The conviction lay upon her that if she refused to the end, Adela would certainly go alone. When an ardent desire, such as this, takes possession of one weakened in spirit and in health, it assumes the form of a fever that must have its course.

The contention delayed them, and it was late when they went down to the carriage. Little Sir Sandy took his seat opposite Grace and Adela.

"I wash my hands of it," he said, amiably. "Do not let your mother put the blame of it upon me, Lady Adela, and tell me I ought not to have brought you."

A few minutes, and the carriage stopped in Grosvenor Square. Other guests were entering the house at the same moment. Adela shrank behind Grace and Sir Sandy, and was not observed in the crowd. Her dress was black net, as it had been at Mrs. Blunt's, though she was not in mourning now; she kept her thin black burnous cloak on and held it up to her face as she passed close to Hilson. The man stepped back in astonishment, recollected himself, and saluted her with an impassive face.

Keeping in the shade as much as was possible, shrinking into corners to avoid observation, Adela lost the others. She heard their names shouted out in a louder voice than Hilson's, "Lady Grace Chenevix and Sir Sandy MacIvor," and she lingered behind looking about her.

How painful to her was the sight of the old familiar spots! She turned into a small niche and halted there; her heart was beating too painfully to go on, her breath had left her. No, she should not be able to carry out this expedition; she saw now how wrong and foolish it had been to attempt it; she had put herself into a false position, and she felt it in every tingling vein.

Just one peep she would give at the drawing-rooms above. Just one. No one would notice her. Amidst the crowds pressing in she should escape observation. One yearning look, and then she would turn back and escape the way she came.

Three or four persons in a group, strangers to her, were passing upwards. Adela glided on behind them. Their names were shouted out as her sister's and Sir Sandy's had been; as others were; and she stole after them, within the portals.

But only to steal back again. Nay, to start back. For a too-well-remembered voice had greeted the visitors: "I am so glad to see you," and a tall, distinguished form stood there with outstretched hands: the voice and form of her husband. Later, she knew how it was. The faintness succeeding to the operation (a very slight one), which had alarmed Mrs. Dalrymple herself, and also the surgeon and the Rector, had passed off, and she was really in no danger. So that when Sir Francis learnt this on his arrival at Netherleigh, he found himself at liberty to return.

Feeling as if she must die in her agony of shame, shame at her unwarrantable intrusion, which the unexpected sight of her husband brought home to her, Adela got down the stairs again unseen and unnoticed, and encountered Hilson in the hall.

"Can I do anything for you, my lady?—can I get you anything?" he asked, his tone betraying his compassion for her evident sickness.

"Yes," she said, "yes. I want to go home; I find I am not well enough to remain: perhaps one of the carriages outside would take me?"

"Can I assist you, Lady Adela?" said a voice at her side, from one who was then entering and had overheard the colloquy: and Adela turned to behold Gerard Hope.

"Is it you?" she faintly cried. "I thought you were abroad, Gerard. Are you making one of the crowd here tonight?"

"Not as a guest. These grand things no longer belong to me. I am in England again, and at work—a clerk in your husband's house, Lady Adela; and I have come here tonight to see him on a pressing matter of business."

Hilson managed it all. An obliging coachman, then setting down his freight, was only too willing to take home a sick lady. Gerard Hope and Hilson both went out with her.

"Don't say to—to any one—that I came, Hilson," she whispered, as she shrank into a corner of the carriage: and Hilson discerned that by "any one" she must especially mean Sir Francis Netherleigh.

"You may depend upon me, my lady. Chenevix House," he added to the friendly coachman: and closed the door on the unhappy woman who was once his master's indulged and idolized wife.

"How she is changed!" thought Gerard, gazing after the carriage as it bowled away. "Hilson," he said, turning to the butler, "I must see your master for a minute or two. Have you any room that you can put me into, away from this crowd?"

"There's the housekeeper's parlour, sir: if you don't mind going there. It's quite empty."

"All right, Tell Sir Francis I bring a note from Mr. Howard. Something important, I believe."

CHAPTER XXXIV

The stately rooms were thrown open for the reception of the guests, and the evening was already waning. Wax-lights innumerable shed their rays on the gilded decorations, the exquisite paintings, the gorgeous dresses of the ladies; the enlivening strains of the band invited to the dance, and rare exotics shed forth a sweet perfume. Admission to the residence of Sir Francis Netherleigh was coveted by the gay world.

"There's a tear!" almost screamed a pretty-looking girl. By some mishap in the dancing-room her partner had contrived to put his foot upon her thin white dress, and the bottom of the skirt was half torn away.

"Quite impossible than I can finish the quadrille," quoth she, half in amusement, half provoked at the misfortune. "You must find another partner whilst I go and have this repaired."

It was Frances Chenevix. By some neglect, no maid was at the moment in attendance upstairs; and Frances, in her impatience, ran down to the housekeeper's parlour. As Adela's sister, and frequently there with Mary Lynn, she was quite at home in the house. She had gathered the damaged dress up on her arm, but her white silk petticoat fell in rich folds around her.

"Just look what an object that stupid—" And there stopped the young lady. For, instead of the housekeeper or maid, whom she expected to meet, no one was in the room but a gentleman; a tall, handsome man. She looked thunderstruck: and then slowly advanced and stared at him, as if unable to believe her own eyes.

"Gerard! Well, I should just as soon have expected to meet the dead here."

"How are you, Lady Frances?" he said, holding out his hand with hesitation.

"Lady Frances! I am much obliged to you for your formality. Lady Frances returns her thanks to Mr. Hope for his polite inquiries," continued she, honouring him with a swimming curtsy.

He caught her hand. "Forgive me, Fanny, but our positions have altered. At least, mine has: and how did I know that you were not altered with it?"

"You are an ungrateful—raven," cried she, "to croak like that. After getting me to write to you no end of letters, with all the news about every one, and beginning 'My dear Gerard,' and ending 'Your affectionate Fanny,' and being as good to you as a sister, you meet me with 'My Lady Frances!' Now, don't squeeze my hand to atoms. What on earth have you come to England for?"

"I could not stop over there," he returned, with emotion; "I was fretting away my heart-strings. So I accepted an offer that was made to me, and came back. Guess in what way, Frances; and what to do."

"How should I know? To call me 'Lady Frances,' perhaps."

"As a City clerk; earning my bread. That's what I am now. Very consistent, is it not, for one in my position to address familiarly Lady Frances Chenevix?"

"You never spoke a grain of sense in your life, Gerard," she exclaimed peevishly. "What do you mean?"

"Sir Francis Netherleigh has taken me into his house in Leadenhall Street."

"Sir Francis Netherleigh!" she echoed, in surprise. "What, with that—that—"

"That crime hanging over me. Speak up, Frances."

"No; I was going to say that doubt," returned the outspoken girl. "I don't believe you were guilty: you know that, Gerard."

"I have been there some little time now, Frances; and I came up tonight from the City to bring a note to him from Mr. Howard—"

"Rather late, is it not, to be in the City?"

"It is foreign post night, and we are very busy. A telegram came, of some importance, I believe, and Mr. Howard has enclosed it to Sir Francis."

"But you owned to a mountain of debt in England, Gerard; you were afraid of arrest."

"I have managed a portion of that, thanks to Sir Francis, and the rest they are going to let me square up by instalments."

"And pray, if you have been back some time, why have you not come to see us?"

"I don't care to encounter old acquaintances, Frances; still less to intrude voluntarily upon them. They might not like it, you see."

"I see that you have taken up very ridiculous notions; that you are curiously altered."

"Adversity alters most people. That bracelet has never been heard of?"

"Oh, that's gone for good. No doubt melted down in a caldron, as the colonel calls it, and the diamonds reset. It remains a mystery of the past, and is never expected to be solved."

"And they still suspect me! What is the matter with your dress?"

"Matter enough," answered she, letting it down and turning round for his inspection. "I came here to get it repaired. That great booby, John Cust, did it for me."

"Fanny, how is Alice Dalrymple?"

"You have cause to ask after her! She is dying."

"Dying!" repeated Gerard, in hushed, shocked tones.

"I do not mean actually dying tonight, or going to die tomorrow; but that she is dying by slow degrees there is no doubt. It may be weeks yet, or months; perhaps years: I cannot tell."

"Where is she?"

"Still at Lady Sarah's. Just now she is making a short stay with her mother at Netherleigh. She went home also in the spring for a month, and when she came back Sarah was so shocked at the change in her that she called in medical advice, and we have been trying to nurse her up. It is all of no use: she grows thinner and weaker."

"You are still at Lady Sarah's also?"

"Oh, to be sure; I am a fixture there," laughed Frances.

"Are the Hopes here tonight?"

"Yes: or will be. They went out somewhere to dinner, and expected to be late."

"Does my uncle ever speak of me less resentfully?"

"Not he. I think his storming over it has only made his suspicion stronger. Not a week passes but he begins again about that detestable bracelet. He is unalterably persuaded that you took it, and no one must dare to put in a word in your defence."

"And does your sister honour me with the same belief?" demanded the young man, bitterly.

"Sarah is silent on the point to me: I think she scarcely knows what to believe. You see I tell you all freely, Gerard."

"Fanny," he said, dropping his voice, "how is it that I saw Lady Adela here tonight?"

"Lady Adela!" retorted Frances, who knew nothing of the escapade. "That you never did."

"But I assure you—"

"Hush, for goodness' sake. Here comes Sir Francis."

"Why, Fanny," he exclaimed to his sister-in-law as he entered, "you here!"

"Yes: look at the sight they have made of me," replied she, shaking down her dress for his benefit, as she had previously done for Gerard's. "I am waiting for some of the damsels to mend it for me: I suppose Mr. Hope's presence has scared them sway. Won't mamma be in a rage when she sees it! it is new on tonight."

She made her escape. Sir Francis's business with Gerard was soon over, when he walked with him into the hall. Who should be standing there but Colonel Hope. He started back when he saw Gerard.

"Can I believe my senses?" stuttered he. "Sir Francis Netherleigh, is he one of your guests?"

"He is here on business," was the reply. "Pass on, colonel."

"No, sir, I will not pass on," cried the enraged colonel, who had not rightly caught the word business. "Or if I do pass on, it will only be to warn your guests to take care of their jewellery. So, sir," he added, turning to his nephew, "you can come back, can you, when the proceeds of your theft are spent! You have been starring it in Calais, I hear. How long did the bracelet last you to live upon?"

"Sir," answered Gerard, with a pale face, "it has been starving rather than starring. I asserted my innocence at the time, Colonel Hope, and I repeat it now."

"Innocence!" ironically repeated the colonel, turning to all sides of the hall, as if he took delight in parading the details of the unfortunate past. "The trinkets were spread out on a table in Lady Sarah's own house: you came stealthily into it—after having been forbidden it for another fault—went stealthily into the room, and the next minute the diamond bracelet was missing. It was owing to my confounded folly in listening to a parcel of women that I did not bring you to trial at the time; I have only once regretted not doing it, and that has been ever since. A little wholesome correction at the Penitentiary might have made an honest man of you. Good-night, Sir Francis; if you encourage him in your house, you don't have me in it."

Now another gentleman had entered and heard this: some servants also heard it. Colonel Hope, who firmly believed in his nephew's guilt, turned off, peppery and indignant; his wife had gone upstairs; and Gerard, giving vent to sundry unnephew-like expletives, strode after him. The colonel made a dash into a street cab, and Gerard walked towards the City.

The evening went on. Lady Frances Chenevix, her dress all right again, at least to appearance, was waiting to regain breath, after a whirling waltz. Next to her stood a lady who had also been whirling. Frances did not know her.

"You are quite exhausted: we kept it up too long," said the gentleman in attendance on the stranger. "Sit down. What can I get you?"

"My fan: there it is. Thank you. Nothing else."

"What an old creature to dance herself down!" thought Frances. "She's forty, if she's a day."

The lady opened her fan, and, whilst using it, the diamonds of her rich bracelet gleamed right in the eyes of Frances Chenevix. Frances looked at it, and started: she strained her eyes and looked at it again: she bent nearer to it, and became agitated with emotion. If her recollection did not play her false, that was the lost bracelet.

She saw Grace at a distance, and glided up to her. "Who is that lady?" she asked, pointing to the stranger.

"I don't know who she is," replied Grace. "I was standing by mamma when she was introduced, but did not catch the name. She came late, with the Cadogans."

"The idea of people being in the house that you don't know!" indignantly spoke Frances, who was working herself into a fever. "Where's Sarah? Do you know that?"

"In the card-room, at the whist-table."

Lady Sarah, however, had left it, for Frances only turned from Grace to encounter her. "I do believe your lost bracelet is in the room," she whispered, in agitation. "I think I have seen it."

"Impossible!" responded Lady Sarah Hope.

"It looks exactly the same; gold links interspersed with diamonds: and the clasp is the same; three stars. A tall, ugly woman has it on, her black hair strained off her face." For, it should be remarked en passant, that such was not the fashion then.

"So very trying for plain people!" remarked Lady Sarah, carelessly. "Where is she?"

"There: she is standing up now. Let us get close to her. Her dress is that beautiful maize colour, with old lace."

Lady Sarah Hope drew near, and obtained a sight of the bracelet. The colour flew into her face.

"It is mine, Fanny," she whispered.

But the lady, at that moment, took the gentleman's arm, and moved away. Lady Sarah followed her, with the view of obtaining another look. Fanny went to Sir Francis, and told him. He showed himself hard of belief.

"You cannot be sure at this distance of time, Fanny. And, besides, more bracelets than one may have been made of that pattern."

"I am so certain, that I feel as if I could swear to the bracelet," eagerly replied Lady Frances.

"Hush, hush, Fanny."

"I recollect it perfectly: the bracelet struck me the moment I saw it. How singular that I should have been talking to Gerard Hope about it tonight!"

Sir Francis smiled. "Imagination is very deceptive, Frances. Your having spoken to Mr. Hope of the bracelet brought it into your thoughts."

"But it could not have brought it to my eyes," returned the girl. "Stuff and nonsense about imagination, Francis Netherleigh! I am positive it is the bracelet. Here comes Sarah."

"I suppose Frances has been telling you," observed Lady Sarah to her brother-in-law. "I feel convinced it is my own bracelet."

"But—as I have just remarked to Frances—other bracelets may have been made precisely similar to yours," he urged.

"If it is mine, the initials 'S. H.' are scratched on the back of the middle star. I did it one day with a penknife."

"You never mentioned that fact before."

"No. I was determined to give no clue. I was always afraid of the affair being traced home to Gerard, and it would have reflected so much disgrace on my husband's name."

"Did you speak to the lady?—did you ask where she got the bracelet?" interrupted Frances.

"How could I ask her?" retorted Lady Sarah. "I do not know her."

"I will," cried Frances, in a resolute tone.

"My dear Fanny!" remonstrated Sir Francis.

"I vow I will," she persisted. But they did not believe her.

Frances kept her word. She found the strange lady in the refreshment-room. Locating herself by her side, she entered upon a few trifling remarks, which were civilly received. Suddenly she dashed at once to her subject.

"What a beautiful bracelet!"

"I think it is," was the stranger's reply, holding out her arm for its inspection, without any reservation.

"One does not often see such a bracelet as this," pursued Frances. "Where did you buy it?—if you don't mind my asking."

"Garrards are my jewellers," she replied.

This very nearly did for Frances: for it was at Garrards' that the colonel originally purchased it: and it seemed to give a colouring to Sir Francis Netherleigh's view of more bracelets having been made of the same pattern. But she was too anxious and determined to stand upon ceremony—for Gerard's sake: and he was dearer to her than the world suspected.

"We—one of my family—lost a bracelet exactly like this some time back. When I saw it on your arm, I thought it was the same. I hoped it was."

The lady froze directly, and laid down her arm, making no reply.

"Are you—pardon me, there are painful interests involved—are you sure you purchased this at Garrards'?"

"I have said that Messrs. Garrard are my jewellers," replied the stranger, in cold, repelling tones; and the words sounded evasive to Frances. "More I cannot say: neither am I aware by what law of courtesy you thus question me, nor whom you may be."

The young lady drew herself up, proudly secure in her name and rank. "I am Lady Frances Chenevix. And I must beg you to pardon me."

But the stranger only bowed in silence, and turned to the refreshment-table. Frances went to find the Cadogans, and to question them.

She was a Lady Livingstone, they told her, wife of Sir Jasper Livingstone. The husband had made a mint of money at something or other, and had been knighted; and now they were launching out into high society.

The nose of Lady Frances went into the air. A City knight and his wife: that was it, was it! How could Mrs. Cadogan have taken up with them?

The Honourable Mrs. Cadogan did not choose to say: beyond the assertion that they were extremely worthy, good sort of people. She could have said that her spendthrift of a husband had borrowed money from Sir Jasper Livingstone; and to prevent being bothered for it, and keep them in good humour, they introduced the Livingstones where they could.

It seemed that nothing more could be done. Frances Chenevix went home with her sister Sarah in great excitement, ready to go through fire and water, if that would have set her doubts at rest one way or the other.

They found Colonel Hope in excitement on another score, and Lady Sarah learnt what it was that had caused her husband not to make his appearance in the rooms, which she had thought quite unaccountable. The colonel treated them to a little abuse of Gerard, prophesying that the young man would come to be hanged—which he would deserve, if for impudence alone—and wondering what on earth could possess Francis Netherleigh to make that Leadenhall house of his a refuge for the ill-doing destitute.

Before Frances went to bed, she wrote a full account of what had happened to Alice Dalrymple, at Netherleigh, saying she was quite sure it was the lost bracelet, and also telling her of Gerard's return.

It may, perhaps, as well be mentioned, before we have quite done with the evening, that the sudden disappearance of Adela caused some commotion in the minds of those two individuals, Grace Chenevix and Sir Sandy MacIvor, who were alone cognizant of her presence in the house. When Grace saw Sir Francis Netherleigh standing in his place as host, she turned sharply round to motion back Adela, following, as she believed, behind. But she did not see her: and at the moment Sir Francis advanced, took Grace's hand, and began telling her about Mrs. Dalrymple.

What had become of Adela? Grace's face went hot and cold, and as soon as she got away from Sir Francis, she looked about for her. Not finding her, unable to inquire after her of any of the guests, as it would have betrayed Adela's unlawful presence in the house, fearing she knew not what, Grace grew so troubled that she had no resource but to seek her mother and whisper the news. Lady Acorn, whilst giving a few hard words to Adela and to Grace also, hit upon the truth—that the sight of her husband had terrified her away, and she had in all probability gone back home. "Hilson will know; he is in the hall," she said to Grace: and Grace went to Hilson, and found her mother's view the correct one.

But, although it had ended without exposure, Lady Acorn could not forgive it. She spent the next day telling Adela what she thought of her, and that she must be getting into a fit state for a lunatic asylum.

The letter of Frances Chenevix so troubled Alice Dalrymple that she showed it to Selina, confessing at the same time what a terrible nightmare the loss of the bracelet had been to her. Selina told her she was "silly;" that but for her weak health she would surely never have suspected either herself or Gerard of taking it. "Go back to London without delay," was her emphatic advice to Alice, "and sift it, if you can, to the bottom." And, as Mrs. Dalrymple was certainly out of danger, Alice went up at once.

She found Frances Chenevix had lost none of her eager excitement, whilst Lady Sarah had nearly determined not to move in the matter: the bracelet seen on Lady Livingstone's arm must have been one of the same pattern sold to that lady by Messrs. Garrard. To the colonel nothing had been said. Frances, however, would not let it drop.

The following morning, saying she wanted to do an errand or two, Frances got possession of Lady Sarah's carriage, and down she went to the Haymarket to see the Messrs. Garrard. Alice—more fragile than ever, her once lovely countenance so faded now that she looked to be dying, as Frances had said to Gerard Hope—waited her return in a pitiable state of anxiety. Frances came in, all excitement.

"Alice, it is the bracelet. I am more certain of it than ever. Garrards' people say they have sold many articles of jewellery to Lady Livingstone, but not a diamond bracelet. Moreover, they say that they never had, of that precise pattern, but the one bracelet Colonel Hope bought."

"What is to be done?" exclaimed Alice.

"I know: I shall go to those Livingstones; Garrards' people gave me their address. Gerard shall not remain under this cloud if I can help him out of it. Sir Francis won't act in it; he laughs at me: Sarah won't act; and we dare not tell the colonel. He is so obstinate and wrongheaded, he would be for arresting Gerard, pending the investigation."

"Frances—"

"Now, don't preach, Alice. When I will a thing, I will. I am like my lady mother for that. Sarah says she scratched her initials on the gold inside the bracelet, and I shall demand to see it: if these Livingstones refuse, I'll put the detectives on the scent. I will; as sure as my name is Frances Chenevix."

"And if the investigation should bring the guilt home to—to—Gerard?" whispered Alice, in hollow tones.

"And if it should bring it home to you! and if it should bring it home to me!" spoke the exasperated Frances. "For shame, Alice! it cannot bring it home to Gerard, for he was never guilty."

Alice sighed; she saw there was no help for it, for Lady Frances was resolute. "I have a deeper stake in this than you," she said, after a pause of consideration: "let me go to the Livingstones. Yes, Frances, you must not refuse me; I have a very, very urgent motive for wishing it."

"You, you weak mite of a thing! you would faint before you were half-way through the interview," cried Frances, in tones between jest and vexation.

Alice persisted: and Frances at length conceded the point, though with much grumbling. The carriage was still at the door, for Frances had desired that it should wait, and Alice hastily dressed herself and went down to it, without speaking to Lady Sarah. The footman was closing the door upon her, when out flew Frances.

"Alice, I have made up my mind to go with you; I cannot keep my patience until you are back again. I can sit in the carriage whilst you go in, you know. Lady Livingstone will be two feet higher from today—that the world should have been gladdened with a spectacle of Lady Frances Chenevix waiting humbly at her door."

They drove off. Frances talked incessantly on the road, but Alice was silent: she was deliberating what she should say, and was nerving herself to the task. Lady Livingstone was at home; and Alice, sending in her card, was conducted to her presence, leaving Lady Frances in the carriage.

Frances had described her to be as thin as a whipping-post, with a red nose: and Alice found Lady Livingstone answer to it very well. Sir Jasper, who was also present, was much older than his wife, and short and stout; a good-natured looking man, with a wig on the top of his head.

Alice, refined and sensitive, scarcely knew how she opened her subject, but she was met in a different manner from what she had expected. The knight and his wife were really worthy people, as Mrs. Cadogan had said: but the latter had a mania for getting into "high life and high-lived company:" a feat she would never be able thoroughly to accomplish. They listened to Alice's tale with courtesy, and at length with interest.

"You will readily conceive the nightmare this has been to me," panted Alice, for her emotion was great. "The bracelet was under my charge, and it disappeared in this extraordinary way. All the trouble it has been productive of to me I am not at liberty to tell you, but it has certainly helped to shorten my life."

"You look very ill," observed Lady Livingstone, with sympathy.

"I am worse than I look. I am going into the grave rapidly. Others less sensitive, or with stronger health, might have battled successfully with the distress and annoyance; I could not. I shall die in greater peace if this unhappy affair can be cleared. Should it prove to be the same bracelet, we may be able to trace out how it was lost."

Lady Livingstone left the room and returned with the diamond bracelet. She held it out to Miss Dalrymple, and the colour rushed into Alice's poor wan face at the gleam of the diamonds: for she believed she recognized them.

"But, stay," she said, drawing back her hand as she was about to touch it: "do not give it me just yet. If it be the one we lost, the letters 'S. H.' are scratched irregularly on the back of the middle star. Perhaps you will first look if they are there, Lady Livingstone."

Lady Livingstone turned the bracelet, glanced at the spot indicated, and then silently handed it to Sir Jasper. The latter smiled.

"Sure enough here's something on the gold—I can't see distinctly without my glasses. What is it, Lady Livingstone?"

"The letters 'S. H.,' as Miss Dalrymple described: I cannot deny it."

"Deny it! no, my lady, why should we deny it? If we are in possession of another's bracelet, lost by fraud, and if the discovery will set this young lady's mind at ease, I don't think either you or I shall be the one to deny it. Examine it for yourself, ma'am," added he, giving it to Alice.

She turned it about, she put it on her arm, her eyes lighting with the eagerness of conviction. "It is certainly the same bracelet," she affirmed: "I could be sure of it, I think, without proof; but Lady Sarah's initials are there, scratched irregularly, just as she describes to have scratched them."

"It is not beyond the range of possibility that initials may have been scratched on this bracelet, without its being the same," observed Lady Livingstone.

"I think it must be the same," mused Sir Jasper. "It looks suspicious."

"Lady Frances Chenevix understood you to say you bought this of Messrs. Garrard," resumed Alice.

Lady Livingstone felt rather foolish. "What I said was, that Messrs. Garrard were my jewellers. The fact is, I do not know exactly where this was bought: but I did not consider myself called upon to proclaim that fact to a young lady who was a stranger to me, and in answer to questions which I thought verged on impertinence."

"Her anxiety, scarcely less than my own, may have rendered her abrupt," replied Alice, by way of apology for Frances. "Our hope is not so much to regain the bracelet, as to penetrate the mystery of its disappearance. Can you not let me know where you did buy it?"

"I can," interposed Sir Jasper: "there's no disgrace in having bought it where I did. I got it at a pawnbroker's."

Alice's heart beat violently. A pawnbroker's! Was her haunting fear growing into a dread reality?

"I was one day at the East-end of London, walking fast, when I saw a topaz-and-amethyst cross in a pawnbroker's window," said Sir Jasper. "The thought struck me that it would be a pretty ornament for my wife, and I went in to look at it. In talking about jewellery with the master, he reached out this diamond bracelet, and told me that would be a present worth making. Now, I knew my lady's head had been running on a diamond bracelet; and I was tempted to ask what was the lowest figure he would put it at. He said it was the most valuable article of the sort he had had for a long while, the diamonds of the first water, worth four hundred guineas of anybody's money; but that, being second-hand, he could part with it for two hundred and fifty. And I bought it. There's where I got the bracelet, ma'am."

"That was just the money Colonel Hope gave for it new at Garrards'," said Alice. "Two hundred and fifty guineas."

Sir Jasper stared at her: and then broke forth with a comical attempt at rage, for he was one of the best-tempered men in the world.

"The old wretch of a cheat! Sold it to me at second-hand price, as he called it, for the identical sum it cost new! Why, he ought to be prosecuted for usury."

"It is just what I tell you, Sir Jasper," grumbled his lady. "You will go to these low second-hand dealers, who always cheat where they can, instead of to a regular jeweller; and nine times out of ten you get taken in."

"But your having bought it of this pawnbroker does not bring me any nearer to knowing how he procured it," observed Alice.

"I shall go to him this very day and ascertain," returned Sir Jasper. "Tradespeople may not sell stolen bracelets with impunity. You shall hear from me as soon as possible," he added to Alice, as he escorted her out to the carriage.

But Sir Jasper Livingstone found it easier to say a thing than to do it. The pawnbroker protested his ignorance and innocence. If the bracelet was a stolen bracelet, he knew nothing of that. He had bought it, he said, in the regular course of business, at one of the pawnbrokers' periodical sales: and of this he convinced Sir Jasper.

Frances Chenevix was in despair. She made a confidante of Lady Sarah, and got her to put the affair once more into the hands of the detectives; the same officer who had charge of it before, Mr. Pullet, taking it up again. He had something to work upon now.

CHAPTER XXXV

LIGHT AT LAST

Some weeks later, in an obscure room of a low and dilapidated lodging-house, in a low and dilapidated neighbourhood, there sat a man one evening in the coming twilight: a towering, gaunt skeleton, whose remarkably long arms and legs looked little more than skin and bone. The arms were fully exposed to view, since their owner, though he possessed and wore a waistcoat, dispensed with the use of a shirt. An article, once a coat, lay on the floor, to be donned at will—if it could be got into for the holes. The man sat on the floor in a corner, his head finding a resting-place against the wall, and he had dropped into a light sleep; but if ever famine was depicted in a face, it was in his. Unwashed, unshaven, with matted hair and feverish lips: the cheeks were hollow, the nostrils white and pinched. Some one tried, and shook the door; it aroused him, and he started up, but only to cower in a bending attitude, and listen.

"I hear you," cried a voice. "How are you tonight, Joe? Open the door."

The voice was not one he knew; consequently not one that might be responded to.

"Do you call this politeness, Joe Nicholls? If you don't open the door, I shall take the liberty of opening it for myself: which will put you to the trouble of mending the fastenings afterwards."

"Who are you?" cried Nicholls, reading determination in the voice. "I'm gone to bed, and I can't admit folks tonight."

"Gone to bed at eight o'clock?"

"Yes: I am ill."

"I give you one minute, and then I come in. You will open it, if you wish to save trouble."

Nicholls yielded to his fate: and opened the door.

The gentleman—he looked like one—cast his keen eyes round the room. There was not a vestige of furniture in it; nothing but the bare dirty walls, from which the mortar crumbled, and the bare dirty boards.

"What did you mean by saying you were gone to bed, eh?"

"So I was. I was asleep there," pointing to the corner, "and that's my bed. What do you want?" added Nicholls, peering at the stranger's face in the gloom of the evening, but seeing it imperfectly, for his hat was drawn low over it.

"A little talk with you. That last sweepstake you put into—"

The man lifted his face, and burst forth with such eagerness that the stranger could only arrest his own words and listen.

"It was a swindle from beginning to end. I had scraped together the ten shillings to put in it; and I drew the right horse, and was shuffled out of the gains, and I have never had my dues; not a farthing of 'em. Since then I've been ill, and I can't get about to better myself. Are you come, sir, to make it right?"

"Some"—the stranger coughed—"friends of mine were in it also," said he: "and they lost their money."

"Everybody lost it; the getters-up bolted with all they had drawn into their fingers. Have they been took, do you know?"

"All in good time; they have left their trail. So you have been ill, have you?"

"Ill! just take a sight at me! There's a arm for a big man."

He stretched out his naked arm for inspection: it appeared as if a touch would snap it. The stranger laid his hand upon its fingers, and his other hand appeared to be stealing furtively towards his own pocket.

"I should say this looks like starvation, Joe."

"Some'at akin to it."

A pause of unsuspicion, and the handcuffs were clapped on the astonished man. He started up with an oath.

"No need to make a noise, Nicholls," said the detective, with a careless air, as he lifted off his hat: "I have two men waiting outside. Do you know me?"

The prisoner gave a gasp. "Why, it's Mr. Pullet!"

"Yes; it's Mr. Pullet, Joe."

"I swear I wasn't in the plate robbery," passionately uttered the man. "I knew of it, but I didn't join 'em, and I never had the worth of as much as a saltspoon, after it was melted down. And they call me a coward, and they leave me here to starve and die! Sir, I swear I wasn't in it."

"We'll talk of the plate robbery another time," said the officer; "you have got these bracelets on, my man, for another sort of bracelet. A diamond one. Don't you remember it?"

The prisoner's mouth fell. "I thought that was over and done with, all this time— I don't know what you mean," he added, correcting himself.

"No," said the officer, "it is just beginning. The bracelet is found, and has been traced to you. You were a clever fellow, Joe, and I had my doubts of you at the time, you know. I thought then you were too clever to go on long."

"I should be ashamed to play the sneak, and catch a fellow in this way," cried Joe, driven to exasperation. "Why couldn't you come openly, in your proper clothes—not playing the spy in the garb of a friendly civilian?"

"My men are in their proper clothes,'" was the equable answer, "and you will have the honour of their escort presently. I came in because they did not know you, and I did. You might have had a host of friends around you here."

"Three officers to take a single man, and he a skeleton!" retorted Nicholls, with a great show of indignation.

"Ay; but you were powerful once, and ferocious too. The skeleton aspect is a recent one."

"And to be took for nothing! I know naught of any bracelet."

"Don't trouble yourself with inventions, Nicholls. Your friend is safe in our hands, and has made a full confession."

"What friend?" asked Nicholls, too eagerly.

"The lady you got to dispose of it for you."

Nicholls was startled to incaution. "She hasn't split, has she?"

"Every particular she knew or guessed at. Split to save herself."

"Then there's no faith in woman."

"There never was yet," returned Mr. Pullet. "If they are not at the top and bottom of every mischief, Joe, they are sure to be in the middle. Is this your coat?" touching it gingerly.

"She's a disgrace to the female sex, she is!" raved Nicholls, disregarding the question as to his coat. "But it's a relief now I'm took: it's a weight off my mind. I was always expecting it: and I shall, at any rate, get food in the Old Bailey."

"Ah," said the officer, "you were in good service as a respectable servant, Nicholls: you had better have stuck to your duties."

"The temptation was so great," returned the man, who had evidently abandoned all idea of denial; and, now that he had done so, was ready to be voluble with remembrances and particulars.

"Don't say anything to me. It will be used against you."

"It all came of my long legs," cried Nicholls, ignoring the friendly injunction, and proceeding to enlarge on the feat he had performed. And it may as well be observed that legs so long as his are rarely seen. "I have never had a happy hour since; it's true, sir. I was second footman there, and a good place I had: and I have wished, thousands of times, that the bracelet had been at the bottom of the sea. Our folks had took a house in the neighbourhood of Ascot for the race-week; they had left me at home to take care of the kitchen-maid and another inferior or two, carrying the rest of the servants with them. I had to clean the winders before they returned, and I had druv it off till the Thursday evening, when out I got on the balqueny, intending to begin with the back drawing-room—"

"What do you say you got out on?"

"The balqueny. The thing with the green rails round it, that encloses the winder. While I was leaning over the rails sorting my wash-leathers, I heard something like click, click, click, going on in the fellow-room next door—which was Colonel Hope's—just as if light articles of some sort were being laid sharp on a table. Presently two voices began to talk, a lady's and a gentleman's, and I listened—"

"No good ever comes of listening, Joe," interrupted the officer.

"I didn't listen for the sake of listening; but it was awful hot, standing outside there in the sun, and listening was better than working. I didn't want to hear, neither, for I was thinking of my own concerns, and what a fool I was to have idled away my time all day till the sun come on the back winders. Bit by bit, I heard what they were talking of—that it was jewels they had got there, and that one of 'em was worth two hundred guineas. Thinks I, if that was mine, I'd do no more work. After a while, I heard them go out of the room, and I thought I'd have a look at the rich things, so I stepped over slant-ways on to the little ledge running along the houses, holding on by our balqueny, and then I passed my hands along the wall till I got hold of their balqueny—but one with ordinary legs and arms couldn't have done it. You couldn't, sir."

"Perhaps not," remarked the officer.

"There wasn't fur to fall, if I had fell, only on to the kitchen leads underneath: leastways not fur enough to kill one, and the leads was flat. But I didn't fall, and I raised myself on to their balqueny, and looked in. My! what a show it was! stunning jewels, all laid out there: so close, that if I had put my hand inside, it must have struck all among 'em: and the fiend prompted me to take one. I didn't stop to look, I didn't stop to think: the one that twinkled the brightest and had the most stones in it was the nearest to me, and I clutched it, and slipped it into my footman's undress jacket, and stepped back again."

"And got safe into your balcony?"

"Yes, and inside the room. I didn't clean the winder that night. I was upset like, by what I had done; and, if I could have put it back again, I think I should; but there was no opportunity. I wrapped it in my winder-leather, and then in a sheet of brown paper, and then I put it up the chimbley in one of the spare bedrooms. I was up the next morning afore five, and I cleaned my winders: I'd no trouble to awake myself, for I had never slept. The same day, towards evening—or the next was it? I forget—you called, sir, and asked me some questions—whether we had seen any one on the leads at the back, and such like. I said that master was just come home from Ascot, and would you be pleased to speak to him."

"Ah!" again remarked the officer, "you were a clever fellow that day. But if my suspicions had not been strongly directed to another quarter, I might have looked you up more sharply."

"I kep' it by me for a month or two, and then I gave warning to leave. I thought I'd have my fling, and I had made acquaintance with her—that lady you've just spoke of—and somehow she wormed out of me that I had got it, and I let her dispose of it for me, for she said she knew how to do it without danger."

"What did you get for it?"

The skeleton shook his head. "Thirty-four pounds, and I had counted on a hundred and fifty. She took her oath she had not helped herself to a sixpence."

"Oaths are plentiful with some ladies," remarked Mr. Pullet.

"She stood to it she hadn't kep' a farthing, and she stopped and helped me to spend the change. After that was done she went over to stop with somebody else who was in luck. And I have tried to go on, and I can't: honestly or dishonestly, it seems all one: nothing prospers, and I'm naked and famishing. I wish I was dying."

"Evil courses rarely do prosper, Nicholls," said the officer, as he called in the policemen and consigned the gentleman to their care.

So Gerard Hope was innocent!

"But how was it you skilful detectives could not be on this man's scent?" asked Colonel Hope of Mr. Pullet, when he heard the tale.

"Colonel, I was thrown off it. Your positive belief in your nephew's guilt infected me; appearances were certainly very strong against him. Neither was his own manner altogether satisfactory to my mind. He treated the obvious suspicion of him more as a jest than in earnest; never, so far as I heard, giving a downright hearty denial to it."

"He was a fool," interjected the colonel.

"Also," continued Mr. Pullet, "Miss Dalrymple's evidence served to throw me off other suspicion. She said, if you remember, sir, that she did not leave the room; but it now appears that she did leave it when your nephew did, though only for a few moments. Those few moments sufficed to do the job."

"It is strange she could not tell the exact truth," growled the colonel.

"She probably thought she was exact enough, since she remained outside the door, and could answer for it that no one entered by it. She forgot the window. I thought of the window the instant the loss was mentioned to me; but Miss Dalrymple's assertion, that she never had the window out of her view, prevented my dwelling on it. I did go to the next door, and saw this very fellow who committed the robbery, but his manner was sufficiently satisfactory. He talked too freely; I did not like that; but I found he had been in the same service fifteen months; and, as I must repeat, in my mind the guilt lay with another."

"It is a confoundedly unpleasant affair for me," cried the colonel. "I have published my nephew's disgrace all over London."

"It is more unpleasant for him, colonel," was the rejoinder of Mr. Pullet.

"And I have kept him short of money, and suffered him to be sued for debt; and I have let him go and live among the runaway scamps over the water; and now he is working as a merchant's clerk! In short, I have played the very deuce with him."

"But reparation lies, doubtless, in your own heart and hands, colonel."

"I don't know that, sir," testily concluded the colonel.

Once more Gerard Hope entered his uncle's house; not as an interloper, stealing into it in secret; but as an honoured guest, to whom reparation was due, and must be made. Alice Dalrymple chanced to be alone. She was leaning back in her invalid-chair, a joyous flush on her wasted cheek, a joyous happiness in her eye. Still the shadow of coming death was there, and Mr. Hope was shocked to see her—more shocked and startled than he had expected, or chose to express.

"Oh, Alice! what has done this?"

"That has helped it on," she answered, pointing to the bracelet; which, returned to its true owner, lay on the table. "I should not have lived very many years; of that I am convinced: but I think this has taken a little from my life. The bracelet has been the cause of misery to many of us. Lady Sarah says she shall never regard it but as an ill-starred trinket, or wear it with any pleasure."

"But, Alice, why should you have suffered it thus to affect you?" he remonstrated. "You knew your own innocence, and you say you believed and trusted in mine: what did you fear?

"I will tell you, Gerard," she whispered, a deeper hectic rising to her cheeks. "I could not have confessed my fear, even in dying; it was too distressing, too terrible; but now that it is all clear, I will tell it. I believed my sister had taken the bracelet."

"Ah," said Gerard, carelessly.

"Selina called to see me that evening, as you saw, and she was for a minute or two in the room alone with the trinkets: I went upstairs to get a letter. She wanted money badly at the time, as you cannot fail to remember, and I feared she had been tempted to take the bracelet—just as this unfortunate man was tempted. Oh, Gerard! the dread of it has been upon me night and day, preying upon my fears, weighing down my spirits, wearing away my health and my life. Now hope would be in the ascendant, now fear. And I had to bear it all in silence. It is that enforced, dreadful silence that has so tried me."

"Why did you not question Selina?"

"I did. She denied it. As good as laughed at me. But you know how light-headed and careless her nature is; and the fear remained with me."

"It must have been a morbid fear, Alice."

"Not so—if you knew all. But it is at an end, and I am very thankful. I have only one hope now," she added, looking up at him with a sunny smile. "Ah, Gerard, can you not guess it?"

"No," he answered, in a stifled voice. "I can only guess that you are lost to me."

"Lost to all here. Have you forgotten our brief conversation, the night you went into exile? I told you then there was one far more worthy of you than I could have ever been."

"None will ever be half so worthy; or—I will say it, Alice, in spite of your warning hand—half so loved."

"Gerard," sinking her voice, "she has waited for you."

"Nonsense," he rejoined.

"She has. When she shall be your wife, you may tell her that I saw it and said it. She might have had John Cust."

"My darling—"

"Stay, Gerard," she gravely interrupted; "those words of endearment are not for me. Can you deny that you love her?"

"Perhaps I do—in a degree. Next to yourself—"

"Put me out of your thoughts whilst we speak. If I were—where I may perhaps soon be, would she not be dearer to you than any one on earth? Would you not be well pleased to make her your wife?"

"Yes, I might be."

"That is enough, Gerard. Frances—"

"Wait a bit," interrupted Gerard. "Don't you think, Alice, that you have the morbid feeling on you yet? With this dread removed—which, as you truly express it, must have been to you a very nightmare—you may, nay, I think you will, regain health and strength, and be a comfort to us all for years."

"I may regain it in a measure. It is simply impossible that in any case my life will be a long one. Let me—dear Gerard!—let me make some one happy while I may! Hark! that's the door—and this is her light step on the stairs!"

Frances Chenevix came in. "Good gracious, is it you, Gerard!" she exclaimed. "You and Alice look as if you had been talking secrets."

"So we have been," said Alice. "Frances, what can we do to keep him amongst us? Do you know what Colonel Hope has told him?"

"No. What?"

"That though he shall be reinstated in favour as to money matters, he shall not be in his affection or his home, unless he prove sorry for that past rebellion of his."

"When did the colonel tell him? When did he see him?"

"This morning: before Gerard came here. I think Gerard is sorry for it: you must help him to be more so."

"Fanny," said Gerard, while a damask flush mantled in her cheeks, deeper than the hectic making havoc with those of Alice, "will you help me?"

"As if I could make head or tail of what you two are rambling about!" cried she, as she attempted to turn away; but Gerard caught her to his side.

"Fanny—will you drive me again from the house?"

She lifted her eyes, twinkling with a little spice of mischief. "I did not drive you before."

"In a manner, yes. Do you know what did drive me?" She had known it at the time; and Gerard read it in her face.

"I see it all," he murmured; "you have been far kinder to me than I deserved. Fanny, let me try and repay you for it."

"Are you sure you would not rather have Alice?" she asked, in her clear-sighted independence.

He shook his head sorrowfully. Alice caught their hands together, and held them between her own, with a mental aspiration for their life's future happiness. Some time back she could not have breathed it in so fervent a spirit: but—as she had said—the present world and its hopes were closing to her.

"But you know, Gerard," cried Lady Frances, in a saucy tone, "if you ever do help yourself to somebody's bracelet in reality, you must not expect me to go to prison with you."

"Yes, I shall," he answered promptly. "A wife must share the fortunes of her husband. She takes him for better—or for worse."

He sealed the compact with a kiss. And there was much rejoicing that day in the house of Colonel Hope.

CHAPTER XXXVI

VISITORS AT MOAT GRANGE

Autumn weather lay on the world and on Netherleigh.

Things were coming to a revolt. Never were poor tenant-farmers so ground down and oppressed as those on the estate of Moat Grange. Rents were raised, fines imposed, expenses, properly belonging to landlords, refused to be paid or allowed for. Oscar Dalrymple was ruling with a hand of iron, hard and cruel.

At least, Oscar had the credit of it. In point of fact, he was perhaps a little ashamed of the existing state of things, and would have somewhat altered it if he could. A year ago Oscar had let the whole estate to a sort of agent, a man named Pinnett, and Pinnett was playing Old Gooseberry with everything.

That was the expressive phrase, whatever it might mean, the indignant people used. They refused to lay the blame on Pinnett, utterly refused to recognize him in the matter; arguing, perhaps rightly, that unless he had Mr. Dalrymple's sanction to harsh measures, he could not exercise them, and that Mr. Dalrymple was, therefore, alone to blame. Most likely Oscar had no resource but to sanction it all, tacitly at any rate.

As to the Grange itself, the mansion, it was now the dreariest of the dreary. It had not been let with the estate, and Oscar and his wife still lived in it. Two maids were kept, and a man for outdoor work—the garden and the poultry. Most of the rooms were locked up. Selina would unlock the doors sometimes and open the shutters; and pace about the lonely floors, and wish she had not been guilty of the folly which had led to these wretched retrenchments. Things indoors and out were growing worse day by day.

One morning John Lee called at the Grange: a respectable man, whose name you cannot have forgotten. He had rented all his life, and his father before him, under the Dalrymples.

"Sir," he began to Oscar, without circumlocution, "I have come up about that paper which has been sent to me by Jones, your lawyer. It's a notice that next Michaelmas, when my lease will expire, the rent is to be raised."

"Well?" said Mr. Dalrymple.

"A pound an acre. A pound an acre," repeated the farmer, with increased emphasis. "Jones must have made a mistake, sir."

"I fancy not. But Jones is not my lawyer, you know; he is Mr. Pinnett's."

"We don't want to have anything to do with Mr. Pinnett, or to hear his name, sir. I have always rented under the Dalrymples; and I hope to do it still, sir, with your leave."

"You know, Lee, that Pinnett has a lease of the whole estate. What he proposes is no doubt fair. Your farm will well bear the increased rent he means to put on it."

"Increased by a pound an acre!" cried the farmer, in his excitement. "No, sir; it won't bear it, for I'll never pay it."

"I am sorry for that, Mr. Lee, because it will leave Pinnett only one alternative: to substitute in its place a notice to quit."

"To quit! to quit the farm!" reiterated Lee, in his astonishment. "Why, it has been my home all my life, sir, and it was my father's before me. I was born on that farm, Mr. Dalrymple, years and years before you ever came into the world, and I mean to die on it. I have spared neither money nor labour to bring it to its present flourishing condition."

"My good sir, I say as you do, that the land is flourishing: sufficiently so to justify the advanced rent Pinnett proposes. Two of you were here yesterday on this same errand—Watkins and Rumford."

"They have spent money on their farms, too, expecting to reap future benefit. You see, we never thought of Mr. Dalrymple's dying young, and—"

"Are you speaking of young Robert Dalrymple?"

"No, no, poor fellow: of his father. Mr. Dalrymple did die young, so to say; you can't call a man under fifty old. His death, and his son's close upon it, brought you, sir, to rule over us, and I am sorry to say your rule's a very hard one."

"It will not be made easier," curtly replied Oscar Dalrymple, who was getting angry. "And I will not detain you longer, Mr. Lee," he added, rising. "Your time is valuable."

"And what is to be my answer, sir?"

"It no longer lies with me to give an answer, Lee, and I must request that you do not refer to me again. Pinnett's answer will no doubt be that you must renew the lease at the additional rent demanded, or else give up the farm."

Farmer Lee swung away in a passion. In turning out of the first field he met two ladies: one young and very pretty, the other getting to look old; her thin features were white and her hair was grey. They were Mrs. Dalrymple and Mary Lynn. Close upon Mrs. Dalrymple's recovery from her accident, which turned out to have been not at all formidable, she caught a violent cold; it laid her up longer than a cold had ever laid her up before, and seemed to have tried her greatly. Mary Lynn had now just come again to Netherleigh to stay a week or two with her.

"Is it you, ma'am!" cried the farmer, touching his hat. "I'm glad to see you out again."

"At one time I thought I never should be out again," she answered; "I am very weak still. And how are you, Mr. Lee?"

"Middling, ma'am. Anything but well just now, in temper." And the farmer touched upon his grievances, spoke of the interview he had just held at the Grange, and of its master's harshness.

"Is it right to us, ma'am?" he wound up with. "Is it just, Miss Lynn?" turning to that young lady. "Ah, if poor young Mr. Robert had but lived! We should have had no oppression then."

Mary turned away her face, blushing almost to tears with unhappy remembrances. Robert! Robert!

"I do believe it will come to a revolt!" said the farmer to Mrs. Dalrymple. "Not with us tenants; you know better than to think that likely, ma'am; but with those people at the cottages. They are getting ripe for it."

"Ay," she answered, in a low, grieved tone. "And the worst of it, Mr. Lee, the worst to me is, that I am powerless for help or remedy."

"We cannot quite think—it is impossible to think or believe, that Mr. Oscar Dalrymple should have put all control out of his power. Therefore, his refusing to interfere with Pinnett seems all the more harsh. You must see that, ma'am."

"I have no comfort, no advice to give," she whispered, putting her hand into Mr. Lee's as she turned away. For Mrs. Dalrymple could not bear to speak of the existing state of things, the trouble that had come of Selina's folly and Oscar's rule.

Yet Oscar was kind to her. Continuously so. In no way would he allow her income, that which he allowed her, to be in the slightest degree diminished. He pinched himself, but he would not pinch poor Mrs. Dalrymple. Over and over again had she wished Reuben to leave her, but Oscar would not hear of it. Neither, for the matter of that, would Reuben. He did not want wages, he said, but he would not desert his mistress in her premature old age, her sickness, and her sorrow. A small maid only was kept in addition to Reuben; and the man had degenerated (as he might have called it but for his loyalty) to little better than a man-of-all-work. He stood behind the ladies now at a respectful distance, having stopped when they stopped.

The grievance alluded to by Mr. Lee, ready to ripen into open revolt, had nothing to do with the tenant-farmers. It was this. In a very favourable position on the estate, as regarded situation, stood a cluster of small dwellings. They were for the most part very poor, some of them little better than huts, but they commanded a lovely view. They were inhabited by labourers employed on the land, and were called the Mill Cottages: a mill, done away with now, having formerly stood close by.

One fine day it had struck the new man, Pinnett—looking about here and there to discover some means of adding to the profits he meant to make off the land—that if these cottages were taken down and handsome dwellings erected in their place, it would be a great improvement, pecuniarily and artistically, for such houses would let directly in this picturesque locality. No sooner thought of than resolved upon. Miles Pinnett was not a man to linger over his plans, and he gave these small tenants notice to quit.

It was rebelled against. Some of the men had been in the cottages as long as Farmer Lee had been in his farm, and to be ordered to leave seemed a terrible hardship. It no doubt increased the difficulty that there were no other small dwellings on the estate the men could go into: all others were already occupied: and, if they left these, they must go to a distance whence they would have a two or three miles' walk to their day's work. And so, encouraged perhaps by the feeling pervading the neighbourhood, of sympathy with them and opposition to Pinnett, the men, one and all, refused to go out. The next step would be ejectment; and it was looked for day by day.

For all this, Oscar Dalrymple suffered in opinion. Pinnett could not go to such lengths, oppress them as he was oppressing, against the will of the owner, Mr. Dalrymple, argued the community, rich and poor. Perhaps he could not. But how it really was, no one knew, or what power Mr. Dalrymple had put out of his own hands, and into Pinnett's, when he leased him the demesne.

Farmer Lee's visit to Moat Grange was paid in the morning. In the afternoon the Grange had another visitor—Lady Adela Netherleigh.

Adela had not lingered long at her mother's in London. After a few weeks' sojourn she came down to Netherleigh Rectory, invited by the Rector and his wife, her sister Mary. They had gone to London for a day, had been struck with compassion at Adela's evident state of mental suffering, and they asked her to return with them for a little change.

"It is not change I want," she had answered, speaking to Lady Mary. "What I want is peace. Perhaps I shall find it with you, Mary, at the Rectory."

Lady Mary Cleveland hesitated. Peace? The word posed her.

"Adela," she said, "we should be very glad to have you, and there is plenty of room for you and Darvy. But, as to peace—I don't know about that. The Rectory is full of children great and small, and I'm afraid it is noisy and bustling from morning till night."

Adela smiled faintly. The peace her heart craved for was not that imparted by the absence of noise. She might feel all the better for having the bustle of children about her; it might draw her at moments out of her own sorrow. But another thought struck her.

"My—" husband, she had been about to say, but changed the words. "Sir Francis is not staying at Court Netherleigh? Is he?"

"No. It is said he means to take up his abode there later; he is not there yet."

"Then I will come to you, Mary. And I will stay with you for months and months if I like it—and you must allow me to contribute towards your housekeeping as Sir Sandy and Harriet did."

Lady Mary winced a little at that, but she did not say no. With all those children—she had two of her own now—and the Rector's moderate income, they could not be rich.

So Adela and Darvy went down with them to Netherleigh. That was in summer, now it was autumn: and, so far as could be seen or judged, the change had not as yet effected much for her. Adela seemed just as before; wan, weary, sick, and sorry.

And yet, there was a change in a certain degree. The bitter rebellion at her fate had partly passed from her mind, and therefore its traces had left her face. The active repining in which her days had been spent was giving place to a sort of hopeless resignation. She strove to accept her punishment, strove to bear it, to be patient and gentle always, hardly ever ceasing day or night to beseech God to blot out the past from the book of the Recording Angel. The sense of shame, entailed by her conduct of long years, had not lifted itself in the least degree; nay, it seemed to grow of a deeper scarlet as time went on. Sometimes she would think if she could trample upon herself and annihilate all power of remembrance, she would do it gladly; but that would not stamp it out of her ever-living soul. Adela had erred; wilfully, cruelly, persistently; and if ever retribution came home to a woman, it surely had come to her.

On this same day, when the sky was blue and the afternoon sun lay on the green fields at Netherleigh, Lady Adela went out, and turned her languid steps towards Moat Grange. Selina had called to see her at the Rectory several times; each time Adela had promised to pay return visits, and had not yet done so. The direct road lay, as the reader may perhaps remember, through the village and past Court Netherleigh. Lingeringly would her eyes look on the house whenever this happened, lingeringly they rested on it now. The home, in which she had spent so many happy days with Aunt Margery, was closed to her for ever. Of all people in the living world, she was the only one debarred from entering it. Very rarely indeed was Sir Francis at Netherleigh. It had been supposed that he meant to take up his abode in it for the autumn months; but this appeared to be a mistake; when he did come it was but for a flying visit of a few hours. Mr. Cleveland privately told his wife that he believed Sir Francis stayed away from the place because Adela was in it.

Selina was in the larger of the two drawing-rooms when Adela reached the Grange. Selina rarely used it now, her husband never, but she had gone into it this afternoon. Opening the shutters and the window, she sat there making herself a lace collar. The time had gone by when she could order these articles of a Madame Damereau, and pay a fabulous price for them.

Adela untied her bonnet strings and took off her gloves as she sat down opposite Selina. Not strong now, the walk had greatly tired her. Selina could but notice how fragile and delicate she looked, as the light from the window fell upon her face. The once rounded cheeks were wasted, their bright colour had faded to the faintest tinge of pink; from the once lustrous eyes shone only sadness.

"Let me get you something, Adela," cried Selina, impulsively. "A cup of tea—I will make it for you directly. Of wine—well, I am not sure, really, that we possess any. I can ask Oscar."

"Not anything, not anything," returned Adela, "I could not take it. Thank you all the same. As to my looks—I look as I always do."

"Ah me," sighed Selina, "it is a weary life. A weary life, Adela, for you and for me."

"If that were all—its weariness—it might be better borne," murmured Adela. "And yet I do try to bear," she added, pushing her pretty brown hair from her aching brow, and for once induced to speak of her troubles to this friend, who had suffered too—though not as she had. "But there is the remorse as well, you see. Oh, how wrong, how foolish, how wicked we were!—at least I was. Do you ever think of our past folly, Selina?—of the ease and happiness we then held in our hands, and flung away?"

"We have paid for it," said Selina. "Yes, I do sometimes think of the past, Adela; and then I wonder at the folly of women. See to what folly has reduced me!—to drag out a dead-alive existence in a semi-prison, for the Grange is no better now, with never a friend to stay with me, or a shilling to spend. And all for the sake of a few fine bonnets and gowns! Would you believe it," she added, laughing, "that the costly things have not half come to an end yet?"

"Just for that?" dissented Adela, in her pain, and losing sight of Selina's trouble in her own. "If it had been for nothing more than that!"

"Well, well, we have paid for it, I say. Bitterly and cruelly."

"I have. You have not."

"No?" somewhat indifferently returned Selina, her attention partly given to her lace again, for she was never serious long together. "How do you make that out?"

"You have your husband still. Poverty with him, with one we love, must carry little sting with it. But for me—my whole life is one of never-ending loneliness, without a future, without hope. Do you know what fanciful thought came to me the other night?" she went on, after a pause. "I have all sorts of fanciful ideas when I sit alone in the twilight. I thought that life might be so much happier if God gave us a chance once of beginning it all over again from the first. Just once, when we found out what dreadful mistakes we had been making."

"And we should make the same again, though we began it fifty times over, Adela. Unless we could carry back with us our dearly-bought experience."

Adela sighed. "Yes, I suppose so. God would have so ordered it had it been well for us. He knows best. But there are some women who seem never to make mistakes, who go on their way smoothly and happily."

"Placing themselves under God's guidance, I imagine," returned Selina. "That's what my mother says to me, when she lectures me on the past."

Adela's eyes filled with tears. "Yes, yes," she murmured, meekly, recalling that it was what she had been striving to do for some little time now—to hold on her way, under submission to God.

The conversation turned into other channels, and by-and-by, when Adela was rested, she rose to leave. Selina accompanied her into the hall.

"Won't you just say 'How d'you do' to my husband?" she cried, opening the door of their common sitting-room. "He is here."

Adela made no objection, and followed Selina. Oscar was standing in the bay window, facing the door. And some one else, towering nearly a head above him, was standing at his side.

Sir Francis Netherleigh.

They stood, the husband and wife, face to face. With a faint cry, Adela put up her hands, as if to ward off the sight—as if to bespeak pardon in all humility for herself, for her intrusion—and disappeared again, whiter than death. It was rather an awkward moment for them all. Selina disappeared after her, and shut the door.

"Is Lady Adela ill?" asked Sir Francis of Oscar, the question breaking from him involuntarily in the moment's impulse—for she did, indeed, look fearfully so.

"Ay," replied Oscar, "ill with remembrance. Repentance has made her sick unto death. Remorse has told upon her."

But Sir Francis said no more.

Adela had departed across the fields with the best speed she could command. About half-way home she came upon Mr. Cleveland, seated on a stile and whistling softly.

"Those two young rascals of mine"—alluding to two of his little sons—"seduced me from my study to help fly their kites," he began to Adela. "Here I follow them, to the appointed field, and find them nowhere, little light-headed monkeys! But, my dear, what's the matter with you?" he added, with fatherly kindness, as he remarked her pale, troubled face. "You look alarmed."

"I have just seen my husband," she panted, her breath painfully short. All the old pain that she had been striving to subdue had come back again; the sight of him, whom she now passionately loved, had stirred distressing emotion within her.

"Well?" said Mr. Cleveland.

"Did you know he was at Netherleigh?"

"He came down today."

"He was in the bay-parlour with Oscar, and I went into it. It has agitated me."

"But why should it agitate you?" rejoined the old Rector, who was very matter-of-fact. "It seems to me that you ought to accustom yourself to bear these chance meetings with equanimity, child. You can scarcely expect to go through life without seeing him now and then."

Adela bent her head to the stile and broke into sobs. Mr. Cleveland laid his protecting hand upon her shoulder.

"My dear! my dear! Strive to be calm. Surely a momentary sight of him ought not to put you into this state. Is it that you still dislike him so much?"

"Dislike him!" she exclaimed, the contrast between the word and the truth striking her painfully, and causing her to say more than she would have said. "I am dying for his forgiveness; dying to show him how true is my remorse; dying because I lost him."

The Rector did not quite see what answer to make to this. He held his tongue, and Adela resumed.

"I wish I was a Roman Catholic!"

The good man, evangelical Protestant, felt as if his gray hair were standing on end with surprise. "Oh, hush!" said he. "You don't know what you are saying."

"I do wish it," she sobbed. "I could then go into a convent, and find peace."

"Peace!" echoed Mr. Cleveland. "No, child, don't let your imagination run away with that idea. It is a false one. No woman, entering a convent in the frame of mind you seem to be entertaining, could expect peace, or find it."

"Any way, I should feel more at rest: I should have to bear life then, you know. And, oh, I was trying to do so: I was indeed trying!"

Thoroughly put out, the Rector made no comment. Perhaps would not trust himself to make any.

"I suppose there are no such things as Protestant convents, or sisterhoods," she went on, "that receive poor creatures who have no longer any place in this world?"

"Not to my knowledge," sharply spoke Mr. Cleveland, as he jumped off the stile. "It is time we went home, Adela."

They walked away side by side. Gaining the Rectory—a large, straggling, red-brick building, its old walls covered with time-honoured ivy—Adela ascended to her chamber, and shut herself in with her grief.

How scornfully her husband must despise her!—despise her for her past shame and sin; despise her in her present contemptible humiliation, she reflected, a low moan escaping her—he so pure and upright in all his ways, so good and generous and noble! Oh that she could hide to the end from him and from the world!

Lifting her trembling hands, her despairing face, Adela breathed a faint petition that the Most High would be pleased to vouchsafe to her somewhat of His heavenly comfort, or take her out of the tribulation that she could so hardly battle with.

CHAPTER XXXVII

AN ALARM

It was a few days later. Mrs. Oscar Dalrymple, who had been spending the afternoon with her mother and Mary Lynn, was preparing to return to the Grange. Alice had just come home again, a brilliant hectic on her cheeks, but weaker, as it seemed to them all. Alice was happier than she had been for years, in her sweet unselfishness. The trouble which had divided Colonel Hope and his nephew was at an end; Gerard had been reinstated in his uncle's favour, and was to marry Frances Chenevix. Lying on the sofa by the window, in the fading light, Alice had been giving them various particulars of this; and Selina, greatly interested, lingered longer than she had intended. But she had to go.

Rising hurriedly, she put on her bonnet and cloak. Mrs. Dalrymple rang the bell. It was to tell Reuben to be in readiness to attend her daughter.

"As if I wanted old Reuben with me, mamma!" exclaimed Selina. "Why, I shall run home in no time!"

"He had better be with you," sighed Mrs. Dalrymple: the sigh given to the disturbed state of things abroad. "The neighbourhood is not very quiet today, as you know, Selina, and it is growing dusk."

It was not quiet at all. The summary process, eviction, had been resorted to by Pinnett, as regarded the tenants of the Mill Cottages. He had forced them out with violence. One of them, named Thoms, had resisted to the last. Go out he would not, and the assailants could not get him out.

A meeting was to be held this same evening at Farmer Lee's. It could not be called a secret meeting; the farmer would have disdained the name; but those about to attend it waited until the dusk should shelter them, conscious that they were likely to speak treason against their landlord.

"Thoms is out," cried Farmer Bumford, as he entered Mr. Lee's house in excitement.

"How did they get him out?"

"Unroofed him, Lee. Pulled his place to pieces bit by bit, and so forced him out. He is now with the rest of the unfortunate lot."

"I thought such practices were confined to Ireland," said the honest farmer. "It's time something was done to protect us. Oscar Dalrymple will have his sins to answer for."

It was at this hour, when the autumn twilight was deepening, that Selina started for home. She chose the way by the common: a longer way, and in other respects not a desirable one tonight. Selina's spirit was fearless enough, and she wanted to see whether the rumour could be true—that the unhappy people, just ejected, had collected there, meaning to encamp on it. Reuben, with the licence of an old and faithful servant, remonstrated, begging her to go home by the turnpike road: but Selina chose to cross the common.

Surely enough, the unfortunate lot, as Mr. Bumford called them, had gathered on its outskirts, in view of their late homes, their poor goods and chattels, much damaged in the mêlée, piled in little heaps around them. Men, their hearts panting for revenge, sobbing women and shivering children, there they stood, sat, or lay about. The farmers, Lee and Bumford, would later on open their barns to them for the night; but at present they expected to encamp under the stars.

In the midst of the harsh converse that prevailed, the oaths, and the abuse lavished on Oscar Dalrymple—for these poor, ignorant labourers refused, like their betters, to believe that Pinnett could so act without the landlord's orders—they espied, hurrying past them at a swift pace, their landlord's wife. Selina walked with her head down; now that she saw the threatening aspect of affairs, she wished she had listened to Reuben, and taken the open road. One of them came running up; a resolute fellow, named Dyke.

"You'd hurry by, would you?" said he, in tones that spoke more of plaint than threat. "Won't you turn your eyes once to the ruin your husband has wrought? Look at the mud and mortar! If the walls weren't of new brick or costly stone, they was good enough for us. They were our homes. Look at the spot now."

Selina trembled visibly. She was aware of the awful feeling abroad against her husband, and a dread rushed into her heart that they might be going to visit it on her. Would they ill-use her?—beat her, or kill her?

Reuben spoke up: but he was powerless against so many, and he knew it; therefore his tone was more conciliating than it would otherwise have been.

"What do you mean by molesting this lady? Stand away, Dyke, and let her pass. You wouldn't hurt her; if she is Mr. Dalrymple's wife, she was the Squire's daughter, and he was always good to you."

"Stand away yourself, old man; who said we were going to hurt her?" roughly retorted Dyke. "'Taint likely; and you've said the reason why. Ma'am, do you see these ruins? Do they make you blush?"

"I am very sorry to see them, Dyke," answered Selina. "It is no fault of mine."

"Is it hard upon us, or not, that we should be turned out of the poor walls that sheltered us? We paid our bit of rent, all on us; not one was a defaulter. How would you like to be turned out of your home, and told the poorhouse was afore you and an order for it, if you liked to go there?"

"I can only say how very sorry I am," she returned, distressed as well as terrified. "I wish I could help you, and put you into better cottages tomorrow! But I am as powerless as you are."

"Will you tell the master to do it? We be coming up to ask him. Will you tell him to come out and face us, and look at the ruins he have made, and look at our wives and little ones a-shivering there in the cold?"

Selina seemed to be shivering as much as they were. "It is Pinnett who has done it," she said, "not Mr. Dalrymple. You should lay the blame on him."

"Pinnett!" roared Dyke, throwing his arm before the other men, now surrounding them, to silence their murmurings, for he thought his own eloquence the best. "Would Pinnett have dared to do this without the master's orders? Pinnett's a tool in his hands. Say to him, ma'am, please, that we're not going to stand Pinnett's doings and be quiet; we'll drownd him first, let us once catch hold on him; and we be coming up to the Grange ourselves to say so to the master."

Finding she was to be no further detained, Selina sped on to the Grange. Oscar was in the oak-parlour. She threw herself into a chair, and burst into tears.

"Oscar, I have been so terrified. As I came by the common with Reuben, the men were there, and—"

"What men?" interrupted Mr. Dalrymple.

"Those who have been ejected from the cottages. They stopped me, and began to speak about their wrongs."

"Their—wrongs—did they say?"

"Yes, and I must say it also," she firmly answered, induced by fright and excitement to remonstrate against the injustice she had hitherto not liked to interfere with. "Cruel wrongs. Oscar, if you go on like this, oppressing all on the estate, you will be murdered as sure as you are living. They are threatening to drown Pinnett, if they can get hold of him; and they do not lay the blame on Pinnett, except as your agent, but on you."

"Pinnett is not my agent. What Pinnett does, he does on his own score. As to these harsh measures—as they are called—my sanction was not asked for them."

"But the poor men cannot see it in that light, Oscar; cannot be brought to believe it," she returned, the tears running down her cheeks. "It does seem so impossible to believe that Pinnett can be allowed to—"

"There, that's enough," interrupted Oscar. "Let it end."

"Yes; but the trouble won't end, Oscar. And the men say they are coming up here. There's a meeting, too, at Lee's tonight."

"They can come if they please, and hold as many meetings as they please," equably observed Oscar. "Men who are living in a state of semi-rebellion must learn a wholesome lesson."

"They have been provoked to it. They were never rebellious in papa's time."

He made no reply. Selina, her feelings strongly excited, her sympathies bubbling up, continued.

"It will be cruel to the farmers if you turn them from their farms; it is doubly cruel to have forced these poor men from their cottages. They paid their rent. You should see the miserable wives and children huddled together on the common. I could not have acted so, Oscar, if I had not a shilling in the world."

Mr. Dalrymple wheeled round his chair to face his wife. "Whose cruel conduct has been the original cause of it?" he asked in his cold voice, that to her sounded worse than another man's anger. "Who got into secret debt, to the tune of some seven or eight thousand pounds—ay, nearer ten thousand, counting expenses—and let the bills come in to me?"

She dropped her eyes then, for his reproach was true.

"And forced me to retrench, almost to starvation, and to exact the last farthing that the estate will yield, to keep me from a prison? Was it you or I, Mrs. Dalrymple?"

"But things need not be made quite so bad," she took courage to say in a timid tone; "you need not proceed to these extremes."

"Your father's system was one of indulgence, mine is not; and the tenants, large and small, don't know what to make of it. As to Pinnett, he does not consider himself responsible to me for his actions; and I—I cannot interfere with them. So long as I am a poor man, struggling to pay your debts, Selina, so long must Pinnett take his own course."

Oscar turned back again, caught up the book he had laid down, and went on reading it. Selina took a seat on the other side of the table, and sat supporting her head with her hands. She wished things were not so wretchedly uncomfortable, or that some good fairy would endow her with a fortune. Suddenly a tramp of feet arose outside the house. Oscar heard it, unmoved; Selina, her ears covered, did not hear it, or she might have flown sooner to bar the doors. Before she could effect this, the malcontents of the common were in the hall, their numbers considerably augmented. It looked a formidable invasion. Was it murder they intended?—or arson?—what was it not? Selina, in her terror, flew to the top of the house, a servant-maid after her: they both, with one accord, seized upon a rope, and the great alarm-bell boomed out from the Grange.

Up came the people from far and near; up came the fire-engines, from the station close by, and felt exceedingly aggrieved at finding no fire: the farmers, disturbed in the midst of their pipes and ale, rushed up from Mr. Lee's. It was nothing but commotion. Old Mrs. Dalrymple, terrified at the alarm-bell, hastened to the scene, Mary Lynn with her, and Reuben coming up behind them.

Contention, prolonged and bitter, was going on in the hall. Oscar Dalrymple was at one end, listening, and not impatiently, to his undesirable visitors, who would insist upon being heard at length. He answered them calmly and civilly, not exasperating them in any way, but he gave no hope of a change in the existing policy.

After seeing his mistress seated in the hall, for she insisted on making one of the audience, poor Reuben, grieved to the heart at the aspect of affairs altogether, went outside the house, and paced about in the moonlight. It was a fine, light night. He had strolled near the stables, when he was accosted by some one who stood aloof, under the shade of the walls.

"What's the matter here, that people should be running, in this way, into the Grange?"

"I should call it something like a rise," answered Reuben, sorrowfully. "Are you a stranger, sir?"

"I am a stranger. Until this night I have not been in the neighbourhood for years. But I formerly was on intimate terms with the Dalrymple family, and have stayed here with them for weeks together."

"Have you, though!" cried Reuben. "In the Squire's time, sir?"

"In the Squire's time. I remember you, I think. Reuben."

"Ay, I am Reuben, sir. Sad changes have taken place since then. My old master's gone, and Mr. Robert is gone, and the Grange is now Oscar Dalrymple's."

"I knew of Mr. Dalrymple's death. What became of his son?"

"He soon followed his father. It will not do to talk of, sir."

"Do you mean that he died?" returned the stranger. But before Reuben could answer, Farmer Lee came up and commenced a warm comment on the night's work.

"I hope there'll be no bloodshed," said he; "we don't want that; but the men are growing more excited, and Mr. Dalrymple has sent off a private messenger to the police-station."

"This gentleman used to know the family," interposed Reuben; "he has come to the place tonight for the first time for years. This riot is a fine welcome for him."

"I was asking some particulars of what has transpired since my absence," explained the stranger. "I have been out of England, and now thought to renew my acquaintance with the family. What did Robert Dalrymple die of? I knew him well."

"He fell into trouble, sir," interposed Reuben. "A random, wicked London set got hold of him, fleeced and ruined him, and he could not bear up against it."

"Died of it?" questioned the stranger.

"He put an end to himself," said Mr. Lee, in a low tone. "Threw himself into the Thames from one of the London bridges, and was drowned."

"How deplorable! And so the Grange passed to Oscar Dalrymple."

"Yes," said the farmer. "He married the eldest of the young ladies, Selina, and something not pleasant arose with them. They went to London, and there she ran very deeply into debt. Her husband brought her back to the Grange; and since then he has been an awful landlord, grinding us all down to powder. Things have come to such a pass now that we expect a riot. The poor labourers who tenanted the Mill Cottages have been ejected today; they have come up to have it out with Oscar Dalrymple, leaving their families and chairs and tables on the common. One of them, Thoms, could not be forced out, so they just took his roof off and his doors out."

The stranger seemed painfully surprised. "I never thought to hear this of a Dalrymple!"

But here Reuben again interposed. Jealous for the name, even though borne by Oscar, he told of the leasing of the estate to Pinnett, and that it was he, not Oscar, who was proceeding to these cruel extremities.

"I should call that so much nonsense," said the stranger. "Lease the estate! that has a curious sound. Has he leased away all power over it? One cannot believe that."

"No; and we don't believe it," said the farmer, "not one of us; Mr. Dalrymple can't make us, though he tries hard to do so. He is playing Old Nick with us, sir, and nothing else. It was a fatal night for us that took Mr. Robert."

"You would have been better off under him, you think?"

"Think!" indignantly retorted the farmer. "You could not have known Robert Dalrymple to ask it."

"Robert Dalrymple died in debt, I take it. Did he owe much in this neighbourhood?"

"Nothing here."

"Did he owe you anything?"

"Me!" cried the farmer. "Not he. Why, only a day before his death I had sent five hundred pounds to him to invest for me. He had not time to do it himself, but a gentleman who took a great deal of interest in Mr. Robert, and saw to his affairs afterwards, did it."

"What gentleman was that?"

"It was Mr. Grubb: he is Sir Francis Netherleigh now, and has come into Court Netherleigh. His sister—who is at the Grange tonight with old Mrs. Dalrymple—and Mr. Robert were to have been married. She has stayed single for his sake."

"Robert Dalrymple may not be dead," spoke the stranger.

But this hypothesis was received with disfavour; not to say scorn. The stranger maintained his opinion, saying that it was his opinion.

"Then perhaps you'll enjoy your opinion in private," rebuked Mr. Lee. "To talk in that senseless manner only makes us feel the fact of his death more sharply."

"What if I tell you I met him abroad, only a year ago?" There was a dead pause. Reuben breathed heavily. "Oh, don't play with us!" he cried out; "if my dear young master's alive, let me know it. But he cannot be alive," he added mournfully: "he would have made it known to us before now."

The stranger unwound a large handkerchief, in which his face and chin had been muffled, raised his soft round hat from his brows, and advanced from the shade into the moonlight.

"Reuben! John Lee! do I look anything like him?"

Reuben sank on his knees, too faint to support himself in the overwhelming surprise and joy. For it was indeed his young master, Robert Dalrymple, raised, as it seemed, from a many years' grave. The old servant broke into sobs that would not be controlled.

"But it is nothing less than magic," cried the farmer, when he had wrung Robert's hand as if he would wring it off, and both he and Reuben had had time to take in the full truth of the revelation. "Dead—yet living!"

"I never was dead," said Robert. "The night that I found myself irretrievably ruined—"

But here Robert Dalrymple's explanation was interrupted by a noise. The malcontents, driven wild by Oscar's cold equanimity, which they took to be purely supercilious, were rushing out of the Grange by the front-entrance, fierce threats and oaths pouring from their lips. Oscar Dalrymple might go to perdition! They'd fire the place over his head, commencing with the barns and outhouses!

"Stay, stay, stay! let me have a few words with you before you begin," spoke one, meeting them with assured, but kind authority; and his calm voice acted like oil poured upon troubled waters.

It was Sir Francis Netherleigh. Hearing of the riot, he had hastened up. He reasoned with the men, promised to see what he could do to get their wrongs redressed, told them that certain barns and outhouses of his were being warmed and made comfortable for them for the night, and their wives and children were already on their way to take possession. Finally, he subdued them to peace and good temper.

But while this was taking place in front of the house, there had been another bit of by-play near the stables. Mary Lynn, terrified for the effect of the riotous threats on Mrs. Dalrymple in her precarious state of health, begged her to return home, and ran out to look for Reuben. Mr. Lee discerned her leaning over the gate of the kitchen-garden, gazing about on all sides in the moonlight. A bright idea struck him, quite a little bit of romance.

"I'll fetch her to you here, Mr. Robert," he said. "I'll break the glad news to her carefully. And—you won't turn as out of our homes, will you, sir?" he lingered to say.

"That I certainly will not; and those who are already out shall go back again. But," added Robert, smiling, "I fear I shall be obliged to turn somebody out of the Grange."

"There's Pinnett, sir?" came the next doubting remark. "If Mr. Oscar Dalrymple has leased him the estate, who knows but the law may give him full power over us—"

"Leased him the estate!" interposed Robert. "Why, my good friend, it was not Oscar Dalrymple's to lease: it was mine. Be at rest."

Relieved at heart, the farmer marched up to Mary; managing, despite the most ingenious intentions, to startle and confuse her. He opened the conference by telling her, with an uncomfortably mysterious air, that a dead man had come to life again who was waiting to see her: and Mary's thoughts, greatly disturbed, flew to a poor labourer who had died, really died, that morning.

"What do you mean, Mr. Lee?" she interrupted, with some awe. "You can't know what you are saying. Colter come to life again!"

"There! I know how I always bungle over this sort o' thing," cried the abashed farmer. "You must just forgive me. And you can well afford to, Miss Mary, for it's not Colter come to life at all; it is young Mr. Robert Dalrymple. And here he is, walking towards you."

The farmer discreetly disappeared. Mary tottered into the shade, and stood for support against the trunk of the great elm-tree. Robert drew her from it to the shelter of his faithful heart.

"Yes; it is I, my darling; I, myself—do not tremble so," he whispered. "God has been very merciful to me, more merciful than I deserve, and has brought me back to you and to home again."

She lay there, on his breast, the strong arms around her that would henceforth be her shelter throughout life.

CHAPTER XXXVIII

ROBERT DALRYMPLE

Sundry shouts startling the night-air, combined with the dashing up of horsemen, caused no little stir amidst the crowd. The booming of the alarm-bell somewhat earlier in the evening had been less ominous than this.

They were the police-officers from Netherleigh, sent for by Oscar Dalrymple, and they had come mounted, for the sake of speed. The moon had gone under a cloud, the old structure, Moat Grange, appeared shadowy and indistinct, and to the imagination of these poor excited labourers, assembled to discuss their position, the three officers—for there were but three—looked magnified into a formidable number. Sir Francis Netherleigh had appeased their anger, but he could not subdue the sense of wrong that burnt in the men's minds; and when he left them, they, instead of dispersing quietly in accordance with his recommendation, lingered where they were, and whispered together of Pinnett and of treason.

On the other side of the house was a group, more peaceful, but not a whit less excited. Of all the surprises met with by Francis Netherleigh in his own life, he had never had so complete a one as this, or one so satisfactory. Searching about after malcontents that might have scattered themselves, he came round by the outhouses and the kitchen-garden; and there he saw a stranger talking with his sister Mary, Farmer Lee and Reuben standing at a little distance. The moon was bright then; the stranger stood bareheaded, and there was that in his form and in the outlines of his face that thrilled chords in the memory of Sir Francis.

"Don't be frightened, sir," spoke Farmer Leo to him, in whispered tones, as befitted the wonderful subject; "it is himself, and not his ghost. It is, indeed."

"But who is it?" cried Sir Francis, his eyes strained earnestly on the stranger.

"Himself, I say, sir—Robert Dalrymple."

"Robert Dalrymple!"

"Ay. Come back from the dead, as one may say. He made himself known to me and Reuben; and then I went and broke the news to Miss Mary. And there they both are, talking together."

But Mary had discerned her brother, and they were coming forward. "Is it possible to believe it?" asked Sir Francis, as they met, his hand clasping Robert's with a warm grasp.

"I think you may; I think you cannot fail to recognize me, changed and aged though I know I am," answered Robert, with an emotion that bordered upon tears.

"You have been alive all this time—and not dead, as we have deplored you?"

"Yes, all this time; and I never knew until a little while ago that I was looked upon as dead."

"But what became of you, Robert? It was thought, that dreadful night, that you—"

"Threw myself into the Thames," put in Robert, in the slight pause made by Sir Francis. They were all standing together now, Mary a little apart, her hand upon the gate, and the moonlight flickered on them through the branches of the thinning autumn trees. "I was very near doing it," he continued; "nearer than any one, save God, can know. It was a dreadful night to me, one of shame and despair. Knowing myself to be irretrievably ruined, a rogue upon earth—"

"Hold there, sir," cried Reuben, "a rogue you never were."

"I was, Reuben. And you shall all hear how. Mary,"—turning to her—"you shall hear also. A beggar myself, I staked that night at the gaming-table the money I held of yours, Lee, the five hundred pounds you had entrusted to me, staked it, and lost it. I cannot understand how you—but I'll leave that just now. The money gone, I wandered about the streets, a desperate man, and found myself on Westminster Bridge. It was in my heart to leap into the river, to take the blind leap into futurity my uncle had taken before me. I was almost in the very act of doing it, when a passer-by, seeing my perilous position, pulled me back, and asked what I meant by hanging over there. It is to him I owe my life."

"Under God," breathed Mary, remembering her dream.

"Ay," assented Robert, "under God. It proved to be one Joseph Horn, a young man employed at my tailor's, and he recognized me. I made an excuse about the heat of the night, that I was leaning over for a breath of air from the water: and finally Horn left me. But the incident had served to arrest my purpose; to show me my folly and my sin. I am not ashamed to confess that I knelt down, there and then, to ask God to help me, and to save me from myself; and—He did it. I quitted the dangerous spot—"

"Your hat was found in the Thames, and brought back the next day, Mr. Robert," interrupted poor, bewildered, happy Reuben.

"It blew off, into the river; it was one of the windiest nights I was ever out in, except at sea," answered Robert. "I walked about the streets till morning, taking myself sharply to task, and considering how I could give myself a chance for a better life. I had still my watch and ring, both of value—they would have gone long before, just as everything else had gone, but that they had been my father's, and were given over by him to me on his death-bed. I parted with them now, disguised myself in rough clothes, went to Liverpool, and thence to America."

"But why did you not come to me instead?" asked Sir Francis.

"I was ashamed to do so. Look at the debts I owed; at what I had done with Lee's money! No, there was nothing for it but to hide my head from you all, and from the world. Had I made a fortune, I should have come back in triumph, but I never did make it. I found employment as a clerk at New Orleans, and kept myself; that was all."

"If you had only just let us know you were alive, Robert!" cried Mary.

He shook his head. "I did not suppose any one would care to know it. I expected that the extent of my villainy had come out, and that you would all be thankful if I disappeared for ever. So there I remained, in the Crescent City, passing as 'Mr. Charles,' my second name, and making the best of my blighted life. I"—his tone suddenly changed to laughter—"nearly married and settled there."

"Oh!"—Mary gave quite a start.

"I had an excellent offer; yes, I assure you I had. It was leap-year. A flourishing widow, some few years older than myself, took a fancy to me. She had a fine house and grounds on the banks of the Mississippi, and an income not to be despised; and she proposed that I should throw up my wearisome daily work and become the master of all this—and of her. I took it into consideration, I can tell you."

"And what prevented your accepting it?" laughed Sir Francis.

"Well, the one bare thought—it did not amount to hope—that a turn of good fortune might some time bring me back here, to find"—with a glance at Mary—"what I have found."

"And the good fortune came, sir—and has brought you back!" exclaimed the farmer.

"Yes; it came," replied Robert, "it came: a turn that was very like romance, and once more exemplified the saying that truth is stranger than fiction. You are aware, I think, that my father had a relative living in Liverpool, Benjamin Dalrymple?" added Robert, chiefly addressing Sir Francis—who nodded in reply.

"Benjamin Dalrymple never corresponded with us, would not notice us; a serious difference had arisen between him and my father in early days. But, a year after my father's death, when I chanced to be in Liverpool, I called upon him. He was cordial enough with me, seemed rather to take a fancy to me, and I stayed with him three weeks. He was a cotton-broker, and would take me down to his office in a morning, and show me his routine of business, verily hoping, I believe, that I should take to it and join him. When, later, I became hard up, and had not a shilling to turn to in the world, I wrote to Benjamin Dalrymple from London, asking him to help me. Not by the smallest fraction, he replied; a young man who could run into debt, with my patrimony, would run into debt to the end of the chapter, though his income might number tens of thousands. Well, all that passed away; and—"

Robert paused.

"The house I served in America exported cotton home in large quantities," he continued rapidly. "Benjamin Dalrymple was amongst their larger correspondents. Some few months ago, his confidential clerk, a taciturn gentleman named Patten, came over on business to New Orleans, to this very house I was in. He saw me and recognized me; we had dined together more than once at old Benjamin's table in Liverpool. Patten had believed me dead; drowned; and it no doubt gave him a turn when he saw me alive. I told him my history, asking him not to let it transpire in the old world or the new. But it seems he considered it his duty to repeat it to old Benjamin on his return home: and he did so. The result was, that Benjamin set up a correspondence with me, and finally commanded me to give up my place as clerk and go back to him. I did so; and I—"

Again Robert stopped; this time in evident emotion.

"Go on, Robert," said Sir Francis. "What is it?"

"My story has a sad ending," answered Robert, his tone depressed. "I landed at Liverpool to find Benjamin Dalrymple ill with a mortal illness. He had been ailing for some time, but the fatal truth had then declared itself. He was so changed, too!—I suppose people do change when they are about to die.

From being a cold, hard man, he had become gentle and loving in manner. I must remain with him until the end, he said, and be to him as a son."

"Was he not married, sir?" asked Farmer Lee.

"He had never married. I did remain with him, doing what I could for him, and making no end of promises, which he exacted, with regard to my future life and conduct. In twenty-one days, exactly, from the day I landed, the end came."

"He died?"

"He died. I waited for his funeral. And," concluded Robert, modestly, "he has made me his heir."

"Thank Heaven for that!" murmured old Reuben.

"How much it is, I cannot tell you," said Robert, "but an enormous sum. Patten puts it down at half a million: and, that, after clerks and other dependents have been well provided for. So, every one who has ever suffered by me in the shape of debt will be recompensed; and Moat Grange will hold its own again."

But his return had to be made known to others who were interested in it: his mother, his sisters, Oscar Dalrymple. Of the latter Robert spoke some hard words.

"I had thought to give him a fair portion of this wealth in right of Selina," avowed he. "But I don't know now. A man who can so oppress an estate does not merit much favour."

"Oscar has been worse thought of than he deserves," explained Sir Francis Netherleigh. "Rely upon that, Robert. He has been sorely tried, sorely put to for money for some few years now, through no fault of his own—"

"No; through Selina's," interrupted Robert. "Old Benjamin knew all about it."

"He has been striving to make both ends meet, to pay his obligations justly and honourably, and he could only do it by dint of pinching and screwing," went on Sir Francis. "The great mistake of his later life was leasing the estate to Pinnett. It is thought that he could have arrested Pinnett's harsh acts; my opinion is that he could not."

"I am glad to hear you say so," cried Robert, cordially. "Oscar was always near, but he was just."

They were moving slowly through the garden to the house, when a disturbance struck upon their ears. It came from the front of the Grange; and all, except Mary, hastened round to the scene. It was, in fact, the moment of the arrival of the mounted police. The officers shouted, the crowd rebelled; and Oscar Dalrymple ran out. The police, hasty as usual, were for taking up the malcontents wholesale; the latter resisted, protesting they had done nothing to be taken up for. They had only come up to speak to Mr. Dalrymple, and "there was no law against that," said they.

"You break the law when you use threats to a man in his own house," cried Featherston, the chief constable.

"We haven't used no threats," retorted Dyke. "We want an answer from Mr. Dalrymple; whether he's going to force us to lodge under the wind and the rain, or whether he'll find us roofs in place of them he has destroyed. They've bid us go to the workhouse; but he knows that if we go there we lose all chance of getting our living, and shall never have a home for our families again."

"There's no longer room for you on the estate; no dwellings for you left upon it," spoke up a voice; and the men turned sharply, for they knew it was Pinnett's. Countenanced by the presence of the constables, the agent came out from some shelter or other, and showed himself openly.

"We won't say nothing about mercy," savagely cried Dyke; "but we'd like justice. Justice, sir!" turning to Oscar Dalrymple, as he stood by the side of Mr. Cleveland, who had just come up. "Hands off, Mr. Constable! I'm doing nothing yet, save asking a plain question. Is there any justice?"

"Yes, there is justice," interrupted another voice, which thrilled through the very marrow of Oscar Dalrymple, as Robert advanced and took his place near Mr. Cleveland, who started back in positive fright. "Oscar, you know me, I see; gentlemen, some of you know me: I am Robert Dalrymple, and I have returned to claim my own."

Was it a spectre? Many of them looked as if they feared so. Was it some deception of the moonlight? Featherston, brave policeman though he was, backed away in terror.

"I find you have all thought me dead," proceeded Robert; "but I am not dead, and never was dead; I have simply been abroad. I fell into debt and difficulty; but, now that the difficulties are over, I have come amongst you again."

"It's the Squire!" burst forth the men, as they gradually awoke to the truth; "we've never called the other one so. Our own young Squire's come home again, and our troubles are over. Good luck to the ship that brought him!"

Robert laughed. "Yes, your troubles shall be over. I hear that there has been dissatisfaction; and, perhaps, oppression. I can only say that I will set everything right. The tenants who have been served with a notice to quit"—glancing round at Lee and Bumford—"may burn it; and you, my poor fellows, who have been ejected from your cottages, shall be reinstated in them."

"But, my dear young master," cried Dyke, despondingly, "some of the roofs be off, and the walls be pretty nigh levelled with the ground."

"I will build them up for you, Dyke, stronger than ever," said Robert, heartily. "Here's my hand upon it."

Not only Dyke, but many more pressed forward to clasp Robert's hands; and so hard and earnest were the pressures, that Robert was almost tempted to cry for quarter. In the midst of this, Pinnett thought it time to speak.

"You talk rather fast, sir: even if you are Mr. Robert Dalrymple. The estate is mine for some six years to come. It has been leased to me by its owner."

"That it certainly has not been," returned Robert, his tone one of conscious power. "I am its owner. The estate has been mine throughout; as I did not die, it could not have lapsed from me. My brother-in-law, acting under a mistake, entered into possession, but he has never been the legal owner. Consequently, whatever acts be may have ordered, performed, or sanctioned, are NULL and VOID. Constables, I think your services will not be required here."

Pinnett ground his teeth. "It's to know whether you are Robert Dalrymple—and not an impostor."

"I can certify that it is really Robert Dalrymple; I baptized him," laughed Mr. Cleveland. "There is no mistaking him and his handsome face."

"And I and Mr. Lee can swear to it, if you like," put in Reuben, looking at Pinnett. "So could the rest of us. I wish we were all as sure of heaven!"

Robert put his hand into Oscar's under cover of the darkness. "You know me, Oscar, well enough. Let us be friends. I have not come home to sow discord; rather peace and goodwill. The Grange must be mine again, you know; I can't help that; but, when you and Selina quit it for your own place, you shall not go out empty-handed.

"I don't understand you," returned Oscar.

"I have come back a rich man; and you shall share in the good. Next to endowing my mother, I shall take care of my sisters. Ah, Oscar, these past few years have been full of gloom and trouble for many of us. Now that the clouds have broken, let us hope that the future will bring with it a good deal of sunshine."

The assemblage began to disperse. Mr. Cleveland undertook to break the glad news to Mrs. Dalrymple and Selina.

Reuben crept up to his master with an anxious, troubled face. "Mr. Robert," he breathed, "have you quite left off the—the PLAY? You will not be tempted to take to it again?"

"Never, Reuben," was the grave, hushed answer. "That night, which you all thought fatal to me, and which was so near being so, as I stood on the bridge, looking into the dark water, I took a solemn oath that I would never again touch a card, or any other incentive to gambling. I never shall."

"Heaven be praised!" murmured Reuben. And the old man felt that he was ready to say with Simeon of old: "Lord, now lettest thou thy servant depart in peace."

CHAPTER XXXIX

LADY ADELA

Winter had come, and passed; and spring flowers and sunshine gladdened the land.

In my Lady Acorn's dressing-room at Chenevix House stood my lady herself, her head and hands betraying temper, her tart tongue in loud assertion. Opposite to her, the same blonde, suave dame she had ever been, waited Madame Damereau. Madame was not tart or rude; she could not be that; but nevertheless she maintained her own cause, and gave my lady answer for answer.

Every available place in the room was covered with a robe, bonnet, mantle, or other choice article essential to a lady's attire: on the sofa lay a costly bridal dress. You might have fancied it the show-room itself of Madame Damereau. Lady Frances Chenevix was to be married on the morrow to Gerard Hope. The colonel had been telling them both ever since Christmas that he thought they ought to fix the day if they meant to marry at all, and so arrangements were made, and they named one early in April.

The articles lying about formed part of the trousseau of Lady Frances; the grievance distracting Lady Acorn was connected with them; for she saw great many more spread out than she had ordered, and was giving way to wrath. Madame Damereau, condescending to appear at Chenevix House this afternoon, to superintend, herself, the trying-on of the bridal robe, had arrived just in time for the storm.

"Was anything so unreasonable, was anything so extravagant ever seen before in this world?" demanded Lady Acorn, spreading out her arms to right and left. "I tell you there are fifty things here that I never ordered; that I never should order, unless I lost my senses. Look at that costly silk costume—that shaded grey—why, you'd charge five-and-twenty guineas for that, if you charged a farthing. Don't tell me, madame."

"Plutôt thirty guineas, I believe," equally answered madame. "It is of the richest, that silk. Miladi Frances intends it for her robe de voyage tomorrow."

"She may intend to go voyaging about in gold, but be no nearer doing it," retorted the countess. "I never ordered that dress, and I won't take it."

"Is anything the matter?" interrupted a joyous voice at this juncture, and Frances ran into the room with her bonnet on. "I am sorry to have kept you waiting, madame, but I could not help it. Is my lady mother scolding at my extravagance?"

"Extravagance is not the name for it," retorted the countess. "How dare you do these wild things, Frances? Do you suppose I should accept all these things, or pay for them?"

"No, mamma, I knew you would not," laughed Frances, "I shall pay for them myself."

"Oh, indeed! Where will the money come from?"

"Colonel Hope gave it me," said the happy girl, executing a pirouette. "A few days ago he put three bank-notes of one hundred pounds each into my hands, saying he supposed I could spend it; and I went to madame's at once. What a love of a costume!" cried Frances, turning to the grey silk which had so excited her mother's ire. "I am going away in that."

But the great event of this afternoon, that of trying-on the bridal dress, must be proceeded with, for Madame Damereau's time was more precious than that of ordinary mortals. The bride-elect was arrayed in it, and was pacing about in her splendour, peeping into all the mirrors, when a message was brought to Lady Acorn that Mr. Cleveland was below. He had come up from Netherleigh to perform the marriage ceremony, and was to be the guest for a day or two of Lord and Lady Acorn.

She went down at once, leaving Frances and Madame Damereau. There were many odds and ends of Netherleigh gossip she wished to hear from the Rector. He was bending over the drawing-room fire.

"Are you cold?" inquired Lady Acorn.

"Rather. As we grow older, we feel the cold and fatigue of a journey more keenly," he added, smiling. "It is a regular April day: warm in the sun, very cold in the wind and shade."

"He is getting older," thought Lady Acorn, as she looked at his face, chilled and grey, and his whitening hair; though, for a wonder, she did not tell him so. They had not met for some months. He had paid no visit to London since the previous November, and then his errand had been the same as now—to celebrate a marriage.

And, of the events of the past autumn and winter months there is not much to relate. Oscar Dalrymple was in his own place now, Knutford, Selina with a handsome income settled on her; and Robert and his wife lived at Moat Grange. They had been married from Grosvenor Square in November, Mr. Cleveland, as again now, coming up for it. Lady Adela was still at Netherleigh Rectory. And, perhaps it was of her that the countess wanted chiefly to question the Rector. She did not, however, do that all at once.

"All quite well at home?" she asked.

"Tolerably so, thank you," he replied. "Mary, as you know, is ailing: and will be for some little time to come."

"Dear me, yes," came the quick, irritable assent. "This baby will make the third. I can't think what you want with so many."

The Rector laughed. "Mary sent her love to you; and especially to Frances: and I was to be sure to say to Frances how sorry she was not to be able to be at her wedding. Adela also sent her love."

"Ah! And how is she?"

"She—" Mr. Cleveland hesitated. "She is much the same. Tolerably well in health, I think."

"I suppose Robert Dalrymple and his wife are coming up today?"

"They came with me. Francis Netherleigh's carriage was waiting for them at the terminus. It brought me on also."

"And that poor girl Alice, is she any stronger?"

"She will never be stronger in this world," said the Rector, shaking his head. "But she is pretty well—for her. I think her life may be prolonged some few years yet."

"She and Gerard Hope had a love affair once; I am pretty sure of it. He liked her better than he liked Frances."

"Well, she could never have married. One so sickly as Alice ought not to become a wife; and she had, I expect, the good sense to see that. I know she is pleased at his marriage with Frances. She is most unselfish; truly good; there are not many like Alice Dalrymple. Her mother is surprisingly well," he went on, after a pause; "seems to have gone from an old woman into a young one. Robert's coming back did that for her."

"And now—what about Adela's behaviour? how is she going on?" snapped Lady Acorn, as if the very subject soured her.

"I wanted to speak to you about Adela," said Mr. Cleveland. "In one sense of the word, she is not going on satisfactorily. Though her health is pretty good, I believe, her mind is anything but healthy. Mary and I often talk of it in private, and she said I had better speak to you."

"Why, it is just the case of the MacIvors over again!" interrupted Lady Acorn. "Harriet sent Sandy to talk to me about it, just in this way, last summer."

"Yes, there has not been much change since then, I fancy. I confess that I am very sorry for Adela."

"Is she still like a shadow?"

"Like little else. The fever of the mind is consuming the body. I look upon it as the most hopeless case I have ever known. Adela does the same, though from a different point of view. She is dying for her husband's forgiveness. She would like to live in his memory as one not abjectly despicable, and she knows she must and does so live in it. She pictures his contempt for her, his condemnation of the way she acted in the past; and her humiliation, coupled with remorse, has grown into a disease. Yes, it is a miserable case. They are as entirely and hopelessly separated as they could be by death."

"Ah, Cleveland! You are here, then?"

The interruption came from the earl. He stepped forward to shake hands, and drew a chair beside the Rector.

"We were talking of Adela," said the countess, when the few words of greeting were over. "She has not come to her senses yet."

"I was saying that her case is certainly one of the most hopeless ever known," observed Mr. Cleveland. "She is as utterly separated from her husband as she could be by death, whilst both are yet living, and have probably a long life before them."

Lord Acorn sighed. "One can't help being sorry for Adela, wrong and mistaken though she was."

Mr. Cleveland glanced at the earl. "I am glad you came in," he said. "I wanted to speak to you as well as to Lady Acorn. Adela talks of going into a Sisterhood."

"Into a what?" cried her ladyship; her tone one of unbounded surprise.

"She has had the idea in her mind for some time, I fancy," continued the Rector. "I heard of it first last autumn, when she startled me one day by suddenly expressing a wish that she was a Roman Catholic. I found that the wish did not proceed from any desire to change her creed, but simply because the Roman Catholics possess places of refuge in the shape of convents, into which a poor creature, as Adela expressed it, tired of having no longer a place in the world, might enter, and find peace."

"She'd soon wish herself out again!" cried Lady Acorn: while the earl's generally impassive face wore a look of disturbance.

"I heard no more of this for some time," resumed Mr. Cleveland, "and dismissed it from my memory, believing it to have been only a hasty expression arising from some moment's vexation. But a week or two ago Mary discovered that Adela was really and truly thinking of retiring into some place of refuge or other."

"Into a convent?" cried Lady Acorn.

"No. And not into any institution of the Roman Catholics. It seems she has been corresponding lately with some of her former acquaintances, who might, as she thought, help her, and making inquiries of them. I noticed that letters came for her rather frequently, and I hoped she was beginning to take a little more interest in life. However, through some person or other, she has heard of an institution that she feels inclined to try. I think—"

"What is this institution?" imperatively demanded the countess. "If it's not a convent, what is it?"

"Well, it is not, as I gather, a religious institution at all, in the sense of setting itself up for religion especially, or professing any one particular creed over other creeds," replied Mr. Cleveland. "It is, in point of fact, a nursing institution. And Adela, if she enters it, will have to attend to the sick, night or day."

"Heaven help her for a simpleton!" ejaculated her ladyship. "Why, you might take every occupation known to this world, and not find one to which she is less suited. Adela could not nurse the sick, however good her will night be. She has no vocation for it."

"Just what my wife says. Some people are, so to say, born nurses, while others, and Adela is one of them, could never fit themselves for it. Mary told her so only yesterday. To this, and to other remonstrance, Adela has only one answer—that the probationary training she will have to undergo will remedy her defects and inexperience," replied the Rector.

"But the life of a sick-nurse is so exhausting, so wearying to the frame and spirit!" cried Lord Acorn, who had listened in dismay. "Where is this place?"

"It is in Yorkshire. Three or four ladies, sisters, middle-aged, educated women of fortune, set up the scheme. Wishing, it is said, to satisfy their consciences by doing some useful work in the world, they pitched upon nursing, and began by going out of their home, first one and then another, whenever any poor peasant turned sick. They were, no doubt, good Christian women, sacrificing their own ease, comfort, and income for the benefit of others. From that arose the Institution, as it is called now; other ladies joined it, and it is known far and wide. I have not one word to say against it: rather would I speak in its praise; but it will not do for Adela. Perhaps you can remonstrate with her. It is not settled, I believe," added Mr. Cleveland. "Adela has not finally made up her mind to go; though Mary fears she will do so at once."

"Let her," cried the countess, in her vexation. "Let my young lady give the place a trial! She will soon come out of it again."

In truth, poor Adela was at a loss what to do with her blighted life—how to get through the weary days that had no pleasure in them. Netherleigh Rectory had brought to her no more rest than Sir Sandy's Scottish stronghold had brought, or the bleak old château in Switzerland. She wanted peace, and she found it not.

Some excitement crept into the daily monotony of her life whenever Sir Francis was staying at Court Netherleigh. It was not often. She could not bear to see him, for it brought back to her all the cruel pain of having lost him; and yet, when she knew he was at Netherleigh, she was unable to rest indoors, but must go out in the hope that she should meet him at some safe distance; for she never ventured within view. It was as a fever. And perhaps this very fact—that she could not, when he was breathing the same atmosphere, rest without striving to see him, combined with the consciousness that she ought not to do so—rendered her more anxious to get away from Netherleigh and be employed, mentally and bodily, at some wholesome daily work. Anyway, what Mr. Cleveland stated was quite true: Lady Adela was corresponding with this nursing institution in Yorkshire, with the view of entering it.

One phase of torment, which has not been mentioned, was growing to lie so heavily upon her mind as to be almost insupportable. It was the thought of the income allowed her by her husband. That she, who had blighted his life, should be living upon his bounty, indebted to him for every luxury that remained to her, was in truth hard to bear. If she could only get a living for herself, though ever so poor a one, how thankful she should be, she often told herself. And, perhaps this trouble turned the scale, or speedily would turn it, in regard to embracing this life of usefulness: for there would no longer be any necessity for the allowance from Sir Francis.

The wedding-day, Thursday, rose bright and glorious; just the day that should shine on all happy bridals. Frances was given away by her father, and Gerard was attended by a former fellow-clerk in the Red Tape Office. Colonel Hope had settled an income upon his nephew; but Gerard was still in the house in Leadenhall Street, and was likely to remain there: for the colonel disapproved of idle young men. Gerard had taken a small and pretty house at Richmond, and would travel to the City of a morning.

At the wedding breakfast-table at Lord Acorn's, Grace and Sir Francis Netherleigh sat side by side. Towards its close, Grace took the opportunity of saying something to him in a whisper.

"We have been so confidential on many points for years, you and I, unhappily have had to be so," she began, "that I think I scarcely need make an apology, or ask your forgiveness, for a few words I wish to say to you now."

"Say on, Grace," was the cordial answer.

"It is about Adela." And then she briefly touched upon what her father and mother had heard from Mr. Cleveland the day before: of Adela's unhappy frame of mind, and her idea of entering a nursing institution, to become one of its sisterhood.

Sir Francis heard her to the end in silence. But he heard her apparently without interest: and somehow Grace's anxious spirit felt thrown back upon itself.

"It has troubled us all to hear this, my father especially," she said. "It would be so laborious a life, so very unsuited to one delicate as Adela."

"I can readily understand that you would not altogether like it," he replied, at length. "If money could be of any use—"

"Oh no, no," interrupted Grace, flushing painfully. "The allowance you have made from the first has been so wonderfully liberal. I don't know why I mentioned the subject to you—except that we think it is altogether undesirable for Adela."

"Lord and Lady Acorn must be the best judges of that," was the very indifferent answer.

"Her mind is in the most unhappy state conceivable; as it has been all along. For one thing," added Grace, her voice sinking to a yet lower key, "I think she is pining for your forgiveness."

"That is not at all likely, I fancy," coldly returned Sir Francis. And as he evinced no inclination to continue the subject, but rather the contrary, Grace said no more.

She could not have told herself why she introduced it. Had it been with any hope, consciously, or unconsciously, of being of service to Adela, it had signally failed. Evidently his wife and her concerns were topics that bore no longer any interest for Francis Netherleigh.

CHAPTER XL

AT COURT NETHERLEIGH

"Oh, Robert, what a lovely day!"

Standing at the open window of her own pretty sitting-room, a room that had been built and decorated for her during the late alterations to Moat Grange, was Mary Dalrymple. Robert, heated and flushed, had come swinging in at the gate, and caught the words across the lawn. He had been out since early morning, superintending various matters; for today was the grand fête-day at Moat Grange, and preparations were being made for it.

Robert called it a house-warming. He had talked of it, as a thing to come, ever since his marvellous return—and marvellous the world thought that return still: but he had waited for his marriage with Mary Lynn to take place, and then for the alterations to be completed that were to make the gloomy old house into a new one, and finally for the warm summer weather. For this was to be an open-air entertainment, for the gratification of the poor as well as the rich. Improvements had gone on without doors as well as within. Those cottages by the old mill had been rebuilt, and their humble tenants were reinstated. Gratitude and contentment had taken the place of rebellion, and the once angry men thought they could never do enough for their young Squire, Robert Dalrymple.

"What a lovely day!" repeated Mary.

It was the first day of June, and one of the sweetest days that charming month ever put forth. Excepting for a light fleecy cloud here and there, the sky was of a deep blue; the sun flickered through the trees, that yet wore somewhat of their tender green, and caught Robert's head as he stood looking up at his wife.

"Ay, it is," said Robert, in reply to her remark, "very lovely. But it will be uncommonly hot, Mary; it is so already."

She leaned from the window in her cool white morning gown, smiling at her husband. How good-looking they both were—and how happy! Every now and then, even yet, Mary could scarcely realize the change—the intense happiness which had succeeded to the years of what had appeared irredeemable sorrow.

"And now, Robert," said Mary, "I think you must want breakfast—if you have not had it."

"But I have had it. I ran in to my mother's, and took some with her and Alice. The tents are all up, Mary, and the people are getting into their Sunday best."

"So soon! Don't forget, if you please, sir, that we sit down to lunch today at one o'clock precisely. We can't do without you then, you know, though we did without you at breakfast."

Robert drew a little nearer to the window. "Where are they all?" he asked.

"Gone for a stroll. I told them that I had a famished husband coming in and must wait at home for him. I think Gerard and his wife have only gone to your mother's. I don't know about Oscar and Selina. Perhaps she is gone to see the new baby at the Rectory."

"Selina does not care for babies."

"But she cares for gossip. And Lady Mary is well enough for any amount of that."

"What is that letter in your hand?" asked Robert.

His wife's face changed to sadness. "It contains bad news, Robert; and though I have been chattering to you so gaily and lightly, it is lying on my heart. Francis cannot come."

"No!"

"Some dreadful measure—important, he calls it—has to be debated upon in committee in the House this afternoon, and Francis has to stay for it."

"Well, I am disappointed," cried Robert.

"As we all are. Robert, I do think it is too bad. I do think Francis might have spared this one day to us," added Mary, with a sigh. "He seems to regard politics as quite a recreation."

"Don't be hard on him, Mary. He has little else now in the way of recreation."

Gerard Hope and Lady Frances had come to the Grange for the fête: Gerard having coaxed a three days' holiday out of Mr. Howard, with whom he was a favourite, though the old gentleman had grumblingly reminded him that his honeymoon was not long over. Oscar Dalrymple and Selina had also arrived the previous night from their own place, Knutford. Perhaps in his heart Oscar had not been sorry to give up the Grange and its troubles. At any rate, he made no sign of regret. Peace and plenty had supervened on discomfort, and he and Selina were friends with all.

Mary had guessed rightly: Selina had gone to the Rectory. If not to see the new baby, to see the baby's mother. The baby was more than two weeks old, and Lady Mary was seated on a sofa, doing some useful work.

"It is early days for that, is it not?" cried Selina, as she went in.

"Not at all," laughed Lady Mary. "With all my little ones, I have to be always at work. And I am thankful to be well enough for it. You reached the Grange yesterday?"

"Yes—and found all well. Mamma came up to dinner last night. She is quite young and active. Gerard and Frances have gone to see Alice, who is much better—and then Frances is coming here to see you. Every one seems to be better," concluded Selina.—"And what delightful weather we have for today!"

"Where is your husband?"

"Oscar! He went across the fields to the Mead House to see old Bridport. What a pity you cannot come out today, Mary! And who else do you think cannot come out? At least, not out here."

"Who is that?"

"Francis Netherleigh. Mary Dalrymple heard from him this morning. He is kept in London by some business connected with the House. He would have been the star of the fête. Yes, don't laugh at me—he would— and we are all vexed. I wouldn't be in that House of Commons for the world," resentfully concluded Selina. "I do think he might have stretched a point today!"

"Y-e-s—if he wished to come," was the doubting assent. "The question is—did he wish it?"

"What do you mean?" asked Selina.

Mary Cleveland dropped her needle and looked at Mrs. Oscar Dalrymple. "It has struck me that he has not cared to come here, you know. Instead of taking up his abode at Court Netherleigh, he pays only a flying visit to it now and then. My husband and I both think that he does not choose to subject himself to the chance of meeting Adela."

"I should not wonder. They were talking about Adela at the Grange last night," resumed Selina, in accents of hesitation—"saying something about her joining a sisterhood of nurses. But I'm sure that can't be true."

"It is quite true, Selina."

Selina opened her amazed eyes. "True! Why, she would have to put her hair under a huge cap, and wear straight-down cotton gowns and white aprons!"

Lady Mary smiled. That part of the programme would assuredly have kept Selina from entering on anything of the sort.

"Yes; it is true," repeated Mary. "The negotiations have been pending for some time; but it is decided at last, and Adela departs for Yorkshire on Saturday, the day after tomorrow, to shut herself into the institution."

"And will she never come out again?"

Lady Mary shook her head. "We cannot foresee the future, Selina. All we know is, that Adela is most unfitted for the kind of work, and we shall be surprised if she does not break down under it. Her frame is slight and delicate, her instincts are sensitive and refined. Fancy Adela dressing broken heads, or sitting up for a week with a family of children ill with fever!"

Selina put her hands before her eyes. "Oh!" she cried in horror. "But she surely won't have to do all that?"

"She will. She must take any case she is appointed to."

Lady Mary took up her work again, and Selina, serious and sobered for once in her life, sat revolving what she had heard.

"Surely she will not do this, Mary!"

"Indeed she will. She is fully determined to enter upon it, and she intends that it shall be for life. Her father came down here to remonstrate with her: he has always had more influence over her than any one else: but it availed nothing. They were together for an hour in Adela's sitting-room here—and I could see how distressing to her the interview had been. Her eyes were swollen with crying."

"Well, I can't understand it," concluded Selina, rising. "Had it been a question of necessity, there might be reason in her wanting to make a guy of herself, but it is not so. Those big linen caps are dreadful."

The door of the red parlour was open as Selina gained the hall. Adela sat there sewing: and Selina went in. How fragile and dainty and delicate she looked, this still young and lovely woman, in her simple muslin dress, with a ribbon at her throat and an edging of lace at the wrists. Selina sat down.

"At work today, Adela!"

"I am making frocks for that poor Widow Jeffrey's children. But for Mr. Cleveland I don't know what they would do, now their father is gone."

"But all Netherleigh is en fête today So ought you to be!"

Adela raised her sad and beautiful eyes to Selina's in some surprise. "The fête can have nothing to do with me, Selina. I am very glad it is so fine for it: and I hope every one will enjoy it, yourself included."

"Thank you: I'm sure I shall. Adela, what is this we hear about you?" broke forth Selina, unable to keep silence longer. "You are going to shut yourself up in a grim building, and wear a most disfiguring costume, and nurse cases of fever!"

"Yes," sighed Adela.

"But you surely never will?"

"I must do it. I leave for it the day after tomorrow."

Selina lowered her voice. "Have you sat down and counted the cost?"

"Over and over again. It will be less painful than what I have long been enduring: bodily discomfort is more tolerable than remorse. I shall live a useful life, at any rate, Selina. For a long while now it has been worse than a wasted one."

"They think—Mary does at least—that you will not be strong enough to stand the fatigue."

"I must do my best," sighed Adela. "I hope the strength—in all ways—will come with the need."

"I dare say they give nothing but suet puddings for dinner four days out of the seven!"

Adela faintly smiled. "I don't expect to find luxuries, Selina."

"Do you take Darvy?"

"Darvy!" echoed Lady Adela. "No, indeed. I shall be, so to say, a servant myself."

Selina, in very dismay, gave her hands a slight wring. To her, it seemed that Adela might as well put herself at once out of the world.

"I must be going," she said, advancing to say farewell. "You are sure you will not come to the fête, Adela?"

"I have done with fêtes for ever," replied Adela, as she drew down Selina's face for a farewell kiss. "Perhaps you will write to me sometimes?" And Selina Dalrymple, sick and sorry for the blighted life, went out with her eyes full of tears.

The day wore on to the afternoon, and the business of the fête began. Old and young, gentle and simple, the aristocracy surrounding the neighbourhood, the tenant-farmers and the labourers, all congregated on the lawns, in the gardens, and in the home field, where the tents were placed. Of the attendants, Reuben was chief, his fresh face happy again as of yore.

Amidst games, dancing, and various other entertainments, there was a fancy-fair, the proceeds of it to be distributed to the poor: though indeed it was more for fun than gain, fortune-telling, post-offices, and mock auctions prevailing.

Alice Dalrymple had a corner in this tent for her reclining chair, and watched with pleasure the busy scene. Lady Frances Hope stood by her; her husband was flitting from stall to stall. Robert's coming back had worked wonders for Alice.

"There!" said Gerard, coming up to her, his face gay as usual, his tone light, as he handed a charming bouquet to Alice: "a fine squabble I have had to get you this. Ten shillings those keepers of the flower-stall wanted, if you'll believe me I gave them five, and told them they were harpies."

"You should not have bought it for me," smiled Alice, gratefully inhaling at the same time the scent of the flowers. "You are just what you always were, Gerard—thinking of every one else, never of self."

"Why should I think of self?" returned Gerard, his wife having left them for a distant stall. "But you know you always liked to lecture me, Alice."

"For your good," she answered, raising her eyes to his.

"Was it for my good? Ah, Alice," he added, his tone changing to one of regret, "if you had only taken me into your hands, as you might have done—as I prayed you to do—you would have made a Solomon of me for wisdom—"

"Hush, Gerard. Best as it is," she impressively whispered, gently laying her hand upon his. "I was not fit—in any way. As it is, I have you both to love, and I am supremely happy. And I think you are."

"Ah, well," quaintly conceded Gerard, "one is warned not to expect perfect bliss in this sublunary world, so one can only make the best of what fate and fortune bestow upon us. Would you not like to walk round and look at the stalls, Alice? You can go comfortably, I think, on my arm."

"Thank you; yes, I should like it—if you will take me."

Amidst the few people of note not at the fête was Lady Adela. She had kept to her determination not to go near it. Mr. Cleveland had asked her, when setting out himself, whether she would not go with him just to have a peep at it, but she said she preferred to sit with Mary. She had heard the news, spoken openly by the Rector at the luncheon-table, that Sir Francis Netherleigh was not coming to it. And in Lady Mary's room she sat, pursuing her work.

But as the afternoon advanced, and its hours struck, one after the other, Adela grew weary and restless, needing a little fresh air. She put on her garden-hat and went out: not with any view of going near the gaiety, rather of keeping securely away from it. And little fear was there of her encountering any stragglers, for the feasting was just beginning, and no Englishman voluntarily walks away from that.

These later hours of the day, as the earlier ones had been, were warm and beautiful. Adela walked gently along, until she came to Court Netherleigh. A sudden impulse prompted her to enter the grounds. She had never yet done so during these months of sojourn, had always driven back the almost irrepressible yearning. Surely there would be no harm in entering now: she did want to see the place once more before quitting Netherleigh and civilized life for ever. No one would see her. She was perfectly secure from interruption by Sir Francis—and from all other people besides, the world and his wife having gone a-gadding.

Not by the lodge-gates and the avenue did she enter; but by a little gate, higher up the road, that she had gone in and out of so often in the time of Aunt Margery. Drawing near to the house, she sat down under a group of trees in view of the favourite apartment that used to be called Miss Margery's parlour, the glass-doors of which were standing open. Cool and gentle she looked as she sat there; she wore the same simple muslin gown that she had worn in the morning. Unfastening the strings of her straw hat, she pushed it somewhat back from her delicate face, and sat on, thinking of the past.

Of the past generally and of her own particular part in it—when was it absent from her memory? Of the means of happiness that had been bestowed upon her in a degree Heaven seldom vouchsafes to mortal woman, and of her terrible ingratitude. How different all would have been now had she only been what she might have been!

Not only had she wrecked her own life, but also her husband's. The bitter requital she had dealt out to him day after day and year after year in return for all the loving care he lavished on her, was very present to her now. For a long while past she had pined for his forgiveness—just to hear him speak it; she coveted it more than ever now that she was about to put all chance of hearing it beyond possibility. God's pardon she hoped she was obtaining, for she prayed for it night and day—but she yearned for her husband's.

It was close upon two years since he put her away from him and from her home. It would be two years next Christmas since Miss Margery died. All that time to have been feeding the bitter grief that played upon her heart-strings!—to have been doing perpetual battle with her remorse!

Lost in these regrets, Adela sat on, taking no heed of the time, when a movement caught her eye. Some one, who appeared to have come in by the same little gate, was striding towards the house. With a faint exclamation of dismay, Adela drew back within the trees. For it was her husband.

Of all the world that could intrude, she had deemed herself most secure from him: knowing that he was detained in London, and could not be down. How was it, ran her tumultuous thoughts. She supposed— what was indeed the truth—that he had at the last found himself able to come.

Yes, but only for an hour or two. She did not know that he had got down at midday, had been to the fête, and was now on his way back to the train, calling at home on his road. He made straight for the open doors of Miss Margery's room, and went in.

A strange impulse seized upon Adela. What if she dared speak to him now? to sue for the forgiveness for which her heart seemed breaking? He could not kill her for it: and perhaps he might speak it—and she should carry with her to her isolation so much of peace.

Without pausing to weigh the words she should utter, or the consequences of her act, she glided after him into the room. Sir Francis stood at a table, his back to the window, apparently taking some papers out of his pocketbook. The sudden darkening of the light, for she made no noise, must have caused him to turn: and there they stood face to face, each gazing, if they so minded, at the ravages time had made in the other. She was the more changed. Her once-brilliant eyes were sad and gentle, her cheeks bore the hectic of emotion, all the haughtiness had gone out of her sweet face for ever. And he? He was noble as always, but his hair had grey threads in it, and his forehead was lined.

"May I be allowed to speak to you for a moment?" she panted, breaking the silence, yet hardly able to articulate "I—I—" And then she broke down from sheer inability to draw breath.

He stood quite still by the table, as if waiting, his tall form drawn to its full height, his face and bearing perfectly calm. But he made no answer.

"I beg your pardon," she humbly began again, having halted just inside the window. "I would not have presumed to follow you in, or to speak to you, but that it is the last opportunity we shall have of meeting on earth. I go away the day after tomorrow to seclude myself from the world; and I—I cannot go without your forgiveness. When I saw you come in now, not knowing even that you were at Netherleigh—an impulse I could not resist brought me after you to ask you to forgive me. Just to ask it!"

But still Sir Francis did not answer. Poor Adela, now white, now hectic, went on, in her weak and imploring tone.

"It has seemed to me that if I went away for good without your forgiveness, I should almost die as the days went on—knowing that I could never ask it then. If you could believe how truly, how bitterly I have repented, perhaps you would not in pity withhold it from me. Will you not give it me? Will you not hear me?" she added, lifting her trembling hands, as he yet made no sign. "God forgives: will not you forgive also?"

Advancing, she sank on her knees before him, as he stood; her sad face lifted to his in yearning. He drew a step back: he had listened in impassive silence; but he spoke now.

"Rise, rise, Lady Adela. Do not kneel to me."

She bent forward; she laid her poor weak hands upon him; the scalding tears began to stream down her face, so pitiful in its sad entreaty. Sir Francis gently touched her hands with his, essaying to raise her; a cold, distant touch, evidently not of goodwill.

"Lady Adela, I will not say another word, or allow you to say one, until you rise. You must be aware that you are only vexing me."

She rose to her feet obediently. She stood still, apart from him. He drew back yet, and stood still also, his arms folded.

"Tell me what it is you wish. I scarcely understand."

"Only your forgiveness, your pardon for the past. It will be a comfort to carry it with me where I am going."

"Where is it that you are going?"

"I am going to join some ladies in Yorkshire, who pass their time in nursing the poor and sick," she answered. "It is called a Sisterhood. I have been thinking that perhaps in that retirement, and in the occupation it will entail, I may find peace. Once entered, I feel sure I shall never have courage to leave it: therefore I know that we shall not meet again."

He did not speak.

"And I should like to thank you, if I may dare, for all your consideration, your generous loving-kindness. Believe me, that, in the midst of the humiliation of accepting it, I have been grateful. When once I have entered this refuge, the necessity for your bounty will cease. Thank you deeply for all."

"You are tired of the world?"

"Yes. It has been to me so full of shame and misery."

"Do you know that you brought a great deal of misery upon me?"

"Oh, it is the consciousness of that that is killing me. If I could undo it with my life, I would; and be thankful. The recollection of the past, the cruel remorse ever haunting my conscience, has well-nigh crushed me. I want you to say that you will try to be happy in your life; there will be less impediment, perhaps, now that I shall be far away: I shall be to you as one dead. If I could only know that you were happy! that I have not quite blighted your life, as I have my own!"

"Do you like the idea of entering this retreat?"

"As well as I could like anything that can be open to me in this world now. It will be a refuge; and I dare to hope—I have dared to pray—that I may in time gain peace."

"Could the past come over again, you would, then, be a different wife to me?"

"Don't reproach me," she sobbed. "None can know how cruel my fate is, how bitter my repentance. Will you not be merciful?—will you not say that you forgive me before I go away for ever?"

"Yes, Adela, I will say it," he answered then. "I forgive you from my heart. I will say more. If you do wish to atone for the past, to be my true and loving wife, these arms are open to you."

He opened them as he spoke. She staggered back, unable to comprehend or believe. He did not move: simply stood still where he was, his extended arms inviting her.

"Do not mock me, pray," she feebly wailed. "Do not be cruel: you were never that. I have told you how bitterly I repent—that my remorse is greater than I can bear. If my life could undo the past, could atone to you in the least degree, I would gladly lay it down."

"Adela, I am not mocking you. You cannot surely think it, knowing me as you do. You may come back to me, if you will, and be once more my dear wife. My arms are waiting for you; my heart is waiting for you: it shall be as you will."

Panting, breathless, the hectic coming and going on her wasted cheeks, she slowly, doubtfully advanced; and when near him she halted and fell at his feet. His own breath was shortening, emotion nearly overcame him. Raising her, he enfolded her to his loving heart.

For a little while, as she lay in his arms, their tears mingled together; ay, even his were falling. A moment of agitation, such as this, does not often visit a man during his lifetime.

"There must be no mistake in future, Adela? You will be to me a loving wife?"

Once more, in deep humiliation, she bent before him. "Your loving and faithful wife for ever and for ever."

Quietly enough they walked, side by side, through the park. Who, watching them, could have suspected the agitation just lived through, the momentous change that had taken place in their lives? Sir Francis went on his way to the railway-station, for he had to go back to London. Adela returned to the Rectory.

And that night, in the solitude of her chamber, its window open to the stars of the summer sky, she spent hours on her knees in prayer and thanksgiving.

On the following morning Mr. Cleveland took Adela to Chenevix House. Sir Francis had been there to prepare the way for her. It was great news for the earl and countess; but it had not much diminished my lady's tartness. She had been too angry with Adela to come round at once.

"Do you know where you are going this evening, Adela?" Grace asked her in a whisper, a happy light in her eyes.

"No. Where?"

"Francis Netherleigh has some mission that is taking him to Paris—my belief is, he has improvised it. He starts tonight, and he will take you with him—if you are very good."

"How kind he is!" murmured Adela.

"Have a care how you behave in future, Adela," said her father, in solemn admonition that evening, as Sir Francis stood ready to take her out to his carriage, which waited to convey them to the station.

"I will, papa: Heaven helping me. Good-bye, dear mamma."

"Oh, good-bye, and a pleasant journey to you! It's more than you deserve," retorted my lady.

CHAPTER XLI

CONCLUSION

There is little more to relate.

On just such a lovely June day as described above, and twelve months later, another fête took place. But this time it was at Court Netherleigh. Not an open-air fête, this, or one on a large scale, for only a few chosen friends had been invited to it.

In the morning, in Netherleigh Church, and at the hands of the good Rector, the infant heir of Court Netherleigh had been made one of Christ's fold.

Court Netherleigh was made their chief home by Sir Francis and his wife. Grosvenor Square was visited occasionally, but not for very long together. Adela's tastes had totally changed: fashion and frivolity no longer held chief places in her heart: higher aims and duties had superseded them. Lady Mary Cleveland herself was not so actively anxious for the welfare of the poor and distressed as was Adela, Netherleigh.

"Sweet are the uses of adversity,
Which like a toad, ugly and venomous,
Wears yet a precious jewel in its head."

As she stood this morning at the baptismal font, her child in the arms of Mr. Cleveland, tears of joy silently trickled down her face. Hardly a day or a night of this latter twelvemonth, but they had risen in gratitude, contrasting what had been with what was.

Lord and Lady Acorn were present; and Grace, who was godmother, held the baby in readiness for the clergyman. Mr. Howard had come down with Colonel and Lady Sarah Hope; Robert Dalrymple and Mary were there from Moat Grange, and the Rector's wife.

While walking back to Court Netherleigh after the ceremony, the party were joined by another guest—Sir Turtle Kite.

Sir Turtle's presence was quite unexpected. Deeply sensible of the service he once rendered them—for, had the little alderman chosen to be crusty then, where would Charles Cleveland have been, where Lady Adela?—the Acorn family had not dropped him with the passing moment. Neither had Sir Francis Netherleigh. On this particular day—a very splendid one in London—the knight chanced to think he should like to air himself in the sunbeams, and take a holiday. Remembering the standing invitation to Court Netherleigh—of which he had not yet availed himself—and knowing that Sir Francis was staying there and not in Grosvenor Square, Sir Turtle travelled down, and met the party as they were going home from church.

"Dear me I am very sorry," he cried, somewhat disconcerted. "I had no idea—I had better go home again."

"Not a bit of it," said Sir Francis, heartily, as he clasped his hand. "You are all the more welcome. I am sure you will like to join us in good wishes to my little boy. Adela will show him to you."

So Sir Turtle's beaming face made one at the luncheon-table, none so delighted as he. And he surreptitiously scribbled a note in his pocketbook to purchase the handsomest christening-cup that could be found for money.

Luncheon over, they went out into the charming sunshine, some strolling hither and thither, some taking refuge on the shaded benches under the trees. Adela gained possession of her baby in the nursery, and carried him out to show him to Sir Turtle. He was a fine little fellow of six weeks old, promising to be as noble-looking as his father, and certainly possessing his beautiful grey-blue eyes.

"What is its name?" asked Sir Turtle, venturing to pat the soft little cheek with his forefinger, and rather at a loss what to say, for he did not understand as much about babies as he did about tallow.

"Francis," answered Adela. "Francis Upton. I would not have had any name but Francis for the world, and my husband thought he would like to add Upton, in remembrance of Miss Upton who used to live here."

"Francis is a very nice name; better than mine," observed Sir Turtle, sitting down by Adela. "And who are its godfathers?" he resumed, still at sea as to the proper things to be said of a baby.

"My father is one, Mr. Howard the other. Sir Francis fixed upon papa, and I upon Mr. Howard. Formerly I used not to like Mr. Howard," ingenuously added Lady Adela, "but I have learnt his worth."

"Ay, a worthy man, my lady; first-rate in business. Talking of business," broke off the little alderman, glad, no doubt, to leave the subject of the baby, but none the less inopportunely, "do you chance to know what has become of a young fellow who got into some trouble at Grubb and Howard's—the Rector's son, yonder"—nodding towards Mr. Cleveland—"Charles, I think, his name was. I have often wished to ask about him."

Lady Adela bent over her child, as if to do something to its cap: her face had flushed blood-red.

"Charles Cleveland is in India," she said. "He is doing well, very well. My husband was—was very kind to him, and pushes him forward. He is kind to every one."

Rising rather abruptly from the bench, she gave the baby to the nurse and went into the house. Her mother, standing at one of the windows of the large drawing-room, turned round as she entered.

"What have you been doing to flush your face so, Adela?" called out my lady—for it was glowing still.

"Oh, nothing: the sun perhaps," answered Adela, carelessly.

"You were talking with Sir Turtle Kite."

"Yes, he was looking at baby, and asking me his name. I told him his father's—Francis."

"Ah," said Lady Acorn, with her irrepressible propensity for bringing up disagreeable reminiscences, "I remember the time when you would not have your child's name Francis, because it was your husband's."

"Oh, mamma, don't! That was in the mistaken years of long ago."

"And I hope you were civil to Sir Turtle," continued my lady: "you seemed to leave him very abruptly. He is a funny little round-headed man, and nothing but an alderman; but he means well. Think what your fate might have been now—but for his—his clemency."

"If you would please not recall these things, mother!" besought Adela, meekly, tears starting to her eyes. "Especially today, when we are all so happy."

Somehow the past, with all its terrible mistakes and the misery they had entailed, came rushing upon her mind so vividly that she could not control her emotion. Passing into the next room, and not perceiving her husband, her sobs broke forth. He came forward.

"My love, what is it?"

"Only—"

"Nay, tell me."

"Something mamma said made me think of that cruel time when—when I was so wrong and wicked. Francis, the shame and sin seemed all to come back again."

He held her before him; his tone one of tender reproof. "But the shame and sin never can come back, Adela. My wife, you know it."

"I know how good you are. And I know how merciful to me God has been," she replied, glancing at him through her wet lashes, with eyes full of love and devotion.

"Very merciful: very merciful to me and to you," whispered Francis Netherleigh. "Do you know, my darling, that through all that dark time, I never lost my trust in Him."

MRS HENRY WOOD (aka ELLEN WOOD) – A CONCISE BIBLIOGRAPHY

Danesbury House (1860)
East Lynne (1861)
The Elchester College Boys (1861)
A Life's Secret (1862)
Mrs. Halliburton's Troubles (1862)
The Channings (1862)
The Foggy Night at Offord: A Christmas Gift for the Lancashire Fund (1863)
The Shadow of Ashlydyat (1863)
Verner's Pride (1863)
Lord Oakburn's Daughters (1864)
Oswald Cray (1864)
Trevlyn Hold; or, Squire Trevlyn's Heir (1864)
William Allair; or, Running away to Sea (1864)
Mildred Arkell: A Novel (1865)
The Argosy (1865)
Elster's Folly: A Novel (1866)
St. Martin's Eve: A Novel (1866)
Lady Adelaide's Oath (1867)
Orville College: A Story (1867)
The Ghost of the Hollow Field (1867)
Anne Hereford: A Novel (1868)
Castle Wafer; or, The Plain Gold Ring (1868)
The Red Court Farm: A Novel (1868)
Roland Yorke: A Novel (1869)
Bessy Rane: A Novel (1870)

George Canterbury's Will (1870)
Dene Hollow (1871)
Within the Maze: A Novel (1872)
The Master of Greylands (1872)
Johnny Ludlow (1874)
Bessy Wells (1875)
Told in the Twilight: Containing 'Parkwater' and nine short stories (1875)
Adam Grainger: A Tale (1876)
Edina (1876)
Our Children (1876)
Parkwater: With four other tales (1876)
Pomeroy Abbey (1878)
Lady Adelaide (1879)
Johnny Ludlow, Second Series (1880)
A Tale of Sin and Other Tales (1881)
Court Netherleigh: A Novel (1881)
About Ourselves (1883)
Johnny Ludlow. Third Series (1885)
Lady Grace and Other Stories (1887)
The Story of Charles Strange (1888)
Featherston's Story. A Tale by Johnny Ludlow (1889)
The Unholy Wish and Other Stories (1890)
The House of Halliwell. A Novel (1890)
Ashley and Other Stories (1897)
Victor Serenus (1898)
Johnny Ludlow. Fifth series (1899)
Johnny Ludlow. Sixth series (1899)

Translations

Les Channing. Traduit de l'Anglais par Mme Abric-Encontre (1864)
Les Filles de Lord Oakburn: Roman traduit de l'anglais par L. Bochet (1876)
La Gloire des Verner: Roman traduit de l'anglais par L. de L'Estrive (1878)
Le Serment de Lady Adelaïde: Roman traduit de l'anglais par Léon Bochet (1878)